TRENTON

A Novel by
John P. Calu and David A. Hart

Plexus Publishing, Inc.
Medford, New Jersey

First Printing, 2010

Trenton

Copyright © 2010 by John P. Calu and David A. Hart

Cover photo of bridge and skyline by Ron Saari

Published by:
Plexus Publishing Inc.
143 Old Marlton Pike
Medford, NJ 08055

This is a work of fiction.

Certain names, characters, places, and incidents either are the product of the authors' imaginations or are used fictitiously. Any resemblance to actual persons, living or dead, is entirely coincidental. Painstaking efforts have been made to ensure the accuracy of any historical characters, places, and incidents described, but some license has been taken for purposes of dramatization.

Library of Congress Cataloging-in-Publication Data

Calu, John P., 1953-
  Trenton : a novel / by John P. Calu and David A. Hart.
      p. cm.
   ISBN 978-0-937548-66-0
   1. Trenton (N. J.)--Fiction. I. Hart, David A. II. Title.
   PS3603.A44625T74 2010
   813'.6--dc22
                                                              2010026566

ISBN 978-0-937548-66-0

Printed and bound in the United States of America.

President and CEO: Thomas H. Hogan, Sr.
Editor-in-Chief and Publisher: John B. Bryans
Managing Editor: Amy M. Reeve
VP Graphics and Production: M. Heide Dengler
Book Designer: Kara M. Jalkowski
Cover Designer: Denise M. Erickson
Marketing Coordinator: Rob Colding

www.plexuspublishing.com

For Helaine
In Loving Memory

Also by Calu and Hart

Acknowledgments

The authors wish to express their sincere appreciation to the following:

John B. Bryans, editor-in-chief and publisher, Books Division, Plexus Publishing, Inc., for listening to, believing in, and working with us.

Landrick F. Hart (deceased) for his painstaking research and record keeping of co-author Dave Hart's (his great-nephew) family lineage, which follows the line of Joseph Hart, uncle of John Hart, the Signer.

Wendy Nardi, archivist of the Trentoniana Collection Room at the Trenton Free Public Library, for her invaluable assistance and patience.

Sally Lane, Trenton Historical Society, for her local columns, intimate knowledge, and keen insights into Trenton's past.

Former City Councilman Jim Coston and the Urban Studies Group for a plethora of ideas and wonderful discussions regarding the future of our beloved city.

Ray Williams, national president of the Colonial Coin Collectors Club, Inc. (C4), for his expertise and guidance in matters dealing with colonial currency.

Randy Russell for always keeping us in touch with the Native American perspective.

Marcelo Gandaria for sharing the Latin American dream.

Amy Reeve, Heide Dengler, Kara Jalkowski, and Rob Colding at Plexus Publishing, Inc., for their inspired contributions to the book's success.

Zully, Vanessa, Michelle, Bob and Barbara, Russ and Fran, James and Jonathan, along with all of our family and friends, for their love and support.

Part One

1

New York Frontier: 1763

The cabin door flew open, and Captain Alexander Scott stood there wounded, struggling to balance himself. "Hide!" he gasped to his bewildered family before collapsing head first on the cold, hard floor.

"Daddy!" Penny Scott screamed when she saw the arrows sticking out of her father's back. He lay still, sprawled out and helpless. Lilly Scott dropped the tined clamshell she had been using to comb her daughter's long auburn tresses and rushed to her husband's side, but his stare was already lifeless and vacant. Blood oozed from the corner of his mouth.

"Bolt the door, Penny!" Lilly shouted to her dazed five-year-old daughter as she strained to pull her husband's body through the doorway and into the room. Penny stood there in her nightgown, frozen with fear. "Now!" her mother commanded, drawing her husband's saber from its sheath.

The desperation in her mother's voice prodded Penny into action. She closed the heavy wooden door, momentarily dampening the sounds of gunfire and savage war cries that had erupted around the frontier outpost, her father's command. After last month's offensive had driven the local tribes away from the river and back into the mountains, rumors of marauding Iroquois sacking and pillaging the countryside had run rampant through the camp. Thinking the fort was safe from a direct Indian assault, Captain Scott had ordered a detachment of his best men into the field to seek out and destroy the renegade band. With his finest battle-hardened regiment away, only a small garrison of green troops was left to defend the post. The French fur traders who didn't want this settlement to succeed had no doubt tipped off the Indians.

Lilly ran around the room shuttering the open windows. She could hear the hiss and thud of flying arrows striking the window boards as quickly as she closed them.

The commotion inside the cabin stirred Penny's infant brother James from his peaceful slumber beside the warm, comforting fireplace. Still holding her husband's sword, Lilly lifted the baby from his crib, rocking him gently in one arm. His irritability subsided immediately.

"Penny—quickly," Lilly whispered urgently, "into the crawl space."

This time Penny didn't hesitate. She and her family had rehearsed this scene many times before as an accepted part of their frontier life. Her father had dug a large, rectangular hole under the cabin floor near the center of the main room. Spacious enough to hide both children in the event of an enemy attack, it also concealed Lilly's modest jewelry and the family's few other valuables. A latticed straw mat lay over the hatch, keeping it from plain view.

Penny shoved the mat aside and clawed into the floorboard for the recessed latch ring. Outside the cabin, the bloodcurdling cries of the Indians, driven from their land and beyond the point of all reason, grew louder, closer, and more ominous.

"Hurry!" her mother cried out.

Penny lifted the hatch and jumped down into the pit. She reached up to receive her baby brother. Suddenly, there was an angry pounding on the door, and the baby joined the wailing chorus from outside.

In a split second, Lilly calculated the odds of her family's survival. There were no sounds of gunfire, and she knew the fort was lost. Her gallant husband lay dead by the door. At any moment the rampaging Iroquois would be upon them. Surely they would all die.

"Momma—please!" implored little Penny, her cheeks streaked with tears, her arms outstretched and trembling.

Lilly let go of her husband's sword and dropped to her knees. James was crying loudly and relentlessly. Surely the baby would give both children away, she thought. She had but one choice.

"Penny, listen to me," Lilly intoned over the baby's wails. "You must be brave. No matter what happens don't dare cry or call out. Do you hear me? You must do exactly as I tell you."

On tiptoes, Penny peeked over the floorboards, casting a mournful glance toward her father's uniformed corpse. "But Daddy said—"

Her mother cut her short. "Daddy's dead, Penny! If you want to live, you'll do as I say!"

Before Penny could protest further, Lilly pushed her daughter's head down into the crawl space and slammed the trap door shut. She grabbed her husband's sword, stood erect, and slid the rug back over the floor opening with her foot just as the door burst open and an angry horde of bare-chested savages rushed in.

She slashed at empty air with the sword as she backed toward the rear of the room, the baby clutched in her other arm. She recoiled in horror as a powerfully built Indian warrior, his face ravaged with pockmarks, viciously separated her husband's scalp from the rest of his head. "No!" she screamed, running at him with sword outstretched.

He was too quick for her. She barely scratched his side as he moved to avoid her thrust then grabbed the sword by the blade, pulling it from her hands.

Surrounded by his fellow taunting and jeering warriors, the big man licked his own blood from the saber and bared his teeth ferociously at his intended victim. Lilly wrapped both arms around James protectively.

The war chief's mottled face came within inches of Lilly's own porcelain white one. His coal black eyes burned into her as he grabbed her shoulders roughly, and Lilly was hit by the nauseating odor of smoke, blood, and whiskey. She could see that his face was not only pockmarked from disease but had been partially burned away. Overcome with hatred and revulsion for this savage who had shattered her family, she spat into his face and jerked free of his grasp.

Without a moment's hesitation, Lilly's assailant raised his tomahawk and struck her in the head with the blunt end. A gash opened and blood spurted from her temple. Dazed and nearly senseless from the blow, she watched helplessly as the monster tore little James from her arms and handed the child to another warrior. The man dangled the screaming infant like a rag doll as he swiftly carried him out the door.

From her dark, cramped hiding place, her tear-soaked blue eyes peering through the dusty cracks between the wooden planks at the edge of the straw mat, Penny watched in horror as the savage ripped the dress from her mother's trembling body and then fell upon her with wanton fury.

"Momma!" Penny screamed inside her head. Her whole body shook with fright, but remembering her mother's last words she closed her eyes and bit her lip so hard it bled. Then, mercifully, she lost consciousness.

2

Footsteps Along the Delaware

A smooth, flat stone skipped lightly across the surface of the water before sinking into the shallow shoals on the peaceful Pennsylvania side of the river. Under the shade of a broad-leaved maple tree, John Hart stood watching the current flow gently downstream and wondered what the future would bring for the son whose only concerns today were the ripples caused by skimming stones.

Knowing this was where she would find her husband, Deborah Scudder Hart had arranged an impromptu picnic following the Sunday church service, attended by everyone in the family except John. It seemed that he had other things on his mind; he had appeared distracted for days, and this, she knew, was his special place. Ever since he was a boy, whenever he felt troubled, John could find comfort walking along the banks of the life-affirming Delaware River. Today, Deborah hoped the laughter of his children and the warmth of the summer sun might also lift his spirits.

Nine years her senior, John Hart married Deborah Scudder when she was just eighteen. In the thirty-five years of wedded bliss that followed, she bore her husband twelve children. Rich in family, a working farmer's most cherished asset, the blest couple had amassed vast landholdings, several mills, and a stable full of racehorses. Current 1774 tax rolls for Hunterdon County, New Jersey, listed the Harts among its wealthiest property owners.

Deborah looked over her brood with a mother's mixture of pride and concern. There had been but one casualty thus far—a daughter, the unlucky thirteenth, who died during birth. It was a death Deborah still lamented, blaming herself repeatedly, though unfairly according to the midwife who attended her. Their two eldest sons and four older daughters had all married and moved out, but there was still family enough left on the homestead to fill her days overseeing the domestic chores and tending to her young.

Lost in thought, John bent down and picked up a dull gray stone. Rubbing the time-worn edges gently between his thumb and forefinger, it reminded him of the Indian arrowheads he had discovered as a boy walking this same riverbank with his father Captain Edward Hart, for whom John's strong-willed, stone-skimming fourth son had been named. Captain Hart was the ambitious and outgoing founder of the famed "Jersey Blues"—a celebrated militia unit formed to help the British regulars fight the French and their American Indian allies in Canada. The two European countries were in a state of perpetual conflict, to the dismay of many American colonists who objected to the cost in property and blood.

Having arrived at the Perth Amboy encampment in the summer of 1746 several weeks too late to join up with the rest of the New Jersey military contingent, the Hunterdon County volunteers, which were assembled by Captain Hart, were instead detached to Albany, where neighboring New York—at first—welcomed them into their ranks. However, after spending a dismal winter awaiting engagement orders that never came, the Blues ultimately began to suffer from neglect. Basic necessities such as food and warm clothing were scarce and back pay was long overdue. Soon, despite the efforts of their leader, the morale of the Blues broke. Discouraged and disheartened, they returned home without firing a single shot at the enemy. Thankfully, local renown for their fighting spirit remained untarnished.

John sighed now, recalling the look of disappointment on his father's face when he returned from that misguided campaign. Although the full truth of the ordeal was kept from the public, Captain Hart never did recover from the shame and embarrassment of his misadventure, however well-intentioned it may have been. The experience left him in physical and financial ruin and served as an emotional warning for John and his younger brother Daniel to be self-reliant and careful as to where one's sense of duty led. John sometimes worried that his own son Edward shared more than John's father's name, as the lad harbored an innate hunger for adventure.

During their walks together along this peaceful riverbank, Captain Hart had regaled his son—a much younger John Hart, to be sure—with heroic tales of the hardy Dutch traders and stout Swedish soldiers who first landed at "the falls on the Delaware." Named after the royal governor of Jamestown, Lord De La Warr, the reference stuck to both the river and the indigenous inhabitants living there when a young, enterprising English interpreter recorded the astonishing coincidence that the local Indians called themselves "N-del-a-wowe," meaning "original people" in their native tongue.

The natives that the early English settlers encountered here were actually part of the vast Lenni Lenape nation that, according to legend, had followed a mysterious holy man—a chief called Walomenop—from the Ohio Valley in search of the Great Salt Sea. The remnants of the Unami or Turtle Totem tribe living in scattered lodges south of the falls in Burlington County were all that remained of these "original people."

It was their arrowheads and an assortment of other artifacts that John had found on his solitary jaunts and come to treasure as a child. His father never had much interest in vestiges of the past beyond the tales of the early settlers he told his sons to encourage an interest in their community.

Captain Hart concentrated on the present and moved among an interesting circle of people. Soon after his arrival to the falls area from New York's Long Island, he befriended the Trents. William Trent, the family patriarch, was a Presbyterian who had emigrated from Scotland to Philadelphia. There, he had made a name and a rather sizeable fortune for himself as a merchant and judge. Later in his life, following in the footsteps of his Quaker friends—notably the family of a miller named Mahlon Stacy—William meandered up the Delaware to the eastern shore of the falls. Here, close enough to visit with his former Philadelphia business associates but far from the hubbub of the busy colonial capital, William found the rich, fruitful land promised by his Quaker brethren to be an idyllic place where he could live as Lord of the Manor with his young and pretty new wife Mary Coddington beside him.

Born on the island of Antigua, the second Lady Trent was said to be the precocious stepdaughter of a wealthy Philadelphia brewer whose connection with the rum and molasses trade accounted for her boastful dowry of African and West Indian slaves. Their exotic presence fueled rumors of her lack of inhibition. While William Trent's time as a member of the landed gentry was short-lived, the town where he chose to close out his days kept his memory alive by adopting his name as its own around 1719.

As had the Lenni Lenape, the Quakers, and even the prideful William Trent before him, Edward came to realize that the enchantment of Trenton was a product of its unique geology. Sitting at the distinctive fracture point where the Piedmont Plateau meets the Atlantic Coastal Plain and created the falls, Trenton and its surrounding area offered a soil rich in mineral deposits, clay, slate, and shale; forests abundant with game and wildlife; and a seemingly endless self-replenishing reservoir of fresh water that included a number of crisscrossing creeks and streams as well as a navigable tidal channel that stretched to the Atlantic Ocean.

It was late summer in 1774, and the captain was gone now. The care of his long-suffering wife and John's mother, Martha Furman Hart, had passed to the son. John wished he could make the memory of his carefree childhood days linger and impress his own children with a fanciful tale or two, but he didn't share his father's gift for storytelling. Quite unlike the captain, he was a plainspoken man. Yet his children took whatever he shared with them more seriously than all the sermons they were subjected to on Sundays at the Baptist Meeting House. John believed in his heart that each child would find his own path, in his own good time, through the history and legacy their father and grandfather passed down to them.

In his mind's eye, standing along the riverbank on this mild summer's day, John could easily trace the movements of the nomadic tribesmen and settlers who preceded him as they discovered the wonders and charms of Trenton and vicinity. Indeed, he had walked in their very footsteps many times. And, lest he forget, it was not far from where he now stood, deep in thought, that he had met his future bride, the vivacious Deborah Scudder, whose widowed father's farm skirted the river rapids a quarter mile away on the western corner of town.

As if reading his mind, Deborah came up silently from behind and slipped her arm around her husband's, pulling him from his reminiscence. He turned to admire her pale and lovely face, her full lips, and was met by the scent of honeysuckle and mint she'd been gathering. A hint of mischief registered in her bright, hazel-green eyes.

"Husband, I am pleased to see a look of serenity that has been too long absent from your face," she said demurely, offering him a mint leaf.

John accepted the mint gratefully and smiled. "Dearest, would that it were more than a respite."

Deborah smiled back fondly, nearly blushing. With each passing day, she grew more deeply in love with the handsome, well-respected man she had spent her entire adult life with. Now graying at the temples and slightly stooped with age, he was her rock and she his guiding light through the ever-shifting tides of life. "You speak of the troubles brought on by our daughter's disgrace?"

"Nay," he replied chewing the mint leaf slowly. "Our Mary is but an impressionable child, weak in the ways of this world and cursed with a mind too feeble to know she has been wronged. Though I do fear she may be doomed to a life of misery as a result of her unfortunate affair."

Deborah clutched the reed basket to her breast. "Yes, Mary is but a child, John, and now burdened with a child of her own," she declared bitterly. Biting her lip she added, "All the while, this 'healer' into whose care we entrusted her, Doctor Gideon De Camp, lies nightly in his comfortable bed with his priggish wife as if nothing graver than a change in the wind has occurred. Husband, surely you have not forgiven this?"

John clenched the rock in his hand tightly. "No, good woman, I have not, but the man refuses us all recompense for his indiscretion. We have no choice but to allow the law to intercede."

"Husband, no!" she gasped, placing a hand to her forehead. "Mary will become a public mockery."

He tenderly placed the errant strand of his wife's dark hair that had shaken loose back behind her ear and pulled down gently on her bonnet. "Cease this discourse, Mother, for the deed has been done. I have asked Samuel Tucker to petition the court on our behalf."

"Then I hope he has the good sense to keep the matter as discreet as possible," she concluded sadly.

They turned their attention back to the river and watched as their nineteen-year-old son, Edward, ran into the water without removing his clothes. "He favors your father," Deborah observed.

"Let us hope he does not choose to imitate him."

"Your father was a good man, John," Deborah said, "if perhaps a little too anxious for glory on the battlefield."

John cast the stone he'd been holding across the wide still water, but neither paid attention to its flight nor gave a care to where it landed. "A preoccupation I fear is certain to cause us all a great deal of pain in the years to come, if the King has his way with the colonies."

Deborah gave him a sideways glance. Even though John had been, among other occupations in his long and illustrious career, a duly elected government representative, Justice of the Peace, and Judge of the Court of Common Pleas, this was the first he had spoken to her of politics in some time.

"Father, come quickly!" cried a red-faced young lass struggling up the steep, slippery slope from the river. Her long skirt and petticoat were caked with mud around the pleated hem.

"What is it, Mary?" Deborah asked as John gave his daughter a hand up.

"You must come quickly—both of you!" the girl shouted, tugging on her father's sleeve forcefully. "Edward has found something ... in the river!"

"A dead fish, I'll wager," quipped Deborah to her husband. "He's probably tormenting the younger children with it."

Mary looked up, wild eyed and pleading. "No mother—it's a girl. And she's dead!"

John and Deborah exchanged a glance before quickly making their way down the embankment. They reached the water in time to see Edward, several yards upstream, lifting a limp body out of a partially submerged canoe.

"Heavens, John, it's a child!" gasped Deborah as she dropped her basket of herbs and ran toward her son and the lifeless form in his arms. The first things she noticed were tangled auburn hair and bruised bare feet. "Edward—is she ..." her words hung in the air.

"She's alive, Mother," Edward said as he gained the bank. "But she must have been in the water a long time—she's shivering something terrible."

"Who is she?" asked sixteen-year-old Scudder, setting down his fishing rod.

"Where did she come from?" Daniel and Dee, the youngest Hart children chimed in excitedly as the girl opened her sky blue eyes and struggled instinctively to break free of Edward's grasp.

John quickly removed his waistcoat and draped it over the child. The gesture had the effect he intended. The girl stopped struggling and allowed Edward to continue carrying her up the riverbank.

"Bring her inside by the hearth," Deborah urged, holding the girl's small hand that felt as cold as ice.

3

Death and Taxes

A dozen drunk and disorderly men, dressed in well-worn broadcloth coats and tricorne hats, were gathered around a table near the open hearth on the first floor of the Eagle Tavern at the corner of Ferry Road and Queen Street. Laughing loudly and swilling tankards of frothy ale, they were oblivious to the other late night tavern patrons scattered throughout the dark smoky room who were equally desirous to ignore them.

A gangly man with long flowing white whiskers and a black patch over one eye stood up suddenly and began to sing a tune in a sad, mournful voice: "Why soldiers, why? Should we be melancholy boys? Why soldiers, why? Whose business is to die! What? Sighing? *Fie!*"

Several of the old crooner's cronies stood up around up him and, with glasses raised, sang out the song's triumphant refrain: "Damn fear, drink on … be jolly, boys. 'Tis he, you or I!"

Sitting at a darkened corner table facing the lively old soldiers, Samuel Tucker squirmed a little and leaned in toward his tablemate. "You hear that, John Hart?" said Tucker, lowering his voice. "That's the rabble you and I represent. Voltaire would have them strangle all the monarchs of Europe with the entrails of priests."

John took a generous sip of his claret and studied his fellow assemblyman. In another time and place, with his bald crown and bowl-cropped side hair, Tucker might have been mistaken for a wayward monk. Dressed as he was, however, in a fine, fitted British tweed suit, Tucker would be more at home in the courts of Europe than the dank rooms of an austere monastery. His actual playground was the courtroom of Hunterdon County, New Jersey, and he did quite well for himself therein. Perhaps too well, as some—including Mrs. John Hart—had asserted based on his wardrobe and lifestyle.

Tucker was contemptuous of everything and everyone he couldn't best. But he was a wily and efficient opponent when it came to the law, which at least partly explained why he and John got along as well as they did. John relied on Tucker's legal expertise in matters dear to him, choosing to believe it was wiser to employ him than oppose him. For his part, Tucker maintained the relationship because John was well connected and could afford his fees. Over the years, they had developed a cautious friendship.

"Listen to you, Samuel," replied John smugly, puffing on his clay pipe. "Quoting a Frenchman, and an atheist at that, while missing the real evils in the world!"

Tucker took the bait. "And pray tell, John, what might they be?"

John let out a hearty laugh, clearly enjoying the effects of the wine. "Why, mercenaries, of course—and lawyers like you!"

"Go ahead, laugh all you want," said Tucker, "but it is because of lawyers like me that the innocent are made whole and criminals are brought to justice."

"So, then, you got through to De Camp?" John asked seriously.

Now it was Tucker's turn to be smug. "Let's just say I was able to reason with the good doctor, man to man."

"He may claim to be a doctor, but he is neither good nor a man and we have no need of him around these parts."

"Precisely how *I* feel and as the court ruled," replied Tucker, sitting back in his chair. "Your daughter's honor has been avenged. You will receive two hundred pounds sterling for the care and custody of the unborn child, not to mention damages for the violation of poor Mary. Doctor De Camp does get to keep his license to practice medicine, but he must relocate his sorry arse to the hinterland."

John looked hard into his attorney's dark eyes. Sparkling in the flickering candlelight, they were alive with his sense of victory. "Fair enough," John sighed, the relief of settling the matter evident in his manner.

Tucker could hardly contain his joy as he added up his percentage of the De Camp "damages" in his head, for perhaps the fifth time.

"And what of Penny Scott?" John asked hopefully.

Tucker took a long, slow swig of his ale, holding John's curiosity for as long as he could.

"Ah, the girl from the river. According to my sources there is some truth in what she told you—a measure, anyway. Her given name is Penelope Scott. Penny, if you like."

"She prefers it," nodded John.

"Right, then. Penny Scott. She was born on the New York frontier, where her father was a British officer stationed at Fort Bull. She was orphaned at five years of age when her mother and father were burned alive in their cabin by a renegade band of Iroquois in retaliation for a British-instigated raid on the Seneca winter camp. A tale is told that just before she expired, her mother wrapped the child in wet blankets to protect her from the heat and smoke and hid her under the floor-boards. She was discovered the next day by a detachment of soldiers sent too late to help defend the homestead."

"That would help explain how she comes to be such a brave young girl," John interjected.

Tucker folded his hands together and rocked in his chair. "Brave? You haven't heard the half of it, John." He wet his whistle again before continuing the story. "After some extensive searching, it was learned that Penny's only surviving kin in America was an aunt on her mother's side, by the name of Susan Thomas. Miss Thomas is married to a Mr. Jacob Caldwell. They have no children of their own. Mr. Caldwell owns a blacksmith shop in Belvedere up near the Water Gap. Although smithing is an uncommon trade for a young lady, Penny was made to help Mr. Caldwell out around the shop. She has a way with horses, or so her aunt claimed."

Tucker paused long enough to notice that John was focused on his every word. He smiled inwardly and continued. "Fearing they might never be able to fully recover the cost of their 'kindness' should Penny find a man of her own, the Caldwells made the girl sign an apprenticeship agreement at the age of twelve, effectively making her an indentured servant until she reached her nineteenth birthday."

"That's inhumane," snorted John.

"Despicable," agreed Tucker. "And after she signed the agreement, the Caldwells' treatment of her grew even more loathsome. She was required to work fourteen-hour days, sometimes without food or drink for an entire shift. And she was forbidden to attend school or have friends. They told her that everything she needed to know, she would learn from them."

"Why, they've deprived her of her very childhood!" John shouted, banging his fist on the table. Tucker jumped in his seat. Conversations quieted around the room, and then, almost as quickly, returned to normal.

Tucker picked up the story. "That may be so, John, but this Penny is not one to lie down easily. She's got real backbone. Around the time she turned sixteen she found help in the person of one of her uncle's customers, a former schoolteacher who had taken a shine to her. This kindly gentleman viewed the girl's situation as intolerable and expected that it would only worsen if he did not intervene. Secretly, he helped Penny resume her reading and writing, but her uncle caught her at it and burned all her books in his furnace. That was the day young Miss Scott stole the schoolteacher's canoe and paddled down the Delaware—the day she would have drowned had not your Edward found her and pulled her from the river."

"Have you been in touch with the Caldwells directly?" an emotional John asked as cautiously as he could.

"I have my methods, John, and you know me to be competent," Tucker said proudly.

"My wife has grown quite fond of Penny," John said.

"She makes up for the one Deborah lost, I suppose," Tucker replied carelessly.

This was a delicate issue for the Harts, and John was incensed by Tucker's insensitivity. "Hold your tongue, counselor," he said angrily. "It would be wise for you to remember that our cordial relations extend far less than do the strings of my purse!"

Shocked and humiliated by John's outburst, Tucker rearranged his thoughts before responding. He knew secrets about the Hart family that could be potentially damaging if made public, but he was no fool. It would be a mistake to open a rift with such a steady customer, and, after all, John Hart came closer to being called a friend than anyone else in his rather limited social circle.

"Good friend, I beg that you pardon my comment," he said at last, striking his sincerest tone. "I meant only to reflect on the fine qualities of your missus and intended no disrespect by mentioning a matter so private. I should have thought better before speaking so freely of it."

John seemed satisfied and even eager to put it behind them. "The point is, Samuel, all of the children have taken to Penny. She is exceedingly helpful and gracious. She dotes on Edward as her rescuer, looks after Daniel and Dee, and has become a loyal friend to our Mary. It would be a grievous sin to send her back to these brutish Caldwells and their blacksmith shop."

"I am in complete agreement, John. But the devil will have his due. And it will not come cheaply."

"Counselor," John insisted, "the girl does not wish to return to Belvedere under any circumstances, and I am not prepared to allow it. She has become one of us, a member of the family." He stopped and looked around to see who might be eavesdropping. Satisfied the tavern's patrons were all occupied in their own thoughts and conversations, he continued. "Therefore, you have my leave to settle this matter as you see fit, with the usual fee for yourself." He lowered his voice and looked Tucker straight in the eyes. "Samuel, you must promise me that the girl is never to learn of this business."

"As you wish, John. Consider the matter resolved." Tucker raised his glass. "Shall we drink to that?"

***

As the evening wore on, the rabble in the big, open room grew louder and bolder and soon began accusing the matronly serving wench, who just happened to be the barman's wife, of refilling their mugs too slowly. The innkeeper, an Irishman by the name of Seamus O'Grady, hesitantly walked over and asked John and Tucker to do something before the old soldiers attacked his helpless wife, as they seemed ready to do.

Tucker begged off, suggesting that it might prove more lucrative to wait until an actual assault occurred. That way, he assured Seamus, he would have a stronger case to present for award in court. Dejected and fearing the worst, Seamus turned to his former employer for assistance.

Seamus and his family had received their start in the new world from the Harts. Fresh off the boat from Dublin by way of the South Hampton docks when he met John and Daniel Hart, the Irishman, along with his eager freckle-faced teenaged son Crispin, were hired to work in the brothers' gristmill located on the outskirts of town. There, Seamus, a potato farmer by trade, convinced John and skeptical Daniel—who once described all Irishmen as "good for nothin' drunks and lousy poets"—to distill the corn crop the Indians called maize into a potent drink. The enterprise was such a startling success that the Hart brothers paid Seamus a bonus of one farthing for each barrel produced at the mill. In time, Seamus and his son saved enough money to acquire a stake in the tavern, which of course they stocked with O'Grady's corn spirits.

For the Harts, however, the distilling business had contributed to a great family tragedy that still haunted John. Under the influence of the spirits, Daniel's manservant, a slave named Cuffee, drove an axe into his master's back, murdering the younger Hart brother in a drunken rage. Cuffee's corpse was found several hours later, swinging from a tree in an apparent suicide. It was widely reported that he had become overwrought with remorse. Only the two men who had summoned the authorities to the scene, John Hart and Seamus O'Grady, would ever know the whole truth.

"I'll see what I can do, Seamus," John said, rising from his chair.

"Suit yourself, John," Tucker said, pushing further back into the shadows.

"I say King George can kiss my arse!" the old one-eyed soldier was preaching to the choir as John approached the group. "You know what he can do with his bloody tea tax!"

"Bloody it is, all right," a squat tavern patron agreed, spraying his comrades with spittle from his toothless mouth. "Spilt on the Plains of Abraham against them froggies and their heathen allies!"

19

"I lost a son to Montcalm in Quebec," a third patron exclaimed, swaying precariously as he stood up. He threw his cane to the floor. "Death to the butcher!"

"And death to taxes!" shouted an animated John Hart.

The room grew suddenly silent. All eyes were glued on John as he stood with his arms folded looking into the uncomprehending stares. Not a hair stirred anywhere.

"And just what do ya mean by that, good sir?" the wobbly legged man inquired.

John smiled. "What do I *mean*?" he asked pretending surprise. "Don't tell me the good men of the Blues have forgotten their *Poor Richard's Almanac*?"

Several of the old soldiers looked around and scratched their scrawny beards and wispy haired heads.

"Yes? Then let me remind you. It has been written that 'nothing is certain in life except for death and taxes.' And of course, it stands to reason that death means the end of taxes. So I say we raise our glasses to the certainty of death. Are you with me, lads?"

John's brainteaser had the proper effect. The liquored-up old soldiers didn't quite know how to respond at first. Then, as if the dimness of the night had parted …

"Here, here!" a man called out.

"I'll drink to that," said another.

"Aye, I've had enough."

"Me too!"

"All this talk about death and taxes is a bit too much for me," admitted the one-eyed soldier shaking his head.

"Aye, I've got to get home," the toothless old coot agreed.

Slowly, one by one, the old soldiers gathered their wits and possessions and began to take their leave. Their drunken revelry had been cut short by somber thoughts, and they preferred to drink, not think. It was unlikely they would remember much of this in the morning.

"Once again I am beholden to you, John Hart," said Seamus, coming up alongside the older man. As John made his way back to the table where Tucker was downing his ale, Seamus offered him a fresh drink. "I made this batch meself," he whispered surreptitiously, peering over his spectacles and grinning broadly.

"There'll be none of that fine brew for me tonight, Seamus," John said politely. "Otherwise the missus will have me sleeping in my breeches," he added with a touch of his usual charm.

Seamus winked conspiratorially.

John placed a gold coin into Seamus's vest pocket and tossed a few silver ones onto the table. Looking down at his attorney he asked jokingly, "Has your thirst been slaked yet, Samuel?"

"I heard you taking liberties with the bard over there, John. That could be extremely dangerous should the King hear of it."

John laughed. "Even were I to worry about the King's reaction, that quip about 'death and taxes' isn't Shakespeare. It's from our own Doctor Franklin."

"Are you sure?"

"He repeats it nearly every time I see him!"

4

A Day at the Races

"*M*other, hold still or we shall never see your hair pinned properly," said Susanna Polhemus, the Hart's third oldest married daughter, with a dramatic sigh.

"I don't see why you go to such a fuss, Susanna. My bonnet will provide the necessary cover," Deborah responded with typical modesty.

Sarah Wyckoff, the eldest daughter, also married, laughed out loud. "Mother! You will not be seen in the company of the fashionable Hart sisters wearing that ragged old relic!"

"Especially not at the elegant Trent house for the social event of the spring," added Gayle Stout, the youngest married daughter. "That's why our sister Martha is not coming. She says she has nothing to wear."

"Martha may have other reasons, but as you know, the Trent estate has passed into the hands of Doctor William Bryant, and his wife is far more conservative than the former lady of the manor," gossiped Deborah, warming to the subject at hand. "I would not be expecting such an elegant affair."

"Nonsense, mother," answered Susanna. "I hear that Madame DeSange, the French doctor's widow, is invited. You know the Bryants would not entertain a friend of Doctor Franklin's with anything less than their finest!"

"What is this I hear?" John Hart said, entering the room. "Dear old Benjamin's name bandied about as fodder for the social expectations of my fashionable daughters?" Smiling, he greeted each of his girls with a kiss.

"And besides, the event is but a prelude to a horserace in which the Harts' steed will surely prevail with me in the saddle," added a cocky John Hart Jr., swaggering into the room behind his father. Bending to take his mother's hand, he raised it to his lips in a perfunctory, albeit comical gesture. Deborah raised her eyebrow and then gave her son a slightly indulgent smile before pinning a green-and-white garland to his shirt.

"Begging your pardon, sir," Penny Scott addressed the patriarch as she appeared in the doorway in her work clothes. She looked down to avoid the gaze of the curious elder Hart sisters, to whom she had not yet been introduced. "The carriage is fitted as you asked, and I've tethered the extra horses behind. By your leave, sir." She exited quickly, before John or Deborah could make the introductions or, in fact, say *anything* that might pull her closer to the frightening world of women's fashion and upper class social conventions.

"Where on earth did you find her, Father?" Sarah wanted to know.

"Edward pulled Penny from the river, if you must know," he replied.

"Had he allowed her the time to dress," John Jr. mused, "she might actually resemble a woman."

"Not everyone shares your sister's interest in the classics," Deborah said with uncharacteristic sarcasm as she threw down the copy of *Mercure Galant*, the French fashion magazine Susanna's husband had brought back from Philadelphia. She gave John Jr. a hard look. "Shouldn't you be on your way?"

"By all means, if I might be excused," John Jr. responded with a formal bow. "Look for me in the winner's circle!" he added on his way out the door.

Deborah shook her head as she watched her often vexing son depart. "Perhaps someday your namesake will learn to mind his manners," she chided her husband.

"Tomorrow we can work on his social skills," John replied. "Today my only hope is that he rides like the wind." He gave his wife and daughters a wink and a smile. "Shall we be on our way, then?"

"Mother, I'm sure Johnny meant no offense," Susanna said as she trailed Deborah to the door. "Penny is actually quite fetching in her own way."

"It's all right, dear," Deborah said softly. "She's just had a very hard life, and I want her to feel at home here."

***

The eldest Hart sons, Jesse and Nathaniel, along with the husbands of Gayle, Sarah, and Susanna, led the way on horseback. Leaving the younger Hart family members at home with their grandmother, John, Deborah, and their daughters followed in the carriage, with Edward and Penny bringing up the rear, riding side-by-side on a pair of Bulle Rock mares.

The reception had been planned months in advance by local physician William Bryant and his wife Emily. It was her opportunity to show off the recently completed renovations of their stately home, Bloomsbury Court, and his to celebrate a foray into the noble sport of horseracing. The guest list included Trenton's most prominent businessmen and horseracing enthusiasts, including the likes of postmaster and merchant Abraham Hunt, tanner Stacy Potts, and various gentlemen farmers including John Hart, all with horses specially groomed for the occasion. It was rumored that Royal Governor William Franklin—the son of John's friend, Benjamin—might put in an appearance, as he had been in Burlington for the recent General Assembly session. With the day arrived, that prospect now seemed unlikely.

As the Hart entourage drew closer to the former home of the venerable William Trent, the younger Hart women—always eager for news of the world abroad—wondered aloud if they would hear tales of Madame Du Barry, the mistress who succeeded the infamous Madame de Pompadour in the court of Louis XV. What had become of the musical prodigy Wolfgang Amadeus Mozart, introduced to the royal family at Versailles at the age of only eight years? Was it true that the latest novel by Jean-Jacques Rousseau had been banned in France? When will civilization reach the colonies?

When indeed, wondered John Hart as his thoughts drifted to the dangerous events of recent months. Now in his early sixties, John had thought his days in the saddle were behind him. After losing his bid for re-election to the General Assembly in 1771, when his occasional friend and frequent rival Samuel Tucker trumped him by pandering to a coalition of Baptists and Presbyterians—exposing John's lack of affiliation with any organized religion—John was willing to accept retirement from a long life of public service. The good people of Hunterdon County and his colleagues across the colony, however, would neither let him rest nor allow him to spend his golden years tending to his horses and fields in quiet Hopewell. As trouble brewed in Boston, his many loyal friends and acquaintances, even Tucker, sought the benefit of his experience to help guide them through the difficult times that were sure to come.

For many colonists, rebellion against the Crown began in earnest with the Boston Tea Party. Staged in December 1773 by a militant faction known as the Sons of Liberty, a small band of colonists disguised as Indians protested the imposition of Parliament's Tea Act by dumping some 342 chests of East India Company tea into Boston Harbor. When the British Crown retaliated by closing the port of Boston to commercial shipping, many of the colonies grew alarmed and set up committees to correspond with the other colonies in order to keep tabs on the actions of their emboldened British overlords.

In February 1774, the New Jersey General Assembly meeting in Burlington voted to form one such Committee of Correspondence to keep in contact with the other colonies on matters related to their "Rights and Liberties." Samuel Tucker was appointed one of the committee members. On July 8, 1774, at John Ringo's Tavern in Amwell, just outside of Trenton, Tucker chaired a meeting that was attended by John Hart. There, the electorate of Hunterdon County, of which Trenton was the recognized capital, formed its own local Committee of Correspondence. While still expressing fealty to the Crown, the committee proceeded to select a group of men who would meet with similar committees from other counties and appoint a New Jersey delegation to a grand General Congress proposed by Massachusetts.

This First Continental Congress would meet in Philadelphia in the fall of 1774.

The New Jersey General Assembly met soon afterward in Perth Amboy in January 1775. Over the violent opposition of Governor Franklin, the assembly unanimously approved the proceedings of the First Continental Congress to protest certain measures of Parliament, boycott English goods, and state what they believed to be the rights of all Americans.

Tensions with Mother England continued to escalate until, just weeks before the Bloomsbury Court reception now being attended by the Harts, news reached Trenton of armed skirmishes that had occurred on April 19 between British soldiers and Massachusetts militiamen at Lexington and Concord. War had broken out in New England, and the reaction in Trenton was immediate. On Sunday, April 30, a rally was held outside the Baptist Meeting House inciting all men of honor and virtue to take up arms alongside their Massachusetts brethren. John had to forcibly restrain his son Edward from going.

By the middle of May 1775, the Second Continental Congress voted to issue three million dollars in paper money to raise an army of twenty-thousand men to defend the colonies. It was expected that General George Washington of Virginia would be appointed Commander-in-Chief of the Continental Army and that he would soon be passing through Trenton as he rushed to the aid of the good citizens of Massachusetts. In the meantime, a Provincial Congress of eighty-five representatives from the various New Jersey counties was converging on Trenton for a meeting scheduled for May 23.

Only one week ago to this day, as fate would have it, John Hart had witnessed firsthand how bitterly divisive and personal the battle would become. Freshly returned to Philadelphia following years abroad in England serving as an agent for the colonies, Benjamin Franklin enlisted the help of his trusted friend in arranging a private meeting between himself and his estranged son, the governor, at another mutual friend's home just across the river in Trevose, Pennsylvania. Ever the diplomat, Benjamin insisted on keeping the meeting secret so as not to endanger his son's reputation. It was his hope that William could be made to see the wisdom of joining the rebellion against an oppressive crown. Sadly, it was not to be. Father and son parted on opposite sides of the conflict, never to reconcile.

Given these recent events, John was not heavily invested in the outcome of a horserace, but it would afford him an opportunity to size up the loyalties of his fellow men and give the women in his family a much-needed diversion from the impending strife.

When all the guests had arrived, Doctor Bryant and his wife showed their well-groomed visitors around the grounds of the luxurious estate. Afterward, they returned to the front parlor where the servants had prepared a delicious meal of harvest soup, poached salmon garnished with blanched cardoons, slivered radishes, and pickled beets from the garden, topped off with fragrant apple purses. The delightful repast was accompanied by a stunning selection of fine French wines. As the servants cleared the dishes, the women settled in for an afternoon of genteel entertainment that included a lively performance on Benjamin Franklin's own invention, the "glass armonica"—a gift to the hostess from the mysterious, silver-blonde beauty, Madame DeSange.

While the women were thus engaged, the men made their way out to the grounds, which led to the main event. It was easy for John to tell where Doctor Bryant's loyalties would fall. He was a man of property and means, interested in maintaining the status quo. He owned one of the most formidable estates in town and was the head of a syndicate of local moneyed movers and shakers who had recently become involved in the acquisition of racehorses. Their first purchase was a three-year-old thoroughbred named Pride of the Empire, who was scheduled to make his Trenton racing debut this very afternoon. Horseracing was an interest Bryant shared with John, whose prized thoroughbred Northumberland was also scheduled to race today.

John and his eldest sons, Jesse and Nathaniel, made their way across the grounds of the estate full of trepidation. It was no secret that John Hart and Samuel Tucker were among the leaders of the New Jersey Provincial Congress—a kind of shadow government operating under the auspices of the General Assembly but without executive consent, whose sympathies lay with the Massachusetts cause. Many suspected the two men were steering that elected body toward a unified resistance against the authority of the Crown.

Ever the opportunist, Tucker saw this as a chance for personal gain—an opportunity to increase his wealth and social stature. He relished the idea of extending his influence outside the boundaries of New Jersey, perhaps even making a name for himself in the annals of history. John, on the other hand, was more pragmatic and principled than his colleague. Taking a page from the lessons of his childhood, he preferred to keep the interests of the people firmly in mind, and this included a safe and secure future for his own growing family. Life under the rule of British indifference was not what he envisioned for future generations of Americans.

In his wide-brimmed Dutch hat and finely tailored English clothes, Tucker could project an air of duplicity that rubbed people the wrong way, and that included some of those he was chosen to serve. His carefully cultivated appearance and mannerisms often cast doubt on the nature of his character. John, on the other hand, was anything but vain. He projected an intuitive wisdom and an unpretentious manner that served him well in dealings with friend and foe alike.

"I don't believe I've had the opportunity to express my gratitude for the bill you introduced several years back," said Doctor Bryant politely, extending his hand to John as the group began the short trek to Eagle Race Track. "That bridge over the Assunpink near Mr. Trent's old mill has greatly contributed to the growth of commerce southward along the Burlington Road."

"No doubt my good fellow Mr. Tucker would argue the value of that investment," replied John good-naturedly, with Tucker standing within earshot, "as he has done on the Assembly floor."

"Ah, yes, quite so," said Bryant. With a wry smile in Tucker's direction he added, "But then, from the view of Trenton's foremost legal mind, a new jail would certainly be a more worthwhile use of taxpayers' money."

"You are correct, Doctor Bryant," Tucker fired back without the slightest trace of humility, "but not nearly so worthwhile as the advantage gained by my esteemed colleague owing to his eldest son's draying business."

The face of the son in question, Jesse, flushed with anger. As he took a step toward Tucker, his father put a restraining hand on his shoulder. It was not the first time that the acid-tongued Tucker and Jesse—at thirty-three, the son who most resembled his father—had come almost to blows. John was well aware that a confrontation between the Harts and Tucker in this public setting would play right into the hands of a loyalist like Doctor Bryant and might be precisely what the man aimed to provoke.

"I daresay, Doctor Bryant," John began cordially, "that while I do not often traverse the bridge myself, I have been given to understand that its superior stone arch construction has afforded some advantage to *many* of our citizens during the rising of the Assunpink flood waters."

John nodded to the two gentlemen who had just joined their small party on the front lawn of the estate, then added, "If you will not take the word of a simple Hopewell farmer, then may I suggest you seek the advice of Messrs. Hunt and Potts, whose opinions you may weigh favorably in regard to the value of our little extravagance."

"Poppycock!" Tucker blustered, clearly outmaneuvered by his political peer. "We all know that bridge will not endure."

Before Doctor Bryant or the others standing by could add to the debate, a gangly unkempt man with the ripe aroma of rawhide about him interrupted the group, pulling the host aside and whispering in his ear.

John did not recognize the leather-clad man, but Jesse did. "That's John Honeyman," he quietly told his father.

"He's the town butcher," added Nathaniel, careful not to be overheard.

"I'm afraid I have some bad news for you, Mr. Hart," said Bryant, turning to face John directly but speaking loudly enough for all to hear. "According to my good man here, it seems your son John Jr. has turned up rather inebriated. If you are unable to produce another jockey to take his place, I'm afraid Northumberland must be scratched from today's race—that is, unless you wish to employ one of my Negroes, which as a gentleman I am glad to offer."

The crowd gasped at the news, and several of the men began talking animatedly amongst themselves, hurriedly rearranging bets based on this latest turn of events.

"That won't be necessary," shouted Edward Hart, riding up on one of his father's mares with Penny Scott close behind him. "Father, I will ride Northumberland today."

"Son, he's an unpredictable mount," cautioned the senior Hart. "It seems he shares his temperament with your brother, which may explain why they get along so well."

"If I may speak, sir … I can make amends for that," offered Penny quickly but with assurance. "We will not let you down." She gave a nod at Edward, who reached across his saddle and took her hand, warmly acknowledging her support. A keen observer might have seen Penny blush at the touch of his hand, but her feelings went unnoticed by the gathering of race enthusiasts.

John was well aware of Penny's gift with horses. He had seen her in the stables late at night, talking to them and brushing them down when she thought no one was around. He was also pleasantly surprised to learn how well and quickly she had taken to the saddle. Was it a result of Edward's skill as a teacher, or her eagerness to accompany him on his long rides through the countryside? His father's intuition suggested it was a little of both.

Of Edward's skill, he had no doubt. It had become clear at an early age that the soldiering instinct was not only in Edward's blood but coursing near the surface. He reflected briefly on the differences between this son and John Jr., seven years Edward's senior. Where Edward was responsible and hardworking, John Jr. lacked a proclivity for any employable trade but rather demonstrated a perverse affinity for sport and games of chance, which John attributed to his carousing and weakness for drink.

Jesse voiced his opinion. "Father, Edward has the best chance of winning."

"I agree," added Nathaniel, who with his dark complexion and black hair resembled his mother most in looks and demeanor.

"Well, seeing as we don't have much choice in the matter," John said turning back to Edward, "you had best get saddled up."

The guests gathered on the lawn had been observing the familial exchange with reserved amusement as Doctor Bryant now stepped forward. "Ah, very well," he said with a clap of the hands, a hint of disappointment in his voice belying his exuberance. "That's the sporting way, and I'd hate to have my horse win its first race by forfeit," he played to the crowd as they boarded their carriages and made for the track.

A slight drizzle had begun to fall by the time the cavalcade of slow-moving carriages discharged their passengers along Sandtown Road, about a quarter mile east of the local establishment that shared the same name as the track. Eagle Race Track was not much more than a trampled meadow encircled by a post and rail fence, but it had become the sporting mainstay of Trenton's decidedly prosperous and mercantile population, now nearly five hundred strong. For a civil-minded and industrious people, there was nothing better to bring men together than a day at the races.

Today's much-anticipated event would be a four-horse race favoring either the green and white colors of John Hart's celebrated Irish stallion Northumberland, or the Bryant syndicate's royal blue and gold Pride of the Empire; it was generally understood that the other two horses were out of their league.

Currency changed hands as the final wagers were made. Conspicuous among the throng of spectators lining the fence was a detachment of British redcoats. Commanded by Lieutenant Fletcher Radcliff, an ambitious young officer of aristocratic stock, the troops had been sent to Trenton by Royal Governor Franklin—ostensibly to keep the peace and maintain order during the race, but also, it was suggested, to be available if needed when the Provincial Congress went into session the following week.

Edward sat nervously in the saddle astride the gray-white Northumberland while Penny gently stroked the horse's long mane. Speaking softly, she encouraged both horse and rider to do their best while the rest of the Hart contingent stood nearby along the outside of the fence. A disheveled John Jr. lay slumped and snoring against the rails.

Alongside Northumberland, Pride of the Empire was the picture of poise and confidence, standing at fifteen hands—a full foot taller than the Harts' stallion. Riding Pride was Seamus O'Grady's son Crispin.

At the clang of the bell, the horses were out of the gate with a whinny and a splay of mud. As they came round the first turn, Northumberland was out in front by half a length.

"Bloody hell!" Tucker blurted, disclosing to all where he'd placed his money.

"Looks like Northumberland is feeling his oats," Jesse prodded Tucker.

"Your father and I may share a taste for fine Irish whiskey," retorted Tucker, "but no good ever came out of an Irish stable."

"Well, Counselor, shall we double the wager then?" challenged John.

"Done!" exclaimed Doctor Bryant from the stands when Tucker didn't respond immediately.

"I'll take me a piece of that!" yelled Abraham Hunt.

"I'm in for a pound," acknowledged Stacy Potts.

"Kick him, Crispin, kick him hard!" hollered Bryant as he returned to the rail.

By the midway point, Pride of the Empire had eased into his long full stride and galloped past Northumberland by a head. The other horses, the mean-spirited Tempest and the plodding Isle of Wight, were as far behind as expected.

Edward was caught by surprise at the big horse's sudden burst of speed and let up on the reins momentarily, a mistake of inexperience. Pride pulled ahead by a full length. At the sight of the lead change, Penny buried her head in her hands and said a small prayer. John Jr. looked up from his stupor to groan some unintelligible instruction as his brother rode past.

As the two lead horses came around the final turn, they seemed locked in step at the same distance from one another, neither one gaining so much as an inch on the other, as Pride continued to maintain a full length on Northumberland.

"Show him the stick!" Bryant shouted his instructions above the noise of the crowd. It was no longer enough just to win for the doctor;

the race had become something very personal, and he willed his horse to bury the upstart challenger and prove there was no substitute for breeding.

Pounding down the home stretch, Crispin reached for his riding crop but Pride hit a tiny divot on the track, and the stick fell from the jockey's grasp. Distracted, his balance shifted ever so slightly as he turned to watch it ricochet off Edward's leg. Pride became confused and lunged perceptively to the left, breaking his stride. It was all the opening Edward needed. He kicked back on Northumberland's hindquarters and, leaning forward, swept past Pride of the Empire at the finish line by a nose.

Penny jumped for joy, her long auburn hair shaking loose from under her boyish cap. For a brief moment, she revealed that she was indeed a blossoming young woman. Edward waved to the crowd, acknowledging the cheers of congratulation all around as he trotted back to where Penny stood. He climbed out of the saddle and, caught up in the excitement of victory, pulled Penny to him and embraced her. At that moment, he realized a feeling for Penny that he had not allowed himself before.

Across the track, among the redcoats, Fletcher Radcliff took in the whole measure of the triumphant Hart family, including Penny Scott whom he assumed to be their servant. His was not a tender glance.

5

Finder's Keepers

BANG!

A shot rang out, interrupting the tongue-lashing William Bryant was giving young Crispin O'Grady near the far fence where Pride of the Empire was being attended to without fanfare. Lieutenant Fletcher Radcliff waved the smoking pistol in his hand as he and his brigade of redcoats hurried across the open field toward a rowdy group of spectators and gamblers on the verge of a brawl.

"Edward—quickly," commanded John Hart. "Round up the women and get them home. And take your improvident brother with you."

"Of course, Father," Edward accepted his assigned role without hesitation.

"Jesse, Nathaniel—come with me!" John ordered as he strode urgently toward the maelstrom. The older boys hustled to catch up with their father.

"Penny, please take care of Northumberland," Edward said, handing her the reins. "I'll take the carriage and fetch the women. We'll meet back at the farm."

"Be careful," Penny urged as she gracefully mounted the horse.

Edward slapped Northumberland's rump and watched as Penny galloped off. He then turned his attention to the unsteady John Jr. After helping him aboard the carriage, they headed toward Bloomsbury Court to collect their mother and sisters.

"We'll have none of that," shouted Lieutenant Radcliff as his troops reached the group of men. "Move along now. Back to your homes."

"Have you any idea what this stupid Mick just cost me?" Bryant fumed.

"*I* certainly do," Samuel Tucker said scowling at the sullen jockey.

"This is what you get when backward colonials are allowed to soil the sport of kings," the lieutenant scoffed. "You've even got your bloody horses racing arse backward. Every good Brit knows a race is run counter to the clock."

"And every good Irishman knows that a Brit don't know his arse from a hole in the ground when it comes to horses," retorted Seamus O'Grady as he stepped in between his son and the soldiers. A young redcoat corporal silenced Seamus by swinging the butt of his rifle into the innkeeper's midsection. Seamus staggered to the ground, gasping for breath. As Crispin tended to his father, an angry mob surged forward.

The British patrol fixed their bayonets and cocked their rifles.

"Steady men, hold your position," ordered Lieutenant Radcliff.

John Hart and his sons pushed their way forward into the tense epicenter. While appearing calm and in charge, the lieutenant discreetly placed his hand on the hilt of his sword—just in case. He and John locked eyes.

"No need for bloodshed, gentlemen," said John, signaling the crowd for calm with his outstretched arms. "There was a friendly wager on a very close contest, and things got a bit emotional. We can work this out among ourselves," he added, addressing Lieutenant Radcliff.

"You'll get your money, John Hart," Bryant seethed.

A thunderclap rumbled angrily overhead. John gazed upward as thick raindrops fell from the heavens as if to cool the flaring tempers.

"I suggest we continue this discussion over a pint or two, Doctor," John said congenially, "before we all become sodden wretches." Directing a shout toward the anxious crowd he added, "The first round's on me!"

The crowd cheered and headed for the tavern.

Seamus winced and groaned as the rain dancing off his head revived him. "Nathaniel, Jesse—bring Seamus along," Hart said.

Grudgingly, Bryant handed Pride of the Empire's reins back to Crispin. "I'll deal with you later," he huffed as he turned to follow the rest of the crowd to the tavern. Crispin attended to his chores obediently in hopes of minimizing the beating he would likely face.

Lieutenant Radcliff's eyes remained fixed on John as his two sons lifted Seamus to his feet and helped him across the field. The soldiers lowered their guns, and Radcliff slowly released his grip on the sword.

When all were out of earshot, the twitchy young corporal turned to his lieutenant. "A good thing at least one of them has some common sense, sir," he said.

Lieutenant Radcliff turned up his collar and watched the Harts make their way across the field in the driving rain. "It's men like that one you need to worry about," he said. "We'll want to keep an eye on him."

Across the way, Tucker doubled back to join the Harts.

"You have the makings of a fine diplomat, John," he exclaimed in a too-obvious attempt to get back in his friend's good graces. With a self-satisfied grin he added, "But did I not warn of what we could expect when the Brits saw us racing the opposite way around the track? I knew they would be insulted."

John walked in silence, followed by Jesse, Nathaniel, and Seamus, as they made their way toward the hospitable glow and warm comfort of Eagle Tavern.

Tucker scurried alongside of him waiting for a response. "Did you hear what I said, John?" he questioned impatiently.

"Sometimes a man needs to make a statement, Samuel, and sometimes he just needs a drink."

***

It was almost dark by the time Penny arrived back at the Hart homestead. Riding north along Rogers Road from Trenton, she had run into a heavy downpour near Pennytown—a small village that Edward proclaimed had been renamed for her when it was decided she would stay on with the Harts. For a short time she had believed the fairy tale, as she did most everything Edward told her.

As she approached the homestead astride Northumberland, she could see the candles lit and glowing in the main house and a warm fire burning in the hearth, inviting her to come in and get dry. She caught a whiff of the savory dinner the servants had prepared for Grandmother Martha and the younger Hart children, Scudder, Mary, Daniel, and Dee. While it was generally accepted that these children were too young to attend the race, Mary had been upset when Penny, who was not much older than she, had been allowed to go. Sensitive to begin with, Mary threw a tantrum and locked herself in the room she shared with Penny. Deborah excused the fit, noting that it wasn't often Mary had occasion to be in the company of her older married sisters. However, in her precarious late-term condition, her parents could not risk the ridicule and embarrassment that would be sure to accompany Mary's attendance.

Penny turned from the aroma of roast goose and cornbread and cantered down the lane to the old barn. She dismounted Northumberland and slowly pulled the creaky wooden barn door open, leaving it slightly ajar for when Edward returned with the carriage.

She lit a lantern and led the prized thoroughbred to his special stall. There she went about the task of removing his saddle and bridle. Several of the animals were stirred by the commotion. She hung the tacking carefully on the wall to dry, then threw a blanket over the champion horse's back and led him to the water trough.

While Northumberland drank, Penny removed her own wet coat and damp shirt and tossed them over the rail. Next, she removed her boots and shook out the water. She peeled off her wet woolen breeches and laid them alongside the rest of her clothes. She found another coarse blanket and wrapped it around herself.

Holding the lantern aloft, she made her way stealthily to the stacks of grain at the far end of the barn. She turned over one of the sacks and dumped some oats into a slatted wooden pail. Looking around to make sure she was alone, she reached behind the neatly stacked grain sacks and pulled out a jug of homemade corn whiskey she had seen Tolley, the Harts' Negro house servant, hide there a few days earlier.

Tolley was unaware that Penny knew about his secret stash, and she would never tell. Shaking the jug to make sure it wasn't empty, she carried it back with her to the stall. Setting it down, she placed the pail of oats before Northumberland then took the grooming brush and began to gently smooth his sleek coat.

When she'd brushed long enough, Penny pulled the cork out of the jug with her teeth and spit it on the floor. She took a swig and instantly the potent liquid raced down her throat, warming her insides. She pulled the blanket more snugly around herself and then took another sip from the jug.

The chill from the long, damp ride home was gone by her third taste. With the next, all inhibitions were forgotten as well. Magically, the room glowed in a soft amber haze. She felt the hot breath of the braying animals warming her exposed flesh. Softly she began singing a lullaby her mother used to sing to help her fall asleep on cold nights. The song always made her feel happy and safe.

She heard a noise like a creaking floorboard from behind her. Startled, she wheeled around quickly, and the heavy horse blanket covering her slid down, exposing her breasts. She looked up nervously and, in the dim lantern light, saw Edward dripping wet. He was watching her with an intensity that warmed her even more than the whiskey. As their eyes locked, she made no attempt to pull the blanket up. Instead, with an instinct that knew more than her years, she lay back in the hay.

In the next instant, he was on top of her. Wrapping her in his strong arms, he kissed her breasts, pale and lovely in the lamplight. Their lips met and his tongue probed her sweet, soft mouth. She looked deeply into his eyes, her breathing fast and ragged, and pulled urgently at his wet clothes. Shedding them as quickly as he could, he lowered himself over her, kissing her passionately.

He eased her legs apart, his chest brushing against her small firm breasts as he eagerly entered her and felt her warmth envelop him. She trembled at the furthest reach of more than a dozen thrusts, moaning softly as she rose to take him ever more fully inside.

They moved together naturally like horse and rider, bareback and unbridled, faster and faster galloping at full and frantic speed until they reached a breathtaking, body-aching end to their innocence. They lay back on the soft hay together, their youthful limbs entwined, left speechless by the intensity of the tenderness that now washed over them and lingered in their embrace.

When Penny awoke several hours later, a still sleeping Edward lay on his side, pressed against her naked back with one arm draped sweetly around her waist. She pulled the blanket up over the two of them for modesty's sake, smiling inwardly with a pure joy she had never before experienced. She stared at him in disbelief. Was this really happening to her? Had she finally found the happiness that had eluded her all her life? What wonderful providence, she wondered, had led her to escape down that river, to reach this home, to find his heart?

He stirred, as if feeling her eyes on him. "It'll be light soon," he said lazily, propping himself up on one elbow.

"Tell me I am yours, always," she asked anxiously, trying to read his boyish grin.

"Only if you will let me have my way with you again." He kissed her passionately.

"What would your parents say if they knew?" she asked nervously.

"Father would say that since I pulled you from the river, you are mine to do with as I please," he teased. "Finder's Keepers!"

She squinted her eyes in mock disapproval then punched him gently in the arm. "And your mother?"

"Hmmm," Edward thought for a moment. "Mother would ask if I had your permission before I ravished you."

"And?" she said playing with him. "Did you ask my permission?"

"Funny," he said, "I don't recall your response so maybe I should ask again." His lips met hers eagerly as they gave in to sweet passion once more.

6

Blood Bath

C hickens clucked and scattered as the two young lovers stole hand in hand across the plantation grounds. A rooster crowed as the first light of the new dawn carried them toward the house.

"I *will* have you, Penelope Scott," said Edward emphatically, his slate-gray eyes shimmering. "No matter what my family thinks."

"Finder's Keepers," Penny reminded him, touching his lips lightly with her fingertips.

"Forever!" he promised.

Lighthearted and giddy, the two lovers parted. Edward climbed the front porch steps quietly while Penny ran around to the back of the house, startling the Harts' mulatto kitchen servant, Violet, who was getting ready to feed the chickens.

"Weak bladder," explained a blushing and bedraggled Penny.

"Uh, huh," Violet replied, unconvinced. "Ain't that what the pot in your room is for?" she chided mildly.

Penny didn't stop to argue. Boots in hand, she crept up the back stairs quiet as a church mouse. She hoped Mary would still be asleep, or at least that her mood would be improved from the previous day.

She pushed open the door to the bedroom tentatively and peered inside. Mary lay still in her bed, curled up behind her pillows and sheets. Penny let out a shriek when her eyes adjusted to the light in the room, and she realized that the sheets were stained dark red. A bloody fetus lay motionless at Mary's feet, the umbilical cord still attached.

Penny screamed again then dropped to her knees by the bed, choked with panic and fear. John and Deborah burst into the room, dressed in their bedclothes.

Deborah gasped in horror as her eyes fell on her daughter's still form. "Dear God—*no!*"

Edward rushed in, followed closely by the rest of the family. He quickly went to Penny's side as if to shield her from the tragedy. He put his arm around her, and she turned and sobbed into his chest, her eyes tightly shut. John Jr. barred the door so the younger Hart children would not be witness to the horrifying scene.

"Take the children away from here," John barked at John Jr. He turned to Penny and Edward, holding hands and dressed in the same clothes as the day before. He immediately sized up the situation.

"Edward, fetch Doctor Van Kirk," he directed his son in a weary, almost emotionless voice. "Penny, find Violet and get this … this mess cleaned up."

As the two departed without a word, John bent down to comfort his wife. Sobbing quietly, Deborah was holding one of Mary's lifeless hands to her cheek.

"*Why?*" she pleaded looking up at him, her eyes welling with tears.

"Who can know these things?" he said in a hollow whisper, struggling to keep his composure for her sake. "I suppose it was meant to be, as our Mary could never have made it on her own in this hard world."

***

Reverend Isaac Eaton closed his prayer book and offered up one final blessing for the two departed souls now at peace in the company of their maker.

"Twas the devil's work that took her life and that of her unborn child," he said, laying a hand on John Hart's shoulder as the grieving father stared down into the shallow grave.

"She was distraught," Deborah said softly from behind her black veil. "I should have seen it coming."

"We all failed her, Deborah," replied John, looking squarely at Edward and Penny. "You did what you could."

Following the service, Doctor Van Kirk reported to the elder Hart that based on his examination the baby had been stillborn. He suspected Mary might have actually induced labor during the night and, in her dazed and confused state, tried to suffer through the birth in silence. The pain must have been excruciating. To stifle her screams, she bit down on a leather bridle strap while pushing down on her belly and pulling between her legs. Apparently, she bit hard—right through the leather, choking on a piece that had broken off and lodged in her throat, suffocating her. The details were so horrific that John wished he had never heard them. Then and there, he vowed to keep them to himself.

As the mourners began to move away, John walked up to Edward and Penny, who were standing off by themselves away from the other members of the family. Penny dabbed her moist eyes with her sleeve and offered her condolences to the man she'd come to respect as she might her own father. Edward stiffened, alert to something he saw in his father's forlorn face and the manner of his movements.

What John had to say pained him deeply, but it had to be said. To look the other way was to ignore the simple fact that the tragic loss of his feeble-minded daughter could have been prevented if Penny had been in the room that night. It pained him even more because he had grown quite fond of Penny Scott, but they had taken her in with the expectation she would watch over and protect fragile Mary. She had failed them in that regard. Besides, with revolution in the air, Edward could ill-afford to take up with a girl who was herself a mere child. Not a vulnerable child who had lived a sheltered life, like Mary, but one who had been wronged or abandoned by nearly everyone she'd counted on for support.

"Edward," he began slowly. "What I have to say to you, I say with a heavy heart."

The young man fidgeted, knowing what was coming. He had expected it since the morning they'd found poor Mary in bed, a bloody corpse. Relations had cooled between father and son, and he had noticed a new distance between his father and Penny, too. There had been no victory celebration for Northumberland's triumph, and John had offered no word of thanks to his son for upholding the family honor. Instead, in the days that followed the race, they had avoided one other, speaking neither of triumph nor tragedy.

Unlike Edward, Penny blamed herself exclusively for his sister's death. It seemed to her that all happiness was fleeting, and she was doomed to live in sorrow and sadness. Edward tried to convince her otherwise, but the truth of the matter was that neither of them had gone out of their way to be alone together again since the first time. It was as if their romance was over before it had begun; as though being together would be a painful reminder of the day after rather than of the pleasurable journey of the night itself. Penny cursed her cruel fate as she now awaited her benefactor's judgment.

"I will come straight to the point," John said forcefully. "I hold you both accountable for Mary's death. From this point forward, you will conduct yourselves in a respectable manner and refrain from any relations, so long as you remain under my roof."

He didn't wait for an argument. Nor did he expect one would be forthcoming. He stormed away to brood alone, leaving Edward and Penny to pick up the pieces of a relationship forbidden by the one man whose blessing they wanted most.

***

When the New Jersey Provincial Congress met again in Trenton, from the 5th to the 17th of August 1775, John Hart welcomed the distraction. For a man who seemed gratefully headed into political obscurity, he was now equally gratified to find himself at the forefront of a very active New Jersey political scene. His name seemed to be on everyone's lips and lists. By the time the Provincial Congress adjourned on the 17th, he found himself elected to the newly formed eleven-man Committee of Safety. This powerful elite arm of the shadow government was charged with the responsibility of protecting the public welfare when the Provincial Congress was in recess. Fiscally prudent and wary of the potential for abuse, John was glad to be among those chosen to govern these matters—if for no other reason than to keep an eye on Samuel Tucker, who had also been selected.

On the home front, as in the Capital, emotions ran deep. Still dressed in black, Deborah Hart continued to grieve over the loss of her daughter and the grandchild she would never know. Her prolonged mourning only made Penny Scott's feelings of guilt more unbearable. John's aged mother, seeing that her daughter-in-law was not ready to resume care of her young children, began to insert herself into the family's domestic affairs. This led to a confrontation between the two women that was only resolved when John asked his eldest daughter, Sarah Wyckoff, to move back into the homestead to help run the household until Deborah was ready to resume the role.

One day while the family patriarch was in Trenton, preoccupied with the latest affairs of government, Edward and Penny seized the opportunity to go riding together. Their destination was a remote hilltop, high in the Sourland Mountains bordering the Hart homestead to the north and east. There, the young lovers rested their mounts and stood on the ridge to take in the sweeping view of the Hopewell Valley below.

"It's breathtaking!" gushed Penny, emerging from a shallow cave cut in the rock ledge where she and Edward had just made sweet forbidden love. The impromptu love nest was hidden from plain view by thick, overgrown vegetation. She took Edward's arm, "However did you find this spot?"

"My father and grandfather used to hunt in these hills," he said proudly. "I've heard my father say a man could be lost to the world in these woods and no one would ever find him."

"Or us, thankfully," Penny replied absentmindedly before changing the subject. "Your father is a wonderful man, Edward, and I am deeply troubled that we've hurt him so."

"He'll get over it," Edward said. He took her hand and kissed it gently.

"Not while I'm around to remind him," she said pulling away slowly.

"What do you mean?" he questioned sharply.

"You heard what your father said—he will never accept the way we feel about each other as long as we are under his roof."

"He will in time, Penny."

"No, Edward, in his care I am at best another daughter to protect." Looking up into his handsome boyish face, she said, "At worst, I am a reminder of the horror that befell poor Mary, though I know he would not wish that fate upon me in her stead."

"We can be careful," Edward said defensively, taking her in his arms again.

"Yes, we can," she sighed, "but we will always feel a measure of guilt if we must steal our moments of pleasure behind his back." She took his hands in hers and raised them to her face, holding them gently against her cheeks. "He does not deserve that and neither do we."

Edward dropped her hands and turned to gaze out over the ridge. "So what do we do then—give up on one another? Can you deny that what we felt that night remains as strong within us this very moment?"

"I deny nothing, Edward," she pleaded. "My love is yours. It has always been and will always be. That is why I must leave."

"Leave?" He turned to face her as he felt his heart breaking. Looking into her sky-blue eyes, he asked, "Where would you go?"

"Reverend Eaton has graciously agreed to let me stay with his family," she said without hesitation. "And he will employ me to help look after the school children."

"Does my father know about this?"

"Reverend Eaton is planning to speak with him about it when he returns from his legislative responsibilities."

Edward responded with an ironic laugh.

"Why do you laugh?" she asked quizzically.

"Because if you stay with the Eatons, you'll still be under my father's roof—he donated the land the Baptists built their church on before I was born. He's their landlord!"

It was Penny's turn to laugh. "Not anymore, Edward. According to Reverend Eaton, your father recently deeded them the land. The Baptists own it now—lock, stock, and barrel."

"Smart move," Edward admitted with a smirk. "I guess Father learned a lesson from the election he lost to Samuel Tucker after all."

She threw her arms around him. "Whatever your father's motivation, Edward, we will finally be free to love one another the way God intended when He brought me to you. Even your father will not be able to deny us that."

Beholding her in this moment, Edward could not help but think how much the skinny little river rat he'd fished from the water less than a year ago had matured in thought as well as in form. The orphaned child had become a woman—strong, confident, and capable of making her own decisions.

"What about Mother?" he asked. "Have you considered that she will not want you to leave?"

"With Sarah back home, she needs the extra room." She grew pensive. "Besides, I can no longer sleep there. I am tormented by nightmares."

"Poor Mary's death was no fault of yours," he declared.

"I know that, Edward, but don't you see?" Penny unleashed her pent-up thoughts. "My life itself has been full of such horrors. My parents died before I ever had a chance to know them. My baby brother was taken by savages and probably murdered, too. The relatives who came to my rescue stole the only memories I had of my mother along with her jewelry and adopted me for their own advantage, not out of any family loyalty or love. I never knew either of those before heaven brought me to your wonderful family. I want more than anything on earth to belong here, but I cannot stay where I am a constant reminder of sadness and loss."

"In time, they'll come to see you as the woman by my side and forget the pains of the past," Edward offered her sincerely.

"Then you agree?" she said hopefully. "My moving out is for the best. I must find my own way for now."

Edward mounted his horse. "And I must make mine," he said, stoically. "In a few short months, I will be of an age to make decisions without my father's consent. Know this, dear heart of mine, when that time comes, I shall not run from my duty." And with that he turned and galloped away.

7

Breaking Apart

No sooner had John Hart returned from a Court of Common Pleas session and the pressing affairs of the Provincial Congress in Trenton than he found himself packing once again. This time he was bound for a meeting of the Committee of Safety, scheduled to convene in Princeton on August 30. The selected meeting place would give him the opportunity to associate with colleagues John Witherspoon, president of the College of New Jersey at Princeton, and the respected Quaker lawyer Richard Stockton on their home turf. New Jersey was moving headlong on a collision course with destiny, and the students and faculty of the venerable college were leading the charge for radical change.

As John gathered the items he needed for his departure, John Jr. appeared in the doorway of his study. The younger man rapped his knuckles on the door with solemn purpose.

The elder Hart looked up momentarily while continuing to collect his papers. "Yes, John, what is it?" He asked, as he regarded his ne'er-do-well son.

The 27-year-old took a tentative step into the room. "I've come to say good-bye," he replied with some hesitation.

"Good-bye?" John appeared amused but then noted his son's travel attire. "Has the town run dry from your excessive thirst?"

John Jr. grinned. He had prepared himself for this kind of dismissal from his father. He knew full well that his recent behavior had been less than stellar and that he was viewed as a disappointment by his parents. "Uninspired" was a word he had heard his mother use to describe his lack of ambition when compared to that of his brothers—

and that came from a good and kind woman who adored him. Others had taken to calling him "lazy" and "self-indulgent."

What everyone failed to consider was that the legacy the Hart patriarch had crafted for himself—and expected his sons to follow—loomed large in Hunterdon County and was increasingly recognized throughout New Jersey. It was one thing to be the son of the honorable John Hart, Esquire; it was decidedly more difficult to share his illustrious name. In these unsettled times, with men choosing sides and forming allegiances based on deep-rooted political philosophies, the name given as an honor to the third Hart son felt more like a ball and chain.

After much thought, the black sheep had decided there was but one solution—to make a new beginning far from the suffocating presence of the man whose accomplishments he could never hope to match. As his 28th birthday approached, John Jr. felt he had put off making this decision for far too long.

"Yes, Father, I'm afraid it has," he answered respectfully.

"Does your mother know of your plans?" John was well aware of the special relationship his namesake shared with Deborah. It had been a point of contention in many a late night conversation between husband and wife.

"No, Father. Not yet."

"And your brothers?"

John Jr. lowered his head. "No, sir. I've come to you first."

"You'll be needing money then?" the elder Hart quickly surmised.

"A small bond, sir. A good faith loan." John Jr. laid the document out in front of his father.

John scanned the note. "A surety bond to a Philadelphia financier? For what purpose, may I ask?"

"Land, sir. In Louisiana."

"Speculation? You mean to trifle with the Spanish?"

John Jr. stood his ground. "They have no right to refuse me. I know this land. I was born here."

"The Spanish acquired Louisiana fairly from the French, John. What makes you believe they will welcome you, let alone sell their land to a loyal subject of the King of England?"

"It would be a mistake for them to consider me so," he said quickly. "I am loyal to no king and least of all the one in England."

"So this is how you choose to support our common cause? To run from the coming fight?"

"Let Jesse, Nathaniel, and Edward take up arms, Father. They are endowed with our grandfather's martial spirit. I can be more useful in bringing the Spanish over to our side. They have no love for a tyrant, either."

"Son, I feel quite sure your motive for this venture has more to do with personal gain than it does with the hereditary succession of a tyrannical monarch. However, I will grant you that our cause may be better served with you out of harm's way rather than in the thick of it. Indeed, should I never have to make good on this bond I will be pleasantly surprised. And, should you bring the Spanish over to the side of the colonies, I will be greatly impressed. Should either of us live to see a new government based on the guarantee of human rights and privileges in a free society, then the petty dalliances of your past and our present discourse on these matters will seem superfluous."

With that, John signed the bond and thrust it back into his son's hand.

"Thank you, Father," the younger man said as he carefully folded the note and placed it in the pocket of his waistcoat. "Despite how you feel about me, I believe, as others do, that you are the right man to turn to in these troubled times. But I must find my own path—one that diverges from yours and that may someday bear fruitful consequences for the Hart name beyond anything you or I can imagine at this moment."

"I pray let it be so, son," John Hart smiled tenderly. "Let it be so."

***

Samuel Tucker banged the gavel down, formally ending what he hoped would be the final session of the Provincial Congress for the year 1775. As president of the local organization, the October meetings in Trenton had been particularly stressful for him. While the accommodations at the French Arms Tavern were pleasant, and the meeting rooms above the Hunterdon County Courthouse spacious, the matters under discussion were particularly demanding. In the end, it was resolved that the New Jersey militia was to be enlarged, and two battalions of recruits for the regular Continental troops were authorized. John Hart was elected chair of the committee appointed to draft the budget and provide for a means of appropriation. By proclamation, fifty thousand pounds was to be raised.

Tucker was deeply concerned about the precarious situation in which he now found himself. In addition to presiding over the Provincial Congress, he was a duly elected representative of the General Assembly—the legally constituted arm of the colonial government that still had the support of many New Jersey colonists. He expected real trouble to follow the announcement of new taxes in support of increasing the colonial militia, which could be but for one purpose. While Tucker relished his duplicitous role in both legislative bodies for the opportunities it afforded him, he knew he would be blamed by Loyalist Assembly constituents for the actions of the upstart rebel Congress. A nervous young clerk approached and handed him a note, rousing him from the extended moment of self-pity. Tucker read it immediately, then walked over to where John was seated, pen in hand as he worked on his committee's monetary plan.

"Well, it's official," Tucker said, pulling up a chair beside him. "The King has addressed Parliament, branding us as rebels and asking 'his' people to rise up against the leaders of the rebellion."

"Does that make you uncomfortable, Samuel?" John asked as he adjusted his spectacles.

"A little," Tucker admitted.

"My God, man—where did you think all of this was heading? We've taken control of the government, raised an army, and are illegally taxing royal subjects. I daresay George III has got the situation summed up right for once."

"And it's about bloody time," agreed Abraham Clark, a member of the committee, as he moved past the two men.

Tucker changed the subject lest anyone else in the room overhear him airing his personal misgivings. "I must say, John, it was rather brilliant of you to suggest the committee give Isaac Collins the commission to print up our new paper money," he said, trying to sound both flattering and upbeat. "It could be just the incentive Collins needs to move his presses from Burlington to Trenton. We could use the dedicated reporting of a sympathetic local newspaper to carry our message to the people."

"Indeed, Samuel," replied John, dipping his quill in the ink jar. "Trenton does seem to be at the heart of the rebel activity. No doubt in time it will play an even larger role in our fight for freedom." He abruptly paused in his jottings and studied the moon-shaped face and pointed nose of his colleague. In a low voice, he continued, "But I think you know I had a more immediate purpose in mind when recommending Collins."

"Ah, yes—the counterfeiting," mused Tucker, recalling John's measured arguments in front of the Congressional panel hours earlier.

"Precisely," replied John, punctuating the affirmative point with a flick of his pen's feather toward Tucker. "If we allow those without scruples, without loyalty to anyone save themselves, to copy and circulate our new currency, the injury will be greater than anything the King might inflict. Franklin's detailed leaf designs are so intricate as to render them impossible to copy except by Mother Nature herself. Having studied the master's work extensively, I have no doubt that Collins will faithfully execute those designs on our behalf."

Tucker became thoughtful. "It is a shame the good doctor is no longer in the printing business himself. We could use his expertise."

"I have little doubt he will serve our cause in ways too numerous to contemplate and with means too few of us possess," John said.

"It would do well for his son to recognize the inevitability of the future," offered Tucker without much thought.

John took measure of his would-be friend and sometimes rival, not sure if Tucker was baiting him or expressing a genuine sentiment. The attorney, he assumed, was aware of the fateful Trevose Summit where father and son could not come to terms on the correct course of action for the colonies. "I fear it is too late to hold out such hope for our esteemed Royal Governor. If a father cannot persuade his son to act on conscience, what hope has the will of the people to prevail upon him to do the same?"

Once again Tucker adeptly changed the course of the conversation. "And what's to become of your family, John?"

John sighed heavily. It was precisely the thought that had been perplexing him since his mission in the new Congress began. "Alas, we too are breaking apart, and I am at wit's end to forestall it."

"Deborah?" asked Tucker with seemingly true concern.

"Her health is little improved, although I thank you for inquiring, Samuel. Recent events have exacted a heavier toll on her than was at first apparent."

"Surely she is supportive of your efforts to reconcile our grievances with the Mother Country?" This was Samuel Tucker at his artful best, mixing politics and personal inquiry to gauge a potential adversary's position on an issue in order to gain advantage. It was not as though John was unguarded in respect to his frequent fishing expeditions. The truth was he rarely felt threatened by Tucker's probing, no matter what the lawyer's ulterior motives might be. Indeed, he often found that conversations with Tucker allowed him to access his own inner thoughts; thus, he spoke quite freely, confident that he could defend himself against whatever he confided.

"The politics of King and Crown are of minor importance to my fair Deborah. She may be the wife of a 'firebrand,' but the children remain her chief concern."

"I'm sure she still mourns the loss of Mary."

"Mary's death was the only the beginning, Samuel. John Jr. has left to seek fame and fortune in the wilds of Louisiana, and Deborah is inconsolable about it. The unexpected departure of Penny Scott also weighs heavy on her heart, not to mention the effect it has had on Edward, whom I can no longer in good conscience restrain from the military service he is so desirous of." John paused to collect his thoughts before continuing. "If all these matters were not trying enough, the latest blow might be the hardest to endure. Only a fortnight ago, according to Jesse, whilst I was here fulfilling my civic duties, our impressionable eighteen-year-old, Scudder, snuck over to the Friends Meeting House, where it seems the Reverend John Brainerd is promoting the development of his Burlington refuge for the Lenape. He has self-righteously named it 'Brotherton' and implies that it is intended for all walks of disaffected people. My sensitive son was apparently so captivated by Brother Brainerd's picture of utopian bliss and communal harmony that he has left home to cast his lot with the Indians."

"And for this Deborah holds you accountable?"

"No, I do," John admitted with a mixture of relief at having expressed it and sadness at having realized it.

8

Common Ground

*C*ommon Sense lit the American spirit in the spring of 1776 like a fully charged bolt through one of Benjamin Franklin's new fangled lightning rods. Written in a confrontational style by an Englishman named Thomas Paine, whose entry into American society was paved by no less a patron than Franklin himself, the forty-seven page pamphlet galvanized colonial leaders up and down the Atlantic coastline, helping to focus and unify them. The call was for nothing short of complete separation from England, and, seemingly overnight, the conflict in the colonies evolved from an uprising, or at best a rebellion, into a full-fledged revolution with "Independence!" as the battle cry.

Paine's treatise was an eloquent product of Enlightenment thinking. Delivered in fiery, evangelical pulpit prose, Paine methodically tore down the vestiges of divine right monarchies and hereditary succession in terms so direct that even the most naive reader understood. He summoned an arsenal of seemingly indisputable arguments, including Biblical quotations, and cited a litany of historical failures on the part of the heretofore-revered English tradition of government that, since the Norman Conquest, had included thirty kings and two reigning minors resulting in no fewer than eight civil wars and nineteen rebellions. In a single stroke, Paine exposed the myth of the vaunted English constitutional monarchy for the fraud it was. He rationalized for one and all the urgent need for a clean break from the feudalism of Europe and espoused the view that an enlightened self-rule of the New World was not only preferable but inevitable.

The popularity of *Common Sense* was unprecedented. Selling for about a shilling, the pamphlet was not only affordable but could be easily copied and shared. Paine's treatise on the "necessary evil" of government was read widely by men, women, and children. His fervent words were discussed on street corners, preached in churches, and proclaimed in taverns, and became nearly sacred among soldiers in the field, yet nowhere was the impact of *Common Sense* felt more strongly than in the households of a colonial America on the brink of war.

Arriving home late for the evening meal, John Hart was both surprised and pleased to find his family waiting for him. Seated patiently around the long wooden dinner table, they were so anxious to hear the latest breaking news that Jesse and Nathaniel had decided to take dinner with their father rather than with their own wives and children. The youngest of John and Deborah's offspring, Daniel and Dee, along with Sarah's four children, had been fed and put to bed early.

John shook the June rain from his hat and coat and hung them on a crowded hook behind the door. Tolley bowed slightly before removing the wet apparel from the hook and taking it to the fireside to dry.

"Make haste to dry them, Tolley," John said. "I will have need of them shortly." He bent over and kissed the top of his mother's head, then gave his frail wife a tender peck on the cheek. She threw him a stern look as she rearranged a place setting at the head of the table. Violet brought him a basin of warm water and a hand towel.

"Violet, bring Mr. Hart a bowl of stew and some bread," said Deborah.

"Yes, mistress," the maid answered, whisking away the basin and towel and heading for the kitchen.

John took his seat with Jesse and Nathaniel at either arm. Edward regarded his father anxiously from the middle of the table. He had news of his own he was bursting to share with the family.

Sarah stood over her father's shoulder with a jug: "Hot cider, Father?" she asked.

"Yes, please, Sarah. I have need of something to warm the innards and soothe the soul. Has everyone eaten?"

"The younger children have been fed and put to bed," replied Jesse, "but we waited for you."

"You look so tired, husband," Deborah said in a voice tinged with both reproach and weariness. "Surely whatever business has come up can wait until the morrow?"

John looked around the table into the faces of his three sons. The mixture of apprehension and fervor he saw in their eyes brought to mind a tribal council of war not unlike the meetings he had recently been attending.

He took a sip of his cider, savoring the pungent juice. "This cannot wait," he said, "for I am to leave for Philadelphia immediately." The excitement in his voice was unmistakable.

"Philadelphia?" gasped Deborah. "That's so far!"

"It's only thirty miles, Mother," corrected Jesse, whose conveyance work took him up and down the rutted roads linking New York to Philadelphia. The perceptive young man knew it was not the actual mileage so much as the distance from the patriarch's strength that troubled his mother.

Violet set a bowl of piping hot stew before John as Tolley and Sarah served the others.

John broke off a piece of crusty bread and dipped it in the bowl. His face was aglow with cider, stew, and purpose. "I have been chosen as one of the five delegates to represent New Jersey in discussions at the Continental Congress, and …" he paused for dramatic effect, "I can assure you we will vote for independence!"

His three sons let out a whoop that John was certain could be heard in the next county. Sarah hugged her mother and grandmother. "Your father would be so proud of you, son," his mother said, wiping a tear from her eye.

"We've got Tom Paine to thank for this joyful news," boasted Nathaniel. "His words set the whole thing in motion."

"Let us not forget George III," Jesse reminded his brother. "He and his ministers deserve a good deal of the credit for their arrogance and folly."

"Will there be a formal declaration of war then, Father?" asked Edward, calculating what the news might mean to the men pressed into military service.

"Yes, Edward, but not a war to be fought by thirteen separate militias. We are to be free and independent states but united as one country with a common cause—to break the yoke of slavery that ties us to the old world and the old ways. Ours will be a new and responsive government made up of people, not kings."

Nathaniel noticed the look that passed between Tolley and Violet as they cleared the empty plates from the table. He mouthed their unspoken thoughts. "In this new country, Father, will everyone enjoy the same promised freedoms?"

John considered his son's question for a moment before responding. "Americans will decide their own fate, determine their own form of government, and elect their own leaders by casting ballots—not by being born into it."

"Who will have the right to vote?" asked Jesse curiously.

"All men of property, of course," was John's quick reply.

"Freeholders, then," noted Edward. "Same as now."

His father nodded as he scooped up more of the delicious stew.

"What about women?" asked Sarah. "Is there to be no suffrage for our grievances in this new country?"

"And slaves?" questioned Nathaniel quickly, with Tolley and Violet listening intently. "Between our servants and our women that's nearly two thirds of the population. Who will fight for *their* needs?"

John held up his hands. "Let us take this one step at a time, shall we?" he said, his tone suddenly a bit defensive. "Once the English shackles are routed from the land, their customs and laws will go by the wayside. Royalty and slavery are both conventions of that old world."

Sarah hid her disappointment. So too did Tolley and Violet.

"Do you really believe that, Father?" asked Edward.

John looked at his wife. Her silent stare spoke volumes to him. In her eyes, he saw the years of secrets, sacrifices, and tears that lay behind them. Only happiness should lie ahead. "It is truly my greatest hope, but let us not lose our focus on the task at hand. We must rid ourselves of our oppressors. That will be work enough for all of us to accomplish."

"What has happened to the Royal Governor?" Jesse wondered aloud.

"He's been placed under house arrest," John said. "It is my understanding he will be sent to a Tory camp in Connecticut for his own protection."

"The poor dear!" exclaimed Deborah. "Can his father do nothing for him?"

"Benjamin will not intercede on William's behalf. He made his choice and now he must live by it, as must we all."

"We are with you, Father," said Jesse.

"Yes, we are," agreed Nathaniel and Edward.

"So it appears, and my heart is glad," John said as he finished his meal. "Each of you must make up his own mind, just as John Jr. and Scudder have apparently done. Sarah, you and Jacob must do the same, as must Gayle, Susanna, Martha, and their husbands. There will be hard times ahead. No one, not even I, can tell you what to do. The choice is yours and yours alone."

As John spoke, Tolley entered the room to summon his mistress. Deborah excused herself and followed him to the kitchen. Not a minute had gone by when Violet emerged with an aromatic apple crisp, placing it before John that he might take the first slice.

"What have we here? Has my wife taken to baking again?"

Deborah beamed as she re-entered the room, a shy Penny Scott in tow behind her. "Not I, husband," she said with a smile. "Twas our Penny who made the pie for this auspicious occasion."

As Penny smiled demurely, it was instantly clear to all that this was not the rough and tumble stable hand they had adopted almost two years earlier. The slight and gangly sprig had blossomed into a full-bodied fruit tree. Gone were the crude work shirts and riding breeches; in their place, she wore a long multilayered skirt of stitched blue indigo and a high-collared white lace blouse. Her long auburn tresses cascaded down over her shoulders.

Edward's heart leaped in his chest. Jesse and Nathaniel stared in disbelief. John smiled broadly, welcoming his runaway "daughter" back to their table. "Please sit with us, Penny," he said, as Sarah pulled a chair out for her, just across from Edward.

"Actually, the reverend and his wife send the pie with their blessings," Penny set the record straight. "Word is spreading quickly through the valley of your important mission, sir," she said, directing her remarks to the elder Hart. "All of our hopes and prayers go with you, sir. Success and Godspeed!"

"We will not let the good people of this colony down," John replied. "Tell the reverend and his missus not to worry. We shall see this new beginning through to a glorious end."

Penny and Edward locked eyes, trying to hold their emotions in check during the family reunion. Try as they might, they could not keep their eyes off one another throughout the remainder of the evening.

As the meal came to a close, John addressed each of his sons in turn.

"Jesse, I have a most urgent request of you," he began. "In my study, I have signed twelve thousand five hundred pounds in New Jersey notes. I ask that you deliver this money personally to the Treasurer Samuel Tucker while I am away. Our very freedom depends upon it."

Jesse accepted the responsibility readily. "You can count on me, Father."

"Nathaniel," John said, "I do not know how long I shall tarry in Philadelphia, but to you I entrust our crops and livestock. Look after the farm."

"Consider it done, Father."

Edward stood up before his father had a chance to address him. "Father, I have an announcement to make," he began excitedly.

"I know of your plans to join the army in defense of New York, Edward. No doubt General Washington will have need of young men with your fighting spirit. Go with my blessing, son. Make us all proud."

"Thank you, Father," Edward said amid hugs and handshakes from his brothers. "I shall do my best."

This news caught the Hart women by surprise. Remembering her husband Edward's failure and disappointment in New York thirty years earlier, Grandmother Martha began to protest in earnest, joined by her daughter-in-law.

Only Penny remained silent, though her heart raced. She knew Edward had been planning this moment for quite some time. His mind was made up, just as hers had been when she decided to leave the only real home she had ever known and the only people she had ever loved. There would be no protest from her; no tears of sadness, no display of fear whatsoever for what the future might hold. Despite how she felt at this moment, she had to find the courage to support Edward, to hope and pray he would return safely to her when his service to his country was completed.

"Stop your whining, ladies, it is decided," John said adamantly, rising from his chair. "We all have our parts to play—let your men do their duty."

With the dinner discussion brought to a conclusion, Nathaniel and Jesse followed their father to his study while Sarah went to check on the sleeping children. Deborah and Grandmother Martha left to supervise the doings in the kitchen, leaving Edward and Penny alone together.

"You don't seem surprised by my decision," he said as he came around the table to embrace her.

"It's not as though you haven't given me plenty of notice," she smiled at him. "You've been waiting your whole life for a chance to prove yourself. You won't find a better one than this."

She reached under her skirt and produced a copy of *Common Sense*, placing it in his hands. "In the event you ever need to remember what you're fighting for, this may help."

"I'll be reminded as much by the giver as by the gift," Edward remarked with a full heart as he spied the inscription she had written on the title page: *To E. H., "Finder's Keepers." Love, Penny.* He bent to kiss her, a gesture warmly returned.

"I have no gift for you, Penny," he said when their lips parted, "and no right to ask you to wait for me."

"You don't have to ask, Edward. Fate will decide."

"And you're all right with that?"

"It was fate that brought us together. Who am I to question what she intends now? She must have some grand purpose in store for me, else I should have perished with my family or been drowned in the river."

"I will return, Penny, but before I do I will avenge my grandfather's shame so that he may finally rest in peace. No army in the world will keep me from my destiny."

"Godspeed, dear Edward. I love you!"

With that, she threw her arms around his neck and pressed her lips to his, hard enough to leave a lasting impression and a heart that beat in him like a drum.

9

Loyal Opposition

I hear that one of their sons has run off to live with savages," Mrs. Emily Bryant gossiped with Mrs. Julia Brennan, one of the social climbers with whom she frequently took afternoon tea.

"I must say I was pleasantly surprised by the appearance of her daughters," Julia offered with a condescending little laugh. "Quite fashionable for a family known for homespun." She helped herself to a sweet roll baked fresh that morning by the Bryants' eavesdropping kitchen help, Mattie.

"I think we could see our way to offer a relationship with one of the younger daughters, in the spirit of *noblesse oblige*, but every time I mention the Hart name, my husband nearly growls at me and walks away muttering," sighed Emily, watching closely for her guest's reaction.

"I can understand your husband's reservations, dear," Julia replied. "We'll need to be sure where their loyalties lie before inviting any of them into our company."

"Oh heavens, Julia—let us leave politics to our husbands! Life here is dreary enough without having to concern ourselves with malcontents. Next thing you know, we'll be worrying whether or not our servants are happy!" Emily spoke loud enough to be certain Mattie had heard and then continued, "Now, tell me more about Madame DeSange. I'm sure you noticed that her décolletage left nothing to the imagination in the presence of so many men."

You poor, naive thing, Julia thought as Emily continued to gossip. *If you only knew how much* I've *revealed to get what* I *want! But, then, you have a rich husband with a backbone—my poor fool barely has a penis, let alone any guts or ambition. Thank heavens his family fortune hasn't been* completely *squandered.* Her eyes narrowed involuntarily. *I will do whatever is necessary to put what's left of it to good use.*

Mattie interrupted Emily's chatter and Julia's musings to clean up the tea service and inquire about her mistress's wishes for the remainder of the day.

"Thank you, Mattie. Mr. Bryant will be late this evening. Plan for supper accordingly and do prepare enough for guests. We may be five or six." She dismissed her servant and turned her attention back to Julia. "You'll be waiting for your husband, won't you, my dear?"

"Oh, thank you for the offer, dear, but I'm afraid I must take my leave shortly. I've already left too much in the hands of my servants today. If I don't watch over them, nothing will get done in time for our move." Julia rose and gathered her belongings. "Now won't it be delightful to be closer neighbors?"

"My, yes, I do hope our husbands can come to terms over the property they're surveying today—it will be lovely having you closer," Emily replied, her sincerity unconvincing. "I understand they've employed Samuel Tucker to arrange the sale. Do you know him?"

"Only by reputation," Julia said as she moved to the door. "Lawyer, sheriff, legislator—I wonder if the poor man ever rests!"

"I wonder if he ever sees his wife." Emily smiled slyly at her companion before calling her servants to ready Julia's carriage.

As Julia departed, Emily turned to her servant. "Mattie, are you certain your source can be trusted?"

"I don't know nuthin' 'bout no source, Ma'am, but Joseph the mule driver tole me he saw that woman alone with Mr. Tucker and they was gettin' more than friendly," Mattie repeated the story to her smiling mistress. "Now, I know Joseph, and he don't lie."

A few hours later, as the sun was setting on a lovely summer day, Doctor William Bryant arrived at his estate on horseback with Robert Brennan and Samuel Tucker riding on either side of him. Apparently the negotiations had gone well, for they were all in high spirits.

"Gentlemen, join me for a brandy here on the veranda while the servants ready supper." As Bryant motioned for one of his slaves to see to the horses, Robert dismounted.

Tucker remained in the saddle. "I'm afraid there is no rest for the wicked," he said with a grin. "Having just returned from my Assembly duties, there are pressing matters that require my attention."

"Well, you had best avoid the free thinkers and rebels, if you can," the doctor replied, only half jokingly.

"You wound me, sir!" Tucker chortled. "I am but a humble businessman trying to make a living."

"If the wages from your work today are those of a humble businessman, then I must try to be more humble," Bryant concluded. Tucker did not reply, but tipped his hat and rode away as Emily came out to the veranda, walking behind the servant who offered drinks to the men.

"Was that Mr. Tucker, and gone so soon?" she asked her husband.

"Off to hustle another shilling or two, no doubt," Bryant said as he took two drinks from the tray and handed one to Robert. "No matter what he's up to, we have cause to celebrate. We paid a fraction of what that land is worth, and there is room enough to suit both your residential interests and my commercial concerns without infringing upon one another's graces."

Emily tried to keep her thoughts to herself as she glanced at Mr. Brennan and saw him, for the first time, as the cuckold she knew him to be.

"Will you be joining us for supper, Mr. Brennan, or should you be headed home to the missus?" Emily thought at least to give the man a hint, but her husband interceded.

"Have the servants set a place for our guest. We still have much to discuss."

Emily left the men to their brandies.

"I don't trust Tucker," Robert said at length.

"I trust him to do what's in his best interest, that's all," the doctor said calmly. "This is a good purchase, Robert, and if you won't have your share I'll take all parts of it."

"I wasn't speaking of the land deal—I'm in for my share of that. I'm just concerned where his loyalties lie. I've heard rumors that he's a ringleader in the rebel cause."

"Just a cover, more than likely. Samuel Tucker will do what is best for Samuel Tucker. Besides, we are the ones who are driving the business his way. This so-called rebel cause is really nothing more than the grumblings of the poor fueled by the support of a few old rabble rousers like John Hart. It will die due to inept leadership or be put asunder by the King's men as we grow our network of successful businesses loyal to the Crown." Bryant spoke with confidence, much to Robert's delight. Eager to show that he understood his host's perspective, he offered an observation of his own.

"In a way, Tucker reminds me of the Quakers. Neither wants a war of any sort, but neither will refuse to do business with the potential winning side."

"Exactly!" his host agreed, enthusiastically raising his glass in a toast to his guest.

***

"Oh, sweet merciful heaven!" Julia Brennan moaned in ecstasy as Tucker took her from behind. "Give me more!" she urged, spurring him to more vigorous thrusts, which she met eagerly. Her husband had never shown her more than the missionary position, and the one time she had mounted him in desperation the poor man spent himself in seconds, appearing shocked rather than excited by her zeal. Tucker was nothing much to look at, but his cunning was not confined to business and he wielded a formidable tool with little inhibition.

Julia turned around to face him like an animal in heat and pushed him back down onto the bed. She rode him with her eyes closed and all the girlish glee of a woman imprisoned in a loveless marriage. She did not necessarily share her lover's political views, but being in the company of such a prominent man during these unsettling times, if only clandestinely, was intoxicating. When she found out that her influential lover would be returning to Trenton from Burlington to conduct business with her husband and conclude the meeting of the Provincial Congress, she hurriedly made her excuses and arranged to meet him at their usual rendezvous before civic duty and domestic responsibility could lure him away from her arms.

Now she could feel herself rushing headlong toward an uncontrollable climax. Instinctively she dug her nails deeper into her lover's fleshy back, encouraging him to quicken the pace. As she arched to take his thrusts more deeply, perspiration dripped between her small, firm breasts, mixing with the scent of cheap French perfume and adding to his excitement.

As Tucker drove harder, she stifled a scream. With a fleeting sense of satisfaction, she felt him burst inside of her. They then lay there, side by side, satiated in the stolen moments of their sinful pleasure.

Suddenly there was a sharp rap on the door.

Her lover's body immediately went rigid. He sat upright, filled with sudden alarm. "Does anyone know you are here?" he interrogated her angrily.

"Of course not," she replied honestly.

"You were followed, then," he said accusingly, the anger in his round cheeks building to a faint red glow.

"Not a chance," she retorted. "I'm the one who has been discreet, although I must say I think Emily Bryant suspects something."

The sharp knock came again. Whoever was at the door was exceedingly persistent.

"Samuel Tucker?" the faintly familiar male voice on the other side of the door called softly.

In an instant Tucker was out of the bed and pulling his nightshirt over his clammy torso. In a moment of conscious vanity, he reached for his powdered wig and set it on top of his bald head. Julia giggled at the sight of the president of the New Jersey Provincial Congress standing before her, wig askew with the remnants of his earlier excitement bulging through his wrinkled nightshirt.

Tucker paid his laughing bedmate no mind. Quickly turning his attention to the door, he opened it a crack and peered out cautiously.

"What do you want?" he snarled as he recognized the intruder.

"Father said if all else failed, I might find you here," replied Jesse Hart, standing nervously in the hallway of the Recklesstown

Tavern, a modest establishment well suited for assignments requiring discretion.

"And so you have," replied Tucker, making no attempt to hide his contempt for the young man. "Pray tell what is so important to your father that he sends you to disturb me at this hour?"

From inside the room, the sound of steps upon the floorboards was heard by both men. Tucker grinned sheepishly as Jesse hoisted a small chest and thrust it toward the older man. "The Proclamation money," he announced. "Father would have brought it himself, but as you know he is in Philadelphia on urgent business."

Motioning for him to keep his voice down, Tucker grabbed the chest and hustled Jesse into the room. Julia stood by the bed, wrapped only in a sheet, a sheen of sweat reflecting on her exposed flesh. She looked the strapping young man up and down, lips parted slightly as she appraised him through her lidded hungry eyes. Flushing in embarrassment, Jesse quickly looked away.

Tucker let the awkward moment pass without an introduction, turning his attention to the trunk. "Is it all here?" he demanded.

"Half," replied Jesse as he handed Tucker the key. "Twelve thousand and five hundred pounds," Jesse carefully whispered in Tucker's ear.

From the bedside, Julia yawned pretending to be uninterested while straining to hear the conversation.

"The bill called for more," Tucker said, eyeing Jesse suspiciously. "Where's the rest?"

"Father will sign the remaining notes and get them to you upon his return," Jesse replied succinctly.

Tucker regarded John Hart's eldest son skeptically. The two men had had their disagreements in the past, but when it came to the word of the father, there could be no doubt. This delivery was in full, and the balance would follow as promised.

"Very well," he concluded, setting the chest on the bed beside Julia and ushering Jesse out the door. "Give my regards to your father."

Julia ran her fingers lightly over the chest, caressing it as lustfully as she had her lover's corpulent body minutes earlier. Though it wasn't Samuel Tucker she was thinking about now, the object of her desire mattered not a whit to him as the sheet fell to the floor. Enflamed by the sight, he threw her to the bed and took her again with savage force.

10

Our Sacred Honor

S o tell me, good Doctor, how do you judge the port?" John Hart asked his worldly companion.

"John, a poor wine imbibed with an old friend is more satisfying than a fine champagne in foul company," responded a very relaxed Benjamin Franklin.

"Thomas Paine may have his common sense, but you, sir, have uncommon wisdom," John said with genuine affection, though it occurred to him that his friend may have just disparaged the port.

"It is most kind of you to recognize the merits of an older mind, John," Ben said. "As to the wine—it is pleasant enough, but in truth I do prefer a beer in summer. That's something we certainly make better than the French. Speaking of which, I do hope the Adams boys bring some of Samuel's father's lager on their next visit. Have you tasted it?"

"No, but its reputation precedes it," John said. "I will gladly raise a pint or two with you and the Adams brothers when the opportunity arises."

"Actually, Samuel and John Adams are cousins, and it is Sam Sr. who is the brewer." Ben smiled, enjoying the conversation. "But no matter—you'll hear enough about them as we work on our Declaration over the course of the next few days. John is quite the orator and will do his best to represent the people of Massachusetts, though he makes no secret of wanting to represent a larger constituency. His cousin Samuel, on the other hand, is a man of action, devoted to the cause and well-respected." Chuckling, he added, "Perhaps owing to the quality of his father's brew!"

"How can you be abroad for so long," John wondered aloud, "yet sit here providing more local detail than I myself have gathered through vigorous participation with representatives throughout the colonies?"

"I have spies in bedrooms and courtrooms everywhere, John. Hopefully, our new nation will be different than any that came before it, but one can ill afford to ignore those men who are moved by greed or a desire for social standing, no matter where one lives," Ben concluded with a touch of sadness.

"Will you stay to help us see this nation born?" John asked hopefully.

"I'm quite sure I can do more for our cause in Europe, my friend, but I will leave you in good hands." Ben smiled at Hart before continuing. "Listen to the Virginian. This young Jefferson is wise beyond his years and has the confidence of General Washington without whom we would have no means to focus our forces."

The two old friends continued their conversation long into the night, discussing their families, the individual delegates, and a host of other topics. They shared a burning passion for independence and for the golden opportunity they had to build a new nation based on liberty and equality. Ben went so far as to admit his abolitionist sentiments, and John admitted that his wife shared those ideas, while he himself was somewhat more conflicted on the issue. For Ben, in his seventies, and John, in his sixties, no subject was out of bounds for discussion. Their mutual respect had been built upon years of honest business together and a desire to see the best in those around them.

When John returned to his modest accommodations that night, he was pleased to find that the rest of the New Jersey delegates had arrived. He regarded each of his peers for the individuals they were. He and Abraham Clark of Elizabethtown had maintained their association for several decades owing to their mutual service in the Colonial Assembly. The Reverend John Witherspoon was an educator by trade, a Scotsman by blood, and a rebel by choice. Thereafter, and only thereafter, was he a man of the cloth. He did not proselytize, and therefore John held him in warm regard. Francis Hopkinson was a legislator poet, and Richard Stockton was a polished Princeton lawyer. The five of them were empowered by the New Jersey Provincial Congress to vote singularly or in accord on all aspects that favored independence.

During the heated debates on the convention hall floor, the New Jersey delegation remained relatively silent and, as Benjamin Franklin had predicted, John Adams spoke forcefully and often on behalf of Massachusetts. What he lacked in stature he made up for with his single mindedness. While at first he struck John and his companions as a contentious, insecure little man who valued no one's opinion more than his own, they had to admit that his dedication to the cause of liberty was unwavering and that his arguments if not his demeanor were persuasive. He ultimately won over the New Jersey contingent when he mentioned having supped at William's Ferry Tavern and pronounced Trenton "as pretty a village" as any he had seen during the whole of his travels throughout the colonies.

Ben smiled across the room at John, as the tall, young redheaded Virginian Thomas Jefferson took over the room with an unerring calm manner. His eloquent yet purposeful prose was as compelling as his casual speaking style; his speech a welcome respite from the brashness of John Adam's pronouncements. The only time Ben Franklin was heard from was when the elder statesman used his considerable powers of persuasion to convince Jefferson to amend the words "sacred and God-given" to read "self-evident" in the opening of the Declaration, in recognition of the separation of church and state, which all present realized must be preserved.

Throughout the convention, the New Jersey delegates never uttered a dissenting word. They understood their duty and accepted their responsibility. Thus, it was without hesitation that each man in turn formalized his commitment for posterity by signing the Declaration of Independence.

Returning to their lodgings after the historic signing, the five men gathered for one last toast together in their adjoining rooms before retiring for the night. They stood side by side as Reverend Witherspoon offered up a prayer of thanksgiving to Providence for guiding their hands in the signing of the Declaration. He then suggested a moment of silence for those young lives lost in the fighting so far and for the battle about to commence in New York. John silently added his own personal prayer for the safety of his son Edward and that of his daughter Susanna's husband John Polhemus.

"Gentlemen, a toast," Reverend Witherspoon concluded, raising his glass, "to we the members of the New Jersey delegation, who by our signatures today bear witness to the birth of a new and glorious nation!"

"Here, here!" the others agreed and then, one by one, each man repeated the oath he had sworn at the conclusion of the signing ceremony: "We proclaim our support for this Declaration of Independence from England ... and mutually pledge to each other ... our lives, our fortunes, and our sacred honor."

They downed their drinks then threw their glasses into the fireplace.

Filled with inspiration and the camaraderie of the occasion, John Hart looked around the room. "Friends, as Doctor Franklin so aptly put it, 'Pray that we all stand together or surely we shall hang alone.'"

"How is it that Samuel Tucker missed this little party, John?" inquired a curious Francis Hopkinson.

"He's busy campaigning in Trenton to become 'Governor' Tucker," John replied with a hint of sarcasm.

"Poor fool," said Abraham Clark. "Livingston has a lock on that office."

"Indeed," mused Richard Stockton. "I personally think it was foolish to entrust Samuel Tucker with our treasury. The electorate would certainly not turn over the militia to him as well, if that's what he thinks!"

"It matters not, Richard," Reverend Witherspoon said, patting John on the back. "With our good fellow John Hart as speaker of the General Assembly to keep him in check, Samuel Tucker has little chance of becoming the prince of the realm his ambition would make of him."

***

Samuel Tucker ascended the stone steps of the Hunterdon County Courthouse slowly, deliberately. He could sense the mood of the crowd. It was electric. Though July 8 was an oppressively hot summer's day with a clear bright blue sky, this was an historic occasion and he saw a chance to seize his part in it. John Hart and the other notables were safely sequestered in Philadelphia, and he alone, Samuel Tucker, president of the Provincial Congress, could command center stage. Could the governorship be far behind? He doubted it.

Only moments earlier, an express rider dispatched from Philadelphia had delivered the news directly into Tucker's hands. He held the first copy of the Declaration of Independence from the Provincial Congress now in session at Trenton. As word leaked out, hundreds of citizens mixed with the committee members and flooded into the courtyard, anxious to hear from their officials.

Tucker let the emotional power surge through him. He imagined that this was what Cicero, Caesar, and all the great orators of the Roman Empire must have felt like in the Forum, addressing the adoring throngs. Initially, Tucker had felt slighted that he was not selected to be among the signers in Philadelphia. But several colleagues assured him that as president of the Provincial Congress, it was vital he remain at home to help orchestrate the transition of government from royal colony to independent state. He still harbored some regret that John Hart had been chosen to bask in the limelight of Philadelphia, but he decided to take this as an auspicious sign that it was his turn to shine here in New Jersey, where it mattered most.

Tucker was confident that he was in the right place at the right time and that the electorate would surely take notice. Destiny was at his doorstep. Not even William Livingston could control the tempo of the day as he now could. Amid the shouts and cheers, Tucker carefully unrolled the parchment. He cleared his voice. All eyes were fixed on him.

"Citizens of Trenton," he began as the crowd settled down. "I have urgent news from Philadelphia. I hold in my hand a document so momentous that it will be celebrated for millennia to come. With this piece of paper 'we the people' of New Jersey—and of all the thirteen colonies—do declare ourselves to be free and independent states!"

The crowd roared its approval, with several spirited "huzzahs" all around. Guns fired freely, and perfect strangers embraced each other.

Tucker went on to read the Declaration in its entirety to the enthralled crowd. When he had concluded, he ordered the church bells to be rung. Drinking in the day and stepping into the revelry, it did not escape him that the Bryant family was conspicuously missing from the rally.

He was neither surprised nor dismayed to realize that Mr. and Mrs. Robert Brennan were absent as well.

11

Midnight Confessions

While the events of July 1776 were cause for celebration, the Continental Army did not distinguish itself with military prowess or valor against the British Empire when put to the test on the battlefield. The Commander-in-Chief knew he needed to capitalize quickly on whatever gains they could make.

After sending the enemy packing at Bunker Hill in the spring, General Washington's plan called for the defense of New York City, which he knew instinctively would be the next British target. Since the Royal Navy ruled the seas, he and his officers expected major port cities to figure heavily in the enemy's war plans once they had the opportunity to regroup and strengthen their numbers. The general, therefore, ordered fortifications built on the bluffs overlooking both the East and Hudson Rivers.

As the ink was drying on the Declaration of Independence, the British fleet under Sir William Howe anchored in New York Harbor. Although Washington had guessed right, the defense of such a wide arc of islands proved to be problematic. Not knowing precisely where the British would strike once they entered the waterway, Washington was forced to scatter his forces thinly along many potential fronts. Howe quickly recognized the weakness in Washington's strategy and exploited it, engaging the Continental troops in small feints at several key points. This strategy distracted Washington from Howe's main force of some 20,000, which he landed on Long Island. Aided by New York Loyalists, the British troops were able to move stealthily northward along the Jamaica Road, outflanking Washington's defenses and inflicting heavy casualties.

For many new recruits like Edward Hart, the first real taste of battle ended in bitter defeat and prolonged retreat. Betrayed by Loyalists, plagued by fever and dysentery, and lacking sufficient intelligence on enemy positions and troop movement, the American forces fell into disarray. Long Island was only the beginning of their suffering. By the end of August, Washington's army faced the threat of a British siege at Brooklyn Heights and had to be secretly evacuated across the East River. By the fifteenth of September, New York City was in British hands. Within a month, Fort Washington, the last American stronghold in and around New York City, fell with more than 3,000 American prisoners taken during the surrender.

With the Hudson River essentially controlled by the British, there was little strategic value left in maintaining a garrison at Fort Lee. Thus, the New Jersey fortification was hurriedly abandoned on November 20, leaving behind a large quantity of American supplies. The British were now on New Jersey soil, forcing Washington south to Newark where he established a temporary headquarters.

In the meantime, the New Jersey State Legislature gathered for its first meeting at Nassau Hall in Princeton, with William Livingston installed as governor and John Hart presiding as speaker of the General Assembly. In the field, amid the daily marching, the nightly encampments, and the continuous fighting, Edward Hart wrote his father regularly, keeping him apprised of the fighting and movement of American forces from New York to New Jersey.

No sooner had Edward enlisted than he found himself dispatched to New York where he was quartered on "Holy Ground," the center of the flesh trade in the city. Despite repeated warnings from Washington about the dangers of consorting with "lewd women," many of his troops—most of them farm boys away from home for the first time—succumbed to drink and desire, resulting in an epidemic of venereal disease. Drilling by day, Edward took to reading *Common Sense* and writing letters home at night to avoid temptation. Frequent thoughts of Penny Scott did much to fortify his resolve.

New York, August 2, 1776

Dear Father,
Time did not permit a proper farewell but know that I am
well and proud to serve the cause of Liberty. What you
have accomplished in Philadelphia must be defended. I do
regret that I will not be home to assist with the harvest but
I am certain Nathaniel and Jesse can manage on their
own. Kindly extend my best wishes to all including Penny
Scott should she happen by.

Your devoted son,
Edward

Whether working by candlelight in the quiet hours late in the
evening or rising early before riding out to the next Assembly meeting, John Hart responded to his son's letters. Thus began a correspondence that informed and deeply touched both men through a
most trying time. Though he was generally known as a man of few
words, John enjoyed the chance to communicate with his son and
tried to impart as much fatherly wisdom as he could. Nonetheless, the
brevity of their letters reflected the great emotional strain he faced
and the physical constraints his son endured.

Hopewell, New Jersey, August 15, 1776

My Dearest Son,
The work I do for our new state pales in comparison to the
sacrifices you and your brothers-in-arms are making for
the sake of our struggling new nation. I am deeply proud
of your service.
  The summer heat is oppressive, but the humidity is good
for the crops. Your brothers will have much to do this har-
vest season, but I will keep an eye on them since you are
not available for the task. I chanced to walk a moment by
the river yesterday and was reminded of how you love to
swim. Please remember though to keep your footgear dry

no matter what the weather, as this small care will greatly preserve good health.

Regrettably, I must confide your mother's health is not so good of late. Ever since we received news that John Jr. had been expelled from Louisiana and sits incarcerated in Cuba, she has taken to her bed and given to long fits of tears. Someday you will know how deeply runs a parent's affection for their children, even when they are the cause of such pains.

All here wish you well.

Your loving father

Soon Edward's correspondence began to reflect the painful realities of war. From afar, his father offered steadfast encouragement to help him through those dark days when friends and neighbors standing beside him were felled by musket balls.

Brooklyn Heights, New York, August 27, 1776

Dear Father,
Today we lost Long Island to the British. Many men died including James Merrel. You may remember him as Nathaniel's friend. Crispin O'Grady did not make it back to camp and we fear the worst for him. Sadly, there are many others we have not heard from either. Why does England persist in denying us our freedom?

We will prevail.

Your loving son,
Edward

Hopewell, New Jersey, September 11, 1776

My Dearest Edward,
I, too, am certain that you will prevail. I have confidence in your Commander-in-Chief. He is making many improvements in the area of intelligence gathering and

considering various strategic maneuvers on the front. In due course, defeats like those you faced in New York will be avoided. Alas, I fear the duties of state have kept me too long from your mother's side. She suffers greatly by my absence.

Your humble and grateful father

Fort Washington, New York, September 25, 1776

Dear Father,
Today we glimpsed General Washington for the first time, and you are right about him. Even in retreat, he is truly an imposing figure. We fought bravely but we are badly out-numbered and ill-equipped. I beseech you to please use your influence to persuade the Assembly to grant us more provisions.

Your loving son,
Edward

Even in the remote confines of rural Hopewell, far from the war-front, reality came crashing in on John Hart as father and son found themselves exchanging stories of tragic loss. For Edward, soldiering became a rite of passage, as the starry-eyed youth who had entered the service of his country was compelled to steel his will in order to deal with the cruel certainties of war. For John, the loss of one single being was analogous to the loss of an appendage he had depended upon for his entire adult life. Even the pressing affairs of state would finally have to wait for mourning so profound.

Hopewell, New Jersey, October 8, 1776

My Dearest Son,
It is with deep sadness that I must inform you of your mother's passing. I am lost without her and care not whether I take another breath. Though she did not often express herself openly on matters of politics, she believed

deeply in liberty and freedom for all mankind. Her dying wish was that upon my death, all our servants shall be set free. With this letter, I am binding you and your brothers to this solemn pledge.

Your grieving father

After John wrote these words, alone and teary-eyed in the dead of the night to a son he believed he might never see again, a son whose dirty blonde hair reminded him of his only brother, he sat reliving the one secret he had tried to keep from his devoted wife; a secret so terrible he thought she would never forgive him should she learn the awful truth. It had troubled him so deeply for so many years that he tried to tell her on her deathbed, only to find out that she already knew.

She had known from the moment her husband arrived home late one night, almost ten years ago, without his thick black belt. Now, with his secret out in the open and his conscience somewhat eased, he closed his eyes to relive the incident that had haunted him for so long. From his brother Daniel's initial outcry, to the assertions of his nephew and neighbors, John's recollection of that night had been cobbled together from his own memories and those of others. Yet now the events unfolded moment by moment in his mind's eye, replaying as clearly as if they had occurred yesterday …

It is early in the morning at the mill-side home of Daniel Hart. A strapping black man named Cuffee, dressed in woolen trousers and a dirty, plain spun white shirt, is lying on a straw mat in his quarters propped up against one wall. An uncorked jug is on the dirt floor beside him. Daniel stands over him, a look of severe annoyance etched on his face.

"Cuffee no work today, Massa Dan'l," protests the groggy servant. "Cuffee no good. Cuffee mighty sick."

Daniel picks up the jug. Tipping it over he sees it is empty. "You lazy, lying dog!" he shouts. "You've been into the jack again!"

Cuffee ducks as the jug smashes against the wall just above his head.

"Get up," Daniel says angrily, showing Cuffee the whip. "You've got chores to do."

"I tole you, I is sick," says Cuffee slowly rising to his feet.

"You goddamn ingrate. I'll teach you to know your place!" Daniel calls for his adolescent son, "Levi!" and grabs a hot poker from the fireplace. He lunges at Cuffee.

Cuffee twists away from the hot poker, which lodges in the wall. Cuffee jumps to his feet. He pushes the much smaller Daniel Hart aside and heads for the door.

Daniel pulls the poker from the wall. Straightening up, he lashes Cuffee across the back with it, ripping open Cuffee's shirt and searing his flesh. Cuffee roars in pain.

Cuffee knocks the poker out of Daniel's hand and pounces on him. He and Daniel lock arm-in-arm and wrestle around the room. They back into the fireplace, upsetting a plate holding a knife and spoon. The pewter ware falls to the floor, clanging loudly.

Young Levi appears in the doorway. He is frozen, afraid, and cannot believe what he is witnessing.

Daniel reaches for the knife but Cuffee is too quick. Cuffee grabs Daniel by the wrist and butts him head to head. As Daniel staggers unsteadily on his feet, Cuffee picks up the knife and stabs Daniel in the stomach.

"Pa!" Levi screams, unable to move.

"Levi—go get help," Daniel gasps. He sinks to his knees.

Cuffee turns on the frightened boy.

Levi grabs an axe that is propped against the wall outside the cabin door.

Cuffee looks around for an escape route.

Levi lifts the axe over his head and charges at Cuffee, swinging away.

Cuffee grabs the axe and pulls it away from the boy, slicing Levi's cheek in the process.

Levi puts a hand to his face and feels the warm blood oozing between his fingers.

Daniel reaches up from the floor and grabs Cuffee around the knees. "Run, Levi! Run!"

Levi turns and bolts back out the door.

Cuffee spins around and buries the axe into Daniel's back.

Daniel's eyes widen momentarily, then close.

As John Hart recalls the sight of his dead brother, his mind races forward …

It is nighttime, later the same day. Cuffee is running through the woods brandishing an axe. A pack of hunting dogs and a party of men wielding torches, muskets, and pistols are in hot pursuit. Cuffee mumbles as he runs, "Cuffee no work today, Massa Dan'l. Cuffee no good. Cuffee real sick."

A shot rings out. Cuffee ducks his head and quickens his pace.

A faceless band of armed men are running through the brush and leaping over stumps. The hounds are sniffing and wailing at the scent.

Cuffee stumbles and falls. He gets up quickly, muttering, "I tole you! I is sick!"

The baying of the hounds is loud and mournful as they catch up with Cuffee at the brook. He wades hurriedly across a shallow stream. A shot rings out, biting into his calf as he emerges on the other side of the stream. He drops to one knee and drags himself into the woods.

The armed posse joins the dogs in the clearing at the far side of the stream.

Cuffee slumps against the base of an old willow tree, exhausted and out of breath.

The hounds are leashed and yelping as members of the armed posse beat and poke the bushes looking for the fugitive.

Cuffee grimaces as he tries to get up. He sets down the axe and reaches for his bleeding leg. He cries out in agony. He looks up into the weeping canopy of tree limbs. He can hear the muffled conversation of men and the baying of dogs close by. Slowly he unties his rope belt and removes it from his trousers. He looks up into the tree once more.

A man whose face is covered in shadows bends down to inspect a drop of blood on a leaf: "Over here!" he shouts to the others in a deep Irish brogue. "This way!"

The men and hounds hurry to follow him. The armed band stomps through the thick underbrush excitedly until they come to a clearing under a large willow. The hounds are yelping uncontrollably, straining against their leashes as the men try to restrain them.

A young man moves forward and raises his torch to the tree. Silhouetted against the pale moon, a large black man in tattered trousers and a torn white shirt is hanging on a limb, dangling from the end of a rope.

Two other men join the young man at the willow tree. Their torches illuminate their angry faces as they speak.

"It's him!" cries Levi Hart, raising his hand to touch the purple gash that graces his own face.

"He's still alive!" announces Seamus O'Grady, standing beneath the swaying body.

"What should we do, Father?" asks an excited Jesse Hart.

"Cut him down and bring the murderer to me," John Hart replies solemnly, removing his thick black belt. "Then leave us."

In the dancing torchlight, as John does what honor demands, he silently curses his brother's cruelty that led to this waste of lives.

***

When Edward posted his last letter to his father, the General Assembly was en route to safer quarters in Burlington. It was a letter his father would be unable to answer.

Hackensack, New Jersey, November 22, 1776

Dear Father,
Fort Lee has been abandoned. We are once again on Jersey soil but so is the enemy. Thomas Paine is in camp with us. If ever we needed the power of his pen again, the time is now. Tomorrow we march south. What fate has in store for us, we cannot know. I pray we shall all be reunited one day soon. Mother's strength of character shall be a treasure for me always.

Please tell Penny I ask for her, if you see her.

Your loving son,
Edward

12

Crisis

*I*s it true?" Penny asked breathlessly, her voice bordering on panic as she rushed into the ministry office.

Reverend Eaton calmly stopped packing the church ledgers into a wooden crate and gazed into the flushed face of his young charge. "Yes, it's true," he replied in his dry, matter-of-fact tone. "Trenton is under British occupation, and they have brought along a contingent of paid Hessian mercenaries with them to keep us in line."

"I've heard stories about those cruel Germans, but is there any news of our own soldiers?" Tears welled in Penny's eyes, conveying her worst fears. "Will they do battle here?"

Reverend Eaton stiffened visibly and pursed his lips, knowing full well the real question behind the ones she'd asked. "I don't think so," he said calmly. "Washington's army is safely camped across the river. The general has commandeered all that floats within a fifty-mile radius of Trenton on the Jersey side. For awhile, at least, the enemy is staying put."

Penny blinked repeatedly, waiting for the obvious.

The reverend could deny her no longer. "Edward is with Washington's troops in Pennsylvania."

"So close and yet so far!" Every nerve in her body tingled at the thought of Edward moving closer to home—and to her.

"Thank our Lord in heaven he is safe," the reverend responded in a gentle and reassuring voice. Sighing, he added, "That's more than one can say for the rest of the Hart family, forced to flee their home." He shook his head sadly. "No one knows where John Hart is—which, of course, is for the best considering the handsome price they've put on his head."

Penny's thoughts went immediately to the remote cave in the Sourland Mountains, where she and Edward had last made love. Surely that's where the hunted patriarch had gone to seek refuge. But it was December and winter's chill hung heavy in the night air. How long could he survive?

"Jesse and Nathaniel are with their families in the care of the neighbors," the reverend continued, "and Sarah and her sisters are with friends in Belle Meade. I've made arrangements to take in stubborn old Martha along with the little ones, Daniel and Dee. We'll hide them in the church's root cellar should anyone come looking."

"What about the farm? Who will care for the animals?"

"My concern is for human souls, Penny," he said gravely. "Still, I'm sure Tolley and Violet will look after the livestock until their master is able to return."

Penny shrugged and then quickly turned on her heels to leave.

"Where are you going?" he asked.

"I cannot tell you, reverend," she said. "But might I take what remains of yesterday's supper?"

He gave her a tender smile. "Of course, my dear, but please be careful. Your heart is in the right place—let's try and keep it safe, too, shall we?"

***

John Hart shivered as the damp cold bit deeply into his aged muscles and brittle old bones. Gone was the resiliency, the suppleness of youth that his body and mind could no longer remember. His legs were sore and cramped. His neck ached badly. Even greater pain was concentrated in the small of his back, which his doctor had attributed to an advancing case of gravel. In the solitude of his surroundings and the agony of his circumstances, the kidney stones persisted with a woeful vengeance.

John had not had a decent meal in three days. The salted beef and stale biscuits he had hastily pilfered from the family pantry were long gone. Determined to conserve the last precious drops of water in his canteen, he pressed it to his lips and allowed himself a short moistening sip.

The hollowed out rock ledge in which he now hid had often sheltered John Hart and sons from sudden storms during hunting expeditions. He thought how much he missed those happier times, knowing now that Providence had never intended this cave as more than temporary lodging for any man, especially not one of his ripe age in the dead of winter.

There was nowhere else he could go without endangering the lives of innocent people—friends and neighbors he valued too dearly to put at risk for the sake of his own protection and comfort. On his infrequent ventures away from the cave to scrounge for food and water, he had to watch and listen closely for roving bands of British soldiers. They continuously patrolled the woods in search of him and other local rebellion leaders, and, in one close call, he had recognized the booming voice of Lieutenant Fletcher Radcliff, the troop leader he'd confronted during the scuffle at the horse race. From that brief encounter, John felt certain Radcliff was not an enemy to be taken lightly. He seemed both confident and cruel—the type of hunter who would relentlessly pursue then take pleasure in the suffering of his prey.

How much longer he would have to remain holed up in this cave like a wild beast, John did not know. Nor could he know how long he would be separated from his family. What he *did* know was that his loneliness and anxiety over the fate of his children was more difficult to bear than the physical pain and deprivation.

He groaned as he tried to stretch out a kink lingering in his stiff calf. He wondered about the welfare of Daniel, his sensitive son, and sweet little Dee. He hoped that by now they had reached safety, along with his long-suffering mother, in the care of the Reverend and Mrs. Eaton. While Deborah was constantly in his thoughts, he took some comfort in knowing she had escaped the indignity and hardship he was now forced to endure.

In a desperate moment, half-crazed and wracked with self-doubt, he cried out in anguish into the black night: "What is to be done with me?" Off in the distance, he heard the mournful cry of a lone coyote. Or was it the echo of his own pitiful bellowing, coming back to taunt him? No. He could not be certain until … there it was again. This time the cry sounded closer, much closer.

For an instant, he thought he glimpsed a shadowy figure pass in front of his hiding place. He edged back further into the cave until he felt the solid wall behind him. He reached for his pistol and cocked the hammer back slowly, taking aim at the cave opening. Dare he risk a shot and give the enemy his position?

***

Edward stirred the dying embers of the campfire slowly, absentmindedly. His thoughts were miles away … about fifteen, he reckoned, from his inviting home across the river; from his noisy loving family and the woman he wanted to spend his life with. What would he find there? He thought of his mother, whom he would never see again on Earth, then of his father. Had John Hart survived?

The wind whipped across the desolate camp, rattling pots, pans, and tent flaps. Edward's military cap went sailing, but he didn't bother to chase after it. He'd get a replacement when the next man fell beside him, whether from the cold or enemy fire. It didn't matter which, he decided. Either way, he thought, one's end was the end, indifferent and inglorious.

He heard his fellow soldiers, huddled together like cattle, grumbling and growling as they cursed the winter wind. Snow was in the air. One didn't need to consult an almanac to know it—the dull ache in your bones told you it was coming. The damp raw air ripped through tattered coats and torn breeches. Threadbare blankets were wrapped around bare and bloody feet, replacing soleless boots whose leather had been sacrificed for soup.

Edward had never imagined that soldiering could be so bleak, so cold and dreary. Where were the victories to be recounted in song? Where were the parades, the banners, the cheering crowds and smiling faces of happy children? Was all that an illusion?

Defeat after defeat had followed the Continental Army from summer into fall and now into winter with no respite. The dead were the lucky ones, he thought at times, having escaped the real hell of the here and now.

Rumors abounded, including that General Washington was to be sacked. The old man had lost his touch, if he'd ever had one. Congress would ask General Lee to replace him—Charles Lee, the despised dog lover who cared more for his mutts than his men. But, wait! Lee had been captured … while having breakfast … at a tavern … four miles from his troops. Or was that just another rumor?

Edward tried to shake the depressing thoughts from his mind. Who cares, anyway? In a week, with enlistments up for renewal, there will be no army left to command. No one will re-up under these conditions with home so close, he thought. He could walk off in the night and no one would care, if they even noticed. Desertion? Why not just think of it as an early leave?

***

Julia Brennan sat in a well-stuffed wingback chair, facing Doctor William Bryant across his massive desk. Emily Bryant sat beside her, gently caressing her hand. Behind them, Lieutenant Fletcher Radcliff paced the planked floor, the clicking of his polished boots resonating off the high ceiling and mauve stucco walls of the tidy office like a metronome.

Julia fidgeted with the lacy collar of her blouse as her eyes darted nervously back and forth from husband to wife. Her feet tapped against one another uncontrollably.

"Just repeat for the lieutenant what you told Mrs. Bryant earlier, my dear," said Bryant, "and your husband need not know anything of this sordid little affair."

"I couldn't!" pleaded Julia. "He would know it was me!"

"The rules have changed, Mrs. Brennan," Radcliff said in a clipped, condescending tone through clenched teeth. "*We* are in charge here, and in a few short days this little rebellion of your Mr. Tucker's won't be worth a footnote in the history of the Empire."

"Consider your husband, Julia," offered Emily slyly. "Once he learns you helped the King's men recover a large cache of illegal funds, he will have to look quite differently upon your actions … should the full story even come out."

Julia pulled her hand away from her so-called friend. Bitter tears were turning her eyes red, despite the belladonna drops she had used to brighten them.

"You may find yourself handsomely rewarded," offered Doctor Bryant with an obvious look to Radcliff for support.

The lieutenant's pacing stopped abruptly. His response was circumspect. "Of course, I cannot promise anything specific," he said hesitantly, "but I can speak to the King's generosity with respect to his *most loyal* subjects."

"There—you see, Julia?" Emily added encouragingly, "The King could not ignore such a noble deed as yours!" She threw her husband a determined look.

Julia glanced helplessly around the room before closing her eyes. She was trapped. There was no escape. Her husband would be arriving any minute from business in another part of town, expecting to join a dinner party welcoming the British and Hessian officers who now controlled Trenton. Julia had come early at the request of her hostess, ostensibly to assist with the preparations. In the course of their conversation, she had mentioned to Emily her fear that some of the rebellion leaders might go into hiding permanently, fleeing to Europe in some cases.

"But that would take considerable financial means to accomplish," Emily had argued. "Not for some," was Julia's reply. And then she'd added, unwisely, "The New Jersey treasury has the money, and those close to it have the means."

"You speak of *your* Mr. Tucker, of course," Emily said, her tone deeply insinuating. The younger woman was betrayed instantly by the look of shock and horror that contorted her pretty face. Without missing a beat, the doctor's wife had confronted her with the allegations of her servants, Mattie and Joseph, then repeated the tale told by the proprietor of the Recklesstown Tavern, a man her husband had recently treated for typhoid.

Julia's distressed thoughts of that earlier conversation were interrupted by a sharp knock on the door. The manservant Joseph opened the door, and a squat mustachioed man in the forest green uniform of a Hessian Jaeger swept into the room.

"Ah, Colonel Rall," said Doctor Bryant as he rose to greet the German officer who had been given command of the garrison at Trenton. "You are just in time. Mrs. Brennan was about to tell us where the rebels have hidden their war chest."

Colonel Johann Gottlieb Rall walked over to Julia, snapped his heels together, and bowed crisply. "Where is it, my dear?" he asked abruptly in German and without preamble. Bryant translated with equal impatience.

Radcliff came around to join him, his imposing figure and cold stare adding to Julia's sense of anxiety. All three men stood before her.

"You'll find it at the Abbott place on the outskirts of town," she said with resignation, adding, "Samuel took it to his friend's farm for safekeeping."

***

The bright glow of a lit torch flooded the mouth of the shallow cave, and John Hart shielded his eyes.

"*Hello!*" a female voice called. "Is anyone there?"

"Who wants to know?" John demanded, training his gun on the opening.

"Mr. Hart? Sir, it's me, Penny. Penny Scott." She popped her head through the narrow opening. "I've brought you a few things," she said squeezing into the neatly concealed hollow and dropping a sack at John's feet.

John released the hammer and lowered his pistol. "I thought I heard a coyote," he said in a vain attempt to explain the pointed gun.

Penny transferred the flame to a tallow candlestick and extinguished the torch. Her cheeks glowed red in the eerie light. "You did," she said, smiling sweetly. "But he'll be looking elsewhere for a meal tonight."

John grinned appreciatively.

Penny rummaged through the stuffed grain sack and removed a jug. John studied it with interest as he accepted it from her.

"It's only cider," she said, then smiled and passed him a small flask. "You might add a little of this."

Next, she unwrapped a cloth napkin revealing a loaf of cornbread. "There's a mutton chop in the other," she added, noticing how his eyes widened at the sight of the food. "The reverend and his missus were quite insistent," she added with some exaggeration.

"How did you find me?" he asked after taking a healthy swig from the flask.

"Edward brought me here."

John gave her a weak knowing smile. Then sitting upright, he asked anxiously, "Edward? Is he home?"

Penny thought for a second before answering. Even in the poor light, she could see that worry weighed heavily upon him. He appeared gaunt and tired, not robust as she'd seen him last, at his wife's funeral. When he spoke, there was a quaver in his normally commanding voice.

"He might as well be," she said, trying for a breezy tone. "Washington's army is just across the river."

"And the rest of the family—Sarah, the children, my mother?"

"All safe and well, sir."

He studied her facial expression through deep-set eyes, wanting to be convinced.

"Any news of my colleagues?" he winced as he shifted his position. "Samuel Tucker and the others?"

Penny let her eyes fall. "Not a word," she lied. "Except … except for Mr. Stockton." She continued as he gave her a curious look. "Reverend Eaton heard he was captured by a band of Loyalists in Monmouth. They've taken him to the British authorities in New York."

"Poor Richard," John lamented. He rose to stand and reached for her hand. "I'm afraid I've misjudged you, dear Penny," he said, his brown eyes welling with emotion. "My pronouncement upon you and Edward was harsh and unwarranted. I hope you will find it in your hearts to forgive me."

"You meant only to protect me," she replied with genuine affection. "Edward and I know that, sir. You are a wonderful father and a kind man to whom I owe a great debt of gratitude."

"I fear *your* kindness could get you killed."

"My kindness is nothing compared to the generosity you have shown me over the years."

Through the cave's opening, John could see morning's first light beginning to bathe the world outside his sanctuary. "You should be going," he urged her, bending over to kiss her forehead lightly, still holding her hand gently in his own. "The enemy will give no quarter to an old man whose defiance of the King's authority is signed upon the document of our self-determination. Nor will they look kindly on any person who comes to the aid of such a traitorous wretch."

Before Penny could protest, the distant baying of hounds drifted into the cave, seeming to underscore John's poignant words. Without hesitation, he blew out the candle.

"You must leave at once, daughter," he implored her, the alarm in his quaking voice unmistakable. "Radcliff is relentless."

"Wait—I have an idea!" she exclaimed excitedly. "Give me your coat and put this around you." She thrust a heavy blanket into his arms.

Grudgingly, he complied. He understood what she was planning and knew it would be useless to try and dissuade her.

"If I guess your plan, you'll be needing this, too," he said, handing over his black tri-corner hat. "You realize that if you are caught, they will kill you."

"There's no chance of that, sir," she boasted as she stuffed her auburn tresses into the tricorne. "Not while I'm riding the fastest thoroughbred in Hunterdon County."

"You came on Northumberland!" he blurted, his heart swelling with joy at the revelation.

"I did, indeed!"

"You are wise beyond your years, Penny Scott. Even so, you may need this." He pressed his hunting knife into her hand, which she immediately stuffed in her boot. "Good luck!"

"And to you, sir!" she replied emotionally, sealing her words with a daughter's tender good-bye kiss.

As she galloped off, John heard a soldier's voice call out from afar, "There he goes, men! After him!" quickly followed by the thundering hooves of a half-dozen horses.

13

Victory or Death

B y noon, word had spread throughout the camp: Prepare to march and to fight. Although it was Christmas Day, there would be rest neither for the weary nor for the wounded, so long as they could walk and carry a rifle. All able-bodied men were to report for assembly at the appointed hour.

The unexpected news was met with mixed emotions in Edward's unit. For some, the forced holiday march could mean only one thing—another imminent retreat. For others, the orders held the promise of redemption and glory on the battlefield at long last; of one final opportunity to prevail over the enemy before most enlistments ran out on New Year's Day 1777. At the moment, Edward's sentiments were with the despondent group. While continuing to obey orders, increasingly he weighed the option of desertion and had even begun to watch for the opportunity.

Certainly, he reasoned, Washington knows the stakes. This march *must* represent a calculated risk rather than an act of final desperation. Either way, he knew it would be difficult if not impossible to motivate these tired, sick, hungry, and ill-clad men, most with but a week left as soldiers, to march—let alone to engage an enemy that had dominated them at every turn.

By midafternoon, the weather had taken a turn for the worse and the sky was growing more ominous with each passing moment. For several days, there had been bitter cold winds and subfreezing temperatures harsh enough to cause ice dams on the Delaware, but with only a light, intermittent dusting of snow on the ground. Then the wind shifted and, with it, perhaps, the outcome of Washington's plan as well. Coming out of the north and laden with moisture, the weather for the next twenty-four hours did not bode well for a long march. If there was to be a fight at the end of it, keeping the gunpowder dry and the artillery operable would itself be a feat bordering on miraculous.

All hope for the artillery lay squarely on the shoulders of a young Caribbean-born captain named Alexander Hamilton, Washington's aide-de-camp. Though Hamilton's artillery unit had distinguished itself repeatedly at Battery Park during the New York campaign, a decisive encounter had eluded him as it had Washington these many months.

Just after mess, the final orders were given. It was to be an overnight march culminating in a crossing of the Delaware River. The destination was Trenton, where a garrison of approximately 1,600 Hessian mercenaries had been assigned by the British to defend the town against the Continental Army.

The soldiers did not have to speculate on Washington's mindset any longer. The password was "Victory or Death!"

***

Colonel Johann Rall was in a foul mood. Hurrying through the doorway, he practically bowled over Abraham Hunt and Stacy Potts as they arrived. He had summoned the two respected Trenton merchants and outspoken Quaker pacifists to Bloomsbury Court at the suggestion of his host, Doctor William Bryant, to help facilitate "a most urgent matter."

"See if you can get him to cooperate," Rall snarled as he continued past them. "It would be in his and your own best interest. *Mach schnell!*"

Entering the room, Abraham and Stacy found John Honeyman and Doctor Bryant standing over a barely recognizable fellow Trentonian. Slumped in a chair with his hands tied behind him was Samuel Tucker, his face welted and bloodied. He looked up at his old "friends" through swollen eyes.

"Who sold me out?" he spat at them through swollen lips.

"Does it really matter, Samuel?" questioned Abraham Hunt with gentle resignation.

"I take it they didn't find the money?" Stacy Potts asked the others.

John Honeyman shook his large furry head. "If it was ever there to begin with."

The doctor hovered over Tucker like a gleeful warden. "The way I see it, Samuel, you have two choices. You can wait until your patriot friends come and rescue you—assuming they survive the occupation. Then, of course, you'd have to explain to the governor and the Assembly what has become of their money ..." He gestured to John Honeyman, and the butcher pulled out his knife, deftly slicing through the rope that bound Tucker. As the attorney rubbed his bruised wrists, Bryant shoved a paper in his face. "Or you can sign this, foreswearing your allegiance to the Crown and going your merry way while Cornwallis and Rall mop up what's left of Washington's army."

Tucker could hardly believe his ears. He looked around at the others for confirmation. "That's it? I'd be free to go?"

Abraham and Stacy looked at each other and shrugged. "Apparently the King wishes to show he can be ... merciful," Abraham suggested somewhat doubtfully.

"Indeed—along with recognizing the symbolic value of your turnabout," Stacy added diplomatically, making the more convincing argument. "I'm sure that's been factored in."

As Tucker grasped for the quill in Doctor Bryant's hand, the doctor pulled it quickly out of his reach. "First we must have the name."

"The name?"

"Of the man to whom you have entrusted the treasury funds," John Honeyman finished for him. "We know it wasn't all to Abbott, as was first suggested, because only worthless unsigned notes were found at his farm."

Tucker hesitated as he felt the walls of the room collapsing around him. Rall had been cunning to engage these men, whom he knew, to reason with him. Now he was trapped. Yes, he could escape execution and walk away a free man, but only by making a sacrificial lamb of someone. Not just any name would do. Bryant would need to be convinced, as would the others. As townsfolk, they would easily spot a fraud where Rall could not.

"Jesse Hart," he said at last.

Surprise registered on the faces of all the men.

"The Signer's son?" John Honeyman blurted, incredulous.

"That's right," Tucker replied without a second thought. "John Hart's eldest."

"But surely—" Stacy Potts started.

"He only delivered the half," Tucker said, thinking on his feet.

"*Half?*" Abraham Hunt repeated.

"As you know, to become legal tender the bills require three signatures. After John Hart signed the last of the batch, he asked Jesse to deliver them to me while he was away in Philadelphia, but he only brought me half of them."

"How can you be so certain?" Bryant asked with some skepticism.

"When next I saw John, he asked if I had received the twelve thousand five hundred pounds from Jesse. At the time, John's wife was on her deathbed, and I didn't have the heart to tell him the truth about his son. It would have crushed him."

"So where is the rest of that money now?" John Honeyman asked, watching for a telltale flicker or twitch in Tucker's eyes.

"Who knows? The Harts are scattered. Jesse's business takes him far and wide. It could be anywhere."

"So how did you explain the missing money in the Treasury ledgers?" Abraham probed.

Tucker grew agitated. He had had enough of this charade. It was time for the courtroom attorney to make his summation. "Look around you, gentleman. There's a war going on. Bad things happen every day. Supplies are lost, artillery breaks down. There are desertions and unexplained deaths. No one can account for every shilling."

Bryant dipped the quill in the ink jar and handed it to Tucker. The attorney signed the protection paper with a steady hand.

***

Lieutenant Fletcher Radcliff was seething. He and his men had been on a wild goose chase since sun-up, following a ghost rider through hill and dale, coming up empty-handed. But he refused to give up.

Though his troops were cold, damp, and hungry, the lieutenant decided to play a hunch before returning to the barracks at Trenton for the night. He did not, however, think of it as a hunch but rather as an example of his keen mind. Radcliff was a firm believer that to be successful in His Majesty's service, an officer had to be sharp-witted enough to outmaneuver the wiliest enemy, and he looked with scorn upon those who relied on instinct over intelligence. He judged his intellect to be superior to that of any of his fellow officers and was thus convinced that he was the only man for the detail he had requested: to round up the rebel leaders in the area.

He had handed Tucker over already and had a strong lead on John Witherspoon's hideout. He would have had Richard Stockton all to himself but the Princeton legislator had fled the area and been caught on the road to the coast. This John Hart, on the other hand, presented a challenge. He rode with remarkable stamina for a man of advanced years, eluding Radcliff's best men. When did he rest? And where did he sleep?

The Hart homestead was quiet and still as the riders approached. Dismounting, Radcliff ordered his men to break down the front door. They obediently put their shoulders to the task only to have it swing open on its own.

Two servants stood nervously in the foyer.

"Where is he?" Radcliff demanded.

Tolley and Violet remained mute and motionless.

"Answer me!" Radcliff ordered, grabbing Tolley's collar and shaking him violently.

"If by *he* you mean Mr. John Hart," said a young woman with cascading auburn locks from behind the servants, "I'm afraid you have missed him. He's taken his family to Philadelphia."

"Right," Radcliff responded dryly as he turned to his men. "Search the house and the grounds!" he barked. "You there," he pointed to Tolley and Violet, "fetch food and drink for my men."

Turning back to Penny, Radcliff eyed the fair young woman with suspicion, trying to recall where he had seen her before. "I suppose you're the kitchen help," he said derisively, taking note of the riding clothes she'd had no time to change out of.

"I take care of the horses," she replied calmly.

He moved closer to her. "Do you, now? You wouldn't happen to have a gray stallion in that stable, would you?"

She hesitated. "Are you looking to make a purchase?"

Radcliff smiled, showing a set of perfect white teeth; too perfect, she thought as her whole body shivered in the coldness of his gaze.

"Not a purchase but a trade," he sneered, grabbing her arm and twisting it. He drew his sword expertly and brought the blade quickly to her throat. "His life for yours."

His grip was tight as he pressed the blade against her flesh. A trickle of blood ran down her neck.

She tried not to show her fear. "I told you he is in Philadelphia," she managed, despite the blade against her throat.

"Then who was it we were chasing all day?" he rasped between clenched teeth. "A phantom?" He slid the blade down her blouse, slicing off a button. "Or was it someone else?" He twisted her arm violently, pinning it behind her back and driving her to her knees.

"You're hurting me!" she cried out.

"That's the idea, stable girl." Grabbing a handful of her hair he forced her face into his crotch, still holding his sword to her throat with the other hand. "You're either my horseman or my whore. Either way, you know what I want, now make it quick!"

Her mind raced desperately for some way out of her predicament. She could feel him swell inside his pants as he held her against him. Slowly, buying as much time as she could, she began to undo the buttons on his uniform trousers.

"Miss Penny, no!" yelled Tolley as he reentered the room with a tray full of drinks.

Releasing his grip on the girl's hair, Radcliff pulled out his pistol, aimed quickly and fired. The shot caught Tolley in the shoulder, sending the tray and stoneware crashing to the floor.

Without hesitation, Penny pulled John Hart's hunting knife from her boot. In one swift motion she slammed it home into Radcliff's groin. Reflexively, he drew his sword across her neck, slitting her throat.

Tolley raced to her side, catching her head as she fell backward. Her eyes grew fixed and dilated. He laid her gently on her back as the floor ran scarlet with blood.

Radcliff's sword dropped with a thud. Using both hands, he pulled the knife from his bloodstained crotch. He held the bloody blade up to his face in disbelief.

Tolley picked up the discarded saber and jammed it into the officer's chest. Radcliff stumbled, then spun like a corkscrew before falling dead to the floor.

14

Turning Point

*E*dward Hart stood at the stern of a shallow draft Durham boat, as lookout for a group of skilled New England seamen guiding their long poles across the swift current of a freezing river.

The Delaware was Edward's river. He fished it, he swam in it, and here, near a place called Johnson's Ferry, he once rescued a damsel in distress who had floated downstream and into his heart. But in all his years he had never experienced the river in this condition. Many of the ice floes were jagged and sharp. Some were the size of boulders, large enough to use as stepping stones—if only Edward could see that far in front of him. Between the darkness of a blustery winter night and the blinding effect of snow whipped by the winds, visibility and temperature were both near zero.

The river crossing was proving far more arduous than the high command had anticipated. This risky maneuver was only the first step on a long road leading to a surprise sunrise attack against the Hessian garrison at Trenton, and it had put the Continental troops hours behind schedule. It was about four in the morning when the last of the men, horses, and artillery pieces reached the other side. During the treacherous crossing, Edward had pulled a man from the icy waters, only later realizing they would both face a nine-mile march to Trenton in the dead of the night, over uneven terrain in chilled, ragged wet uniforms.

The next test of the troops' mental and physical toughness came on turf even more familiar to Edward. It required the army of nearly twenty-four hundred to ford an overflowing Jacob's Creek in total darkness. Ropes and strong backs lowered the artillery and munitions wagons down one side of the steep slippery slope for the difficult crossing, then hauled them up the opposite bank. This Herculean task accomplished, the army headed south along Bear Tavern Road.

A mere nine miles away, Colonel Johann Rall, commander of the Hessian troops at Trenton, was enjoying some late night Christmas cheer at the home of the prominent merchant Abraham Hunt. Food and drink were in plentiful supply, and the festivities included a fierce game of whist for Rall, Abraham Hunt, John Honeyman, and Stacy Potts, whose spacious and comfortable home on the corner of Second and Queen Streets had been turned into Rall's personal headquarters. Some of Rall's men and a contingent of uprooted loyalists, meanwhile, were housed at the barracks built by Hunterdon County taxpayers twenty years earlier for use by British troops during the French and Indian War. These were spartan accommodations, to say the least.

As the game raged on, a messenger who may have been sent by Doctor Bryant arrived to warn the German commandant that based on information provided by his Loyalist spy network—which at times included the likes of John Honeyman—an attack on Trenton was imminent. The suspicious and somewhat disheveled man was turned away at the door by Hunt's Negro house servant, who had been given strict orders that the colonel was not to be disturbed. Before taking his leave, the courier scrawled a hasty note, which he insisted be delivered to Rall immediately.

Evidently, the would-be informant had chosen an inopportune moment to pass the note to Rall. The colonel and his partner were on the verge of completing a slam, having already won eleven hands straight. He pocketed the note rather than break his lucky streak.

***

Entering the tiny hamlet of Birmingham on the northwestern fringe of Trenton, General Washington divided his troops, sending a small force south along the river road under the command of General John Sullivan. He led the main body of his troops, along with the main artillery, southeast along Pennytown Road and placed them under Field General Nathanael Greene. Washington's plan was to pin the

Hessians between the groups in a three-pronged attack, with the third wave coming ashore to the south at Bristol under the cover of heavy gunfire.

Edward found a spot for himself in Captain Hamilton's artillery division after the gunner's mate he had rescued from the river earlier stopped for a rest in the woods. While waiting for others to bring the cannon up from the rear, the man fell asleep and froze to death. Numbed by the tragedy all around him, Edward somehow viewed the opportunity to march beside General Washington along a road that shared the same name of the girl he loved as a good omen. He volunteered immediately for the assignment.

Meanwhile, farther south in Mount Holly, Madame DeSange, the merry widow who counted Benjamin Franklin among her intimate friends, was entertaining Johann Rall's fellow officer Colonel Carl Von Donop. The colonel, who had earlier been enticed from his post in Burlington by a light American feint, found himself enchanted by the attractive widow and decided to linger in her comfortable residence for several days. This distraction kept the principal force intended as Rall's reserve much further from Trenton than was prudent.

Wearing a golden wine goblet for a crown and a majestic fur-trimmed purple robe with nothing on underneath, the voluptuous Madame DeSange flounced across the fire-lit boudoir for the amusement of her captive colonel.

"Madame, King Louis himself could not possibly be as imperial or as naughty as you," chortled Von Donop. He was dressed as Marie Antoinette in a silk corset, courtesan's wig, and a faux mole his paramour had insisted upon for authenticity in their decadent little game.

"Monsieur, if her Highness possessed *your* equipment," she said, licking her lips lasciviously and grabbing his corseted bulge, "she would have the makings of a great king!" She threw herself onto the canopied bed, stretching her delightful frame across it and batting her long lashes at him.

He laughed heartily, then tossed back the last of his brandy before turning momentarily serious. "I find it hard to imagine a woman like you in the company of Doctor Franklin," he confessed. "Is it true you have consorted with the enemy?"

"My darling colonel, politics makes for strange bedfellows, no? How can you be so certain I am not consorting with my enemy *now*?"

With a wicked laugh she pulled back her robes, revealing all her glory as he mounted her with abandon.

***

Freezing cold, hungry, and exhausted, Edward fretted whether the powder in his musket would be dry enough to fire properly when the lines were finally drawn. As he marched, his thoughts turned from his father's safety to Penny's warm inviting body, her intoxicating scent. To keep himself awake and moving, he whistled the little tune he had heard her singing on the night following the horserace, when he'd stumbled upon her half-naked in the stable.

How ironic, thought Edward as he willed himself onward in foul weather and darkness, to be marching over land owned by his maternal grandfather, Richard Scudder, and not be able to duck in out of the cold for a pint of warm grog and a bit of news about his family. But there were spies everywhere, and his troop had been warned to stay in their ranks.

In the pocket of his frayed uniform jacket, he still carried the copy of *Common Sense* Penny had given him to read and remember her by. It had been a long, depressing six months of soldiering since he'd seen her last. How would she greet him—if at all—should this battle fail? He feared but dared not consider the worst. Instead he contemplated, with uncanny clarity given his present situation, the opening words from Tom Paine's latest treatise *American Crisis*, which General Washington had read aloud to his men just before they broke camp for the march to Trenton.

> *These are the times that try men's souls. The summer sol-*
> *dier and sunshine patriot will, in this crisis, shrink from*
> *the service of their country. But he that stands it now*
> *deserves the love and thanks of man and woman.*

Words never meant more to a man than did these to Edward Hart at this moment. Whatever the outcome of the battle, he was grateful to have survived his own personal crisis of conscience, making the choice to stay and fight.

The paltry sentry post guarding the northern end of town near Kings Road was quickly and efficiently dispatched. Washington ordered Captain Hamilton to place his artillery on the high ground atop a gentle sloping hill that overlooked the center of a sleeping town. All was quiet in the early morning light, shrouded by an intermittent mix of freezing rain and snow. Despite the prolonged delay in their arrival, the element of surprise remained in their favor.

Every nerve and fiber of Edward's body was taut as he waited for the battle to commence. He read the same anticipation on the filthy, damp, runny-nosed faces of the men around him. The line of armed-and-ready soldiers exhaled frosty breaths, seemingly as one, and in the distance Edward heard the first rounds of gunfire as Sullivan's men encountered the enemy pickets placed in the western quadrant of the town.

Within seconds, the order was given to commence firing, followed by the incessant booming of Hamilton's artillery shells as they pounded the slumbering Hessian barracks.

Nearby, in his headquarters, Colonel Rall was roused from his sleep by the noise. At first, he thought he was dreaming; then it crossed his mind that the men might be engaged in a show of arms to mark the holiday. It was not until he ran to the window and threw open the sash that he heard the captain of the night watch shouting up to him, "*Die Fiend! Die Fiend!*" and knew they were under enemy attack.

Rall dressed hurriedly and rushed out to join his troops in the streets. "We are outnumbered and completely surrounded," his captain reported. In fact, while the three Hessian regiments were indeed outnumbered, they were hardly surrounded. At Bristol, the crossing had been aborted by Colonel John Cadwalader due to the impassable condition of the river, thus one flank remained uncovered.

Yet Rall's own assessment was even more deeply flawed. Convinced he was facing the same army that had run from New York with its tail between its legs, he made the brash decision to counter-attack. He rallied his troops for a frontal assault aimed at Washington's strength instead of pulling back to a more defensible position beyond the Assunpink. As Sullivan's men advanced from the west, forcing the Germans toward Washington's waiting troops, the Continental Army fanned out throughout Trenton under cover of the artillery bombardment, going from house-to-house to dry their weapons and harrying the Hessians under a constant barrage of musket fire. In the confusion, many of the German guns were turned and trained on their fellow soldiers.

In an apple orchard north of town, the end came swiftly for Johann Rall and his remaining troops. Fatally wounded, the colonel was carried back to Stacy Potts's house, where George Washington had already accepted the surrender of the garrison from a subordinate. Rall's body was hastily interred in a grave beside the Presbyterian Church.

Washington wasted no time in gathering up his men, along with some nine hundred Hessian prisoners, and scurrying them back across the Delaware. His casualties were "a trifling," with apparently no Continental troops killed during the exchange, while enemy losses were reported to number twenty-two dead and eighty-three wounded.

Washington was elated by the victory, but with large numbers of enemy troops stationed in nearby Princeton and Burlington, he lacked sufficient forces to hold the town for any length of time. Unwilling to expose his tired and hungry men to further danger, he chose to return them to safety across the river to Pennsylvania rather than linger in Trenton.

As Edward headed with his company for the ferry down below Eagle Tavern to make the crossing, excitement was high among the men. Several barrels of rum had been confiscated from an enemy storehouse and liquor flowed freely along the docks as the victorious but physically exhausted soldiers fortified themselves for the long cold return across the river. While waiting for his transport, Edward stole a moment to venture into Eagle Tavern's familiar walls and search out its warming hearth. Seamus O'Grady welcomed him with a pint but could not provide him with any news of his father's whereabouts, other than to say, "He must be safe or surely I would have heard of it, as I have of Samuel Tucker's turnabout and Richard Stockton's capture." In truth, until the area was clear of the enemy, Seamus would have no news of the Harts or any other rebel leaders who remained in hiding.

Comforted for the time being by the idea that "no news is good news," the two men drank a toast to the Continental Army's stunning victory and to Crispin O' Grady's memory. Edward recounted for a tearful Seamus how he had read passages of *Common Sense* to his courageous, though illiterate, son by firelight in camp. He told how this ritual had helped ease the pangs of homesickness the young men shared, and he tried to pass on to Seamus his well-worn copy of *Common Sense* in memory of Crispin's bravery.

Seamus thanked him but given the inscription he felt the book held far greater sentimental value for a young soldier in love than it ever could for a grizzled Irishman nearing the end of his days. When Edward insisted, Seamus agreed to hold on to it for safekeeping until he returned. As they parted, the old man gave Edward a pair of warm mittens to replace his wet worn ones.

Within a week of the battle, Washington was back on Jersey soil again—this time to fight a defensive battle, and Edward Hart was among the troops. The American triumph over the Hessian garrison at Christmas had greatly boosted the morale of the fledging Continental Army and patriots all throughout the thirteen former colonies. A good many enlistments were renewed, rallied in large part by Washington's personal charisma and a stirring speech he made on the eve of the New Year. Riding atop his great white steed, he addressed the assembled troops with compassion and commitment:

> *My brave fellows, you have done all I asked you to do, and*
> *more than could be reasonably expected; but your country*
> *is at stake, your wives, your houses and all that you hold*
> *dear. You have worn yourselves out with fatigues and*
> *hardships, but we know not how to spare you. If you will*
> *consent to stay only one month longer, you will render that*

service to the cause of liberty and to your country which
you probably never can do under any other circumstances.

Additionally, for those who stayed on another month, a bonus of ten dollars was promised. Nearly all assembled stepped forward.

While Washington was anxious to capitalize on the victory and keep the momentum going, he feared that a sleeping giant had been awakened. His assessment proved to be an accurate one. Before "Trenton," as the battle came simply to be known, the British had prepared to settle in for the winter. General Charles Cornwallis was in New York waiting to sail for England to visit his ailing wife. After Trenton, Cornwallis's leave was canceled as Sir William Howe's ablest field commander prepared for a forced march from New Brunswick to Princeton down the Post Road to confront the Continental Army. With an amassed force of some eight thousand troops, Cornwallis's goal was to destroy Washington's ragtag army and all rebel resistance once and for all.

The remnants of Colonel Rall's garrison that had managed to slip off to Burlington before Trenton's final capitulation eventually joined up with Colonel Carl Von Donop's troops. The amorous German officer had finally recognized the seriousness of the military situation and perhaps even the consequences of his extended dalliance at Madame DeSange's. His reconstituted force later joined up with a wayward unit of British Light Dragoons that had until recently been led by an ambitious young lieutenant named Fletcher Radcliff. Eventually, Radcliff's eviscerated body was found in a pigsty behind the barn of a still-at-large rebel leader's farm in Hopewell. The surprise attack and defeat at Trenton postponed a full military inquest and forestalled any opportunity for immediate recriminations.

Knowing he would be within spitting distance of his home, Edward got himself assigned at the start of the second day of the New Year to the vanguard of riflemen, primarily Pennsylvanians, under the command of Colonel Edward Hand. Their mission was to delay the enemy advance on Trenton as long as possible, and their tactics were simple: snipe away at the bright red column marching in tight formation along the road, taking out as many of their opponents as possible. Each hit-and-run ambush took its toll on the British and gained precious time for the Continental Army to prepare its defense of the town.

From behind rocks and trees, over hedgerows and down ravines, Continental rifle fire thwarted the enemy advance at every turn as they marched single file in their bright crimson coats down the Post Road from Princeton. Confusion reigned on both sides and, whether by chance or fate, Edward suddenly found himself separated from his unit and without his powder horn. Under fire from a detachment of British light infantry, he ran back through the tiny hamlet of Maidenhead to the Presbyterian Church grounds. His father had been baptized at this same old white church in 1714, but he had no time to consider the coincidence as a young Jaeger officer on a black steed came charging toward him, his saber drawn.

Edward blocked the first slashing blow with the barrel of his rifle, but the backswing of the rider's blade grazed him on the right cheek, opening a two-inch gash. The officer wheeled his mount and headed back for the kill.

With his adrenaline pumping, Edward's next move was one of pure desperation as he charged the horseman. Brandishing his rifle like a club and shouting at the top of his lungs, he sprinted forward on foot to meet the enemy head-on. It was a bold move that caught horse and rider by surprise. The braying stallion reared up on its hind quarters, pitching the officer backward, his saber flying from his grasp as he hit the unyielding frozen ground.

Edward dispatched the young German with the butt of his rifle as the infantry closed in and shots began peppering the ground in front of him. Moving behind the officer's horse to evade the barrage, he recognized that the powerful animal was about the same height as his father's prized stud, Northumberland. Without a second thought, he grabbed the reins and leapt into the saddle in one motion. Blood ran down his face and neck, mixing with tears as he sped away to rejoin his regiment.

The sun was going down as Edward's weary detail of expert rifle-man made their way back into town from the north. Washington sent out support to help cover their retreat across the lone bridge over the

Assunpink Creek that separated the two armies. Bodies began to pile up and clog both the advance of the British regulars and the retreat of the rebels as the creek ran red with blood. From his position atop a small rise adjacent to the old Mahlon Stacy Millworks, Washington concentrated his weaponry on the defense of the narrow stone bridge. It was like a turkey shoot as a continuous volley from sharpshooters repelled the enemy advance. Safely across the bridge, Edward found himself shoulder-to-shoulder with Seamus O'Grady as the enemy fell back to regroup.

"What are you doing here?" asked a startled Edward.

"Protecting your arse," smiled Seamus, "like you did for me boy."

Edward lowered his head as his mind filled with a bitter memory. "But in the end I failed," he choked out.

"So say you," said Seamus. "But I've never known a Hart to fail an O'Grady. Besides, it was either come out here and defend this bridge—built, I might add, on the strength of your father's reputation—or tar and feather that Brit lover William Bryant. And I just ain't liquored up near enough to go and do that yet."

A cry went up as the British unleashed another assault on the stone bridge. Smoke and shot poured out from both sides, but the Americans held their ground with darkness closing in and the British casualties mounting. A cheer went up on the American side as the enemy again fell back in retreat. Edward reeled around to congratulate Seamus on his fine marksmanship. Blood trickled through the old man's hand as he clutched his chest.

"Help!" Edward called out as he looked around for aid. Too many others were attending to their own wounds to respond.

Seamus pulled tightly on the younger man's coat. "Forget about me," he coughed.

"Don't try to talk, Seamus," cautioned Edward. "Save your strength."

"Listen," Seamus wheezed. "I have news of your father. He's alive and well and very proud of you, lad. You are your father's son. The rest of the family is also safe."

At this point the enemy had returned to formation for another assault. It would be full strength with the remnants of Rall's inflamed mercenaries leading the charge, looking to retaliate for their embarrassing defeat a week earlier.

Seamus pulled a folded scrap of paper from his jacket and pressed it into Edward's hand.

"What's this?" asked Edward, his entire body shaking from the thunder of pounding feet charging the bridge.

"I was saving it for me son," Seamus rasped. "It's the recipe for our Jersey Corn Jack. There's an inn that'll need tending when this war is over, and who knows, young Edward, but you may find yourself in need of a job." He smiled weakly and more blood ran between his fingers. "I offer this ... in tribute to the bond our two families have shared." Edward staunched the blood flowing from the old man's chest with his mitten and then stuffed the paper in his coat pocket.

Shots were flying back and forth across the bridge as the assault continued. O'Grady pulled Edward's ear down to his quivering lips as a musket ball whizzed past the young man's head, a narrow miss. "Don't you let them take this bridge, Edward! It's what separates us from tyranny. Do it for your father. Do it for ..." his eyes widened, "for your Penny, who died at their hands!"

"*No!*" Edward screamed at the top of his lungs. The torrent of pain that shot through his whole body blinded him with rage. He let go of the old man, picked up Seamus's pistol, and without a thought of the danger, raced for the bridge. As he ran directly at the enemy, waving the gun, his voice boomed, *"I am Edward Hart, son of John Hart. He built this bridge and I shall die defending it!"*

Inspired by their half-mad comrade, men began standing up from behind the safety of their cover, raining volley after volley down on the enemy to protect him. Before he could reach the bridge and certain death, a fellow patriot reached up and pulled him down, throwing him to the ground and out of harm's way.

Under blistering fire and demoralized by their enemy's resolve, the mercenary Hessians turned on their heels and ran. Their third and final assault on the little stone bridge Samuel Tucker had once callously predicted "would not endure" had been beaten back by the Continental Army. To avoid the loss of even more men, the British command called a temporary halt to its offensive as night fell.

With Washington's back against the river, Cornwallis arrogantly remarked to his commanders, "We shall bag the fox in the morning."

But when morning came, the "fox" was gone, having escaped under the cover of darkness to fight another day. After midnight, Washington ordered his men to wrap the wagon wheels with rags to dampen their sound and his army moved out. To further disguise their departure, he left some five hundred men and two cannons behind, with orders to keep the campfires burning and the enemy on edge. The general made an end run south around the British lines before turning north toward Princeton. Ironically, a few Hessian troops had avoided an American capture a week earlier by taking a similar route.

As the Continental troops marched on to Princeton, basking in the glow of their spirited showing against the greatest army in the world, at least one soldier walked in silence with a heavy, heavy heart.

15

Legacy

Nathaniel Hart found Edward sitting off by himself picking at moldy rations, lost in morbid thoughts.

After Washington's calculated withdrawal from the standoff at Assunpink Creek, his army surprised the enemy rearguard in Princeton, and within the course of ten crucial days, snatched up yet another brilliant military victory for the American cause. The unorthodox tactics and embarrassing results so unnerved the British high command that Sir William Howe decided to take a defensive posture for the first time in the war and relocated the bulk of his troops to Amboy for the rest of the winter. With port access directly across from New York, Howe could evacuate his forces if need be to avoid further losses until a spring offensive could be mounted.

Although the British presence was still felt in New Jersey, the Continental Army was free to roam where it pleased. From their winter quarters in Morristown, Washington's troops—bolstered by a growing number of citizen-farmer militiamen and encouraged by the victories at Trenton and Princeton—harassed enemy foraging parties at every turn.

"They told me I might find you here," said Nathaniel, sitting down beside his younger brother and warming himself by the campfire. Edward clasped his brother's hand in welcome and smiled sadly.

Taking notice of Nathaniel's freshly issued "Jersey Blues," Edward poked fun at his agrarian-minded sibling, "Where'd you leave the pitchfork?"

"When I heard about the hero of Trenton," said Nathaniel admiringly, "I asked myself, why should my little brother have all the fun?"

"Hero?" laughed Edward bitterly. "Is that what they call a fool with a gun and nothing to live for?"

"You're not the only one suffering from this war, Edward," Nathaniel chastised him mildly.

"Did Father send you here to tell me that?" Edward tossed his tin plate aside.

"Father is ill, Edward. But he'd be dead if not for Penny. That's what I came to tell you."

Edward looked at his brother sharply. "Don't trivialize her death for me, Nathaniel. I loved her, no matter what you or the rest of the family thought of her."

"In truth, we were all quite fond of her, and her actions were anything but trivial. She took half a regiment that was after Father on a wild goose chase, then brought down an English officer by his bloody balls."

Edward fought back tears. "She died a hero," he said. "But right now that is of little solace to me who shall never see her again."

A big burly sergeant had been staring at the two brothers for some time, as if he was waiting for them to do something. Edward looked over at him, annoyed.

"Friend of yours?" asked Nathaniel using his thumb to point.

"You've come to the camp at a bad time, Nathaniel," said Edward in a low voice. "The pox is about, and the general has given orders to have us all inoculated. I've refused. The sergeant here would like nothing better than to clap me in irons for insubordination."

Nathaniel peeled off his jacket and pulled down the collar of his shirt below his shoulder, revealing a round purple welt.

"Don't tell me they got to you already!" Edward said incredulously.

"They didn't have to, Edward. I got mine before I came here."

"You *what*? Why?"

"An epidemic of small pox broke out at John Brainerd's Indian mission," Nathaniel began, his voice suddenly sounding thin and high. "Half the population was wiped out, Edward, and … Scudder was among them. Father sent me to bring his body home."

Edward rose to his feet. "No, dear God—not that sweet boy!"

"I wanted to wait to tell you, Edward, considering the … the heartache you've already had … losing Penny, and all."

"To think he did not live to see twenty," Edward lamented. "Imagine the man he might have grown to be. If there is a heaven, he's with Mother now."

A moment of silence passed between the men over the fate of their nineteen-year-old brother before Nathaniel continued.

"Father insisted I be inoculated before going. He knew about the treatment from Doctor Franklin, who lost his own son Francis before it was perfected. Franklin has been an outspoken advocate for inoculations ever since." Nathaniel grimaced. "He also suggested the British might be behind this latest outbreak, as a means of thinning out our troops."

Edward let out a low moan as he sat back down by the fire, pulling his threadbare blanket around his shoulders

"As I said, Edward, you're not the only one who has suffered from this war. Now go get yourself inoculated or this old farmhand is going to give you a thrashing you won't soon be able to forget," Nathaniel grinned, nudging his tired younger brother.

***

Several men on horseback and wearing the blue uniforms of Continental officers approached the homestead of John Hart early one hazy June morning. Behind them trailed a long, dusty column of infantry, mostly empty wagons and assorted artillery.

Despite Britain's overwhelming force of arms, the Continental Army under the leadership of General George Washington had proven a formidable opponent. As the war moved well into its second year since independence was declared, Philadelphia, rebel capital and cradle of liberty, had fallen into enemy hands, but word was spreading that Benjamin Franklin's mission abroad had been successful. The French were poised to enter the conflict on the American side.

Viewed from the road, the Hart farmhouse, barn, and stables all appeared to be in need of repair. In many places, the post and rail fence had fallen down and lay rotting on the ground. The trees and shrubs that shaded the buildings were badly overgrown, and the once fruitful grain fields and orchards were in decline. Yet, a spring-fed water lily pond still glistened in the sun, the sound of croaking bullfrogs gently punctuating the summer afternoon.

Leaning on his walking cane for support, a frail but keen-eyed John Hart watched the approach of the troops from his front porch steps with mounting excitement. Alongside Hart stood his sons, Jesse and Daniel, his daughter Sarah Wyckoff and her family, little Dee with Grandma Martha, and the Hart house servants, Tolley and Violet.

At length, a tall distinguished-looking officer on a great white steed separated from the troops and cantered up to the house, removing his hat as he drew close.

"Your Excellency," John greeted the man with a bow.

"Please, John, we can dispense with the formalities here," the general said graciously. "This is your home!"

"And you and your men are our honored guests, General. What is ours is yours." Smiling broadly, John indicated the whole of his once glorious estate with a wide sweeping gesture. "I hope you will make yourselves at home here."

Washington raised his hand and several of his military advisors rode forward, dismounted, and introduced themselves individually to John Hart and his family. Two men who needed no introduction followed close behind the officers.

Edward dismounted first and ran to embrace his father. Nathaniel followed more slowly, walking with a pronounced limp.

"Nathaniel may try to tell you he fell off his horse, Father," explained Edward in response to the puzzled look on his father's face. "The truth is he took a musket ball in the hip at Germantown."

"Just trying to keep up with Edward," Nathaniel prodded his brother good naturedly.

"Take it from me, John," Washington exclaimed, "your sons both fought bravely. You should be very proud." The contingent of officers surrounding him registered enthusiastic agreement.

"I am indeed proud of you, my sons," John said, tears forming in his eyes as he embraced them both. "Jesse, Sarah—please see to the general's comfort. Nathaniel, Edward … I believe you know the way to your rooms." He stepped aside.

"With all due respect, Father," said Edward as Washington and his advisors were led inside, "we are most eager to join you for dinner tonight, but our place is otherwise with the men."

***

After dinner, John Hart and George Washington strolled the grounds, taking inventory and inspecting the accommodations. The large army had made camp on every habitable inch of ground on the Hart plantation. Washington's adjunct followed them, preparing a meticulous accounting of all John Hart provided so that he might eventually be reimbursed from the national treasury, including rails split for firewood, hay and straw for bedding, and corn for the horses. Washington remarked that John Hart could not imagine how thankful he was to see the men bathing and laundering their uniforms in the pond, while their horses drank to their heart's content.

John noted the incursions on his property with interest, while neither expecting nor counting on any future remuneration. He was content to do his part for the cause of liberty without complaint, but he couldn't help but think there was something more on the general's mind than a monotonous inventory he could have easily assigned to any officer on his staff.

In the shade of an old elm tree, Washington pulled the Signer aside and queried in a low voice, "John, is it fair to assume that in your good offices you have traversed this state up one side and down the other?"

"Aye, General, in my time I have traveled many roads to get where I needed to go," John responded with growing curiosity. "But surely you can see by my appearance that long days in the saddle are behind me, so why do you ask?"

"John, while I admire your strength of character and years of service, I won't prevail upon you to lead another charge," Washington remarked amiably. "Your instincts serve you well, though, for I am in a quandary. It has been reported to me that the enemy encampment at

Monmouth Courthouse may be vulnerable to a surprise attack, but I do not know the terrain from here to there all that well."

"General, I would ride with you to hell and back, but fortunately for both of us there are within my household several able-bodied young scouts who, as it happens, know a little-traveled shortcut that should preserve the element of surprise you desire."

***

Later in the evening, John asked Edward to meet him in his study. There was much that remained unsaid between them, though neither man was loquacious by nature.

"About Penny ..." the elder Hart began. "I shall never forget her sacrifice, Edward. She was worthy of your love, and I was wrong to try and keep you apart. I am sorry for my harsh words to you both."

There was nothing Edward could say that the gratitude in his eyes for these words did not already reveal. As he embraced his father, he was struck by how frail he had become in the two long years since all the trouble began.

"Your mother loved her, too." John Hart's voice broke. "Dear Edward, what are we to do without those two good women in our lives?"

Edward stood strong for his father's sake. "We'll have to lean on one another a bit, I expect, sir," he said.

With a grateful smile, John sank down into his leather chair and bid Edward bring his brothers into the study. With three of his five surviving sons thus assembled, he relayed his earlier conversation with General Washington. Jesse, the eldest and most widely traveled of the three, agreed to take the lead as the primary scout to Monmouth. Nathaniel and Edward would stay within their ranks, ready to supply back-up intelligence and preserve the secrecy of the mission at all costs.

There, with his sons in his long neglected study, the scene of so many past checks and balances, John decided the time had come to lay out his legacy. With the light of the full moon filtering in from the outside, he took a sip of water from an iced pitcher and cleared his throat.

"None of us knows how much longer this war will last," he began, "but it seems doubtful I will live to see the end of it."

"Nonsense, Father, there are years ahead of you," protested Jesse.

"How I wish that were true, son," John said wistfully. "But even if it were, it will not be possible, in my lifetime, to see our homestead and mills restored to their rightful glory. No, it is time I pass the responsibility for the future on to each of you."

John rose to his feet unsteadily, leaning on his cane. As he struggled to keep his balance, Nathaniel got up to support him but faltered on his own bad leg. While Edward moved to help Nathaniel, Jesse put a steadying arm around their father.

Grateful, the old man put his arm around his son's shoulder as Jesse eased him back into the chair.

John gently patted his son's cheek with a mottled hand stiffened by arthritis. "Jesse, you are the oldest son, and this farm is your birthright, but I think we all recognize the severity of Nathaniel's injury. I hope you'll forgive me when I say that Nathaniel belongs here at the homestead as caretaker for what remains of our estate. It will be his duty to provide for the younger children, for as long as they have need, and to see to it that my pledge to your mother regarding the release of the servants is honored when I pass on."

"Father, that is not fair to Jesse," exclaimed Nathaniel, caught completely off guard by his father's decision.

Jesse silenced his brother with a compassionate look before he could say anything more. "It is right and you know it, Nathaniel. Besides, my plans for after the war are the same as before it and will leave me precious little time for farming, even if I were so inclined—which I am not. My place is on the road. But first there is a little matter of Samuel Tucker and some missing Treasury funds that I must clear up."

John grew pensive. "Boys, Samuel and I have shared a long history together, and although we have often found ourselves on the opposite sides of an issue, I am convinced that in time, under the right circumstances, he will make amends for his past transgressions. If for no other reason than to recast his own legacy, as he knows history will be the judge of his role in these momentous events."

"What about John Jr.?" asked Nathaniel, genuinely concerned that all the surviving Hart sons be accounted for in their father's largesse.

"If he's still alive, you mean?" added Jesse with a hint of sarcasm and doubt. "We've heard nothing from him since he was expelled from Louisiana and imprisoned in Cuba!"

"Ah, the prodigal son," John sighed. "Should John Jr. survive his adventures abroad and return to these shores, he will receive nothing from my estate and no monetary assistance from any of you. Is that clear?"

"But, Father—he is our brother and carries on your name," pleaded Nathaniel.

"Which is why he shall see nothing of his inheritance until and unless the debts he has amassed," John said, angrily shaking a fist full of documents he had picked up off his desk, "are settled by him alone."

"Yes, Father," Nathaniel acquiesced.

"However," John continued, his tone softening, "should any of his progeny come forward, they are to be accorded all the rights and privileges inherent in the Hart name as surely as if they were my own children."

The Hart patriarch now cast his attention to Edward. Of all his children, none had been so deeply scarred, more changed by war than this dashing, handsome soldier who carried so much unspoken sadness within him. The innocence that once glowed brightly from boyish eyes had been all but extinguished by the human suffering he had witnessed and the personal losses he had endured.

Edward had sat quietly during the discussion of the future, of family and inheritance, none of which seemed to involve him. There was a time when all he could think to do was fight for glory and honor, as the grandfather he'd been named for had endeavored to, and, when it was over, settle down to a quiet life in the country with a beloved wife, surrounded by happy children for whom he could spin exciting yarns by the fireplace for nights on end.

But now Edward had no idea where his path might lead. Certainly, Penny had been taken from him, and with her, the idyllic life he had envisioned. He believed his father had surmised correctly that after the war the Hart landholdings would be the family's sole measure of wealth, and he also agreed that it was appropriate to place the estate in the hands of Nathaniel—the only Hart boy who seemed truly tethered to the soil.

Fidgeting in his chair, with the eyes of his father and brothers upon him, Edward found himself reaching unconsciously into his breast pocket, feeling for his faithful copy of *Common Sense.* Instead, his hand came to rest upon a folded scrap of paper. It was the recipe Seamus O'Grady had entrusted to him as he lay dying in his arms, after defending a seemingly insignificant bridge at Trenton that, in the Irish innkeeper's last words, "separates us from tyranny."

In that one crystal clear moment, Edward saw a glimpse of his future. He was standing in his tavern keeper's apron alongside that beautiful little bridge, now trussed up and decorated with a wide floral arch, and there, in front of him, across that fateful stone structure rode a stately gentleman on a white steed, waving to the celebrating throngs that had come out to greet him as he made his way to New York to be installed as the first elected president of a new nation.

Part Two

16

Eagle Tavern Redux

"W hat *is* this place?" asked Tina Alma as she slipped through a narrow gap in the boards covering the first floor window of an old abandoned building. Her cautious tone telegraphed the teen's anxiety to her companion as she followed him in through the opening like Alice down the rabbit hole.

Darius Hudson slid the splintered board back into place, concealing their point of entry. He flicked open his cell phone. The pale blue light illuminated his dark, handsome face.

"It used to be a tavern," he said nonchalantly, "dating back to the Revolutionary War, but it's been closed up for years."

"A bar?" Tina asked incredulously. "It's our first date, and you take me to a bar? What kind of girl do you think I am?" she asked with mock seriousness, placing her hands on her hips in a defiant pose.

Darius took her gently by the hand. "Not just any bar," he answered, his dazzling smile in contrast to the darkness that surrounded them. "It's called the Eagle Tavern. There's a lot of history in these walls."

"*¿Aguila?*" Tina muttered the word for eagle in Spanish and her best friend Isabel Aguilar popped into her head warning her not to get involved with this handsome black guy. *Your father will kill you if the Latin Kings don't get you first.*

"It gives me the creeps. When you told me we were going to an old tavern, I thought it was to get something to eat," Tina said, swatting at the cobwebs clinging to the long, dark, beautiful hair she had just spent an hour straightening. "My father would not approve of your choice of restaurant," she chided mildly, trying to mask her growing apprehension. "Come to think of it, neither do I."

"I wanted you to see where I work," explained Darius, inching toward the stairs, "and show you something really special."

"I thought you were a ticket taker for the Trenton Thunder."

"That's for pocket change. I love baseball, but this is where I really want to spend my time." The former varsity first baseman beamed at his date.

"In a boarded up old bar?" Tina was unimpressed. "Okay," she sighed with real exasperation. "Show me what you found in here that's so special."

He was pleased. At least she was paying attention. From inside the musty, old clapboard building, the two teens could hear the sound of cars sloshing down South Broad Street on the rain-slicked roadway. Luckily, the rain had let up by the time they parked in the alleyway behind the old tavern.

"I ride down this street all the time, but I never noticed this place before," Tina rambled on nervously. She crept alongside Darius, the wooden planks creaking underneath them as they went. "Couldn't we just come back here in the daytime when we can see where we're going?"

"And spoil the surprise?"

The thought of a "surprise" waiting for her at the end of this secret escapade had initially intrigued Tina, but the sheltered high school senior was starting to have second thoughts. What did she really know about Darius anyway? He was a year older than her and had graduated from Trenton High last year. He used to play on the baseball team. He was really handsome. He had an athlete's build and was sexy, at least according to some of her friends. She had seen him at the high school with some of his friends who still went there. Apparently that's where he noticed her, too.

She and her friends started hanging out after school with Darius and a group of his pals about a month ago, and the two of them managed to sneak in a brief conversation once in awhile. Last week when the weather was nice, they all took a ride to Cadwalader Park and she rode shotgun in his car. That was when he asked her out on this "date." Tina didn't know how to break the news to her parents that she was seeing a boy from the other side of the tracks. She knew that her devoutly Catholic, hard-working parents, who had their sights set on their seventeen-year-old daughter going to college, would frown upon her dating anybody, let alone a boy from Trenton's seedy North Ward—the housing projects near the Trenton Battle Monument.

"But aren't we trespassing?" she inquired, a telltale quiver of suspicion rising in her voice.

"Oops!" said Darius as the light from his cell phone went dead and darkness surrounded them. "Forgot to charge the battery," he admitted sheepishly.

"That's not funny, Darius," she said, standing in an ink black hallway. She rested her hand against the plaster wall for support and found a gaping hole filled with rough lath and loose horsehair. She screamed.

"Don't move," he said, crawling away from her on the floor.

"Wait! Darius, where are you going?"

She could hear him shuffling his way down the corridor.

Tina couldn't move even if she wanted to. She was too frightened. Here she was in a spooky old building, trespassing with a boy she barely knew. What was she thinking?

A stream of bright light burst from down the hallway near the foot of the stairs.

"And the Lord said let there be light," joked Darius coming toward Tina. He flicked the flashlight off and on playfully as he drew nearer. "I was hoping no one saw me leave this here today."

"Darius, I want to go … now!" Her hands were trembling. "Why did you bring me here?"

"I'm sorry, Tina," he said, reaching out to stroke her cheek with his free hand. "I didn't mean to scare you. It's not much farther. I hid it under the staircase."

She didn't budge. "What could be so important that you had to drag me out on a rainy night and break into an old abandoned building? What kind of *work* do you do here anyway?"

"Excavating," he replied, his deep brown eyes twinkling in the dancing light.

"What?"

"I'm taking a class at Mercer County Community College. We're involved in an archaeological dig at this site. Last week we turned up a cannonball; before that a hairbrush with some buttons, and lots and lots of pottery shards."

"That's what you brought me here to see? Pottery shards?"

He laughed hard and the pure spontaneity of it brought a welcome moment of relief to his skeptical date.

"Of course not," he said smiling. "Tina, this old place is a relic, a time capsule full of mysteries and wonders from the past just waiting to be discovered."

"I thought baseball was your passion. Isn't that what you told me?"

"It was … I mean, it is," he fumbled. "I love playing baseball. I really do, but not too many guys ever make it to the big leagues. Besides, I've always wanted to find something else I could get excited about."

"And you think you found it in dirt?"

"No, not in dirt—in the past … in history."

She gave him a quizzical look.

"Look, I know this might sound crazy," he said, "but you know how people give President Obama credit for helping to break down racial barriers? Well, I just want to be remembered as the first African American to write a book on the history of Trenton."

She shook her head. "Wait a minute, isn't black history all about slavery and segregation?"

"That's my point. I'm not talking about black history or white history. I'm talking about *Trenton* history. Too many people are still slaves to the notion that there's no place for us in our own communities. History made us who we are."

"Darius, you can't rewrite history."

"I don't want to rewrite it. I just want to make it accessible to *everyone*. Do you have any idea how important Trenton was in the War for Independence?"

"Hey, don't look at me. While your ancestors were in the cotton fields of Georgia, mine were in Cuba harvesting sugar cane and making rum. What do I care about the American Revolution other than to get a passing grade in school?"

He sighed, disheartened by her lack of interest.

"Darius," she said smiling, trying to recover his upbeat mood, "if you're trying to impress me with your studies and your conviction—hey, I'm all for it, but I still don't understand why you brought me *here*. Couldn't you have told me all this over pizza?"

"Tina, this place might not be standing much longer, and I wanted you to see it, to get a sense of its past the way I did. That's why we're doing the dig. Some big shot developer is trying to buy this place, and for all we know he's gonna turn it into a Burger King."

"Can they do that?"

The sound of shattering glass spoiled the surprise he had been building up to. She looked at him with fear in her eyes, and he quickly pulled her down the hallway with him and then crouched near the staircase. He reached up underneath the stairs from behind, quietly pried a board loose, and pulled out a bundled parchment stitched into a booklet with thin leather strips.

A board creaked loudly somewhere in the building. He switched off the flashlight and grabbed her by the shoulders. "Ssshhh," he warned.

"Yo, Darius!" called a deep-throated voice from the room down at the other end of the hall. "C'mon bro, we know you're in here!" said another.

"We saw your car in the alleyway," came the first voice again.

"Yeah, nobody else would drive such a shitwagon," echoed a third higher-pitched male voice. A peel of raucous laughter rang out from the group.

Darius put his face within an inch of Tina's. He could hear her heavy breathing and if he had placed his hand on her chest, he was certain he would have found her heart pounding as loudly as his own.

"Tina, listen to me," he whispered softly so as to not cause her added alarm. "Do you know the way back to where we came in?"

"I ... I think so."

"Down the hall, all the way to the end then left into the pantry," he said calmly. "You'll see a streetlight through the cracks in the window boards."

He paused to let her process what he had just said. "Please take this book and keep it for me. I'll explain later. Here, you'll need the flashlight. I'll meet you at the car." He handed her the keys. "If I'm not out in twenty minutes, drive away."

"Darius, what's going on?"

Down at the other end of the hall someone stumbled over a chair and a bottle smashed onto the floor. "Watch where you're going, ass-hole," shouted the deep-voiced intruder. Sounds of pushing and shoving ensued.

"Just do what I say, Tina. Go!"

"Darius, who are those guys?" she asked in a voice laced with panic.

"Trust me, Tina," he said spinning her toward the way out, "you don't want to know."

17

The Grass Is Always Greener

*T*o Luis Alma, the traffic along Calhoun Street seemed heavier than usual. The potholed boulevard was one of only two local arteries connecting Trenton to Morrisville across the Delaware River without a toll, but the volume of cars made it seem more like a weekend than a typical Friday morning in late September. The forty-three-year-old landscaper watched with growing interest as more and more cars turned into the parking lot next to the Shiloh Baptist Church as if it were a Sunday.

Leaning on his rake, Luis thought back to his phone conversation with the redneck Deputy Commissioner of Parks who had chosen Luis's firm to clear away the overgrown grass and debris littering the dry canal bed running along the south side of the church. "The place is an eyesore and a refuge for homeless derelicts just like the rest of the neighborhood, but the church members are complaining. I'd send in my own crew but we ain't got nobody available for Cal*coon* Street, if you catch my drift. So just get in, do the job and get outta there as fast as you can."

Thinking about his bid and how quickly it had been accepted, Luis wished he had gone higher. At the time, he was looking at the contract as a stepping-stone to more county work for Alma's Quality Landscaping and doing everything in his power to keep his three crews busy. The season was almost over, and his men could use whatever money they could make now to help them get through the winter.

Had he known the canal's history, this first-generation American, the son of Cuban immigrants, would have appreciated the irony of an engineering marvel of the industrial era: hand dug by countless Irish immigrants—now being cleaned up by three Latinos armed with a power mower and weed whackers.

Brought back from his musings by the sound of car doors slamming, Luis suddenly realized he wasn't the only one distracted by the traffic motoring up and down Calhoun Street. His crew had also stopped to take in the steady stream of well-dressed men and women stepping out of trendy cars and parading into the church. This must be a funeral service for somebody pretty important, Luis thought to himself.

"*Ay, Mamita*," muttered one of his men leaning over the fence to admire a leggy blonde in a form-fitting blue suit. As she made her way up the church steps, she paused briefly to pull her long hair back into a ponytail and adjust the hem of her skirt. Luis made a mental note to buy his wife a suit just like it and to keep his teenaged daughter away from his horny crew. As if on cue, his other worker let out a wolfish whistle of approval.

"¡*Basta*!" exclaimed Luis. "Hector, Felix—*vamonos*. Back to work!" He appreciated the sight of a pretty woman as much as any man, but this was his business, his livelihood. He had grown it from a father-and-son operation into a thriving enterprise with a payroll, uniforms, trucks, and equipment to maintain, and he knew when it was time to keep his men in line.

Grumbling, the two men turned their attention back to the work at hand.

***

Inside the modern, sand-color brick church, Reverend Lionel Evans was nervously greeting guests as they arrived for the funeral service of Reverend Hollis Markham. Tiny beads of sweat formed on his smooth, bald head and trickled under his stiff white collar. The wife and daughter of the deceased had been the first to arrive and the hardest for him to receive. Leaning on each other for support, the two women were led to their seats by the fashionable daughter's impeccably dressed husband, local real estate developer Randal Whittaker. To the others gathered around the casket paying their last respects,

Reverend Markham was a revered community activist who had spent most of his eighty years working on behalf of the poor and needy. But to his family—the grieving widow, daughter, and son-in-law—he was a husband and father first.

Following Reverend Evans's rather lengthy eulogy, which he delivered with conviction, if not flair, Trenton Mayor James "Jimmy" Dodd approached the podium to share an intimate account of his first meeting with Hollis Markham.

"We met at 'Tony Goes,' which some of you still insist on calling the Casino Restaurant," the four-term mayor and former high school guidance counselor recalled, warming up his audience.

"I was seeking office for the very first time," Mayor Dodd continued. "The Reverend had summoned me because we had a difference of opinion about what to do with a particular abandoned lot on the corner of Hanover and Montgomery streets. I don't have to tell you that when Reverend Markham summoned you, you went." The people were nodding their heads in agreement.

"You see, at the time, I was in favor of building a state office high-rise, and the state boys assured me that the money would have been good for the city, but to his credit, the reverend was adamant that what Trenton really needed was decent low-income housing. Well, he won that battle—and I'll bet I wouldn't be mayor if he hadn't." Scattered laughter filled the room as Dodd went in for the close.

"I learned a lot from the right Reverend Markham. We all know how much he loved this city. We owe it to him to keep on making it better." The mayor paused for effect and then stepped down from the podium and moved to the far side of the room as if swept there by his emotions.

In life, Reverend Hollis Markham could be a powerful ally or a formidable foe. The son of an Alabama preacher, in the early 1960s he and his family were part of the second great migration of poor blacks out of the south. Arriving in Trenton with high expectations, the family found only menial work and no less segregation than they had left behind. With little more than the hope he carried in his heart, Hollis joined Reverend Martin Luther King's Civil Rights crusade.

The pursuit of equal rights became his passion, and he carried the torch until the day he died.

Along the way, he held various elected and appointed positions in city and state government. While he gave 100 percent in every situation, those closest to him knew that his most cherished work was serving as mentor to the many youth organizations in the adopted city he had come to know, love, and call home.

As a man of God, Hollis also made quite a name for himself, preaching with rare conviction from the pulpit at the Shiloh Baptist Church until his retirement two years earlier. In the last few years of his ministry, he had come to terms with the anger and impatience of his youth, and—just as he had once shorn his trademark Afro and replaced his colorful leisure suits with three-piece pinstripes—he had softened his tone and embraced a broader mission of racial and economic harmony for all Trentonians, regardless of race, religion, or means.

Today's ceremony was a reminder of the many hearts and minds he had touched in many different ways. From soul-searching parishioners to at-risk youths, from radical activists to right-wing politicians, men and women had packed the church to say farewell to an individual who had earned everyone's respect, whether you agreed with his views or not.

Yet despite the many positives of the life now being eulogized, a dark cloud shrouded the mourners as they listened to one touching story after another. While nobody spoke of it directly, preferring to address their loss obliquely as a "tragedy," the question on everyone's mind was *Who murdered Hollis Markham?*

***

Outside, behind the church at the far end of the parking lot, Luis Alma and his crew were putting their equipment into the back of a white Chevy pickup. The warmth and brightness present earlier in the day had given way to shadows and clouds as the sun left the sky for longer and more frequent intervals. Luis didn't need a weatherman to tell him a storm was coming.

As Hector and Felix climbed into the rear of the truck and reached into the cooler for bottled water, Luis walked around to the driver's side to log in their finishing time and check his cell phone for messages from his other two crews. Suddenly, a nearby car alarm shattered the peace and quiet of the late afternoon.

Hector and Felix jumped down from the tailgate and joined their boss in the cab. The piercing shrill of the alarm drowned out any thought of conversation as they watched an old brown Pontiac Bonneville, dragging a tail pipe, slam over a curb and swerve into the street. Sparks flew as the pipe bounced up and down on the poorly paved road. A "Save the Old Barracks" decal waved from the corroded bumper. Luis couldn't make out the face of the driver, only the dark color of his skin.

Intended for traffic control, the police cruiser positioned at the front entrance of the church made a quick U-turn and screeched off, siren wailing in hot pursuit of the Pontiac. A patrolman on foot came around from the front of the church and ran toward the sound of the car alarm. He crouched down and disappeared behind the car.

Watching the whole scene through the window of his cab as though he were at a drive-in movie, Luis could feel the tension building in his temples. When the cop on foot patrol didn't resurface and the car alarm continued to wail, his concern grew serious. The instincts that had earned him medals for his Army service in Iraq during Operation Desert Storm came back to him in an instant and he knew what he had to do. "Stay put," he shouted to his men as he climbed out of the truck, slamming the door. Felix and Hector were more than willing to obey.

Luis kept low as he moved toward the spot where he had last seen the officer. He bent down and checked under the cars. Nothing. He headed in the direction of the car that was making all the racket, a late-model silver Mercedes coupe parked about four cars away.

By now, most of the crowd from inside the church had moved outside, including the striking blonde who had distracted Luis's crew earlier. She was visibly upset as she exclaimed, "That's my car alarm!" to nobody in particular. Standing on either side of her were

Mayor Dodd and Reverend Evans; the two men looked and gestured toward the parking lot but appeared frozen to the church steps.

Moving cautiously among the parked cars, Luis's foot struck something soft. He looked down and saw the cop lying there, face up, silent and still. The hair on the back of Luis's neck and arms stood straight up.

It was clear to Luis that the officer had suffered stab wounds to the chest and arms. He checked his pulse; it was faint, but he was alive. Luis pulled out his handkerchief and folded it over a deep puncture in the officer's chest to staunch the flow of blood. Next, he removed his own belt to use it as a tourniquet on the man's badly slashed right arm.

Before Luis could think of what to do next, two things caught his attention. The first was a man in a gray hooded sweatshirt running from the parking lot and disappearing down the canal bank. The second was an image that only registered in his mind after he had started off in pursuit.

The officer's gun was missing.

18

Save the Old Barracks

*R*unning and dialing a cell phone at the same time is difficult enough under normal circumstances, but Luis was in pursuit of a suspected armed felon while moving between parked cars. He finally had to stop, keeping his eyes on the fleeing fugitive as he dialed 911.

"Officer down," he shouted into the receiver when the operator answered. Catching his breath he added, "340 Calhoun Street, Shiloh Baptist Church." He repeated the message then flipped the phone shut and stuffed it into his pocket.

Sprinting down Calhoun past Spring and Passaic streets, Luis caught sight of the gray hooded sweatshirt again at West Hanover. There, the suspect made a sharp turn onto another portion of the old canal. Racing through backyards littered with rusted cars, broken toys, bags of trash, and angry dogs, Luis dashed by the old canal keeper's house where he ran into a set of white sheets hung out on a line to dry.

Stumbling as he tried to shake off the clinging white sheets covering his chest and face, Luis drew icy stares from the residents huddled on porches and behind windows, terrified by what looked like a Ku Klux Klansman in pursuit of one of their own.

The suspect slipped down Greens Place and across West State Street, where he was almost hit by an oncoming car. Luis had just rid himself of the sheets and was gaining ground again when he suddenly found himself in the path of a yellow school bus leaving the New Jersey State Museum. He narrowly dodged the bus then hurried across the road behind it.

The sudden burst of activity caught the attention of a trooper stationed at the entrance to the grounds of the State House. He radioed for back up.

As the fugitive reached the outside balcony of the museum, he looked back to see if he was still being followed. At that moment, Luis thought *he's just a kid* and then saw the fear flash in the boy's eyes as he reached behind his back and pulled out the officer's revolver. Luis stopped dead in his tracks and then dove to the ground. In the next instant, with police sirens screaming, the boy leaped over the concrete barrier and disappeared from sight.

As Luis got back on his feet he heard the sound of a muffled gunshot just beyond the wall. Racing to it, he peered over the top. The fugitive was sprawled out on the road below, holding his right foot. The police revolver had apparently gone off when he fell and skidded some ten yards away.

For a split second, Luis would have been content to let the police take it the rest of the way, but when the suspect rose unsteadily to his feet and began to limp across Route 29 toward the river, he vaulted the concrete barrier and resumed the chase. He had invested far too much time and energy in the ordeal to let this creep get away now.

Luis's thoughts wandered momentarily to the cop who was clinging to life in the parking lot at the Shiloh Baptist Church. Without a thought for his own safety, he plunged down the museum steps two at a time.

Dodging the speeding highway traffic, Luis was right behind his quarry at Stacy Park as the boy waded into the swift flowing Delaware. Clearly his plan was to ride the current downstream, but he was hobbled and slowed by injury and Luis tackled him from behind.

With a forearm to the throat, Luis knocked the boy into the water and wrestled the knife out of his hand. Dragging him cursing and kicking out of the water, he gave him a quick knee to the midsection and all resistance ceased. Wet and exhausted, Luis sat on the young man's chest and waited for the police to arrive.

***

The switchboard at Trenton Police headquarters was lit up like an air traffic control panel. The mayor's office at City Hall on East State Street was buzzing with the news. Questions were pouring in from all corners of the city. Coupled with the mysterious and as yet unsolved murder of the Reverend Hollis Markham, concerned citizens wanted answers. Was Trenton witnessing the second coming of the Ku Klux Klan?

Hours after an all-points bulletin went out on the brown Pontiac Bonneville with the hanging tailpipe and the Old Barracks decal on the bumper, the alert yielded results. The car was found abandoned behind the old Roebling Building across from the Sun National Bank Center, formerly known as the Sovereign Bank Arena, by laborers from the Office of Public Safety. The car's owner, Darius Hudson, was taken into custody for questioning.

Officer Joe McKenna, the patrolman injured in the church parking lot, had been taken to the Helene Fuld Trauma Center on Brunswick Avenue, where he was in critical condition with multiple stab wounds and a punctured lung. His wife and his partner were keeping vigil at his bedside.

Abigail Treadwell-Tucker, the owner of the silver Mercedes with the loud alarm, was in the mayor's office when Dominic Rosetti, the crusty director of public safety, burst in with the news that his boys had found the abandoned Pontiac. Dominic made no apology for the interruption and proceeded to ogle Ms. Treadwell-Tucker, who appeared completely unfazed by her ordeal. In fact, one might have thought she was enjoying the attention. Her hair and lipstick were photo perfect, complementing an ivory complexion, a dimpled chin, and wide-set blue eyes above a slightly upturned nose. Designer eyeglasses contributed to a Palinesque, sexy-smart appeal, while her tightly fitted suit revealed a slender, shapely figure and long, silken legs.

Even though her breasts were a little too concealed for his taste, those amazing legs, which were currently crossed as this confident young woman sat laughing with the mayor of New Jersey's capital city, held Dominic's attention for a moment longer than was advisable. When Mayor Dodd introduced Dominic to Abby, she removed her glasses, clenched one stem between too-perfect white teeth, and looked into the leering director's eyes until he had to blink and turn away.

In her statement to the police, Abby alleged that nothing but her cell phone was missing from the car. The officer she spoke with assured her the police would be able to track it by way of a GPS signal, if anyone tried to use it.

"Do you know anything about the Old Barracks, Abby?" Dominic asked, his tone a bit condescending in her estimation.

"Sure, what would you like to know?" she replied, repositioning her legs to assure his undivided attention. "The barracks have a fascinating history, though personally I gravitate to more … private accommodations."

A rare blush warmed Dominic's face. As Mayor Dodd cleared his throat nervously, the door opened and Luis Alma was ushered in by the mayor's chief of staff. Still dressed in his work clothes, exhausted from the chase and wet from the river, Luis addressed the mayor without seeming to notice the others.

"You wanted to see me, Mr. Mayor?" The weariness of the long day showed on his handsome, grimy face. His eyes appeared glazed under heavy lids, and it was easy to see he was in desperate need of a shower, a shave, and especially a good night's sleep.

Dodd rose from his chair and walked around his desk to greet Luis with a practiced smile and handshake. "So, you're the gardener who saved Officer McKenna's life and kept the perp from escaping. Mr., ah …"

"Alma. Luis Alma," Luis said, glancing from Abby to Dominic and back again. She gave him a smile; he merely nodded.

"Well, Mr. Alma," the mayor said clapping him on the shoulder, then wiping his hand with a handkerchief when he realized just how wet and filthy Luis was. "I'm going to make sure you get a citation for heroism. What do think about that?"

Luis suddenly recognized Abby as the woman on the church steps. He looked at her pretty hands with their manicured nails and noticed she wasn't wearing a ring. She met his gaze and responded with an inviting smile.

Turning back to the mayor, Luis said, "I'm honored, Mr. Mayor, but with your permission I'd like to go now. My wife is waiting for me."

19

Columbus Park

R aul Antonio Alma had lost his wife to cancer two years ago, just shy of his seventy-first birthday, and subsequently moved in with his son Luis. They shared a three-story brick row home at 31 Roebling Avenue with Luis's wife Maria, a nurse at St. Francis Hospital, and their two children, high school senior Tina and her nine-year-old brother Roberto. It was a cozy place and Raul did have his own room, but he wished he could visit his family back in Cuba—especially with winter coming on.

Raul grabbed the morning paper before anyone else woke up and made himself a cup of strong coffee, or *cortadito* as he called it. He shuffled across the faded linoleum floor in his bathrobe and worn-out slippers to sit down at a big round Formica-topped kitchen table with padded chairs. He hadn't even had time to glance at the headlines when his daughter-in-law Maria joined him.

"Hola, Papi, how would you like your eggs?" She always made breakfast on weekends. On weekdays it was all she could do to get the kids dressed and off to school before she had to leave for work herself. She kissed him on the cheek, noticing he hadn't shaved.

"Oh, Maria, you don't have to go to any trouble for me. Scrambled with chorizo, if you have any left over, and tomato …" His mouth watered.

"And onion and *queso*," she added with a gentle laugh, "and warm tortillas on the side."

Raul smiled at his good fortune and opened up the newspaper. "Holy Crap!"

"¡*Papi*!" Maria chastised him.

"You gotta look at this!" Raul exclaimed as the rest of the family joined him at the kitchen table.

The Trentonian was better known for its Page Six girls, lottery numbers, and sleazy tabloid fare than hard-hitting news, but today's front page headline ran above an undated U.S. Army file photo of Luis Alma posing in his Desert Storm military fatigues and appearing years younger: "LAWNMAN HERO FOR LAWMAN." The lead story was about a "quiet, unassuming Hispanic everyman who became a hero overnight when he risked his life to save an injured city cop. The courageous ex-serviceman, who had seen combat duty in Iraq, doggedly pursued the fleeing thug responsible for the attack on foot through the backyards and alleyways of Trenton's rundown West Ward until he cornered the desperate criminal, disarmed him of the policeman's revolver, and apprehended him as he tried to swim across the Delaware."

There were sidebar stories including a sensational editorial in the early edition that was even more flattering. Written by the popular, rough-and-tumble Irish-American columnist P. J. Moore, it saluted the dreamy iconic image of a decorated American veteran returning from the horrors of war abroad to fight injustice at home. The piece ended with an impassioned plea on behalf of all Trenton's law-abiding citizens, begging Luis Alma to take up arms against the city's evil "Big Three," which, according to Moore, were "Corruption, Crime and inCompetence!" The entreaty came across more as a challenge than a request, daring Luis to make a formal run for any political office, be it police commissioner, mayor, or dog catcher—anything that might help Trenton's citizenry sleep more soundly at night. And P. J. Moore would guarantee the paper's support.

Raul spread the newspaper out on the breakfast table for everyone to read, pushing aside the scrambled eggs and chorizo, fresh-squeezed orange juice, and warm tortillas. A nonstop barrage of comments was thrown at Luis from his usually sarcastic but noticeably proud father, his doting wife, and his two impressionable children as they read the articles about him. As it was difficult for Luis to get a word in edgewise, he just listened and tried to enjoy his meal.

"It says here the guy you nabbed was a nineteen-year-old hoodlum named Bobby Jackson," Raul said looking up from the paper. "He's got a rap sheet a mile long—dealing drugs, stealing cars, fencing stolen property ..."

"He's also a suspect in several recent burglaries," Maria added as she refilled her husband's coffee cup.

"He dropped out of school last year," Tina said, adding, "My friends say he's in the Bloods." She avoided her mother's gaze lest her eyes give away the real source of her inside knowledge.

Tina wasn't about to point out that the last paragraph in the same article, which she had scanned quickly, mentioned one Darius Hudson who had been taken into custody for questioning as a possible accomplice. The article indicated he was later released on his own recognizance after stating that his car, spotted at the crime scene, had been stolen. The police were skeptical of his story because he hadn't filed a stolen vehicle report, and when they later found it abandoned they determined it hadn't been hot-wired. Darius had broken a date with Tina yesterday after school, saying there was something important he had to take care of. He didn't offer her any more than that and she hadn't heard from him since.

"He's a gang member?" her brother Roberto squealed. "I knew it."

"What do you know about gangs?" his mother questioned him like a police interrogator.

Roberto took a big bite of eggs and sausage so he wouldn't have to answer.

"Well, it sounds to me like this punk Bobby Jackson is headed for the pen," Raul said.

"He's not much more than a kid, Pop," Luis said, thinking of the fear he had felt when that "kid" pulled a gun on him.

"Well, I don't like it," Maria said as she served Luis more eggs with a wooden spoon. "The crime in this city is getting out of hand. Take that Markham case. The police say it may have been a botched burglary, but they still don't have a clue who did it! So, the reverend comes home early, surprises a burglar before he can take anything, and then has his throat slit, just for kicks. We see this all the time in the emergency room."

"Oh, mother," Tina moaned. "Not again."

But Maria would not be deterred. She had brought up the subject many times before and always got the same reaction from her family, but this time the events had hit too close to home. "The point, Tina, is that your father could have been killed." She took a seat at the table across from her husband and reached for his hand. "Honey, I think it's time we put a deposit on that property we looked at in Hopewell."

Luis recognized the seriousness of her tone and felt the worry in her slightly trembling hand. The news caught the rest of the family totally off guard.

"Property in Hopewell?" Raul repeated incredulously.

"I was going to tell you about it, Pop, when I thought the time was right. We haven't made up our minds yet, but it is worth thinking about. The business is growing, and Maria makes good money at the hospital. We don't need to live like this."

Raul was crestfallen. He felt betrayed that his son didn't think enough of him to talk about such important matters. After all, wasn't he the one who had started the family business that was now doing so well, according to his ungrateful son?

"Pop, look around," Luis continued. "There isn't even a safe place to park my truck. We may have outgrown the neighborhood."

"Hopewell, huh?" Raul said again, scratching his two-day stubble. His temperature continued to rise even though he looked into his son's honest and caring eyes. "That's what white folks do, Luis. They leave the city when the going gets tough."

"I don't want to leave!" Tina blurted out. "Daddy, please don't take me out of Trenton High. I want to finish where I started. It's important to me."

"No way, Jose," Roberto piped up. "I vote we go. The sooner the better. My school sucks—nothing but bullies and dope addicts."

Maria was stunned. She had never heard her young son speak so bluntly about his elementary school, even though she was aware of its sinking reputation.

She squeezed her husband's hand. "Luis, it's worse than I thought."

Luis stood up and stretched his arms out. "¡*Calmate*! Everybody just take it easy. We're not going anywhere yet, and I promise you this will be a family decision. We'll talk about it tomorrow. I've got to get to work."

It was Saturday, and Alma's Quality Landscaping had only one job scheduled for the day, but Luis was anxious to get out of the house. This wasn't the way he had wanted to bring up the subject of moving with his father. Maria should have known better ... and what was up with Tina? Was Roberto's elementary school really that bad? Where did they get that picture of him for the newspaper?

With his thoughts careening, he couldn't wait to start pruning back the rose bushes and planting fall mums in the botanical gardens at the Trent House off Market Street. It was such a beautiful place, and working with his hands usually helped take his mind off of his troubles. He felt progressively more relaxed as he drove away from his house, picturing himself on the grounds of the restored colonial mansion that was once the home of the man they named his city after. *His* city. That was how he thought of it, so maybe his father was right.

He had to pick up Hector and Felix on the way. For once he was thankful that they couldn't read a newspaper, but he hadn't counted on the Spanish language radio stations picking up the story.

***

After seeing her husband off to work and cleaning up the breakfast dishes, Maria stopped by her daughter's bedroom and gave the closed door a gentle knock before entering. She found Tina sitting cross-legged on her carefully made bed, gingerly leafing through the pages of some old booklet. Tina slipped it under her bedspread and picked up a fashion magazine.

Feeling slightly worn-down by all the early morning drama, Maria snuck a look at herself in her daughter's mirror and brushed back a coiled strand of silky black hair that had escaped its place. She tucked it neatly back behind her ear.

"Is there something you want to tell me about?" she inquired sweetly, in a tone her daughter knew all too well. Maria had an uncanny way of being consoling and direct at the same time. She was also adept at reading her teenage daughter's deepest emotions.

"Not that I can think of," Tina replied airily, flipping through the magazine. "What did you have in mind?"

Maria ignored her daughter's clipped tone and plowed ahead. "Well, for starters," she said, taking a seat on the edge of the bed, "you can tell me how you know this gang member who almost killed your father."

Tina's guard went up immediately. "I didn't say I knew him. My friends do."

"Uh huh, you mean friends like Isabel?"

"Maybe," Tina said, trying to sound noncommittal but failing.

"Tina, you and Isabel Aguilar have been friends since you were babies. You attended each other's *quinceañera*. I would find it hard to believe that Isabel knows anyone in this town that you don't."

Tina sighed heavily. Maternal perception was in overdrive, and all she could do was remain silent so as not to give her mother anything more to work with.

Maria reached for Tina's hand and started gently massaging her cuticles. "Does this have anything to do with the boy you are seeing?"

Tina withdrew her hand in a hurry. "I'm not seeing anyone," she said defiantly.

Maria turned her face away. She couldn't bear to look at her daughter when she knew she was lying. Maybe she was protecting someone, but who and why?

"Then why do you sleep with your cell phone under your pillow every night?" She turned back around and looked directly into her daughter's nervous eyes. "I am sure Isabel has better things to do than call you in the middle of the night to discuss algebra."

Tina thought quickly. "I'm hiding it from Roberto," she lied again. "I don't want him playing Astrosmash or changing my ring tones."

Maria stood up slowly, almost as if in pain, and gave her daughter a peck on the cheek. "Okay, *mija*, we'll do this your way."

"Mom, I don't want to start all over at a new high school." Tina looked like she might cry.

"I know you don't, sweetie," her mother said as she paused in the doorway. "And when you're ready to tell me the real reason why, I'll listen."

Her mother left the room without looking back. Just in time, too. Tina's cell phone vibrated under her pillow. It was a text message from Darius:

> *meet me @ columbus park tonite 8 pm I'll explain every-*
> *thing ... bring the pamphlet.*

***

Tina sat alone on a wrought iron bench beneath the massive stone statue of Christopher Columbus in the city park named in his honor. The park was empty except for a group of kids playing a pick-up game of basketball on a court at the far end of the recreational area. The fall night air was crisp and clear. She was dressed in blue jeans and a suede jacket. A tied leather pouch lay across her lap.

Darius greeted her with a big wave and then came over to give her a kiss. Her reception was chillier than the night air. She turned her cheek away. He had expected an icy reaction but wasn't easily discouraged. Undaunted, he sat down beside her and looked up at the surrounding night sky while rubbing his hands on his knees.

"Just imagine," he began looking straight ahead. "Not so long ago I would have been shot on sight for venturing into this park."

Tina gave him a puzzled look.

"My kind wasn't welcome here," Darius continued. "Chambersburg was a little Italian enclave here in Trenton, and Columbus Park lay at the heart of the fortress."

She was still annoyed. "Fortress?"

He forced her to look at him, hoping she wouldn't turn away again. "Sorry, I forgot—you weren't around for any of this."

"Neither were you," she replied peevishly.

"Yeah, but I've heard all the stories. After the riots in '68, the Italians would sit on their rooftops with rifles, waiting to pick off any colored person who had the nerve to show his black ass in the Burg."

Tina looked up at the rooftops and spires of the cozy little row homes, St. Joachim's Church, and a few cafés and restaurants that now rimmed the park. She tried to imagine a city at war with itself.

"Darius, what's going on?" she said, wanting to confront the issue before he tried to charm her again. "Bobby Jackson was one of those guys looking for you at the Eagle Tavern, wasn't he?"

"Yes," he replied without betraying any emotion.

"Is he a friend of yours?"

Darius hesitated. "Sort of," he admitted reluctantly.

She pushed for more specifics. "What's *that* supposed to mean?"

"It means he's from the hood. Okay? Can we leave it at that?"

"That doesn't make him your friend." Her voice was more strident than she'd intended, and she realized with some embarrassment that she was starting to sound like her mother.

"It doesn't make him my enemy, either," he countered, trying to control his frustration with this line of questioning.

"Isabel says he's a member of the Bloods. Is he?"

"He's in trouble, Tina," said Darius with a heavy sigh, "and he needs help."

She folded her arms across her chest. "Yeah, I would call trying to kill a cop some pretty big trouble!"

"He didn't know what he was doing," pleaded Darius. "He wasn't in control."

"In control of what? Darius, were you with him? Were you trying to help him …" Her voice trailed off.

"No, I wasn't with him, but yes, I *was* trying to help him," Darius conceded, shrugging his shoulders.

"Is that why your car was seen at the church?"

"It's a long story."

She couldn't believe what she was hearing. "Darius, don't you get it? That was my *father* who chased after him!"

"I know."

"My father could have been killed. Tell me you're not okay with that."

He bent over and put his head in his hands, rubbing his throbbing temples. "Of course I'm not."

She shook her head. "Then why were you helping him?"

"You wouldn't understand," he said looking away.

"You've got that right. I don't understand. Just like this pamphlet." She threw the leather pouch at him. "Was I stealing it for you?"

"No!" he answered quickly.

"Then why did we take it, instead of giving it to your professor?"

"Because the owner told me to keep it," he said, turning back to face her.

"What the hell are you talking about? Darius, this is an old copy of *Common Sense*. It may even be an original. It could be valuable."

"Did you read the inscription?" he asked.

"Inscription?"

He removed the booklet from the leather sheath and held it under the streetlight to read it for her. "*To E. H., 'Finder's Keepers.' Love, Penny.*"

"Who's E. H.?"

"Me," he replied unexpectedly. "My real name is Ernest Hudson. But I go by my middle name, Darius, so as not to be confused with the actor, Ernie Hudson."

Tina made a sour face. "Are you kidding me?"

He smiled broadly and with a soft laugh added, "Yeah, but I had you there, didn't I, Tina? Oh, and by the way, you're absolutely right—this thing is *very* valuable. It's from the first printing of Thomas Paine's famous work published in Philadelphia in January 1776."

"How can you tell that?" she asked, sidetracked by the old charming Darius, come to life again. "His name doesn't appear anywhere on it. It's credited to 'an Englishman.'"

"That's exactly how you can tell," he said with undeniable enthusiasm. "Thomas Paine couldn't afford to use his name when it was first printed. He would have been a marked man."

"All the more reason for you to take it to someone who knows about these things and can handle it properly," she said forcefully.

Darius was steadfast. "Not until I find out who E. H. and Penny were. That's my new mission. And yours—if you want to help." She frowned and shrugged.

"In the meantime," he said sliding the delicate booklet back into the leather pouch and handing it to her, "you better keep this. It's safer with you."

20

Alma Arms

*M*ore than any other single image, the golden Capitol Dome towering above the New Jersey State House is, by all accounts, the most recognizable symbol of the City of Trenton. Never in his wildest dreams had Luis Alma imagined that one day he would be standing alongside his family in the building's magnificent rotunda, looking up at the dome from the inside, as a distinguished guest of the governor of New Jersey.

According to the guide who escorted them on the grand tour, the New Jersey State House was originally built in 1792 and was considered the second oldest state capitol in continuous use. Home to the New Jersey State Senate and Assembly, the elegant building was severely damaged by fire in the late 1800s and had been restored and renovated several times since. Modern restorations completed in 1987 painstakingly refurbished the gilding, millwork, masonry, and decorative molding of the legislative chambers down to the most minute detail.

Luis and Raul had often talked about the family's struggles in Cuba and of the opportunities available to anyone willing to work hard and obey the law here in the United States. Today, father and son were awestruck as they walked in the footsteps of Abraham Lincoln, Andrew Jackson, and Woodrow Wilson, all of whom had passed through these State House halls.

"Thanks for coming to America, Pop," Luis said with complete sincerity.

"Thanks for making me so proud," Raul answered with tears in his eyes.

"Papi, Daddy—come take a look at this!" Tina called excitedly. She and Roberto were gazing up at the portraits of the five New Jersey Signers of the Declaration of Independence that hung on the wall outside the governor's office.

"It's incredible!" Maria exclaimed.

"What is it?" asked Luis.

"Can't you see it, Papi?" Roberto could barely contain his excitement.

"The resemblance." Tina pointed to the portrait of John Hart.

Raul put on his reading glasses as he and Luis stepped closer for a better look. They squinted hard at the sober facial features—dark, intelligent eyes, thin smile, and arched brow—of a man about Luis's age captured in oils.

"The kids are right," Maria said. "Change the hairstyle, Luis, and—"

"It's you, Dad!" Roberto finished for her.

"If you say so," said Luis, unconvinced.

"*¡Dios mío!*" said Raul. "He looks just like my father!"

***

"I still don't understand why we couldn't have the ceremony at City Hall," whined Mayor Jimmy Dodd as he climbed the State House steps. "This was *my* idea. Markham was a city activist, McKenna is a city cop, and Alma is a Trenton taxpayer."

The state director of Historic Preservation and Cultural Affairs, otherwise known as the HPCA, Helen Nelson, a shapely, attractive fifty-something in a smart mocha business suit accented by a colorful Hermès scarf, was striding step for step with Dodd. When she reached the top ahead of him, she replied, "Because the governor thought it would get better press coverage at the State House, and we all know how you like the media, Mr. Mayor. Besides, Hollis Markham was a saint who held numerous official *state* positions, as you may recall."

"I still don't like it—it's all about politics, isn't it?" Dodd wheezed. "Markham was black. Alma's Latino. This little power play is about votes, isn't it, Helen?"

"And I suppose the award isn't?" she shot back, her expression bemused.

"What's the matter, Your Honor," Abigail Treadwell-Tucker teased as she followed them through the security scanner, "don't care to share the spotlight?"

"If your police department finds Markham's killer," Helen challenged him as they crossed the hall and entered the rotunda, "you can have center stage all to yourself."

"My goodness," Abby gushed as she encountered Luis and his family admiring the gallery, "I almost didn't recognize you out of your wet work clothes!" Looking directly into Luis's warm brown eyes she noticed they were flecked with fiery green sparks. His mother had joked that they were a gift from a Portuguese sailor on leave whom she'd met before marrying Raul.

As Luis fidgeted uncomfortably with his tie and blazer, Raul stepped between them. "I don't believe I've had the pleasure," he oozed in his best imitation of a Latin lover, taking Abby's hand and gazing deeply into her pale blue eyes.

Sensing Maria right behind him, Luis recovered quickly. "This is my wife, Maria, and our two children, Tina and Roberto." With a smile he added, "My father, Raul, you've already met."

Abigail shook Maria's hand firmly and smiled with confidence. "I'm Abby Treadwell-Tucker. You must be so proud of your husband."

"I am," replied Maria slightly taken aback, wondering how this pretty blonde woman and Luis knew each other.

Helen Nelson, standing with the mayor just outside the circle formed by Abby and the Alma family, cleared her throat.

"Luis, I'd like to introduce Helen Nelson, state director of the HPCA," Abby said, taking the hint. In a stage whisper, she added, "Be nice to her, she's my boss," then motioned to the mayor. "I believe you've already met Mayor Dodd."

Helen stepped forward ceremoniously to shake Luis's hand. "Always a pleasure to meet an honest-to-goodness hero," she said with a furtive glance toward Dodd. "Lord knows this town can use one."

"I was in the right place at the right time," Luis responded modestly. "That's all."

"Ah, and a humble hero at that," Helen added with a knowing wink at Abby.

Acquiescing to the press, the mayor posed with Luis, shaking his hand and smiling for a half-dozen flashing cameras.

"Your Honor, I see that Senator Howard Stevens and Randal Whittaker have just arrived," Helen interrupted the photo-op. "The senator is standing in for the governor," she explained to the Almas. "We'd better get this show on the road."

Dodd scowled at Helen. "What the hell's Whittaker doing here?"

"Mr. Mayor," Abby moved quickly to change the subject, pulling the mayor and Maria together. "How about a picture with the woman behind the hero for tomorrow's *Trenton Times*?"

At the mention of the *Trenton Times*, Raul and Luis glanced at each other with eyebrows raised. They had often talked about the differences between the city's two most popular newspapers. *The Trentonian* pandered to the lowest common denominator with scandal, the police blotter, and other tabloid fare. You read that one for fun. The *Trenton Times* was respectable and represented what this immigrant family aspired to. You read that one for business and a larger worldview. Raul had already told his cronies about the articles in the other paper. He couldn't wait to share what they wrote about his son in the *Times*.

Portly, baldheaded Senator Howard Stevens took his position behind the podium beneath the Great Seal of New Jersey. Beside him stood a tall, handsome African American man in a hand-tailored suit from Harrod's of London. He took in the whole room in one observant glance as Stevens introduced Director Nelson and Mayor Dodd to an eager crowd of about thirty people.

After reading a prepared statement from the governor, who had unfortunately gotten stuck in traffic on the Garden State Parkway while returning from Cape May on state business, Stevens stepped aside and the mayor presented Trenton's Citizenship Award to Luis

Alma in recognition of his heroism. Heartfelt applause and more picture taking followed. Dodd seized the moment to ham it up with the media, until the senator reclaimed the podium to make "a very special introduction." This announcement seemed to take the mayor by surprise.

"And now, it is my privilege to present the president and CEO of Triumph Development Corporation—Mr. Randal Whittaker."

Dodd looked up suspiciously as the dapper black man, flanked by Helen Nelson and Abby Treadwell-Tucker, stepped forward and adjusted the microphone.

"Good afternoon, ladies and gentleman, good citizens of Trenton, dear friends," Whittaker began in a deep, velvety voice, holding out his hands as if he were Moses parting the Red Sea. "As many of you know, Triumph Development is committed to the preservation and rebirth of our magnificent city. It gives me great pleasure today to unite Triumph's commitment to that most worthy of causes with the acknowledgment of a truly valiant, selfless deed by one of our own. An ordinary citizen. A common man like you and me. Luis Alma."

There was a barely noticeable undercurrent of levity from the press corps, who didn't believe for an instant that this multimillionaire businessman considered himself in the same class as "common folk."

Whittaker ignored the buzz and continued. "As we gather on this momentous occasion to recognize Mr. Alma's fearless actions, it is my honor and privilege to announce a major new city building project spearheaded by Triumph Development Corporation: to demolish the blighted, dangerous, and substandard sprawl of housing on Tucker Avenue near the Trenton Battle Monument and replace it with a safe, comfortable, and modern residential complex of single family homes named in honor of a hero whose very name is Spanish for the word 'soul'…"

The tension and anticipation was expressed nowhere better than on the mayor's ashen white face as Whittaker cued Abby. As she removed a royal blue velvet cloth from a large easel with a flourish, revealing a colorful poster, the developer reached the climax of his announcement. "I give you Alma Arms—the Soul of Trenton!"

For a fraction of a second there was nothing but stunned silence in the sunlit rotunda, broken suddenly by enthusiastic applause first from Director Nelson, followed ardently by Senator Stevens and Abby Treadwell-Tucker until the rest of the crowd fell in and followed suit. Dodd joined in somewhat reluctantly.

Maria hugged her husband. Tina and Roberto jumped up and down holding hands. Only Raul and his son exchanged skeptical glances. Everywhere else emotions erupted with great joy. Even the jaded media joined in. Whittaker came around from behind the podium and posed for pictures with Luis, Senator Stevens, and Mayor Dodd like a proud parent.

Dodd's enthusiasm ebbed slowly as he leaned in and whispered to Whittaker, "Why wasn't I told about this?" When he didn't get a response he added, "Don't you think this is a bit much?"

"Go with the flow, Jimmy," Whittaker said at length. "Just go with the flow."

Still in shock, but curious about the theatrics of the announcement as well as the name of one of the streets Whittaker had mentioned, Luis shot Abby a questioning glance. Instinctively, she knew what he was thinking. She gave him a cryptic smile and a little shrug before turning away to continue applauding with everyone else.

***

Luis sat on the edge of his bed and removed his shoes. After a long, grueling day of smiles, handshakes, and speeches, he felt more exhausted than if he had mowed a hundred lawns. He held the hand-crafted walnut wood and gold engraved plaque in his hands. "Where should we put it?" he called over his shoulder.

"On the floor," Maria replied slipping her naked arms around his neck and plying the plaque gently from his grasp. "I don't need anything to remind me I married a hero," she whispered seductively in his ear while playfully removing the knot from his tie. She leaned forward, brushing her fully aroused nipples against his powerful back.

Luis felt the fire down below spark to life.

She sensed his reaction and began lightly massaging his neck and shoulders to encourage him. He kissed her welcome hands, tenderly.

"Where are the kids tonight?" he asked, sighing and rolling his neck from side to side as she rubbed him.

"Tina went to the library, and your father took Roberto to De Lorenzo's for tomato pie."

"The one on Hudson or Hamilton?"

"Oh, no," Maria sparred playfully with her husband. "We're not going to have that debate again, are we?"

"That all depends on what else you had in mind." His body tingled with anticipation.

"I'd like to know how it feels to be held by those powerful *Alma Arms*," she said, pulling him around to face her and burying his face between her breasts.

21

Night Owls

*A*s Luis was being recognized for heroism by his passionate wife, a few blocks away a plump hostess with a bouffant hairdo, false eyelashes, and too much makeup was showing a party of three to a secluded booth in the back of Amici Milano. The table was set for four, with clean pressed white linens and a candle barely flickering under a miniature tiffany lampshade.

A waiter in a white tuxedo shirt, black slacks, and red-striped apron came over immediately. He pulled an order pad from behind the small of his back.

"Drinks, gentlemen?" he inquired with a noticeable Spanish accent.

"Glenlivet, straight up," said Senator Stevens removing the candle from the table and placing it on the window ledge.

"Make mine a double, Carlos," the mayor said with a distinct air of familiarity.

"Grey Goose martini, extra dry, two olives," ordered Randal Whittaker, who was seated facing the other two.

"Very good, sir," replied Carlos, turning toward the bar.

"I can't believe it's come down to this," Whittaker griped as he glanced around him. "I like this place, but there used to be a dozen great Italian restaurants to choose from in the Burg. Is this really the last one left?"

"There's still Rossi's, Randal," Mayor Dodd offered with enthusiasm. "For my money they still serve the best burger in town."

"So why didn't we go to Rossi's tonight?" queried Stevens before quipping, "Almost forgot—it's a *Republican* watering hole. Hizzoner was afraid we might bump into his public safety director."

"Well it *is* Rosetti's hangout," Dodd confirmed, both embarrassed and annoyed with himself for bringing it up in the first place. "He's become a royal pain in the ass lately."

"*Royal* is quite an appropriate word choice, Mr. Mayor," Stevens snickered, "with old Dominic running his own little fiefdom over there."

Dodd scowled. "That started long before my administration."

"You know, I've heard that Rossi's locks their patrons in after nine o'clock," mused Whittaker, changing the subject and observing Dodd closely. "For their own protection," he clarified.

"Since when did Joe DiMaggio Corner become Fort Apache, the Bronx?" asked Stevens.

"Since the day Jimmy Dodd was sworn into office," Whittaker joked with a sadistic grin.

"The Chambersburg exodus started way before me," Dodd said defensively.

"Relax, Jimmy, it's been happening all over the country," Whittaker offered congenially. "Superhighways and suburban shopping malls have played a part in the decay of Trenton as much as any other city, and *you* can't be blamed for them."

"I think it's the ratables that kill us," countered Dodd. "The state's presence here has been stifling local growth. They own everything and pay next to nothing for it."

"Careful, Jimmy," cautioned the senator as Carlos arrived with their drinks. "State money is about all you've got to look forward to, unless you can manage to pull off the rebirth of fine dining here in the Burg."

"If that's going to happen at all, it'll be like the dining district in Newark's Ironbound neighborhood, with a certain Spanish flair," Whittaker said with a nod toward Carlos, who had just placed their drinks before them.

"That reminds me, Randal," Dodd said, lowering his voice. "What was the deal with today's little announcement? When were you going to clue me in?"

"You mean about Alma Arms?" Whittaker smiled at Stevens, who was enjoying the warmth of his scotch. "That was spontaneous—a spur-of-the-moment stroke of genius, don't you think?"

"Yeah, real fucking brilliant," Dodd groaned downing his double in a single gulp. "Next time I would appreciate your running it by me first so I don't look like a complete idiot."

"What are you worried about?" Stevens said, studying the menu. "We all know Hollis didn't want us to call it the Markham Towers."

"I guess we don't have to worry about what the reverend thinks anymore," said Dodd with a shrug.

"Speaking of which, what's the latest on the case?" Whittaker inquired casually. "Have your men in blue come up with anything?"

"No," sighed Dodd. "It's the damnedest thing."

"What do you mean?" Stevens pursued.

"It seems he may have known his killer."

"Why do you say that?" questioned Whittaker.

"Because nothing was taken and there were no signs of a struggle."

"Have they found the murder weapon?" asked Stevens.

"Are you kidding me?" Dodd groaned. "Every criminal in this city owns a blade of some sort, and there doesn't appear to be anything distinctive about this one."

"I've read that the Sex, Money and Murder branch of the Bloods has put out a training video on mercy killing," Helen Nelson said as she approached the booth.

"Just what we need, as if random acts of violence weren't enough," replied the mayor sarcastically. "See if you can get me a copy to watch the next time I'm feeling too optimistic about life."

"Where's your sidekick?" Whittaker asked Helen.

"Waiting for you," she said, ordering a drink in the same breath.

***

"I wish you could have been there," Tina was telling Darius as they made their way up the concrete steps of the Trenton Free Public Library. "The history in that place is incredible, and there was a painting of some famous guy who looked just like my dad. You should have seen how nervous he was getting his award."

"Somehow I don't think I would have made it any easier for him," Darius said. "Especially not if he saw me drive up in my car."

"You *do* know you'll have to meet my parents some day, right?" she teased him. "I can't keep you a secret forever."

"So, you think we'll be together *forever*?" Darius moved closer, flirting as he opened the library door for her.

"You must really have a high opinion of yourself," she played him expertly. "You barely know me, and I know even less about you." She stopped in front of the windowed wooden doors that led into the Trentoniana Room on the second floor. "You haven't told me *anything* about your family."

He placed his hand on the doorknob but didn't turn it. "That's because there's nothing to tell. My father left when I was young. My mom works at the Thrift Shop. End of story." Opening the door to the large cluttered room, he moved in quickly, distancing himself from her question.

"Wow, it's like being in a Charles Dickens story!" she exclaimed as she took her first look around. The spacious former classroom of the old Trenton Academy School was covered from floor to ceiling with books in stacks and on dusty shelves. Various and sundry artifacts, along with countless black-and-white photographs, lined the walls, desktops, and staircases that led from one wood-paneled room to another.

A middle-aged woman seated on an antique stool in front of an even older looking microfilm reader swiveled around to face them. She had long, graying hair and her bangs overlapped a pair of thick eyeglasses set in black oval frames.

"Well, what do we have here?" she greeted them. "A couple of late-night scholars?"

"Are you the librarian?" asked Tina hesitantly.

"Nope, I just help out around here on Thursday nights," the woman answered cheerfully. Sensing their confusion she added, "And occasional Saturdays."

"Hey, I know you," said Darius. "You wrote those columns for the *Trenton Times*—'A Time to Remember,' right?"

The owl-eyed woman folded her arms across her chest and scrutinized Darius from head to toe. "Yep, that's me. Shelly Reed, at your service, but that was over twenty years ago. My eyes may not be what they used to be, but don't you dare try to tell me you followed my column at the time."

Darius laughed. "We've been reading them in Professor Collins's history class at Mercer County. He says you're an authority on just about everything."

"Everything old!" she laughed. "You mean Daniel Collins, right?" She didn't wait for an answer. "He and I go *way* back—all the way to the Revolution, some people say." She laughed at her own joke. "So what can I do you for?"

"We're looking for information about the old Eagle Tavern on South Broad Street," Tina said.

"Is this for a school project?" Shelly asked, turning off the overheating microfilm unit.

"You could say that," said Darius before Tina could respond. He wanted to keep his interest in the tavern under wraps, at least until he could establish some facts about the pamphlet's owner.

"I just did," Shelly retorted, standing and peering over her glasses at him. "What type of information are you interested in?"

"When it was built, who owned it, that type of thing," Tina said studiously.

"If you're looking to buy it," Shelly started jokingly, "I think you're too late. Triumph's got their eye on it, and they usually get what they want in the way of Trenton real estate."

"So I hear," agreed Darius. "But I understand the sale isn't final yet."

Shelly removed her glasses and twirled them in her hand. "You are correct, young man. Although they have made a formal offer, the building is on the historic register so the acquisition must be approved by the HPCA."

"HPCA?" Tina questioned.

"Historic Preservation and Cultural Affairs," replied Shelly directly. "The state governmental agency responsible for oversight on such matters."

"Don't the mayor and city council also have to approve such a sale?" asked Darius.

"A mere formality under the Dodd administration," Shelly replied with a dismissive wave of her hand.

"Then you can't help us?" Tina said disappointedly.

"I didn't say that," was Shelly's response. "It just so happens we have a file on Eagle Tavern." Standing, she motioned the teens to follow her to the card catalog. There, she opened a drawer marked *De–F* and pulled out the card rack. Rifling through it, she came to "Eager, Thomas," followed in sequence by "Eagle Tavern."

"Second cabinet on your right." Shelly pointed to an old army-green steel filing cabinet. As Darius and Tina watched her with increasing curiosity, she sauntered over to the cabinet, opened it, and reached in. She removed a musty old folder and placed it in Darius's hands, then pointed to a huge antique desk overflowing with loose papers, file folders, and film canisters. "Knock yourselves out," she said as she turned back to her own research.

Darius and Tina walked over to the desk, pulled out two chairs, and started looking through the fat legal-sized folder. From numerous faded articles and an assortment of other documents, in the course of an hour they had pieced together a considerable history on Eagle Tavern.

Apparently, a man named Robert Waln initially built the tavern in 1765 as a private home. A sizeable addition was added in 1830 when the tavern and the adjacent Eagle Race Track were at their peak. It continued to be run as a tavern by an assortment of owners until 1890.

By the turn of the century, the building had become a boarding-house, changing hands through various owners until 1942, when one Frank Nonziato tried to turn it into restaurant but failed because he couldn't obtain a liquor license. After he sold it, it was used as an apartment building for about decade until it went vacant in the mid-1950s. The City of Trenton purchased the building in 1965 and still owned it. As Shelly Reed had indicated, the building was on the National Register of Historic Places.

After extensive renovations, it opened briefly in 1980 as an operating tavern, run by a company called the Heritage House. By 1983, lacking patron support, it closed again. In 1988, a group called Tavern Friends, Inc., took over the building and tried a restaurant venture, again unsuccessfully. After several break-ins, the unprofitable tavern was closed for good in March 1992 and remained boarded up ever since.

With its three stories, quaint rooms, numerous working fireplaces, and original beams and floorboards essentially intact, locals kept hoping that someday Eagle Tavern would soar again. Sadly, with each passing year, the cost to make necessary repairs and upgrade the structure to code put the dream further out of reach.

"Find what you were looking for?" asked Shelly, jacket on and car keys jingling in her hand.

Tina rubbed her eyes and looked at Darius. His face was impassive. "No," she replied for them both. "Not all the owners are listed."

"Naturally," replied Shelly. "For that kind of extensive search you would probably have to spend a day at the State Archives. But I should warn you: They're still pulling things out of boxes from various county seats and cataloging them for online searches. So don't be surprised if you don't find what you're looking for there, either. It's a mess."

"How comforting," Darius groaned.

"What period of ownership are you interested in?" Shelly asked helpfully.

"We don't really know," Tina said, trying to read Darius's expression.

"Maybe sometime just before or even during the Revolutionary War." His sheepish smile told Tina he might be ready to open up and ask for help.

"A couple of Revolutionary War buffs, eh? Well, if you come back next Saturday, I'll show you some really cool things we have here. Authentic stuff like books purchased by Benjamin Franklin and donated to this library."

A few minutes later, in the library parking lot, Darius and Tina were in his car waiting for the guard to open the gate.

"You should ask her to help you, Darius. She seems to know a lot."

"Yeah," he replied. "I'll think about it."

As he pulled out of the lot onto Academy Street, Tina screamed, "Stop!" Hitting the breaks hard, he stopped the car just inches from a young black male in a dark leather jacket, black beret, and sunglasses, gold chains dangling conspicuously from his neck. The young man slapped his hands on the hood and reeled backward as if he'd been hit. As Darius started to pull away, the man followed, calling his name and pounding on the trunk.

"Darius, that guy knows you—aren't you gonna stop?" There was alarm in Tina's voice.

"No."

"Darius, he might be hurt!" she pleaded.

Cursing mildly, Darius pulled over and rolled down the window.

"Yo, Darius—you almost hit me, bro!" the boy sang out as he reached the car and peered in the driver's side window. Tina saw a diamond stud in his nose as she judged him to be fifteen, tops.

"What do you want?" Darius barked.

"Whoa, is this your new babe?" the boy said, eyeballing Tina. "*Mamacita!*"

"I said, what do you want?"

"I need money, bro—for the man. I need it quick."

Darius let out an audible sigh. "How much *this time*?"

"Make it a deuce, bro."

"What? Are you kidding me?"

"Hey, I'm good for it. You know that. And you know what happens if I don't pay up."

"I don't have that kind of money on me."

"Hey, that's cool. When can you get it?"

"I'll go to the bank on Monday."

"Cool. You wanna hang out later?"

"You'll have the money on Monday, now go home!" Darius said angrily as he rolled up the window and pulled away from the curb.

Tina was seriously confused. "Who *was* that, Darius?"

"My kid brother."

22

Bank On It

G rowing up on the streets of Trenton had taught Darius to take precautions where money was concerned, and he instructed the teller to divide the money equally into two separate envelopes. Although it was broad daylight and the Wachovia Bank branch on West State Street was bustling with government employees on their lunch break, his instincts told him a more perfect crime scene could not have been invented.

After his transaction, Darius felt even more uneasy at the sight of an armed guard milling around the ATM machine in the front lobby. It might have been the guard's familiar face, or maybe it was the fact that he was a uniformed Trenton cop and not a bank security guard that unnerved him. He half imagined the guard knew what he was going to do with his money.

To avoid scrutiny, Darius took a leisurely walk to the rear of the grand old bank with its vaulted gold ceiling, red marble columns, and wood-paneled stalls to view a huge painting of George Washington, triumphantly parading on horseback through Trenton while little girls laid flowers before him.

"You have a good eye for art." The familiar male voice had a distinctly British accent. Darius spun around. "It's a Wyeth," the man said.

"Professor Collins!" Darius said in surprise. He stuffed the two envelopes into his back pocket to avoid any questions then turned back to the painting. "It's so *big*."

"Perhaps that's because it commemorates a *big* event," the amiable history professor suggested. He was dressed in a maroon sweater, tweed jacket, and charcoal gray slacks. "Here we see George

Washington returning to the city of his most important victory over we Brits and our hired German hit men." The professor leaned toward Darius, cupping a hand to his mouth as he said conspiratorially, "I daresay dear old George wouldn't recognize the place if he saw it today." He chortled.

"No, sir, I suppose he wouldn't," Darius said, feeling a little out of his element with this conversation and not sure where it was going.

"I didn't see you at the last dig, Darius," the professor continued. "Is everything all right?"

"I was busy," he said unconvincingly.

"Not laboring over excessive homework in history, I trust," the professor grinned.

Professor Collins was better known for his lighthearted classroom style than for giving out too much homework. The spontaneity of Darius's smile told him he was right.

"You didn't miss much, actually," Collins continued. "Our work had to be suspended. Apparently there was a break-in at the tavern. Kids, most likely."

"What makes you think it was kids?" Darius asked, thinking of his night at the tavern with Tina and hoping they hadn't left anything incriminating behind. "It could have been a homeless person trying to get warm," he offered hopefully.

Professor Collins studied Darius curiously, his brow wrinkled in concentration. "Just a guess," admitted Collins. "Yes, the homeless can be desperate, Darius, but by and large they aren't mean-spirited or stupid. If a vagrant had wanted to get into Eagle Tavern for shelter, I doubt he would have demolished a window so completely—let alone broken an expensive bottle of Cristal inside. You can bank on *that*," he chuckled, amused by his own little pun.

The professor's dry, self-effacing sense of humor suddenly reminded Darius of Shelly Reed, the woman he and Tina had met at the library; no wonder the two of them got on so well, he thought. And it was true that he had managed to get into the tavern without breaking anything, while Bobby Jackson and company left a path of destruction in their wake. It was obvious the professor had given the break-in some thought.

"Did you notice this wooden arch?" Professor Collins asked, returning to the painting. "It was erected on the bridge across the Assunpink Creek, the site of Washington's celebrated tactical retreat during the second battle of Trenton. You can actually still see part of the original stone bridge under the roadway on South Broad Street. If it hadn't been for the Continental Army's unyielding defense of that modest little bridge, you'd probably be speaking a bit more like me today."

The remark rekindled the smile on Darius's face, encouraging the professor to continue with his quaint history lesson. "If you're really into this kind of thing, Darius, I would encourage you to visit the Trentoniana Room at the public library. Among the collection of artifacts and memorabilia is a portion of the Triumphant Arch. It's quite fascinating."

"I'll definitely check it out," replied Darius, making a mental note to look for the arch on his next visit.

The professor grew circumspect. "Curious thing about the word *triumphant*: *Tri* is a root word meaning a union of three. Very symbolic—the triangle, the shamrock, and even the arch are examples." He pointed to the painting.

Darius gave him a confused look.

"Right," said the professor when he realized Darius was not following him. "An arch essentially has three parts: two sides and an apex at the center.

"The arch is often mistakenly thought of as a Roman invention. While they may have perfected the design and surely did leave many examples behind for the world to admire, the Romans borrowed quite liberally from the Greeks who borrowed from the Egyptians who borrowed from the Mesopotamians, etc., etc. Nothing is new under the sun, eh, my boy?" He gave Darius a friendly slap on the shoulder.

"Ah … Shakespeare?" nodded Darius, remembering his English Lit class.

"Perhaps," mused Collins, "although the Bard may have borrowed it from Ecclesiastes. But stay with me on this point, it's important: In Masonic lore, the arch and the triangle represent the union of two forces to support a third, unseen higher power—that of the common good. In the middle ages, stonemasons improved upon the Roman design by adding what appears to be a decorative crown called a *capstone* to the top of the arch. This capstone also served to distribute the weight evenly down the two sides. Dome designs like the one on the State House Capitol are a variation of the same principles—hence the word, *capitol*."

Darius's head was spinning. The professor had a way of connecting one thing to another, and everything to history. He thought back to the first day in history class when a smart-ass student asked Collins why an Englishman was teaching American history. "Because," the professor said, "after the Revolution, everything of significance in the world came from America." Then as now, he always seemed to be able to reel Darius into his lectures. You never knew where they would end up.

"So, are you saying the Masons built the State House?" asked Darius, trying to piece together everything the professor had explained.

"Oh, my—it would be difficult to imagine it any other way," Collins chortled again. "Indeed, the Mason's Lodge, which today is the Visitor's Center on Barrack and Lafayette Street, is just a 'stone's throw,' if you'll pardon the pun, from the original State House. Their construction dates are within a year of each other."

Darius's interest was peaked. "You said *original* State House. Why?"

"Because the State House we see today is the result of many additions and restorations. The building was substantially destroyed by fire in 1885. Little is left of the original structure, except perhaps part of the front facade and some roofing struts—which, by the way, offer another representation of the triangular arch. Of course, we're merely scratching the surface …"

***

Exhausted hardly described how Maria felt as she said goodnight to the nurses staying behind for the emergency room nightshift. She had worked a double shift after agreeing to cover for a sick coworker, and "dead on her feet" was a more apt description.

Her regular shift had started at six in the morning and, while she usually had energy to burn, she was emotionally and physically drained by yesterday's award ceremony and the prolonged session of lovemaking that followed it. By 8 P.M. she was wiped out, and she still had the walk home to look forward to. It wasn't that far, less than a mile, down Hamilton to Anderson then on to Roebling, where she knew Luis and the kids would be waiting for her with something special for dinner. Special if for no other reason than that she wouldn't have to cook it.

As she passed by the 500 block of Hamilton Avenue, the colored lights on shop signs and window displays made her think about the approaching holiday season. It was a favorite time of year in the Alma household, full of baking and singing and general merriment. Except for odd jobs and snow plowing, Luis took off a lot of time in the winter, and he and Raul would take care of the shopping and put up the Christmas decorations. Tina and Roberto would be off from school soon … she was glad they were still young enough to get excited about opening gifts on Christmas Day.

As far back as Maria could remember, a Michele Lorie cheesecake had been an integral part of the Alma holiday meal; cherry and New York–style were particular favorites. Walking by the bakery that locals had patronized for generations, a twinge of nostalgia was swallowed up by sadness as she saw the sign in the window, thanking customers for their years of support and saying good-bye forever.

So many good things come to an end for no apparent reason.

She stopped by the drycleaner's to drop off the sport coat Luis had worn for his special occasion and to pick up the full-length suede coat they'd given Tina last Christmas. The coat had not come cheap, but the fact that Tina loved it so much meant a lot to her mother, who had saved for it and picked it out. She and her daughter might be going through a rough time right now, but Tina was a good kid and Maria knew she would come around.

Washington and Anderson streets run parallel, and the distance between them narrows as they get closer to Hamilton. As Maria crossed Washington and was about to turn left onto Anderson, she heard the roar of car engines in the distance. Looking down both streets at once, she saw two cars racing recklessly in her direction. She imagined a terrible crash, and two young drivers being rushed to the emergency room. She hoped they would survive and learn a lesson.

Deep in her thoughts on the plight of others, Maria was momentarily blinded by the oncoming headlights. Frozen in her tracks, she was caught in a crossfire between the two cars that passed on either side of her.

23

A Better Place

Patrolman Joe McKenna put a hand on Luis Alma's shoulder as he thought back to another funeral at Shiloh Baptist Church, when Luis had attended to Joe's wounds. Now the roles were reversed, and Luis's wounds were also far from superficial.

"I'm sorry," the officer said evenly, fighting to control his emotions. "I wish there was something I could do for you."

Luis did not acknowledge the officer's heartfelt remarks. He couldn't. He was numb. Staring vacantly as they lowered the shiny bronze casket into the freshly dug grave at Greenwood Cemetery, he was only vaguely aware of the sobbing around him.

If he could have focused his attention, he would have seen the tears streaming from his son and daughter's eyes as they stood beside him, but he wasn't there. The shock was more traumatic than anything the war had done to him, and he had shut down. He couldn't *feel* anything—no arms, no legs, no heart beating. And he didn't care to feel anything ever again.

Closing his eyes, he imagined himself falling face forward into the grave, then the dirt being shoveled over him and Maria. All it would take was a slight breeze or a false step for it to happen. He would be reunited with the only woman he'd ever truly loved.

Raul grabbed him by the sleeve. "Luis, we should go. There is nothing more we can do here. She has gone to a better place."

"Papa, please," said Roberto through tear-streaked eyes. "Can we go home?"

Tina took her father's hand and walked with him in silence to the hearse. It was the first time he had felt connected to anyone all day.

The mourners parted, mouthing their condolences like flowers tossed on the descending coffin as the family passed.

She's gone to a better place. Luis heard his father's words ringing in his head. *Where is that? Take me with you. I don't want to stay here without you.*

He felt the sorrow, the guilt, the love, and the anger ... all those pent-up emotions welling inside of him. *I should have picked her up at the hospital. It was too late for her to walk home alone. This goddamn city! The streets aren't safe for anyone. Crime runs like a cancer here. It's out of control. We can't stay in this fucking place any longer ... I hate this town and everybody in it!*

Darius Hudson stood behind a sycamore tree, careful to remain out of sight. Tina had told him not to come, but he couldn't stay away. He wanted her to know he cared, that he shared her grief, that he was there for her. And yet he dared not show his face. Somehow, he felt as if it was his fault. Even though he knew it was irrational, he couldn't help the feeling.

Tina had seen him but hadn't changed her mind. She didn't want him there. Her mother's death wasn't his fault, but he was a reminder of something she wanted to forget. She couldn't shed the guilt she felt over lying to her mother during the last intimate conversation she shared with her. Her mother had known it, too, even if Tina hadn't owned up to it. It was a lie about her relationship with Darius.

"She's gone to a better place, Luis," someone from the crowd repeated as Luis stepped into the limousine. He looked up as the door was closing and saw it was Reverend Lionel Evans, flanked by Mayor Jimmy Dodd, Randal Whittaker, Helen Nelson, and Abby Treadwell-Tucker, all picture-perfect in their black suits. *Can the cameras and reporters be far behind?* he thought in disgust.

As the limo pulled away, it hit Luis like a lightning bolt: Everything that had happened since the day of Reverend Markham's funeral was connected; it had all happened for a reason. Just as suddenly as the insight came, he decided he didn't want to know anymore. He wanted to give it all back—the canal job, the chase, the award—and go back to the life he'd had before.

But where to begin? He put his arms around his children and held them tight. Together, as a family, they cried.

24

A Christmas Story

C *hestnuts roasting on an open fire …*" Nat King Cole's silky tones threaded their way through the speakers outside the Archives Restaurant at the Trenton Downtown Marriott. Having finished dinner, Randal Whittaker and Abby Treadwell-Tucker sat on a cozy couch beside a fireplace, decorated for the holidays but without the family pictures or stockings on the mantel. Still dressed from the funeral, they sipped snifters of expensive cognac.

"You hardly touched your dinner tonight," Whittaker said. "If it was the food, just say the word and I'll have them fillet the chef."

"I seem to have lost my appetite," she replied dispassionately.

"Good, then we can skip dessert." He smiled and juggled a pair of hotel room key cards in front of her.

"I can't do this anymore, Randal," she sighed.

"C'mon Abby, you know we don't have much time," he said impatiently.

"Exactly," she said sharply. "You're off to the Bahamas with your wife tomorrow, while I'm stuck here pushing papers to finalize your Eagle Tavern deal."

"Just make sure Dodd signs them," he responded coldly. "Meantime, why this sudden attack of conscience? You knew the ground rules when we started."

"Your wife is a good person, not to mention a friend," she said shaking her head. "How the hell could I have let this happen?"

"I thought you liked it this way—no strings, just a few laughs and a lift up the ladder. You scratch my back and I scratch yours." He was all business.

"As I said before. I seem to have lost my appetite."

"It's your call. You know where I'll be." He tossed one of the key cards on the table and walked off toward the elevator.

As Abby sat there collecting her thoughts, she found herself distracted by a little girl with Shirley Temple curls in a frilly party dress, playing with a snow globe. Noticing the attention she was getting, the girl skipped over to Abby, smiling, to show her how the snowflakes floated all around the country scene. Abby was suddenly reminded of her family in upstate New York, and her mind became flooded with the scent of pine needles and memories of Christmas past. Like so many of her friends, including Randal's wife, hadn't she once thought of marrying a decent and loving man, having children, and raising them in a place like home?

She had, but that was before the accident. Before that fucking car slid into her old Chevy on Pine Hill Road at sixty miles an hour on Christmas Eve. The drunken bastard killed her only brother and turned her father against her as if the whole thing was her fault, the steering wheel in her abdomen making sure she would never have kids of her own.

Happy Holidays.

"Penny," the little girl's mother called from across the room, "come to mommy and leave the nice lady alone."

Abby forced a smile, swished the amber liquid in the snifter slowly and watched it settle in the glass. She took a long, soothing swallow of the cognac, picked up the room key, and headed on her way.

***

Luis was having trouble coping with the realities of life without his Maria. They had been a good team, building on their individual strengths to create a stable home and give their children opportunities that neither of them had known. They balanced each other. He was a hard worker but impatient with others less diligent. She was compassionate and equally hard working. He always said she let people take advantage of her. He tried to protect her from those who would abuse her generosity.

He wanted to hold it together for Tina and Roberto's sake, but he had been wracked with grief and loneliness since Maria's death. The prospect of enduring a joyless Christmas in the home they had shared together, so full of memories from happier times, was just too painful for him to bear. There were reminders of her loving touch everywhere: in the rose-color flannel bed sheets; the living room lampshades he had teased her about belonging in a bordello; and in the delicate, white lace curtains she made to cover the kitchen window frames, still badly in need of the paint job he had promised but never gotten around to. The thought brought tears to his eyes.

When Raul suggested they travel to Miami to satisfy his longstanding desire to spend time with relatives, Roberto, Tina, and even Luis thought it was a great idea. Luis's older brother Miguel, a Catholic priest, lived on the north shore of Miami Beach and when he was up for Maria's service he suggested they come visit him, their sister Rosa, and their Great Uncle Rodrigo.

Though they weren't the best of travelers even under ideal conditions, the Alma family was finding all the miserable things they'd heard about holiday travel to be especially true on this trip. At the security checkpoint in Philadelphia, an Iranian couple pushing a young child in a wheelchair held up a long line snaking through the metal detectors and body scanners. When the couple refused to be separated from the sickly boy, a scene erupted into a shouting match in which neither side knew what the other was saying. Calm was restored only after a fellow turbaned traveler overcame his fear of being subjected to the same type of treatment and volunteered to translate.

The US Airways flight from Philadelphia to Miami International was bumpy but uneventful. Somewhere over St. Augustine—the oldest city in North America—while the rest of the family slept, Luis ordered his third rum and coke with lime. He avoided calling it a *Cuba Libre* so he didn't have to hear the story of the drink's origin from Papa Raul for the hundredth time. The Sandra Dee look-alike stewardess gave him a reproachful glance when she finally came by to collect the empty bottles.

At the baggage claim in Miami, Luis found the wait interminable and the crowd even less agreeable. He paced around the carousel like an expectant father. Despite Raul's assurances to the contrary, Luis was certain that their luggage, including a few presents they had brought for their relatives, was on its way to San Francisco aboard the US Airways flight that had boarded at the next gate over from theirs.

The wait was torture for Luis, and he was having second thoughts about the whole idea of this trip. Patient Maria would have known how to calm him down, he thought painfully. He had no help from Tina. She had been silent the entire trip, her iPod headphones stuck in her ears and her cell phone at the ready. Roberto was engrossed in his Game Boy and only occasionally broke away for meals and bathroom emergencies. Only Raul remained upbeat, excited as he was by the prospect of seeing his Uncle Rodrigo, the older brother and only surviving sibling of his long deceased father.

Luis wasn't fooled by Raul's false bravado and his outward show of hopeful anticipation. Inside, he was smarting over the loss of Maria, whom he had regarded as a daughter and whose kindness and warmth had gracefully supplanted those faithful attributes belonging to his own dearly departed wife Anna, during his dark days after she passed away.

Father Miguel Alma picked up the beleaguered family in the church van he used to transport kids to Sunday school for *La Voz Católica*, the Catholic Charities in Miami Shores. Until Maria's service, Luis hadn't seen his older brother for a long time—not since Miguel transferred from a tough neighborhood church in Newark to this wonderful assignment in the Sunshine State five years earlier. Their spinsterish sister Rosa, who taught English as a Second Language to immigrant children and performed secretarial duties for the foundation, was waiting for them in the passenger seat.

"It's so great to see you again, Papi," said Rosa, looking in the rearview mirror. She was unable to turn her head to greet them properly due to a neck brace that was compliments of a recent fender-bender. The accident had kept her from attending Maria's funeral in New Jersey. Her dark hair was pulled into a tight bun and covered by a floral print kerchief.

"*Sí*, Rosita, and you are looking very well, all things considered," joked Raul, kissing her on the cheek before settling back into his seat. "What's the other guy look like?"

"Looks can be deceiving, Papi," she said with a forced smile that hinted at a physical malady she was trying to suppress so as not to spoil the reunion. "I am so sorry about Maria, Luis. She was a wonderful person. She did not deserve such a cruel and senseless ending."

"*Gracias*, Rosa," Luis acknowledged sadly. The effects of the long day of travel were starting to catch up with him. "*Perdóname* if I'm not myself right now. I've lost the best part of me."

Tina had temporarily ditched her iPod and now she dabbed her eyes with a tissue and stifled a sob. For the fifth time since landing, she checked her cell for a reply to her texts to Darius. Nothing. She looked out the window, trying to keep her focus on the leafy palm trees and other sights of Miami.

"You and the children are welcome to stay as long as you wish," Miguel said with a warm, comforting smile. "*Mi casa es su casa.*"

"We are very grateful, Miguel," Luis said, gripping his brother's arm affectionately.

"How is Rodrigo?" Raul asked, anxious to change the subject and the tone.

"Same as always, Pop," replied Miguel. "Ornery as can be and fit as a fiddle for ninety-one years old. He goes to the beach every morning and sits there all day, smoking his *puros* and eating his fresh fruit, listening to the waves. He says the sea sings to him, tells him stories."

"What kind of stories?" asked Raul curiously.

"You'll have to ask him that yourself," Miguel said pleasantly as he turned the car onto the 79th Street Kennedy Causeway heading toward the ocean.

"Why is that?" Raul seemed befuddled by Miguel's remark.

Rosa spoke up while fussing with her hair. "Call it old age, senility, or second sight to make up for the eyesight he's lost, but Uncle Rodrigo sees things. He knows things that will happen before they do. He even predicted you and Papi would be coming to Miami, Luis," she confided with a sideways glance at Miguel.

"That's utter nonsense," Luis responded impatiently showing the effects of liquor and fatigue. "Miguel invited us."

"Yes," replied Miguel, "but this time *Tio* Rodrigo told me you would finally accept."

***

Later that evening, Padre Miguel said grace before a simple yet traditional Cuban meal prepared by Rosa. They dined gratefully on stewed chicken and fried plantains with rice and beans. After homemade flan for dessert, Tina helped Rosa clean up and Roberto went into the living room to watch television. Miguel excused himself to prepare for tomorrow's mass. Raul and Luis joined Uncle Rodrigo on the balcony sitting in a worn-out wicker rocker smoking a cigar and listening to the sounds of children playing soccer in the street below as darkness approached.

The slight but steady old man had been uncharacteristically quiet throughout dinner. His hair was only thin white wisps where once a thick, full dark mane reigned. Dark sunglasses covered his injured eyes, damaged long ago in an explosion at the cigar factory in Tampa where he used to work. A hickory walking cane lay across his lap.

"They tell me the moon over Miami is quite a sight to behold," Rodrigo said as the two men, drinks in hand, joined him on the terrace. There was a cool, pleasant breeze blowing in off the ocean as evening began to settle over the modest apartment building. "Tell me, Raul, what do you see?"

Raul set his glass down and peered over the railing toward the eastern sky. "A big, bright yellow *globo*," replied Raul. "So close you can almost reach out and touch it with your fingers."

"Ah," said Rodrigo with a satisfied sigh, "not unlike the moon we used to see on warm nights in Havana."

"*Si, Tio* Rodrigo," answered Raul sitting down beside him. "The very same."

"Then I have missed nothing," concluded Rodrigo.

Luis stirred the ice in his glass with his fingers. "What is it like, Uncle Rodrigo," he began, searching for the right words, "to live in darkness every day?"

"You adjust, Luis," replied Rodrigo, rocking gently. "You learn to look at things differently. To trust in your other senses and find light where you can."

Mulling his great uncle's words, Luis downed his drink. The old man smelled the rum and heard the ice cubes clink against the glass. "We all see things differently, Luis, but I can tell you this from experience: There are few great insights at the bottom of a bottle."

Luis had expected this type of lecture from his older brother the priest, but coming from an old blind man the words struck a nerve, leaving him feeling exposed and fragile.

Roberto came out onto the balcony and beckoned his father and grandfather to come watch *CSI: Miami* with him "just like at home." Although both men were anxious to continue their conversation with Uncle Rodrigo, they knew how important it was for Roberto to keep things as normal as possible. They bid Rodrigo good night and went inside. After the show there would be unpacking to take care of, and they knew from Miguel that Rodrigo turned in early.

***

Early the next morning, Rodrigo walked the three blocks from his apartment at 84th and Harding to the North Shore Recreation Area and made his way to the beach, an hour before his houseguests had even woken up. Luis slept better than he had in weeks and figured it was a combination of the hours in the air and a home-cooked meal. He had to admit, it was nice to be around family again.

Miguel and Rosa had promised to take the children to Aventura Mall for some last-minute Christmas shopping. This would give Luis and Raul some time for a walk on the beach and a chance to catch up with Uncle Rodrigo. Tina was torn between a day at the beach or the trip to the mall. The decision got a little easier when Aunt Rosa mentioned that the mall had a Forever 21 store; Luis and Raul made it a no-brainer by contributing cash to the cause.

The gentle rolling surf and warm sun on his face was like a tonic to Luis. All thoughts of the harsh winter weather back home vanished as soon as his toes touched the soft sand. He wished his troubled mind could be as easily soothed as his tired body.

They found Rodrigo near the edge of the water, nestled in a sand chair, peeling a mango he had brought along for his noontime meal. As skillfully as any sighted person, he ran a paring knife around the skin of the ripe, juicy fruit. He tossed the scraps into the air to a waiting flock of grateful gulls.

Luis and Raul laid down bamboo mats and sat on either side of their ancient family treasure. Rodrigo offered them a slice of mango, but Rosa had just fed them a hearty breakfast and both declined.

"I often think of where we might be, *Don* Rodrigo, if the Bay of Pigs had succeeded," Raul offered up for conversation, using a term of respect before his uncle's name.

"Yes, I think of this sometimes, too, Raul," the old man said slowly. "Maybe your father and I would have become citrus farmers like we wanted to instead of American émigrés. You know, he wanted to call our business 'A & R Fruit Company,' insisting that Antonio came before Rodrigo." He smiled recalling his younger brother.

"Do you miss home?" Luis asked.

"Home is where you say it is," Rodrigo said, poking holes in the sand with the point of his walking stick.

"That's what I've been trying to tell *you*, Pop," Luis said to Raul. "Things have changed in our hometown. Trenton is not what it used to be. We need to find a new home."

"Maybe it is *you* who has changed and not the town," Rodrigo suggested diplomatically.

"Hopewell has crime, too, son," Raul said. "It just doesn't make the papers like in Trenton."

"They don't have random drive-by shootings with innocent people gunned down in the street," answered Luis, the anguish shaking his voice.

Uncle Rodrigo stopped his poking and sat upright. "This Hopewell is a better sounding place than Trenton … it has good farmland, yes?" he asked cautiously.

"Yes," Luis responded curiously. "How did you know?"

Rodrigo inclined his head to Raul. "You never told him, Raul?"

Raul sighed. "I never saw the point," he said wearily.

"What point? What didn't he tell me?" asked Luis, red-faced but inquisitive.

Rodrigo rested his chin on his cane and gazed blindly out into the open water. "A story handed down for many generations in our family tells that the founder of the Alma bloodline was a farmer from Hopewell, New Jersey."

Luis looked at his father incredulously.

"It's just a story," Raul scoffed.

"As the story goes," Rodrigo continued, undeterred by Raul's skepticism, "this gentleman came from a very important family said to have counted George Washington and Benjamin Franklin among their friends."

Raul played with the sand, spilling it from hand to hand as Luis gave Rodrigo his undivided attention.

Feeling Luis's keen interest focused on the story, the old man continued. "As a young man, this son of an important family ran up considerable debts and got into trouble with the Spaniards who controlled Louisiana at the time. He was put in irons and shipped to a debtors' prison on Cuba where this rogue, who was said to have a big heart and even bigger *cojones*, charmed his way out of prison, made and lost a fortune, and bedded a chambermaid who later bore him a son she named Juan Antonio Alma, taken from the pet name 'Mi Alma' which he had called his mistress."

The old man paused in his story to take a sip of water from a plastic bottle. He resumed poking his cane into the sand.

"*Chisme*," ridiculed Raul with the Spanish word for gossip. "It's a tall tale told by a promiscuous young maid to conceal the identity of the real father or to satisfy the curiosity of her bastard child."

"Whatever happened to the gringo?" Luis asked, strangely drawn into the story.

"He sailed back to the colonies after they had won their independence from England and was never heard from again," Rodrigo said. "His parting words to the boy's mother were said to be a promise to welcome them as family should they someday choose to follow him to America."

Luis looked at his father, who was making the "loco" gesture with his hand. Turning back to the old man he asked, "And you believe this story is true, Uncle Rodrigo?"

"It's not up to me to say the story is true or not. Like your father and his father before him, each Alma must look into his own heart and soul and decide for himself what truth is." With this dramatic pronouncement, Rodrigo slowly rose to his feet and stretched.

"Raul, walk with me along the surf," he said. "I want to feel the ocean. Luis, try to relax, *mijo*. I'm sure this is a very trying time for you, but today is beautiful and you don't want to miss it. When the sun hits our backs, it will be time to leave. Padre Miguel will be very upset if we are late for mass on Christmas Eve. Plus, you won't believe the feast your sister Rosita is planning for midnight!" A toothsome grin lit up the old man's face. "Just like the old days, isn't it, Raul?" he said, grabbing his nephew's arm and leading him toward the water.

"Even better, *Tio*. We never had enough to eat in Cuba," Raul said, sharing a bittersweet laugh with his uncle.

25

Building Bridges

The sojourn in South Florida had been therapeutic for Luis, but returning home was a total shock to the system. He had to face the cold reality of life all over again. It wasn't the harsh, bone-chilling winter weather they flew back to that struck the hardest blow.

During their pleasant stay with Miguel, Rosa, and Uncle Rodrigo, life was simply put on hold. It was precisely what they needed and, unfortunately, all they got. Raul, Luis, and, to a lesser extent, Tina and Roberto were too distracted adjusting to the unfamiliar routines of an enlarged, if quirky, family and the wonderful tropical weather to dwell for any length of time on what their return to a "normal" existence would be like.

For Tina, the week away was both an instant and an eternity. She enjoyed the beautiful beaches, the holiday shopping, and the quaint domestic life of her peculiar relatives, but she also missed hanging out with Isabel and her other friends, especially Darius Hudson. Their relationship had just started to advance in the trust and intimacy departments when the unexpected happened. The hole in her life left by the sudden loss of her mother was huge, and she needed someone she could look up to and depend upon to fill that void. She wasn't sure Darius was that someone, but her feelings for him seemed to keep growing.

For his part, Darius had kept a low profile, trying his best to give Tina the time she needed to heal while wanting desperately to be a part of her healing process. In the days immediately following the funeral, he had been content to give her that space. Even when she announced the sudden trip to Miami, he managed to show the kind of support he knew she needed. The reality was that he missed her more than he could have imagined, and their separation only increased his desire to take the relationship to the next level. And there was something else: He couldn't wait to share with her, in person, the progress he'd made on their "research project" since she'd left for Florida.

Roberto was another matter. He returned from vacation feeling like he hated school and had started to think almost daily about dropping out. Lately, gaming seemed to provide his only enjoyment in life. While he may not have shared as obvious a bond to his mother as Tina did, at nine he had been more dependent on her psychologically than he realized. For better or worse, Roberto's relationship with his father seemed co-opted by his grandfather, who spent much more time with him than Luis's work schedule allowed.

For Luis, the ghostly company of his wife would never suffice. While he often felt her presence in the home they had made together, it was no substitute for her touch, her smile, or her reassuring words in a world that no longer made sense to him.

Nothing could protect Luis from the well-meaning Mrs. Garcia, the widow next door who watched the Alma house and collected their mail while they were away. She was a plump, cheerful older woman with a soft spot for Raul, in particular. She couldn't do enough for the Almas, nor could she avoid poking around in their business when the opportunity presented itself. She was clearly disappointed when Luis and not Raul stopped by to pick up the mail, but she managed to be pleasant nevertheless, making quite a fuss over a package that had arrived the day the family left for Florida. She felt certain it was addressed in a female hand, which piqued her curiosity, but Luis seemed disinclined to open it in front of her and anxious to be on his way. The conversation ended with Mrs. Garcia, a naturalized Mexican-American, promising to make *chili con carne*—her specialty—and bring it over before the end of the week.

Returning home, Luis set the UPS package aside as he took a seat at the kitchen table and began sorting through the mail. After separating the bills from the junk mail, he turned his attention to the sympathy cards that were still pouring in. He put them in a pile for Tina, who had agreed to handle the responses for the family after school.

From the size of the stack, Luis reasoned that this would keep her busy and out of mischief for several nights to come.

Luis had forgotten all about the package as he caught up on the local news. He was reading his newspapers, from the most recent issue back, when Raul returned from his dentist appointment. Pulling up a chair beside his son, Raul moved the package out of his way, grinning confidently to display his newly cleaned teeth. His smile faded quickly when Luis mentioned Mrs. Garcia's inquiry into his health and her promise to bring over some chili.

"That woman will be the death of me," Raul muttered.

"Come on, Pop, her chili isn't *that* bad," goaded Luis.

"You know exactly what I mean," Raul grumbled.

"I don't believe this!" said Luis excitedly. He folded the paper in half and read onward. "Bobby Jackson is out of jail."

"Isn't that the hood you nabbed after he knifed the cop and stole his gun?" asked Raul incredulously.

"Yeah, that's him," replied Luis, his eyes glued to the story. "He's out on bail."

"Bail," echoed Raul. "What's bail for a would-be cop killer these days?"

"It says here that bail was set at two hundred thousand dollars."

"*¡Madre de Dios!* Where did he get that kind of money?"

"A lawyer named Solomon Sachs is representing him," Luis read on. "Apparently he posted it."

"Something smells fishy," Raul sniffed. "Sachs is a big-shot attorney. He's been involved in a lot of high profile cases. What's he doing representing this punk?"

Luis kept reading. "Apparently Jackson used to belong to the Trenton Youth Club, and Sachs is on their board of trustees."

"It doesn't make sense," Raul insisted. "Putting a kid like that back on the streets is just asking for trouble."

"I'll bet it's gang money, Pop. They can get their hands on that kind of dough, no problem."

Raul shook his head in disbelief. "But how does the Trenton Youth Club fit in? And what about Sachs? He can't be connected to one of these street gangs. Jewish Mafia, maybe, but the Bloods? No way!"

"Wait, Pop," Luis held up a hand, "there's more. The cops have a lead on a possible accomplice—the driver behind the wheel of the car I saw pull away. And according to the reporter, P. J. Moore, the cell phone stolen from Abigail Treadwell-Tucker's Mercedes that day has been used recently."

"She's the great looking blonde, right?" Raul remembered fondly.

"Yeah, that's her. Calls from her stolen cell phone led the police to the projects in the North Ward and to the arrest of another youth whose name is being withheld because he's a minor." Luis set the paper down, shaking his head.

"What does all this mean, Luis?" Raul asked.

"It means that Hopewell is looking better and better, Pop," replied Luis without skipping a beat.

"Tina will be crushed," Raul said, then let out a laugh. "So will Mrs. Garcia!"

Luis ignored his father's attempt at soap opera humor. "It will be a good move for Roberto, and he's the one I'm most worried about. Tina will graduate in a few months, and it will take that long to get into a new place, anyway. But Roberto still has years of school ahead of him, and I'll be damned if it's gonna be in the Trenton system." He slapped the page of the paper for added emphasis. "This is just further proof there's no future in this city."

Raul tapped the UPS package. "Better check this baby for explosives before you open it," he joked as he stood to leave.

"Where are you going, Pop?"

"Where do you think I'm going?" Raul said putting his jacket back on. "School's letting out, and I'm going to meet Roberto at the corner. Got to keep these old legs from getting stiff."

Luis smiled approvingly as his father went out the door. Raul was not only a great support system for Roberto, but he seemed to be gradually accepting the idea of a move to Hopewell. And why shouldn't he? The evidence was everywhere and gaining momentum. Trenton was no longer the future of the Alma family, if indeed it had ever been.

Luis turned the package over in his hand. Thinking of his father's mock warning, he shook it lightly. It felt heavy, but nothing rattled.

He put it to his ear and nothing was ticking either. There was no name on the sender's line, and he didn't recognize the local return address other than to notice it was from an apartment in the recently renovated upscale Broad Street Bank Building. And, supporting Mrs. Garcia's unspoken suspicion, the label was handwritten in a flowing and legible script, presumably by a member of the gentler sex.

Studying the label closely, Luis saw that it was addressed to *Mr. Luis Alma*. That was odd, Luis thought. The package was addressed to him rather than to the family. What was it, and who could have sent it?

Slowly, he pulled away the tab and turned the box upside down. A hardbound book slid out onto the table. Picking it up he saw it was *The Roeblings: A Century of Engineers, Bridge Builders and Industrialists* by Hamilton Schuyler.

Opening the book, Luis found an unsealed white envelope tucked under the cover. He pulled out a small Shoebox greeting card featuring a rainbow bridging the sky between two clouds—one fluffy and white, the other a stormy, granite gray. The caption read, *"Into each life some rain must fall. Stronger is he who builds bridges, not walls."*

With mounting curiosity, he flipped open the card and scanned the message. Written in the same elegant confident script as the label was a note:

> *Dear Luis,*
>
> *I know words cannot begin to describe the grief you are feeling so I will not even try. I only wanted you to know that my thoughts and prayers are with you and your family in your time of need.*
>
> *I hope you can find comfort, as I have, in the lives and struggles of great men and women. Taking a cue from the street on which you live, I pass along this book about the Roebling family in the hopes that, through an understanding of the obstacles they overcame, you may find a common bond upon which to rebuild.*

A life well lived takes courage and the force of will I know you possess.
With both my deepest sympathies and my fondest wishes,
Abby

P.S. "The future of many rests in the fate of a few."
(p. 127)

Luis took a deep breath, then reread the note with an almost guilty pleasure. He slowly savored each sentence and, with each new word, found it exceedingly difficult to shake the image of Abby Treadwell-Tucker from his mind.

26

Long Range Plans

S enator Howard Stevens lay naked, spread-eagle on a king-sized bed in a motel room he'd paid cash for, across the river from Trenton in Langhorne, Pennsylvania. His hands and feet were strapped to the corner posts. A black satin blindfold covered his eyes.

"Howie, you've been a naughty boy," said the dominatrix in a husky voice that he did his best to pretend wasn't Helen Nelson's. She was clad in a tight black leather bra and thong, fishnet stockings, and stiletto heels. Her long black wig and velvet mask gave her the appearance of a voluptuous black widow spider.

"You've made a mess of your room!" she scolded him as she poured warm melted chocolate over his genitals. "And now you've gone and soiled yourself. What am I to do with you?"

"Please don't spank me, mommy," the senator begged in an innocent little boy's whine, relishing the pain and degradation. "I'll clean it up."

"Oh, yes you will, Howie," she chided him disdainfully. "But mommy will help you. That's what mommies are for."

The dominatrix clapped her hands sharply and out of the walk-in closet came two scantily dressed hookers attired as French chambermaids. The girls giggled and cooed as they stripped.

"Is that Gigi and Yvette?" Stevens inquired excitedly.

"Yes, Howie," replied his surrogate mother. "They're here to clean up your mess."

Yvette was a well-endowed twenty-two-year-old African American stripper. She took a feather duster and began lightly dusting the senator's ears and nose. She bent down and rubbed her nipples across his pursed waiting lips.

Gigi, a petite Asian girl with delicate features, produced a small plastic pail filled with warm water and began giving the senator a sponge bath, starting at his bare feet and toes.

The two women expertly dusted and sponged the naked senator from head to toe, coming face-to face at his throbbing, chocolate covered epicenter.

Helen sat in a hardback chair across the room with a perfect view of the two young vixens adroitly plying their trade. Just beyond them she saw her reflection in the hotel mirror, putting her squarely in the middle of the erotic scene. Fondling her breasts with one hand, she reached between her legs and began to stroke herself with the other.

As Yvette and Gigi licked and sucked their way through the senator's gooey mess, Stevens erupted loudly. Helen, panting and moaning softly, came quietly in the pleasure of her own relief.

A few minutes later, as the girls climbed into the shower together, Helen untied the senator's wrists and ankles and began to dry him off with a soft towel.

"I'm thinking we need new blood," he said assertively.

"You've tired of the French maids *already?*" she asked with a note of surprise in her voice.

"No, not the girls," Stevens insisted. "I'm talking about Dodd. Whittaker thinks he's outlived his usefulness and I agree."

"You don't think we can get one more term out of him?" she said as she dressed. "He's worked well for us in the past."

"I think he might interfere with our long range plans. Listen, candidates are coming out of the woodwork to challenge him, which could postpone the election until mid-June. Now's the time for us to get our back-up plan in place."

She picked his tie off the chair and handed it to him. "Who do you have in mind to replace him?"

"How about that hotshot Latino hero, Luis Alma?"

"Good choice," she purred, reaching down and running her hand up his crotch. "I'll set it up."

***

Nervous and perspiring, Luis started to think he'd made a big mistake in accepting Abby's invitation. Even though it was just lunch, he hadn't been out alone with a woman other than his wife for almost twenty years. He felt as awkward as a teenager on his first date.

Maria had only been gone for a little over two months. Was it too soon?

He wasn't sure he could trust his own judgment, so he'd tried to remove any dangerous elements from the situation, suggesting an *early* lunch in a *public* place that did not serve *alcohol*. She seemed bemused but not bothered by his conditions as she recommended Café Ole on South Warren Street, across from the Classic Book Shop.

It was Saturday morning at 11, and Luis was already there. The streets were eerily quiet, devoid of the workday pedestrian and vehicular traffic he was accustomed to. None of the state offices were open, and even the State Museum was closed for renovations, which had been going on for three years. Although it gave him extra time for nervousness, being early did have its advantages, Luis thought. For one, he could leave before she got there if things didn't feel right. Coming up with an excuse shouldn't be too hard, if she even bothered to call him on it. He smiled at the thought. She wasn't the type who would let it slide if he stood her up.

He ordered a decaf cappuccino grande rather than his usual espresso, thinking it would just fuel his nerves. He took the coffee and walked back to a secluded table at the rear of the shop, close to the emergency exit. His failsafe.

He hadn't told Raul or the children where he was going, only that he had to run some errands. He felt a sudden pang of guilt and stood to leave. Just then he saw her at the counter, impossible to ignore in tight faded jeans and teal cashmere sweater, brown leather bomber jacket and white silk scarf. Latte in hand, she spotted him and waved. Too late for failsafe.

He stood quickly as she approached him, and she gave him a quizzical look as she eyed the emergency exit. "You weren't thinking of bolting on me, were you?" she said by way of a greeting, her lips set tight, almost pouting, arms crossed. He noticed the silky radiance of her blonde hair as a shaft of noonday sunlight caught it through a window.

"No, I was, I was just, ah, waiting—" he stammered as he struggled to maintain composure, feeling simultaneously annoyed and smitten.

"Then why don't we sit down?" she offered.

He smiled nervously at her as they pulled their chairs up to the table. "I looked on page 127 of the book you sent me," he said, trying for a casual tone but missing the mark. "That quote—'the future of many rests with the fate of a few'—it wasn't there." It sounded almost like an accusation.

"I'm sorry," she replied in a confessional tone. "I should have made that clearer." She took a sip of her coffee, realizing that she would have to lead the conversation for awhile. She was comfortable in that role and even confident that some Roebling family history would put him at ease.

"That quote is actually from page 127 of *my* unfinished manuscript on the life of Mary G. Roebling—I know, how could I expect you to figure that out?" She gave a small, self-deprecating laugh, shaking her head before continuing. "The Roebling story is fascinating. John Roebling founded the iron rope company that was famous in Trenton until about fifty years ago. They built the rigging for steamships and cables for elevators. Their most famous job was the Brooklyn Bridge. As a matter of fact, John Roebling died building it, and his son Washington had to take over."

She took a moment to sip her coffee, noticing how intently Luis was following her every movement. He was a good listener, she decided as she picked up the story.

"Washington was a gifted engineer who made important improvements to the bridge design, but he came down with caisson's disease—the bends—while working underwater with his men. He almost died, and he never fully recovered. His wife Emily had to learn engineering so she could relay his instructions to the workers. They never gave up, and somehow they finished building that bridge."

"That's quite a story," Luis said, finally starting to relax a little. "But who was Mary Roebling?"

"Mary was Washington Roebling's granddaughter by marriage, and she was way ahead of her time." Abby sipped her latte, licked the foam off her lips, then continued. "She was the first female bank chairperson in the history of the U.S. and managed to be a patron of the arts at the same time. She was a remarkable woman. That quote I sent you was one she had used to describe Emily, but I meant it to suggest that one person's greatness can lift us all."

"I'm not really sure where you're going with all this," Luis said a bit suspiciously.

"Look," Abby said, leaning forward, "can we just start over?" She held out her hand. "Hi, I'm Abby Treadwell-Tucker. My mother was a Treadwell, which means she had her own money. My father was a Tucker, which meant he knew how to use other people's money."

"So you're a Tucker," Luis said, trying to discern the true color of her wide, beautiful eyes without staring. At the moment he would have said teal, but he thought they might be reflecting her sweater. Her eyes caught his gaze momentarily before he looked away, feeling a sense of danger he couldn't pinpoint. "As in Tucker Street?" he managed to finish his thought.

"Guilty as charged," she said with no remorse. "Descended from a long line of lawyers, liars, and land robbers."

"Have you ever been married?" he asked incongruously. She took it in stride.

"Weak men bore me," she said as if challenging him, "and most powerful men don't understand why any woman would want to have her own career. They seem to honestly believe that every woman's dream is to live vicariously through the goals and accomplishments of her husband."

"But not you." He was enjoying the banter.

"Not me."

It was his turn to be amused. "So why do you use both surnames?"

"For professional reasons."

"Oh, really?" He took another sip of his coffee. "This ought to be good."

She ignored the sarcasm. "I came to Trenton to research the life of Mary Roebling. Like I said, she was quite a woman—smart, confident, headstrong. Yes, some might say she was opportunistic, but ultimately she cut her own path apart from her husband and his powerful family out of necessity. She had no choice after he died."

"I never heard of her before today," he replied honestly.

"She reminds me a lot of Helen Nelson."

Luis hadn't completely made up his mind about the forceful HPCA director. He had only actually spoken with her once, on the day he was honored at the State House, but observing her at Maria's funeral, he felt as if she treated it like a political fundraiser and that had angered him. He suspected she had no honest feelings for anyone. Of course, that might also be true of the woman sitting in front of him … but, God, she was something to behold.

"I never did finish the book," Abby continued, "but Mary Roebling's spirit must have stayed with me. I took this job working with Helen at HPCA, and I've never looked back. In my professional life, people know me as Abby Treadwell-Tucker—AT&T? You have to admit it has a certain ring to it."

"So, tell me," Luis said, "is a housing project named after *me* really going to be built on a street named for *your* illustrious family?"

Abby smirked. "Depends on who you ask. And by the way," she added, "I didn't know anything about Alma Arms until Randal Whittaker announced it at your award ceremony. My family *is* originally from Trenton, but my great grandparents moved to upstate New York and my parents never dwelled on the past. Shelly Reed, the local historian who works in our office, thinks the street may have been named for John Tucker, who was an early Trenton mayor, but I think it might have been named after Samuel Tucker, who was apparently a big high muckety-muck in local politics at the time of the Revolutionary War. That's supposedly him on the mural behind the bank, reading the Declaration of Independence."

"You know, I've looked at that mural a hundred times and always wondered who that guy was," Luis admitted. "What's his story?"

"Samuel Tucker? From what I've heard, he dropped completely out of sight after the war," she said, shaking her head. "Shelly Reed says he and his wife are buried on the grounds of the Trenton Psychiatric Hospital out on Sullivan Way. Apparently the headstones are in a terrible state of decay."

"I know where that is," he said, leaning toward her. "It's out near the Trenton Country Club. There's a big insurance company on the corner."

"That's the place," she confirmed with a winning if calculated smile. "The country club is actually on a farm that once belonged to the Woodruff family. And New Jersey Manufacturers, the insurance company, is situated on land once owned by the Scudder family— that's another old pioneering family linked to the Harts of Hopewell."

Luis was impressed. "You really know your local history."

She wouldn't accept the flattery. "Well, I did quite a bit of research for the Roebling book, but when your office is within earshot of Shelly Reed, you can't help but pick up a lot of history. The woman is a walking encyclopedia."

"So do you think she has any information about the Harts?" he asked, picking up on her last reference. "The ones from Hopewell?"

"Sure, if anyone around here does," she said, her curiosity piqued. "Is there something in particular you want to know?"

Luis looked at his watch. He was enjoying Abby's company and wished he'd allowed himself more time. He'd been so sure his "date" wouldn't go well that he had promised Roberto he would be back by one o'clock to take him to Manny's for a haircut. After that they planned on hitting the Quakerbridge Mall to shop for shoes. While he looked forward to spending some time with his son, right now the overriding emotion was a feeling of guilt over enjoying a woman's company so much, mixed with disappointment at having to leave her.

He finished his cold cappuccino. It made no difference. He hadn't noticed the taste let alone the temperature since the moment she walked into the café.

"Can we hold that thought for another time?" he asked furtively, tossing a twenty dollar bill on the table to cover a ten dollar tab and hoping to impress her. "My son is waiting for me." He stood to go.

Her smile faded. "Only if you promise there will be another time."

"You can count on it." As he moved toward the entrance he stopped and called back over his shoulder, "Do you like pizza?"

"Love it!" she exclaimed as he passed the lunch counter and headed out the door.

27

History or Hijinx?

*L*et me see if I've got this straight," said Tina with a hint of sarcasm. She was in the passenger seat of Darius's car on their way to the library for another round of research. "It was your little brother my father saw pulling out of the church parking lot behind the wheel of your car?"

"Like I already told you," Darius said. "He borrowed my car without asking."

"But he's only fifteen," she reminded him. "He doesn't have a license!"

"That never stopped him before."

"He's taken your car before?" She was having difficulty believing what she was hearing.

"Yeah, more than once," he said matter-of-factly.

She gave him a hard look. "Why don't you just hide your keys?"

"I have," he replied defensively. "But he went and made himself a copy."

Tina looked out the window. A light March drizzle had begun to fall gently against the windshield. She collected her thoughts as she considered what to say next.

"What was he doing at the church?" she asked cautiously, a part of her didn't want to know the answer.

"Playing wheelman for Bobby Jackson is my guess."

"You're kidding," she said skeptically.

"I wish I was," he said as he made a right onto Perry Street.

She gave him a thoroughly perplexed look. "Your brother hangs out with that creep?"

Darius shrugged. "He lives in the hood."

"So how did the police catch your brother?"

"Stupid kid used the cell they stole from that Mercedes to call Bobby after he was released."

"Was that what he needed the money for?" she asked, reluctantly turning to face him. She wasn't sure she trusted him to answer truthfully.

"More or less."

"What do you mean? Was that what your brother needed the money for or not?"

He met her searching eyes. They were glowing, illuminated by the dashboard lights. She was grilling him hard, and he didn't like it.

"The owner of the Mercedes decided not to press charges. Her insurance company replaced the smashed window, plus she works for the state, so they gave her a new phone. The money was just to cover the deductible on her insurance."

Suddenly it dawned on Tina that she had never even bothered to ask Darius his brother's name.

"My brother's name is Curtis, by the way," he said as if reading her mind.

"Where is he now?"

"Mercer County Youth House," he said with a look of disappointment on his face. "He got off easy. Thirty days in juvie."

"That's good, I guess," she offered.

"No it's not." His face turned serious. "My brother is the state's main witness against Bobby Jackson. Thirty days detention was supposed to be protective custody, but Jackson is back out on the streets, and the minute Curtis is released from the Youth House he's dead."

They rode the rest of the way to the library in silence, each lost in their own thoughts, listening to the metronome-like squish-squish of the windshield wipers.

"So what's new on the E. H. and Penny front?" she asked at length as they pulled into the Trenton Free Library parking lot.

"Dead end," he admitted sullenly. "I thought I was onto something when my professor got me into the archives, but I couldn't find anyone with the initials 'E. H.' among the owners listed for Eagle Tavern."

"Maybe he wasn't an owner. How about a bartender?" she asked hopefully.

"They don't even list all the owners. How the hell am I supposed to find out the name of a bartender? For that matter, what bartender would be stupid enough to leave behind a priceless first edition pamphlet?" He was starting to vent his frustrations over a lot more than the subject at hand. She responded in kind.

"First off, I don't like your tone of voice. I didn't think there would be a list of bartenders. I just thought maybe he wasn't one of the owners. Secondly, it wasn't a priceless first edition when he left it—it was the *only* edition. And third, I've had about enough of your attitude. Take me home!"

"I would if I was allowed to drive anywhere near your house!" he threw back at her with increasing anger. "Let alone ever meet anyone from your family. I guess I'm just not white enough."

"What do you want from me?" she cried out loud, letting her emotions rip. "It has nothing to do with you being black. Even though I wanted you to meet my parents, the timing had to be right. I lied about going out with you to my mother because I wasn't ready. I was nervous, okay? Then she gets killed before I can tell her about you, and my father hates the whole city and wants to leave. And how do I know if you really care about me, anyway?"

She continued before he could answer.

"You make me steal some artifact from a boarded-up old tavern, and we go on a wild goose chase trying to find out who owned it, then your brother just happens to be the driver for a guy who tried to kill my father, and you yell at me like I'm the one who's making *your* life hard!" She broke down in tears.

He slowly wrapped his arms around her and held her tightly, as she let out a sigh that sounded as if the weight of the entire world was on her shoulders.

"I am so sorry, Tina. I never stopped to think of how it looked from your side of things." He gently wiped a tear out of the corner of her eye. "You've been nothing but good to me. I'm really sorry I never had the chance to meet your mom. She must have been one very special lady."

She cried uncontrollably as he held her close.

"Your dad seems like some kind of superman, taking on a crazy bastard like Bobby Jackson to save somebody he didn't even know. My dad left us when I was only two or three years old. He got out of jail long enough to knock my mom up with Curtis a couple years later, and none of us have seen or heard from him since. My mom works all the time just to put food on the table, and her health's not that good. I worry about my kid brother, but he never listens to me. I warned him not to hang out with guys like Jackson, but I can't watch him 24/7."

"How did you manage to avoid the gangs?" she asked as her tears subsided.

"It was easier for me. I was into sports when I was younger and then, I know you're gonna laugh, but history saved me. I swear to God. I fell in love with history in school and not because of some cute teacher, either." He smiled down at his gradually relaxing friend and brushed her hair back away from her tear-stained eyes. "I just have a passion for learning what some pretty amazing people did with their lives and what they left behind."

"Well, then we better get back into that library, huh?" she said, smiling tenderly at him and straightening herself out.

"You know, we may never find out who E. H. and Penny were," he admitted painfully.

She paused as he held the door open for her. "It might be better that way," she offered conciliatorily.

He couldn't leave it at that. "Tina, try to see it my way. History needs to breathe, and it's the job of every researcher to bring the characters he encounters to life. Without that, it's just a series of unconnected events. Through living history, we look to the past to understand the present and work for a better future."

She blinked. "I see your point, Darius." And in truth she did, as never before. He had finally revealed himself to her, and she was happy to share this adventure he was committed to. "So, where does that leave us?' she asked, entering through the turnstile.

The question brought Darius to a complete stop even though he was not quite through the turnstile. "Do you mean you and me, or the pamphlet?"

"The pamphlet," she replied as the desk clerk shooed him forward through the gate. "I know where *we* stand."

"Okay, that makes one of us," he said under his breath.

They found Shelly Reed behind her big oak desk chatting animatedly with a male visitor dressed in a gaudy kelly green pullover. He had a distinct if subdued British accent. Darius introduced Tina to Professor Daniel Collins.

"Ah, here to check out the Revolutionary War paraphernalia we spoke of when last we met?" asked the owl-eyed Shelly Reed with a flutter of her lashes, a reflexive action that appeared magnified beneath her lenses as they slid down her slightly pointed nose.

"Actually—" Darius began.

"Actually, with Darius, one can never tell whether it's history or hijinx he has in mind," Professor Collins finished theatrically with a playful wink.

"It's history today, professor," Tina replied for the suddenly tongue-tied Darius Hudson.

"Then you're in luck," Shelly chimed in with her lilting chirp, "because Professor Collins and I were just discussing this item of New Jersey colonial currency." She gestured to a worn, faded colonial note displayed in a glass case.

"It's a fifteen shilling note printed by Isaac Collins, no relation, dated February 20, 1776," the professor said, the enthusiasm evident in his voice. "It was presumably part of the proclamation money the New Jersey Provincial Congress authorized to help fund their war effort against we Brits."

"Notice the signatures," Shelly said, pointing to them with the eraser end of her pencil. "There are two—John Hart and Samuel How. But it took three signatures to make this note a legal tender. So as currency, it was actually worthless."

"Whose signature is missing?" Darius frowned as he concentrated his attention on the barely legible scrawl of the two signers.

"Right, that would be one Samuel Tucker," said the professor with a nod in Shelly's direction. "This bill is believed to be from the horde confiscated by the British at the old Abbott place on December 9, 1776. Tucker, who was state treasurer at the time, sent it to his friend's farm on the outskirts of town for safe keeping just before the British occupied Trenton."

Shelly picked up the story. "But Tucker was ratted out by a loyalist sympathizer named Julia Brennan for reasons that remain unclear. He was captured a few days later and inexplicably switched sides, taking an oath of allegiance to the King."

"The British were duped, though," Professor Collins said almost gleefully. "They expected to find the entire treasury—roughly twenty-five thousand pounds' worth of the original proclamation money. But all they found were some six thousand pounds in worthless bills—worthless because they bore only two of the three necessary signatures."

Tina twisted and braided her hair as she processed the story. "What happened to the rest of the money?" she asked. The smile on Darius's face told her he was about to ask the same question.

"Ah," exclaimed Shelly with a Cheshire cat grin, "that is the age-old mystery we local historians have been trying to solve. Each note had to be individually signed. The process could take months, even though there were nineteen persons authorized to sign them. These two signers probably split the notes between them. We know from John Hart's biographer, Cleon Hammond, that Hart signed all twenty-five thousand pounds, nearly fifteen thousand, six hundred notes of varying denominations. So, we can conclude that Hart turned over the first half for Tucker to sign, while he and How worked on the other half."

"Right," said Collins as Shelly stopped to catch her breath. "So, Tucker had about thirteen thousand pounds' worth of notes on hand—it would be reasonable to assume that he was able to sign some of them before the occupation."

"But not all," concluded Tina.

"Bingo!" said Shelly.

"So why did the British only get half of the money and only the unsigned notes?" Darius asked.

The professor couldn't stand still, he was so anxious to tell the next part of the story. "We know that later, in 1778, after the British had vacated Trenton and been swept from most of New Jersey for that matter, Tucker decided to change sides again. He apparently was ready to serve the good citizens of New Jersey once more, and as an act of contrition, he wrote Governor Livingston claiming to have suddenly found a missing trunk containing various 'official bonds and documents' he thought had been confiscated by the British at Abbott's farm."

Shelly walked around the desk to join the engaged group and continued the narrative, "But Livingston didn't take the bait. He rebuked Tucker's entreaty."

"So what happened then?' Darius was eager to know.

"Unfortunately," replied Professor Collins, "you bloody Americans have either very short memories or a very forgiving nature. I am not sure which, but in any event Tucker was eventually re-elected to the New Jersey Legislature."

"And the money?' asked Tina excitedly. "What happened to the missing six thousand five hundred pounds?"

"It vanished, lost to history," Shelly said. "We do know that Tucker was planning to make a trip to England with his wife, but they never got to make the voyage."

Darius tapped the glass plate containing the colonial note. "This John Hart," he said, choosing his words carefully, "did he or any member of his family happen to own Eagle Tavern at one time?"

Shelly let out a short bemused laugh. "I don't believe so. He was one of the signers of the Declaration of Independence and the first Speaker of the New Jersey Assembly, but he remains a bit elusive. We know he had twelve children—six boys and six girls and, come to think of it, he was also known to raise horses, so it is likely that he and his sons frequented Eagle Tavern during racing season. However, I don't remember reading anything about him owning it."

As she tapped her pencil on the case, deep in thought, a light bulb seemed to switch on. "Give me a minute," she said, slipping back behind her desk and pulling open a drawer. Retrieving a stuffed folder, she placed it on the desk and began to scan the contents. "I did a piece on the Hart family awhile back …"

Tina and Darius huddled around her. "Now, let's see—yes, the boys were named Jesse, Nathaniel, John Jr., Edward, Scudder, and Daniel.

Darius perked up. "Edward? One of the sons was named Edward Hart?"

"Yep," she replied reading from her own article. "Now I remember."

"Did he have a wife named Penny?" Tina inquired excitedly.

"No, his wife's name was Nancy," Shelly replied without a pause. Darius and Tina looked at each other dejectedly.

"But this is peculiar," said Shelly with her nose buried in the folder. "Edward Hart *did* run a tavern. It was called the Horse and Groom. And now *this* is just too damn funny," she added with obvious glee. "The tavern was located just outside of Pennytown—that's the borough of Pennington today."

"Too bad you can't use any of *these* pieces to fit whatever puzzle you're putting together," the professor offered, trying to gauge the confused look on the teens' faces.

"Yeah, too bad," Tina agreed, dismayed but unconvinced. "Is that a picture of John Hart?" she asked with renewed interest, peering over Shelly's shoulder.

"It's what passes for his picture," the professor said. "Historians have been unable to authenticate it."

"That didn't stop the politicians from hanging it as his official portrait in the State House Gallery," Shelly added with a wry smile.

"That's where I've seen it!" exclaimed Tina excitedly. "It was the day my father got his citation from the city—we all thought there was a family resemblance."

"Well, considering the fact that John Hart had twelve children and they scattered far and wide after his death, I wouldn't rule anything out," Professor Collins responded with raised eyebrows.

Oblivious to the professor's innuendo, Darius looked around the room for anything that could help him unravel the mysteries and something caught his eye. "Hey, I recognize that thing over there from the bank painting," he said pointing to a curved dark wooden beam arched over the top of the card catalog. He went to get a closer look. "Is this the piece of the arch you were telling me about in the bank lobby, Professor Collins?

"It is indeed, Darius," his impressed history professor replied. "You have a keen eye."

Darius frowned and stood on a stool to get a better look. "Professor, what are these markings in the lower right hand corner?"

Professor Collins squinted. "Markings? What markings?"

Darius traced the faint impressions with his finger.

"Shelly, could you hand me that magnifying glass?" Collins asked as he traded places with Darius.

"Incredible," the professor remarked. "I never noticed this before. Here, have a look." He stepped down and handed Darius the lens. Darius got back on the stool and studied the carvings through the glass.

"What do you see?" Tina asked impatiently.

"This first thing looks like the crest over the State House entrance."

"That would be the Great Seal of New Jersey," Shelly said, looking at Collins with growing curiosity on her face.

"This other thing I can't seem to place—it looks like two triangles overlaid and facing each other."

"That would be the Masonic square and compass," said Professor Collins, directing his comment at Shelly.

"Shazaam!" she said then let out a low whistle. "Now that *is* something!"

28

Hope

*A*re you *crazy*?" Luis exploded in laughter. He was sitting across from Abby, crammed into a booth in the boxcar-like room on the second level of the no-frills De Lorenzo's Tomato Pies on Hudson Street. "*Me* run for mayor? You've got to be nuts. Besides the fact that I don't want to, haven't you noticed that I'm Latino?"

Abby had certainly noticed. She had noticed his dark good looks, his straight chiseled nose, and those coffee-color truth-or-dare eyes with green highlights that seemed to release burning copper when she met his gaze. She was intrigued by the careless five o'clock shadow of a tortured artist look and the roughly calloused yet well-kept hands of an honest man who worked his butt off for a living. She had definitely noticed, in spite of her best efforts to ignore, the feelings this particular Latino evoked in her.

More than a few of De Lorenzo's other patrons, munching on savory slices of thin-crusted, old-fashioned tomato pie, paused momentarily to gawk at the animated Luis. From the framed, faded black-and-white photographs lining the wood-paneled walls, New York Yankee greats seemed to look down on him disapprovingly.

Abby ignored the crowd reaction and addressed him head on. "You're aware that Latinos now make up twenty-five percent of Trenton's population? It's a largely Democratic constituency, and our fastest growing ethnic block."

"Maybe, but half of it is here illegally," he said sarcastically.

"What are you saying, Luis? That you were smuggled into the states?" she asked with mock curiosity.

"Not me," he replied candidly.

"Then who, Luis? People you know, people who work for you—your family?"

"Let's change the subject," he suggested, looking away from her.

"You're overreacting, Luis," she said, glancing around the cramped room that forbade any semblance of privacy. Not exactly the place she would have picked to have this conversation, she thought to herself, but then the choice hadn't been hers.

"Overreacting?" Luis said, scratching his head. He searched her beryllium eyes for an answer to his next question. "Why me, anyway?"

"Because you're you," she answered without the slightest hesitation. "You're an intelligent, charismatic self-made man and a decorated war veteran with a successful small business."

"I'm surprised you didn't throw in hero," he said with a chuckle, hoping she couldn't see how flattered he actually felt.

"I think we can agree the word has been a little overused since 9/11," she said with a coy smile, meeting his gaze.

He took a sip of his birch beer and looked away self-consciously. He was having trouble thinking straight. He'd been in this restaurant a hundred times before, but never sitting across the table from a companion like this. Her sales pitch felt a bit brash, but her features seemed to be softening by the minute, her blonde hair revealing soft, sun-kissed highlights. Her lips—too thin by his normal standards—were moist and inviting, and her upturned, aristocratic nose crinkled appealingly when she smiled. He didn't know for certain what her intentions were, but he was interested enough to see how it all played out.

"What makes you think I'll do any better than Dodd?" he asked.

She smiled. A confident smile. "Good, then you're considering it?"

"I didn't say that," he answered quickly, "but humor me. What qualifies me?"

"You run a successful business," she said. "We'd expect you to run the city the same way." Taking a sip of her Diet Coke, she watched his reaction closely. "You've got a bottom-line perspective, and you represent family values. It's a nice package. Minority, veteran, businessman, family man."

"It takes more than that to be a politician," he said deliberately.

She was gauging her progress. "You're right. It takes integrity, something our current crop of politicians may never have had to begin with."

"It takes money and organization," he said as their pie arrived with the toppings of his choice—sausage and sweet peppers. He handed her a steaming slice on a chipped green melamine plate.

"You're right, and we're in luck this year," she said, biting into her unevenly cut slice and catching the stringy cheese before it dripped down her chin. She set the pie aside and wiped her mouth with a paper napkin. "There are candidates coming out of the woodwork and that's sure to undermine Dodd's chances, but the elections are set for the middle of May and that doesn't give us much time if we want to win, or at least force a runoff. I'm sure Triumph will provide major funding if you declare your candidacy now. Plus, I think we can convince Senator Stevens to back you." She looked him straight in the eye. "Look, Luis, I'm prepared to help you in any way I can, if you want me."

Something about the way she said "*if you want me*" nearly made him choke on his tomato pie. A long swig of his soda helped him get his voice back. "Why do I have the feeling these discussions have been taking place without me?"

"Luis," her tone was both intimate and inevitable as she leaned across the table, "Dodd is a *loser*. We've been lucky no competent Republican has run in ten years, but that's about to change and the party knows it needs new blood." She reached across the table and covered his hands with hers. "You're different, Luis, and we ... *I* am convinced you can bring hope and change to Trenton."

He was speechless, caught completely off guard. It had been months since he had felt the touch of a woman's hand, and the effect of Abby's was electric. Yet, at the moment, the feeling was bittersweet as he wrestled with the thought that her motives were purely political.

"That's a lovely sentiment, Abby," he said withdrawing his hands, "but I believe you have to live here to run for mayor."

"And ...?" she said, not sure where he was heading.

"That leaves me out. I'm moving my family to Hopewell."

"What? And leave all *this*?" she deadpanned, gesturing around them with pale, slender arms.

He finished chewing a mouthful of pizza before reacting. "Come on, Abby," he said. "What do you care, anyway? You're set for life with a cushy state job."

"Maybe, but I live here, and I work downtown every day," she shot back. "Do you have any idea how frustrating that is?"

"Why? Because you can't find a good pesto or a place to get your hair done after six?"

"Right, you've got me all figured out," she glared at him.

"Then tell me, Abby, why *do* you care so much about what happens to Trenton? You must be pretty cozy in your luxury apartment, and I'm sure you can get out of town any time you want in that fine Mercedes of yours."

Her porcelain complexion turned crimson as his words found their mark, but rather than rage against his hurtful arrogance, she took a deep breath, then a drink of water. When she found her voice, the passion of her convictions bubbled beneath a firm measured tone.

"Listen, Luis, you may think I'm some kind of rich bitch dilettante, but I've worked hard for everything I have. Sure, I could work in New York or Washington, take home three times what I make here, and become a media whore for the network news, but *this* is my town and I get really pissed off that most people don't know there wouldn't *be* a 'Land of the Free' if not for Trenton. There's no reason it can't be a great place to live, with economic, social, and educational opportunities for everyone. That's the way it started out, and I do what I do because I believe it can be that way again."

For a moment, Luis just looked at her, astonished at the depth of her feelings and his own stupidity. "I was way out of line, Abby," he began. "The truth is, I'm flattered that you think I'd be a strong mayoral candidate, but the timing couldn't be worse. I've got a growing business to run and a family that needs me. Now more than ever." He paused before adding, "And I've still got my principles."

"I know you do," she agreed wistfully, "and the way I see it, those are all pluses for a winning campaign."

"Maybe," he said, "but those things would all suffer if I got involved in politics."

"I think you're wrong, Luis," she said, fairly certain he was right but unwilling to give up the point. "You have so much to offer," she pressed her case. "We could work on school improvements, better jobs, and public safety, and you know we could create more opportunities for Hispanics."

"Yeah, well there *was* that one columnist who wanted me to run for dog catcher," he laughed. "Tell me, though, why do you think Stevens would support me? He doesn't know me."

"You'd be surprised what he knows," she said with a practiced flutter of her long lashes.

"From you? Or Helen Nelson, maybe?" he countered.

She tried a different approach. "Luis, don't you think it's your duty—"

Luis held up his hand to cut her off. "Please don't say it's my duty, Abby. I've served my country already."

Before he'd responded, she knew she'd miscalculated with that old party trick. She changed tack. "Are you really moving to Hopewell?"

"I'm thinking about it … Maria and I looked at property there." His expression was forlorn. "I just want to do what's best for my family. To raise my kids in a safe place and grow my business. That's all there is to it."

"And let Trenton rot?" she inserted pleadingly.

"Hey, it's not my fault the city's in such bad shape. The problems are far bigger than any one person can fix."

"Change can begin with just one person," she said with seemingly complete sincerity. "In the hands of the right person it can be contagious." She looked directly at him. "Will you at least consider it?"

He shrugged his shoulders, but didn't answer.

"Dodd's support has really eroded in the last year, but without a strong opponent he could return to City Hall," she said. "Independents are changing the balance, as we've seen in some of the gubernatorial elections recently, and it looks like the Republicans have a couple of viable candidates. But if Dodd survives for another term, it's just going to be more of the same." She tried appealing to all the sensibilities she could think of. "Luis, if you want to be mad at someone for your wife's death, be mad at Jimmy Dodd. He hasn't done anything to stop the gang violence."

Luis wasn't interested in exploring his personal feelings right now. "I have no stomach for politics, Abby. Isn't there anyone else you can run?"

"The field is thin," she said. "The last legitimate candidate was Hollis Markham."

"Christ, Abby," he whispered. "He was an old man."

"My point exactly, but people trusted him. He had integrity."

"And a presence in the community," Luis agreed. Lowering his voice, he added, "More than half the population would have voted for him just because of the color of his skin. I'm thinking that blacks *and* whites would vote against a Latino candidate."

"Unless you gave them all the same thing Markham promised," she said with conviction.

He took the bait. "And what was that?"

"Hope." She left the word hanging in the air and silently finished her second slice of the delicious Trenton treat, looking at him with wide eyes as she chewed and swallowed.

He didn't trust her, but he couldn't deny he felt a dangerous attraction toward her.

She shifted in her seat and her leg made contact with his under the table, sending a wave of sensual energy straight through him. Sensing his reaction, she was quick to capitalize.

"Would you mind giving me a lift home, Luis? My car is in the shop, and I've been using my boss's car service privileges to get me around these last two days."

"Are you going to continue with the political pressure?" he asked with mock resistance.

"No, but I might show you a side of Trenton you've never seen."

***

For a ride that felt much longer than it was, Abby and Luis sat in his truck in awkward silence, each lost in their own private thoughts about where the night was headed. Luis hadn't anticipated playing chauffeur to a lovely lady, or he would have cleaned up the truck. Suddenly it smelled like the men's locker room at the local YMCA. If Abby was offended by the manly odors she didn't say so, though she did admonish him good naturedly for the lingering stale smell of cigarettes, a habit she incorrectly assumed was his.

"It's two of my men," he said. "I only smoke cigars and only on special occasions." He told her his favorite Cuban cigar was a *Cohiba*.

"So, you've still got Cuban connections?"

"Sure I do, but don't tell Uncle Sam," he grinned. "It could hurt my chances of becoming mayor."

The incessant chime of a cell phone interrupted their banter, and Abby reached inside her Vera Bradley bag to pull out her slim pink BlackBerry Pearl. The name illuminated on the caller ID made her visibly tense. She decided to let it go to voicemail.

"Nothing urgent, I guess," Luis said.

"No, nothing important," she said dismissively, setting the phone on the car seat beside her. Randal Whittaker would have to wait.

Neither the uncomfortable silence at the start of the ride nor the phone call that interrupted a possible better outcome could have prepared Abby for an awkward goodnight handshake offered by Luis, who left the engine running. As she rode up alone in the elevator, she rationalized that somewhere between De Lorenzo's and the doorstep of her building, Luis had either lost his nerve or found his conscience. Either way, she had rarely experienced this type of rejection, and it left her feeling confused.

As she turned the key to the door and entered her dark apartment, she was still trying to shake off her disappointment. Flipping on the light switch in the hallway and catching her image in the antique Victorian mirror that had always made her think of *Snow White* and the queen asking "Who is the fairest of them all?" there was no hiding from the truth. With one finger, she traced the age lines that had recently become noticeable around the corners of her eyes, as if she could make them disappear. She wished her lips were fuller and thought for the umpteenth time about collagen injections. Damn that mirror on the wall.

She quietly undressed and sat on the corner of her bed, debating whether to shower or return Randal's call. Even though his temperature hovered around the melting point of butter, she suspected there was still enough evening left for a private rendezvous. But was she really in the mood for a megalomaniac and his humiliating games? The doorbell rang before she could decide. She slipped into a soft terrycloth robe and went to open the door.

It was Luis standing in the doorway, a sheepish look on his face and her cell phone in his hand. "You forgot something," he said.

Reaching for the cell, her hastily tied robe fell open. As his eyes devoured her, she blushed, surprised but not embarrassed. He stepped into the room intending to help her cover up, but as his hand made contact with her arm there was no turning back. Her robe fell to the floor, and he kicked the door closed behind him.

The sight of her in nothing but a satin thong was all-consuming for Luis as he reached out to hold her small beautiful breasts, her nipples taut and swollen as he touched them, gently, then bent to take each of them in turn between his lips. She kissed his hands and fingers, then guided them urgently inside her thong. Moaning, she flicked her tongue across his ears, noticing the slightly salty taste of his skin as he felt her melt in his arms. Their eyes met and locked, burning into one another, his heart pounding as she led him urgently to her bedroom.

Hurriedly undoing his belt buckle, her hands fumbled with his trouser clasp and zipper before finally freeing him. She pulled him down on the bed, on top of her, their mouths melding hungrily. He kept one hand against the small of her back as she arched to take him inside her, moaning softly as wet heat began radiating from the locus of his thrusts, then allowing herself to cry out as she came once, then again, and then a third time.

Later, as they lay side-by-side on her canopied four-poster bed, she whispered, "I could sure go for a *Cohiba* right now, Luis, if you've got one." When he didn't respond, she rolled on top of him to gaze down into his face. There was a tear in the corner of his eye.

"Are you okay?"

"I'm sorry," he said gazing up into her eyes. "It's been twenty years since I've been with a woman other than my wife, and I guess I'm feeling a little guilty."

She thought for a moment before responding. "I can handle the ghost, Luis," she said, "but I draw the line at the guilt." Shrugging her bare shoulders, she sighed and added, "I have enough of my own."

"Please, Abby, don't get me wrong. What happened here tonight, between us—it's amazing. I just don't know if I'm ready for a relationship yet."

She smiled tenderly. "Luis, it's just *sex*. You haven't done anything wrong, and there's nothing to worry about, so let's just take it slow and see where it goes. As long as we're honest with each other, nobody will get hurt."

After a glass of champagne, she made him lie on his back as she teased him with her tongue, kissing him in places that hadn't been visited by a woman's lips in years. Building his excitement slowly, denying him immediate release, she caressed the length of his shaft with her hands and mouth, smiling playfully as she prepared him for another round.

When he was ready she mounted him, swaying slowly from side to side as she took him deeper and deeper. As her pace and breathing quickened, he kissed beads of sweat from between her sweet pear-shaped breasts. He reached down and held her tight little buns in his strong hands, lifting and lowering her again and again as she stretched luxuriously atop him, eyes closed, riding him with a deep and sensual abandon. The expression of pure pleasure on her lovely face was more than he could stand as he finally exploded inside her, their bodies shaking and shuddering before they collapsed on the bed together, delighted, exhausted, and utterly spent.

29

No Surprises

Y ou're late," Luis said gruffly, the darkness broken only by the light from a muted television screen. He flicked on the table lamp and the family room lit up. "The library closed more than an hour ago."

Tina removed her coat. "We stopped at Dunkin' Donuts on the way home."

"You and Isabel?" he asked slyly.

"Yeah," she said quickly, shifting her weight nervously from one foot to the other. She was uncomfortable lying to her father, but given the circumstances she thought it was best for both of them.

"I thought she was grounded," he probed.

"Uh, yeah, she was," she stammered digging the hole a little deeper, "but not any more. She's allowed out if it's related to school work."

"Why didn't she drop you off in front of the house like she usually does?" He turned his gaze from the television screen and softened as he looked at his daughter's beautiful face.

"I took a walk past Mrs. Garcia's to make sure she was okay. She hasn't been feeling well lately." She waited for her father to call her bluff.

"And?" He paused to see if she would elaborate. When she didn't, he turned back to the TV. "Is she okay?"

"Oh yeah," she gushed. "I mean, I think so. Her lights were off so I figured she must be asleep."

She waited for the next question from the Grand Inquisitor. This was so unlike her father, she knew something must be wrong.

"Roberto had a problem in school today," he said somberly. "He came home with a black eye."

"Oh, no," she exclaimed, sitting down on the couch beside him. "What happened?"

"He wouldn't tell me." As he turned and gazed into his daughter's eyes, it was like looking into his own.

"Do you want me to talk to him?" she asked hesitantly.

"That's okay," he said. "He's with Papi."

She rested her head on his shoulder. "Can I get you anything, Dad?"

"No, thanks, honey, but listen—I've made up my mind. As soon as you're finished school, we're moving to Hopewell. Your mom would have wanted it that way, so I'm going to use the life insurance money to buy the land we looked at before … before she left us. I'm calling the realtor tomorrow."

Tina turned and looked deep into her father's eyes. She could sense the hurt, the pain, the suffering he was feeling, and she was suddenly overcome with guilt. A tear trickled down her cheek. "Okay," she whispered in his ear as she reached to hug him.

He held her tightly, stroking her hair gently as he struggled to hold back his own tears.

"Promise me something, Tina," he said at last, his voice choked with emotion.

"Dad?" she said, biting her lip.

"No more surprises, *por favor,*" he said flatly as he pulled back and looked her square in the eye. Somehow, he knew that part of his being so hard on her had to do with his own mixed feelings about the romantic encounter with Abby.

She threw her arms around him once more and proclaimed, "¡*Te prometo!*"

***

As a practical matter, Luis had always deferred to Maria on the day-to-day aspects of raising their children. He'd been too busy working to provide for them, and they had grown up fast, as children tend to do. With their mother gone, instead of growing closer, he felt the distance between them more acutely than before. Tina had been spending so much time at the library that Papi Raul only half jokingly suggested she apply for a job shelving books. As for Roberto, Maria had always relayed his daily activities to Luis during the evening meal, and now he had to rely on whatever his son shared with his grandfather. So few words had ever passed directly between father and son that they had no idea how to talk to one other.

Thus, instead of bringing the family closer together, Maria's tragic death seemed to drive them further apart, with Luis the most alienated of all. Through the long dreary winter, he had been an emotional recluse—not void of thoughts and feelings but unwilling to share them openly. He had always counted on his father's pithy insights, and Raul did occasionally offer words of support, but with Mrs. Garcia now a fixture in the Alma household—cooking, cleaning, and pursuing Raul relentlessly—the older man was increasingly finding excuses to stay away from home.

Too often, at least in the eyes of his family, Luis retreated to the den alone to wallow in his own grief. In truth, he was both tormented and terrified: tormented by the absence of Maria from his life, and terrified by the feelings Abby had revived in him during their one amazing night together. He now found himself torn between two worlds, unable to reconcile the flesh and blood of real life with the idyllic dreams of his past.

Eventually he finished the book Abby had given him about the Roeblings, but while he was impressed by the family's fortitude and good fortune, their story failed to inspire a greater sense of loyalty toward his hometown or any faith in his ability to make a difference.

Of course, he was flattered by Abby's ardent attention, but he found himself wondering what lay at the heart of it. Why the sudden interest in him? Did she really believe in him? Could he trust her?

Abby was nothing like Maria, and while he wasn't shopping for a replacement, he found himself thinking he might be more comfortable with someone a little less driven. Abby was a born career woman who gave the impression that business always came first for her.

Maria, on the other hand, was a born nurse who had always put the needs of her patients and family first.

Luis not only resisted the impulse to call Abby, he avoided her calls. She was persistent, however, and on her third attempt he agreed to meet for lunch again—if only to prove to himself that he could see her without tearing her clothes off. She selected the time and place and attempted to control the mood. Sensing the emotional tug of war he was suppressing, she chose a less obtrusive and more intimate meeting place—a Spanish-Portuguese restaurant called Malaga in nearby Hamilton Township. She hoped the familiar cuisine and a soft ambience would help to put him at ease.

It was a Sunday afternoon, and the restaurant was crowded with local patrons. One table was occupied by a family Luis knew from the neighborhood, who greeted him warmly, while a number of other diners recognized him from the newspapers. More than a few came over to express their condolences and to ask how he and the children were holding up.

This outpouring of support deeply embarrassed him, at the same time stirring guilty feelings about the beautiful young woman he was seated with. Every time he opened his mouth in reply to a well-wisher he put his foot in it, and his attempts at meaningful conversation with Abby during the uninterrupted moments fell completely flat. To make matters worse, a barrage of calls were directed at her cell. Helen Nelson called repeatedly, clearly irritating her, while another unidentified caller seemed to push her into a state of sullen distraction. When the phone rang for the fifth or sixth time, she broke with habit and powered it off.

They picked at their food and conversed in forced bursts, skipping uncomfortably from one topic to another and frequently interrupting one another. They tried but failed to find any common ground.

When Abby asked him about his work and his "connection to the community," he seemed hesitant to respond. He had previously divulged far more to her than he'd intended, in the unguarded aftermath of their lovemaking, when he had told her that his employees Hector and Felix were in the country illegally. She hadn't said much at the time, but he knew she must be contemplating the possible repercussions should he run for office. She was too politically savvy not to.

When she finally raised the question of his candidacy, he didn't know whether to feel relieved that it had become a business meeting or disappointed that it wasn't strictly about mutual attraction. On the plus side, he felt less guilty and embarrassed. On the negative side, he wondered if he would ever see her naked again.

Whatever her motives for meeting, she avoided any reference to their night of passion. She did, however, hook him up with a private landscaping job, from an acquaintance who owned an apartment complex, before they parted company. It was work he was happy to have right now, with the start of his busy season still a month off and his business feeling the pinch of a lousy economy. He thanked her, and they shook hands perfunctorily before going their separate ways, each confused about the failure to connect and wondering if the relationship was doomed to be remembered as a one-night stand.

***

On a blustery sunny day in early March, Luis drove his Chevy pickup with his two favorite employees, Hector and Felix, to an apartment complex on Colonial Avenue off West State Street. Though Luis didn't know it, this low-income property was once the site of the grand residence of Revolutionary War General Philemon Dickinson, known in the day as "the Hermitage." Dickinson had watched through a field glass from across the river as Hessian Jaegers billeted in the Hermitage ransacked it, tossing expensive Louis XIV furniture into the yard for spite and into the fireplace for warmth. Fortunately, George Washington had cleared out the Hessians in 1776, and Luis's job would only entail cleaning out the flowerbeds and planting spring flowers.

He was glad to be out in the fresh air and working with his hands again. Although it was not yet officially spring, the days were getting longer and the sun provided a hint of warmer days to come. The winter had been almost unbearable for Luis, though that had little to do with the weather, which by all accounts had been quite mild.

The sunshine had drawn many of the locals outside to sit on their porches, work on their cars, and chit-chat with their neighbors. Luis couldn't understand how so many apparently able-bodied men could idly take in the day instead of working. Children of all ages, from toddlers to teens, were also out in force. Occasionally, one or two of the more curious little "gangstas" would stroll by the job site to watch at close range as Luis and his men—presumably illegal aliens—labored in the dirt among the barren shrubbery. Once, a boy of about twelve lingered a little too long near the pickup, but Luis had had the good sense to lock it.

The first raindrop fell just after lunch. Initially, Luis welcomed the precipitation. It would nourish the new seed they'd planted on the winter-ravaged front lawn of the apartment grounds. Soon, however, the increasing ferocity of the downpour forced him and his crew to run for cover in the pickup. Even the locals withdrew into the shelter of their rundown homes.

After half an hour with the windows fogged and no let-up in sight, Luis sent Hector and Felix to retrieve the tools while he tried to tune in the weather on the truck radio. As his men loaded the equipment into the back of the pickup, he noticed how the cab of the truck seemed to sink into the ground. He got out to take a look and realized that all four of his tires had been punctured. He pictured that twelve-year-old punk smiling as he heard the forecast through the window he'd left open, "Rain, heavy at times, throughout the afternoon and into the night."

***

Dripping wet, Darius emptied his pockets into the plastic container and placed it on the conveyor belt. He waited anxiously until his wallet, keys, cell phone, wristwatch, and pocket change sailed safely through the scanner before he stepped forward. Under the close scrutiny of a massive and heavily muscled State House security guard, he held his breath and walked through the metal detection booth unscathed.

A black female security guard was running a second check on the contents of Tina's pocketbook when Darius caught up with her. The unsmiling guard placed Tina's rain-soaked umbrella into a rack along with assorted others. "You can come back for this when you're done, honey." Her pleasant tone took them by surprise as she handed each of them a visitor's pass.

"Are you sure you want to do this?" Tina asked Darius, unnerved by the tight security they encountered as they entered the hallway. "I should be in school," she added guiltily.

"Relax," he said cheerfully. "You're only missing a study hall. We'll take the tour, and I'll have you home in time to help Roberto with his homework."

"But it's pouring outside," she said nervously. "Besides, I've taken this tour already, with my family—remember?" She was not one to take chances, and cutting class, even if it was only a study hall, was playing havoc with her conscience. Especially after the "no surprises" conversation she had with her father.

When he didn't respond, she asked for the umpteenth time, "What is it we're looking for, Darius?"

"I told you—I don't know exactly," he said. "But since we weren't able to identify the owner of that copy of *Common Sense*, it seemed like other clues were leading us here."

"Clues to *what*?" she asked in exasperation.

"I don't *know*," he grumbled, his voice rising in pitch. "But everywhere I turn, things keep pointing to the State House."

She was flummoxed. "What *things*?"

"Signs, clues, tips," he said. "There's some secret this old building has to tell, and we're going to find out what it is."

"You've been watching too many programs on the History Channel," she groaned. "Not everything old has a mystery behind it."

"Then why are there Masonic symbols on that arch in the Trentoniana Room connecting it directly to this place?" he asked, trying to keep his voice down. "And how is it that two leading local historians didn't know about it? Did you see old owl-eyes and Professor Collins light up after my little discovery?"

His emphasis on the word "my" was not lost on Tina. She rolled her eyes.

Spotting several state staffers conferring in a circle across the hall, the two teens stopped and waited to be helped. Tina recognized the stylish woman she had met at her father's citation ceremony back in October. If she remembered correctly, her name was Abby something. She clearly remembered that her mother had been taken aback by how well this attractive woman—*la rubia,* the blonde—seemed to know her father.

"It's fate, I tell you," Darius concluded as he stood with his back against the wall, below the paintings of the New Jersey signers. "Now all we need to do is beat Professor Collins and Shelly Reed to whatever the secret is."

"Why do you think there's a *secret* associated with that old relic?"

"Because of what the professor told me at the bank, about triangles and arches and their connection to the Masons. The Masons protected secrets, Tina. It's just too coincidental, and Professor Collins knows it, too."

She was about to point out the portrait of John Hart on the gallery wall when Abby walked over.

"It's Tina, isn't it?" she inquired amiably. "You're Luis Alma's daughter—I remember you from the ceremony. I'm really sorry about your mom." She added, "I'm Abby."

"Thank you," Tina said demurely. "This is my ... friend, Darius Hudson."

"Nice to meet you," Darius said with a broad smile, shaking Abby's hand.

"How's your father doing?" she asked, turning to Tina. "I haven't heard from him in awhile. I hope everything's all right."

Tina was dumbstruck by the implied intimacy in Abby's words. "You haven't heard from him?" she repeated, clueless to what Abby was talking about, but afraid to let her know it.

"He hasn't been returning my phone calls," Abby said. "I don't want to be a pest, but I need an answer soon."

Tina glanced at Darius, who just shrugged. "Right, you need an answer," she said slowly, trying not to show her confusion.

Abby misread Tina's reaction as a sign of Luis's rejection, not knowing he hadn't even discussed the matter with his family. "I was afraid he'd turn me down," she said awkwardly. "I guess I shouldn't be surprised, though. Why would a good and decent man like your father agree to run for mayor?"

Tina shook her head. "Yeah, it's a real surprise to me," she offered truthfully.

Helen Nelson suddenly broke from the corner group discussion and stepped over to the center of the Rotunda. "Listen up, everyone," she said, rapping her heavy bracelet on the binder she was carrying. "All those here for the tour, please come forward," she waved sweetly, noting the visitor badges clipped to the small group milling around nearby.

"Excuse us," Darius said to Abby as he and Tina stepped in closer to hear what Helen had to say.

"I'm sorry," the HPCA director continued, "but we've just been informed that due to flash flooding in the area, the State House is closing early today."

As scattered boos greeted the announcement, two uniformed New Jersey State Troopers appeared at Helen's side to enforce an orderly departure.

"Feel free to come back again soon, but for now kindly return your badges to the guard station," Helen added with a practiced smile.

Though he was disappointed the tour had been cancelled, Darius was quick to recognize an opportunity. Slipping his badge into his pocket, he pulled Tina down the hall before Abby could corner her again, rushing her toward the main entrance, avoiding the security station.

"Wait!" she said. "My umbrella—"

"Forget about it," he said without looking back. "I'll buy you a new one." And with that he hustled her through the doors and out into the rain.

30

Still Water Runs Deep

*E*ven as a kid, Dominic Rosetti knew the value of hard work. Growing up in Chambersburg, this second generation American, son of a steel worker and grandson of a stonemason from Calabria, hawked newspapers and shined shoes on the corner of Market and Broad to help his family make ends meet. Those early years formed his character, and although he couldn't have known it at the time, one particular event in the summer of 1955 would cement his most enduring friendship and teach him a lesson that would help him face countless challenges throughout his life.

On a hot steamy day in August, Dominic was camping with his Boy Scout troop on Treasure Island, a liver-shaped tuft of marshy woodland in the middle of the Delaware River just below Frenchtown, when disaster struck. A record-setting flood followed a double thrashing by Hurricanes Connie and Diane less than a week apart. The usually placid Delaware at Trenton reached a peak flood stage of nearly twenty-nine feet on August 19, 1955.

Streets turned into surging rivers, and the Trenton War Memorial became an island surrounded by a sea of swift-flowing muddy water. The Capitol was flooded, and in the low-lying Island Section of Trenton, residents had to be evacuated by boat, with more than a thousand people stranded for nearly two weeks. At least fifty bridges were lost or damaged in the ferocious deluge, including the 902-foot Yardley Bridge when an uprooted bungalow swept downstream and struck it. Two fun seekers from Princeton drowned, and Dominic Rosetti was one of four hundred boys from various Scout troops who were airlifted to safety by Army and Navy helicopters. In surviving, he came to understand that "whatever doesn't kill you makes you stronger."

He also learned that, in time of danger, there are people you can count on to do what's right and these are the people you want in your corner. He formed an instant bond with Charlie Stillwater, a reserved young scoutmaster whose quick thinking had saved his troop from certain death during the flood. Charlie had instructed the boys to string their tents to the trees, forming hammocks that allowed them to hang above the rising floodwaters until the rescue teams arrived.

Their friendship endured and, on countless trips together over the years, the normally reclusive Charlie Stillwater taught Dominic how to fish, hunt, trap, and survive in the wilderness. The summer after Dominic graduated from Trenton Central High School, he and Charlie canoed the entire fresh water length of the Delaware River from Hancock, New York, to the Marine Terminal at Duck Island in Trenton.

During their wonderful summer adventures, while huddled nightly around the campfire, Charlie—a modern nomad with Native American blood running through his veins—told Dominic about growing up in Indian Mills, New Jersey, and learning the ways of the native people from the elders who still practiced the sacred arts of their ancestors. Charlie told the tale of his great-great-grandfather, snatched as a baby by the Iroquois during a raid on a British outpost in upstate New York, before the colonies split with the English Crown. It was told that the entire family perished in the raid, with the exception of the baby who was raised by his captors as one of their own. The boy, who was called "Two Feathers" for the red-tail hawk and blue heron feathers in his headband that symbolized his dual cultural identity, was not only accepted by the tribe but would eventually marry the chief's only daughter.

When smallpox hit Two Feather's village, nearly decimating it, the tribe joined up with a group of Lenni Lenape who had traveled to New York from Brotherton in New Jersey. Later, when a few members of the group decided to return to Brotherton—now a white settlement known as Indian Mills—Two Feathers and his family made the journey with them. There, the family adopted the Anglo surname

"Stillwater" in honor of the calm peaceful Delaware River that had carried them safely to their new home in the Pine Barrens of New Jersey. Members of the family had lived in Indian Mills ever since.

Charlie himself had a face and neck riddled with pockmarks, a reminder of the mixed heredity that had actually saved his ancestors from the disease that killed so many of their pureblooded brethren. As a young man, he developed first a passion for learning and later for teaching survival skills and appreciation for the natural world. The secrets he learned from his elders—using sticks to start a fire, building lean-to's, and foraging for fresh food and water—impressed the Boy Scouts of America. He became a decorated Eagle Scout and later a well-respected scoutmaster for the organization.

Dominic and Charlie lost touch for a number of years after Dominic took a job as a courier with Roma Bank, settled down with a pert teller he'd met there, and started raising three children. While Dominic's kids were growing up and he and his wife were growing apart, Charlie moved up to Titusville where he started a canoe rental business along the river. As fate would have it, Charlie's move was largely responsible for Dominic's defining role in city government.

Dominic was unhappy in his bank job with little opportunity for advancement, and while he would have happily followed his father's footsteps into a factory job, by that time, the rubber, ceramic, and steel industries had already left town. State and local government seemed to offer the best chance for steady employment, and he soon found himself on the municipal payroll.

After less than a year of working a security detail for the Office of Public Safety, Dominic became tangentially involved in a State Police investigation into the disappearance of the teenaged daughter of a well-to-do Jewish doctor. It was a high-profile investigation, both because of the family involved and due to widespread speculation—sensationalized in the press—that the girl had disappeared while on a moonlight river rendezvous with her black boyfriend.

Dominic was aware that Charlie sometimes assisted local authorities in river searches for victims of boating accidents, and on his recommendation, his mentor was brought in on the case. The body turned up precisely when and where Charlie predicted it would: four days later, after the gases of decomposition floated it to the surface, just below the "falls" where the tidal water backs up into a calm eddy. The gruesome find solidified Charlie Stillwater's reputation as "King of the River Rats" and led to Dominic's ascension as Trenton's public safety director.

Eventually, Dominic and his wife ended their tempestuous love-hate relationship in an acrimonious divorce. By this time, their children had grown up and moved away. Dominic stayed in his beloved Chambersburg and rented a modest apartment within walking distance of his favorite restaurant, Rossi's. He also resumed his friendship with Charlie, who had sold his canoe rental business in an act of protest against the state when property taxes reached the level of "government extortion," in his words.

Charlie tried to live for awhile in seclusion, without electricity or running water in a hut he'd slapped together on Rotary Island just south of the Scudders Falls Bridge, but the flood of September 2004 ended life in his little Eden almost before it began.

Still alive and kicking at seventy-three, Charlie had for the last few years been living alone in a rented room in a rundown boarding house on Monmouth Street, paying his rent with the money he earned from the job his old friend Dominic Rosetti had gotten for him—running the ancient electric elevator inside the Trenton Battle Monument. The job provided Charlie with countless hours of happiness. Riding up in the cable car with the park's visitors offered a bird's-eye view of the picturesque Trenton cityscape against the backdrop of his beloved Delaware River.

Whatever else could be ascribed to Trenton, it was, first and foremost, a river town subject to Mother Nature's fury. Few people knew that better than Dominic Rosetti. Thus, it was no surprise that by the time Mayor Jimmy Dodd phoned his public safety director in a near panic, Dominic had already spoken to the National Weather Service, the executive director of the Delaware River Basin Commission, and the governor, and was himself en route to the Capitol Complex to oversee the disaster emergency plan that he and his old friend Charlie Stillwater had designed.

31

Dom

E verything is under control, Mr. Mayor," Dominic Rosetti shouted into his crackling two-way. "My boys got the filtration plant sandbagged. The water's safe, and the National Guard is on alert."

Personally, Dominic considered Mayor Jimmy Dodd a two-faced weasel, and he made no secret of how he felt in face-to-face meetings when they were alone. But on the job, especially in matters of municipal emergencies where protocol mattered, he knew his place and put partisan politics aside. He treated the mayor with the respect he had for the office, if not the man.

Dominic turned his hunter green Eddie Bauer Ford Explorer down Perry Street heading for North Warren, where traffic was backed up coming out of the state employee parking lots. He would have preferred to listen to Sinatra on his CD player, but he turned down the volume and continued his conversation with His Honor the Mayor instead.

"Yes, sir," he continued after a pause. "We've got bedding and hot food in place over at the Holland Middle School. You can give the order to evacuate the Island Section whenever you like. They have a place to go. Once the state workers have cleared the lots, I think we should also close down Route 29 from the tunnel north to Ribsam's. The river is supposed to crest around 7 P.M. Riegelsville is bracing for a surge. No point in letting anyone try out their water wings on those roads tonight."

Dominic checked his watch. It was a little after five. The reports he had received indicated that the heavy rain had clogged storm drains with debris, causing the initial flash-flooding conditions. Construction encroaching on the wetlands did not allow adequate runoff; combined with melting snow and torrential rains soaking the Pocono-Catskills corridor to the north, Dominic recognized a recipe for disaster. He just hoped it didn't reach the same proportions as the Flood of '55.

A burst of static from the two-way interrupted his thoughts. "Chief, this is Haney. We've got a stalled vehicle blocking traffic on West State near Calhoun, do you copy?"

"Roger that, Otis," Dominic barked. "Have the cops redirect. I'll be right there."

Rain pounded his windshield as he shot across Warren over to Bank Street to avoid the rush-hour traffic feeding into East Hanover. He made a left onto North Willow then picked up West Hanover to Greens Place, where he pulled over across from the State Museum. Leaving his Explorer running, he walked down West State toward Calhoun in the driving rain.

"It didn't look that deep—I thought I could get through," Abigail Treadwell-Tucker explained to Dominic through the window of her stalled silver Mercedes, the water up to her wheel wells. A cherry-top police cruiser sealed off the lane as cars snaked around them, turning up West State.

"She sits too low to the ground." He offered her a hand out of the car. "Do you have AAA?"

"Yes!" she yelled above the rain striking the roof and the sloshing of passing cars. "They're on the way."

"Yeah, and I'm Humpy-Dumpty," he said surveying the scene. Rain splashed off his hardhat and into Abby's face. "Come on. I'll have a man stay with the car until the truck comes. Where can I take you?"

"Thank you … Dom," Abby said, reading the nametag stitched onto the pocket of his yellow-and-black-striped nylon vest. She did her best to hide her revulsion as she recalled her first encounter with Dominic Rosetti in the mayor's office after the Markham funeral. She'd done her best to put the leering public safety director in his place, and he was no doubt in the mood for revenge. "I'm fine, really."

"Listen, sister," his voice rose over the noise, "you have two choices—me, or the overworked, underpaid sonofabitch who's coming for you in his smelly rig. You already know *I'm* no good—hell, you've probably figured out that D-o-m stands for 'dirty old man.' But I'm parked right over there, and I can take you some place where you can get warm and dry in a hurry. Or, if you prefer to take your chances, you can wait it out for Mister Goodwrench—assuming he can get through the roadblocks."

She was quick to see the wisdom in his crude assessment. In these conditions, there was no telling how soon the tow truck might arrive. Flashing him a fake smile, she held out her keys. He tossed them to Otis Haney, a sixtyish black man in an orange rain slicker who was standing a few feet away, grinning ear to ear, amused by the interplay between his cantankerous boss and this svelte, pampered fox.

"Now comes the fun part." Dominic turned his back to her and bent over slightly, hoping she didn't catch the grimace on his face or the groan rumbling in his throat. "Unless you want to ruin those fancy new Pradas, you'd better hop on."

In Abby's mind, there were times when dignity must give way to practicality. She removed her shoes and jumped aboard. Wading through the murky, knee-high water, Dominic Rosetti—Sir Galahad in a dayglow nylon vest—carried the damsel in distress to the safety of his waiting transport.

***

Roberto stepped off the bus at Market and Warren, clad in his New York Yankees baseball cap and his Philadelphia Eagles windbreaker—a wardrobe combination that might have drawn stares and recriminations in some U.S. cities, but not in Trenton. In Trenton, if such attire wasn't commonplace, at least it was acceptable.

His grandfather had gone so far as to tell him that this was what was wrong with Trenton: "divided loyalties." Without a major sports team of its own and stuck between New York and Philadelphia, Trenton was a sort of no-man's land where people on the same block—even in the same household—chose their "home" teams from different cities, frequently mixing and matching as Roberto did.

There was a lot more than sports on Roberto's mind right now, as he sloshed south along Warren Street, his cap pulled down low over his new buzz cut, bracing his slight frame against the wind and rain.

He was a nine-year-old boy who had recently lost his mother to an act of violence. He couldn't communicate with his hero father, whom he adored. He was scared to death he'd never measure up to his standards, and he had just failed a social studies quiz because of a missed question about Cuba, of all things. The walls were closing in on him. His Latino friends teased him, saying his sister was dating a black guy. The black kids beat up on him just because he was Hispanic. The drug dealers were hanging around his schoolyard with their crack cocaine, disguised as students and selling the shit like candy, meting out threats and beatings to the uncooperative. The situation appeared hopeless.

The teachers, administrators, and counselors, for the most part, seemed focused on their own problems: ongoing contract disputes, sick kids and aging parents, extramarital affairs, and addictions of their own. They couldn't completely ignore the problem students, but few noticed or cared about the needs of a quiet fourth grader who did relatively well in school and had never made any trouble.

That left Papi Raul. He was Roberto's rock, but now he had missed that question about Cuba. As if it wasn't bad enough that Mrs. Garcia was already chasing his grandfather out of the house, now Papi would hate him for not studying where they came from.

Roberto crossed the street and climbed up the ramp toward the Lower Free Bridge. The rain had let up a little bit, but the river looked high and angry. Cars with their lights on were crossing the bridge at a snail's pace in both directions.

He stopped for a minute to look at the famous lighted sign: "TRENTON MAKES, THE WORLD TAKES." He remembered his social studies teacher explaining that the slogan was a contest winner dating back to 1911 when Trenton was a totally different place. In those days the city was known for pottery, steel, rubber, cigars, oyster crackers, and pork roll, selling its products proudly all over the world. He could remember all that, and none of it mattered to him. Why couldn't he remember who ruled Cuba before Castro?

As he made his way onto the bridge crosswalk, Roberto slipped on the rain-slicked iron grating and took a hard fall. Cars honked as they rumbled past but didn't stop. Roberto simply ignored them as he climbed back on his feet. The loud gurgling sound of swift flowing water echoed up through the openings in the grates.

Down along Route 29, traffic was at a virtual standstill in both directions. Police cars and emergency vehicles were trying to make their way around the stalled traffic approaching the bridge, but even the shoulders were jammed.

Roberto peered over the edge cautiously. He felt the spray hit his face. Garbage of every sort—planking, bottles, cans, tires, weeds—swept past in the rushing brown water. Stabbed with a sudden fit of dizziness, he leaned backward and grabbed unsteadily for the railing. He closed his eyes for a moment to compose himself, then reached into his pants pocket for his cell phone. Flipping it open, he took a photo for posterity then pressed #2 on the speed dial.

32

Floodgates

B y the time Darius and Tina got to the bridge, the police had it blocked off on both sides. Two uniformed policemen were already out on the bridge trying to coax Roberto down from the railing ledge. Facing south with the famous sign illuminated in the background, the wind and rain lashed the boy as he stood on the railing and clung to the "W" in "World."

Darius had been about to drop Tina off at Rossi's half a block away from her home when she got her brother's desperate call. The hurried photo he transmitted, intended as his farewell image, told her where he was. The ride over was a blur except for the two calls she made. First, she called her father's cell, but it went straight to voicemail. Calling home, Mrs. Garcia answered. She said Luis had called earlier to say his cell phone had died, he was getting four new tires put on the truck, and he was going to be late for dinner.

"Sorry, miss," said the cop guarding the bridge entrance on the Jersey side, putting out his hand to prevent Tina from advancing. "You can't go any further."

"That's my brother up there!" she shouted, tears rolling down her cheeks. "Darius, do something!" she pleaded.

Darius stood mute and shaking, unable to speak or move another inch. He was holding onto Tina tightly, as if it was *his* life in peril.

"I'll handle this, sergeant," snapped Dominic Rosetti coming up the ramp behind the kids. "What's your brother's name, miss?" he asked Tina in a gentle voice.

"Roberto," she said between sobs. "We just lost our mother, and I don't know where my father is."

"Whatever happens, you need to stay put," Dominic commanded the two teens. "This bridge is a dangerous place to be with the river rising." He gave the sergeant a look to be sure his order was understood.

That's all Darius needed to hear. He stayed behind Tina and couldn't even look at the scene out on the bridge.

The public safety director ducked under the yellow police tape and walked slowly out onto the bridge. He motioned the two patrolmen who had been talking to Roberto to get out of his way. "Get the boat ready just in case," he whispered to one of them as he moved into place.

Dominic looked up at the petrified boy standing out on the handrail, balancing precariously above the dangerous current. Seeing his baseball cap, Dominic called out, "You a Yankee fan?"

Ignoring the question, Roberto inched farther out on the narrow handrail, still gripping the neon "W" tightly.

"I am," Dominic shouted above the din of the rushing water. "Seen all the greats—DiMaggio, Mantle, Berra. Who's your favorite?"

Roberto turned his face away.

"I'll bet it's A-Rod."

Roberto shook his head.

Dominic breathed a little easier having gained the boy's attention. "Jeter, then. I'm with you on that. He's the best. Did you see him when he played for the Thunder?" he asked, referring to the Yankee's Double-A affiliate in Trenton.

Roberto nodded.

Dominic pursued the small opening. "So you must be a pretty big Thunder fan, too?"

Roberto made no acknowledgment. He resumed his mesmerized gaze into the river below.

"Listen, Roberto," Dominic pressed, afraid he might lose the boy at any moment. "Come down from there, and I'll give you two tick-ets to any Thunder game you want." He pointed to where Darius and Tina were watching with nail-biting intensity. "You can take your sister over there. She loves you, and you have her scared to death right now."

Roberto looked over to where Tina was standing. Her eyes were wide with fear, her hands covering her mouth.

"Papi and Papa, too?" he asked hopefully.

"Yeah, sure," Dominic agreed without hesitation. "And all your friends, too—anybody you want."

Dominic noticed how the boy stiffened up at the mention of the word "friends" and quickly took a different tack. "Listen, Roberto, I know you're upset about your mother, but this won't make things better. Your family loves you. They need you. They want you to come down from there and go home with them. Believe me, they're hurting just as badly as you are."

As he was speaking, a young beaver struggling to stay afloat in the high, raging current, swept past them. Roberto and Dominic watched in the fading light of dusk, as the helpless animal bobbed up and down before disappearing below the water's surface.

Dominic turned back to the boy. "That's what'll happen to you if you go into the river," he said, moving a few inches closer to him. "That beaver had no choice, but you do. Come on, Roberto—what's it gonna be?"

"Do you really have Thunder tickets?" the boy asked, fighting back tears.

"Swear to God," Dominic said crossing his heart. "Any game you want."

Roberto stared hard at him, trying to decide if he could be trusted.

"Tell you what," Dominic said upping the ante, "I'll throw in hot dogs and sodas for everyone, too."

Roberto felt his stomach growl. He hadn't noticed until now just how hungry he was—or how scared. As the reality of his predicament dawned on him, he stood frozen in fear.

Dominic recognized the panic in the boy's eyes. It was the same fear he had seen on the faces of his friends decades ago, during a camping trip on a small island in the middle of the Delaware when the land beneath them suddenly ceased to exist. He knew what he had to do. "Okay, Roberto, I'm coming to get you. You're gonna be fine. Just stay where you are."

Slowly, awkwardly, the heavyset man climbed out onto the catwalk. The spectators on the banks held their breath as the public safety director edged toward the boy.

"I'm scared," Roberto said. "I don't want to end up like that beaver."

"You won't, Roberto, trust me. I've done this a million times. Why, did you know that back in the big flood of '55, me and my buddy Charlie Stillwater fished off the roof of a house that was floating down the river, just for kicks?"

"Nah, uh," Roberto challenged.

"Uh, huh," replied Dominic, trying to keep the boy distracted until he was close enough to grab him. "Caught me a great big Atlantic sturgeon, size of a refrigerator. That was dinner for three weeks straight. I never had sturgeon since, and I don't ever want to eat one again."

He finally reached the boy. The two of them were shaking for the same reason, though Dominic did his best to appear calm. He tossed away his hard hat then his slippery nylon vest, knowing they would just get in his way. "Now, listen carefully, Roberto. Whatever you do, don't look down. Close your eyes if you have to. And when I count to three, I want you to let go. *Capiche?*" The boy nodded his head nervously.

"One." Roberto closed his eyes. From behind him Dominic leaned up on the railing, unsteadily.

"Two." Dominic reached up and laced his arms around Roberto's legs in a bear hug.

"Three!" As Roberto released his grip on the "W," he and Dominic tumbled backward onto the catwalk.

***

A joyful celebration erupted on the Jersey side of the river as Dominic and Roberto walked arm in arm across the bridge. Tina squeezed her brother so tightly he felt she might choke him to death. Raul and Luis, who had arrived moments earlier, thanked Dominic with tears in their eyes as they were reunited with Roberto. Luis wrapped a warm blanket around his sobbing son. "I'm sorry," Roberto said to his father.

"Don't be," Luis said, holding his son close. "This is my fault, Roberto, not yours." He turned to Dominic. "That was an incredibly brave act," he said.

"It's nothing, really," Dominic replied humbly. "I've had plenty of practice."

Tina hesitated for a moment before introducing Darius to her family. Inwardly, she was disappointed at how he'd seemed to cower in the face of the near disaster, but she tried not to let it show. The bridge ordeal had ended happily and Roberto was safe, so she put her feelings aside as her father greeted Darius with a firm handshake.

"So, we finally get to meet your library partner," Raul said, grinning slyly at Tina.

"No more surprises or secrets, Dad," she said to her father.

"That goes for me, too," Darius said taking her hand. "I should have told you on the way over, but I was afraid you'd think I was some kind of wimp. I'm scared to death of bridges."

"It's called *gephyrophobia*," volunteered Abby as she joined the group. "Fear of bridges." She had watched the rescue scene play out through the passenger side window of Dominic's Explorer. "It's like vertigo only worse," she said. "I'll bet you're afraid of heights, too." Darius nodded in embarrassment.

"You mean to tell me you've never crossed this bridge?" Tina asked him.

"Tina, I've never been outside of New Jersey," he confessed.

At that moment, Mayor Jimmy Dodd bounded briskly over to join the gathering, which now included citizens, public officials, and city cops.

"Rosetti," he barked, trying to take charge. "What the *hell* do you think you were doing out there? You should have checked with me before pulling a stunt like that. If you or the boy had been killed, it would have been *my* ass in a sling."

"Then you must be glad we survived, Mr. Mayor," Dominic said in a low even voice, controlling his anger.

"There wasn't any time, sir," Abby said to Dodd. "I can vouch for that." She turned to give Dominic an appreciative smile. "Funny, but before today, I would never have pegged you as the protective type, at least not where women and children are concerned."

"Nobody's perfect, Miss Tucker," Dominic said, giving her a wink. "But in this situation, I think you'd have done the same thing."

Dodd threw her a cold look. "We have experts trained to handle these kinds of situations, Abby," he said in a clipped tone, "and Mr. Rosetti knows that. His rash actions could have endangered the boy's life."

"Excuse me, Your Honor," she said in a frank tone, "but the boy's life was *already* in danger."

"That's not the point, Abby," Mayor Dodd argued.

"What *is* your point?" Luis jumped in. "This man saved my son's life and that's all that matters."

"I'll decide what matters, Mr. Alma," Dodd said poking a finger in his chest. "Is that clear?" His face was as red as a chili pepper. "Everyone wants to be a fucking hero, but who takes the heat when things go to hell? Me, that's who!"

The news reporters and camera crew arrived at the tail end of Dodd's tirade.

"It's all yours, Mr. Mayor," Dominic said stepping aside and motioning to the press. As he walked off toward his SUV, he called back over his shoulder to Abby in a playful tone, "Coming, dear?"

She addressed Luis in a low voice that only he could hear. "Dominic Rosetti may be an arrogant jerk, but when someone needs him, he's there for them, no questions asked. I wish I could say the same of you, but I *am* glad your son is all right."

He stood speechless as she walked off to follow her ride home.

33

A Man's Heart

*T*he way to a man's heart is through a good guacamole," Mrs.
Garcia chuckled to Tina as she removed the seeds from and
diced the tomatoes. She was one of those perpetually posi-
tive people who either cheered you up or got on your nerves. When
Tina had asked her for help in preparing dinner, she had responded
enthusiastically, feeling like part of the family, especially in the company of Raul, who was obviously enjoying the banter.

"Mrs. G, for the life of me, I can't remember what my mom put in
the *ropa vieja* to make it so tender," Tina lamented, referring to the
shredded beef dish her father loved so much.

"Oh, honey, I'm sure she used a touch of cilantro and some good
virgin olive oil," Mrs. Garcia said warmly. "She must have been a
wonderful cook."

"She loved it," Tina said, "but she never seemed to have enough
time."

"That's the problem with this country—nobody has the time to
cook anymore," Mrs. Garcia said, growing nostalgic. "When I was
growing up in Vera Cruz, we used to have the whole family over for
dinner once a week. Aunts, uncles, cousins—everybody brought
whatever they had and it was like a party."

Raul had been listening attentively, and he finally spoke up. "The
problem in Cuba is that nobody has anything to put on the table. Here
at least there's always plenty to eat."

Tina rolled her eyes as her grandfather repeated his often-shared
remark. He dipped a tortilla chip in Mrs. Garcia's guacamole and
gave his enthusiastic approval.

"I told you," Mrs. Garcia whispered to Tina with a wink as he helped himself to a plate of chips and a bowl of her special recipe to take back into the living room.

Raul seemed to be softening to Mrs. G's advances. She was a very nice woman, after all, and she certainly knew how to cook. She was a little too jolly for his taste but not bad looking for sixty-five. Her husband, a few years older than she, had died almost ten years ago, leaving her with a modest home, fully paid off, and a small pension from his thirty years at Congoleum. Raul and his wife Anna had known Jose and Pilar Garcia since the early 1960s when they were two of only four Latino families living in Chambersburg. The other two families were Puerto Rican, and perhaps because they had been the first to break into the traditionally Italian neighborhood, sometimes acted like they owned it.

Little by little, the Almas and Garcias had seen the Burg change as more and more Italians moved out to the suburbs, selling their row homes to families from Mexico, Guatemala, Cuba, and the Dominican Republic. While the Hispanics shared a common language, prejudice ran deep and stereotypes kept them at arm's length until they got to know one another as individuals. The Puerto Ricans had gotten the last of the factory jobs, so the Cubans became groundskeepers and gardeners. The Mexicans found work in restaurants and small grocery stores. The Guatemalans followed as laborers and construction helpers. The only thing left for the Dominicans to become was mechanics and car stereo installers. Consequently, the one-time Italian stronghold was quickly becoming a Latin American melting pot where one was more likely to hear Spanish spoken than either Italian or English.

For Raul, diversity had its rewards. He had discovered a great little cigar shop owned by a young Dominican, a family-style Mexican bar and restaurant run by Guatemalans, a Costa Rican laundry and tailor shop with a Brazilian who did shoe repair, and a barbershop still run by an old *Siciliano*. By the time he retired, he was very happy with the way his neighborhood was shaping up.

***

Luis was sitting on the edge of Roberto's bed for a long overdue father and son conversation. He looked around the tiny room for a clue as to where to begin, his eyes taking in the Derek Jeter poster, the Eagles pennant, a baseball glove, and a soccer ball, before coming to rest on the picture on the nightstand. It was Roberto and Tina with their mother and grandfather on a day trip to the Camden Aquarium from last summer.

He picked up the silver framed photo. "I guess I've been out of the picture for a long time, haven't I?"

"You had to work that day," Roberto said without looking at his father.

"I'm really sorry I haven't been there for you, son," Luis struggled to connect. "You know how much you mean to me, don't you?"

"Sure," Roberto responded without making it any easier.

"I love you and your sister more than anything in this world. I'm sorry I never told you this before, but I know how smart you are and I think you're a great kid. You used to tell your mom about whatever was bothering you, and I wish she was still with us, but you can talk to me about anything—I promise I'll do my best to listen and help. You're not alone in this." With that Roberto crumbled into his father's arms.

"Dad, it's hard in school, and I don't know what to do," he groaned.

"Are we talking about your schoolwork or something else, son?" Luis asked diplomatically.

"My grades are okay except that stupid quiz, but the other kids drive me nuts. Dad, what do the Mexicans have against Cubans? What did we ever do to them? And why do the Puerto Rican kids think they're so great? We speak the same language, so why can't we all get along? I thought that was what America stood for—that's what mom always said."

"Land of the free, home of the brave," Luis mumbled, thinking about what his son was dealing with at nine years old. "Listen, Roberto, people act really stupid sometimes. When I was in the army, I bunked with guys from every ethnic background you can think of—Africans, Italians, Germans, you name it—and you know what I learned?" Roberto shrugged in response. "We're all pretty much the same. There are good people from every race, religion, and culture you'll ever meet, and bad ones, too. No one group is better or worse than any other. You've got to be smart enough to remember that, especially when someone's trying to sell you their bigoted ideas. And when that does happen, the real trick is to stand up for what you know is true." Luis squeezed his son's shoulders warmly. "It's not easy, but I've got your back, soldier." With that, he saw a relaxed smile appear on his son's face at last.

"Dad, what was it like being a soldier?" Roberto wanted to know.

"It was a lot of things," Luis answered, mulling the question. "You know how your mom always told you to do your best in everything you do?"

Roberto nodded his head in agreement.

"Well, when you're a soldier you *have* to do your best, because other people's lives depend on it. There are no second chances."

"Why did you become a soldier?"

"There were a lot of reasons," Luis said thoughtfully. "First of all, I felt I owed it to my country, to America. You know Papi came here from Cuba, where people don't have the right to live where they want, work where they want, or even say what they want to say. But I was born here, in the United States, a country that stands for liberty, freedom, and justice for all. Those aren't just words, Roberto, but ideals we have to fight for and protect. This really is the land of opportunity. That doesn't mean everything is easy, but it does mean you have a real chance here."

"You have a better chance if you're an Anglo," Roberto said, speaking his mind.

"Why would you say something like that?" Luis said, the remark taking him by surprise.

"That's what everyone says at school."

"Well, it's not true," Luis said forcefully. "Everybody in this country has a chance, and I mean *everybody*. People use race as an excuse not to try and do their best, but I don't buy it anymore. There are single mothers, black, white, *and* Latina, working two jobs just so their kids can have a decent home and stay in school. There are rich white guys who volunteer at soup kitchens instead of spending their time at country clubs, because they care about other people. And look at me—my family didn't have a dime when I was growing up, but with the help of the GI Bill, I put myself through night school at the community college and went on to graduate from Rider University with a business degree. Now I've got my own business and a chance to make a better life for you and Tina. There is opportunity out there for everyone, Roberto, whether you're black, white, brown, red, or purple." The remark brought a smile to the boy's face. "All you need is to believe in yourself and be willing to work for it."

"I didn't mean to make you mad, Papa. It's just what they say at school."

"Well, don't buy it, not even for a minute," Luis said. "I know it's tough, son, but I promise you that there are good people ready and willing to help you become whatever you want to be in this life. Don't let racism and narrow-minded people stand in your way."

"Okay, Papa," Roberto said nodding. "I won't."

Luis gave him a smile and mussed his hair, then added in a friendly voice, "I was thinking we might try to talk some of these things over with a school counselor or a priest, Roberto. What do you think?"

"The school counselors don't like us Latino kids," Roberto said, surprising his father again. "They say we're troublemakers."

"Well, sometimes you have to make a little trouble to wake people up," Luis answered, thinking out loud. "But don't worry about it. We can always get your Uncle Miguel on the phone for a talk."

"I don't need a priest, I just need you, Papa," Roberto said, holding his father in a tight hug.

"I hear you, son," he returned the squeeze. "Now, I don't know about you, but I smell something good cooking. We better get to the kitchen before Papi eats it all up!"

***

The table was complete when Tina put fresh flowers in her mother's favorite vase as a centerpiece. Mrs. Garcia said grace, and they loaded their plates with shredded beef, rice and beans, fried plantains, sautéed zucchini, and chips with guacamole. When Luis thanked Mrs. Garcia, she mentioned that it was all Tina's idea and she was only too happy to help, anytime. He winked at his daughter, thinking what a fine young woman she was becoming.

After they'd eaten but before the table was cleared, Luis said, "There's something we need to talk about as a family." He stopped Mrs. Garcia from leaving the table by grabbing her wrist. "Stay, Mrs. G—you're family." She blushed happily and even Raul nodded his head in agreement, although he regarded her in the manner of a kid sister you can't get away from.

"I say you go for it," Tina threw her opinion into the ring.

"I'm not sure it's a good move," Raul responded cautiously.

"It's time for a real change," Tina added, "and you've got enough support to make things happen."

"The grass isn't always greener on the other side," Raul protested.

"Exactly!" Tina said, "and he's just the man to make them understand that."

Roberto and Mrs. Garcia had no idea what they were talking about, and Luis wasn't sure which side of the debate he was on.

"Luis, I don't want to leave the neighborhood," Raul finally admitted.

"Dad, I think you should run for mayor," Tina said with conviction.

"Say *what*?" Raul couldn't believe his ears.

"After school the other day, I ran into that lady we met at the State House, Miss Tucker—she says there are a lot of people who want to see Papa run for mayor, and I think it's a great idea." Tina beamed at her father, positively glowing with pride. "You're just the man to stand up and do something about the problems facing Trenton."

Roberto seemed to catch the fever. "Just like you told me, Papa, sometimes you have to make a little trouble to wake people up. You should go for it!"

"I've never been more proud of you, Luis," Raul said with a tear in his eye for his son and the neighborhood he wouldn't have to leave. "My son, the mayor! But who is going to mow the lawns?"

"¡*Ay*! Mayor Alma—I like the sound of that!" Mrs. Garcia added with enthusiasm.

As his family gushed their approval, Luis stood wordlessly, the once vivid picture of Hopewell's future gentleman farmer fading into the back of his mind.

34

Critical Mass

L uis Alma stood, hands stuffed deep into his pockets, as he studied the strangely familiar portrait of John Hart on the wall outside the governor's office in the New Jersey State House. Could there really be some kind of weird connection, he wondered? His family had commented on the resemblance: the straight sharp nose, the hooded brow, the dark searching eyes, and the narrow pointed chin. There was something about the lips, as well. Instinctively, he reached to touch his face, then laughed and shook his head. *Anyone* could find a family likeness to a historical figure if they wanted to see it badly enough.

On the other hand, he had to admit it *was* curious that within the Alma family a legend persisted, a tale that might conceivably tie his bloodline to this obscure patriot. Since it could never be proven, his decision was to accept any personal connection he felt to John Hart as ideological rather than physical. After all, while a man is made of flesh and blood, his beliefs, his words, and his actions form his character.

More than two centuries earlier, John Hart had cast his fate with liberty and put his faith in a new nation governed by his peers: farmers, merchants, laborers, soldiers—common ordinary men. In the end, Luis reasoned, this was what linked him to Hart. The question of kinship aside, they shared a belief in duty, honor, family, and the inherent goodness of their fellow man.

Luis heard the tip-tap of high heels on the polished marble floor and turned expectantly; it was Helen Nelson approaching him with purpose. The flicker of disappointment in his eyes did not go unnoticed by the perceptive HPCA director.

"I know you were expecting Abby, Mr. Alma. I sent her on an errand so we might have a word in private."

Feeling cornered by the dynamic Madame Director, Luis said a bit nervously, "It's nice to see you, Ms. Nelson."

"You've been admiring our Harrison collection," she observed with an appreciative smile, gesturing to the portraits of the New Jersey Signers. "These paintings were commissioned in 1905."

Curiosity got the better of him. "I'm particularly interested in the one of John Hart," he said. "Is that a true likeness?"

"Good heavens, no!" she exclaimed with a haughty laugh. "Just look at those cascading, shoulder length black locks, the smooth forehead, and keen eyes. This is a portrait of a man in his prime—not more than forty, wouldn't you say? John Hart was sixty-three when he signed the Declaration of Independence. I'd expect a powdered wig and crow's feet!"

"Are you saying the portrait is a fake?" he asked in surprise, his eyes narrowing, fixing on her striking, high cheek-boned face. She must have been quite an eyeful at one time, he found himself thinking, with that voluptuous figure. Yet for him, the woman's physical charms were undone by her acerbic tongue and superior air.

"Not exactly," she said dismissively. "The commission demanded a portrait of all the signers, so Henry Harrison produced one his benefactors could accept. That's how artists serve their government, after all."

"I don't follow," Luis responded, aware of her patronizing tone.

"If you can't paint the real thing," she offered impatiently with a wave of her hand, "then use your imagination. Make it up. Romanticize it. Create an enduring portrait that symbolizes the prevailing image of a bold, dashing, handsome young rebel leader."

"And hope no one questions it."

She drew a deep breath. "Several historians did, indeed, take Harrison to task, but he claimed that lacking a good likeness of Hart he turned to the next best thing: a blood relative. Reportedly, a grandson, also named John, was tracked down and talked into sitting for the portrait. *Voila*! Instant Signer."

"Art *imitating* life," he said in reaction to her dripping sarcasm.

"You catch on fast, Mr. Alma," she said glancing at her watch. "The truth is that the artist could have used any model he chose or simply winged it. Is that the face of John Hart? It all depends on the beholder and what he's looking to find."

Luis was surprised how deeply disappointed he was by the revelation; he supposed the word "sucker" must be imprinted on his forehead, just waiting for her to spot it. He changed the subject before his mood could sag any lower.

"What was it you wanted to ask me, Madame Director?"

"Have you made a decision about running?" she asked with a directness that surprised him, fingering a garish diamond brooch on the lapel of her gray suit jacket.

He shifted on his feet for a moment before responding. "No offense intended, Ms. Nelson, but I'd like to give Abby my decision personally, since she's the one who approached me about it."

Helen wrestled an overwhelming urge to castrate this upstart landscaper where he stood. "Mr. Alma," she said composing herself, "you didn't think this was Abby's idea, did you? I'm sure she was quite *persuasive* ..." she said the word as suggestively as she could, "and I will see to it that she gets credit for doing her job, but let's be clear on one thing, shall we? Time is running out, and there are people willing to get behind you. They call the shots. They hold the power, and they have the money to make your candidacy happen. If you're ready to play ball, we have work to do."

"Is that why you need me?" he probed. "Has Jimmy Dodd stopped playing ball?"

"We need a fresh face—someone the public can relate to," she tried to work her charm on him. She needn't have bothered; he'd already figured out that charm was not her strong suit, at least when things didn't go her way.

"Sure, like a hero," he said.

"Now you get the picture," she bristled in delight. "Everybody wins. The public gets a new image to cozy up to. Hell—it may even be *uplifting*. Once you've learned the game, we might even go national, if you're up for it." She winked at him, thinking she was actually winning him over. "We can use a guy like you."

"That's exactly what it sounds like, *using* a guy like me," he remarked, letting her know what he really thought.

"Don't worry," she assured him. "We'll ensure you maintain a strong reputation in your community."

He had quickly taken stock of her gambit and found himself wishing Abby wasn't part of it. "Sounds like you've got it all figured out, Ms. Nelson, except for one thing."

"And what would that be?" She tapped her foot impatiently.

"I may decide not to play along," he said succinctly.

Her face flushed, and her whole body stiffened. She hadn't expected this type of resistance. Apparently, she was going to have to play hardball.

"Look, *Luis*, the party is offering you the chance of a lifetime. I was hoping to appeal to your civic pride, but if I have to I won't hesitate to call my friends over at Immigration. I'm sure they'd be very interested in the legal status of some of your employees."

Although it was Helen Nelson who had him by the balls, he could feel the knife guided by Abby's hand deftly twisting in his back. "You people really know your business," he exploded, drawing stares from startled state staffers leaning over the railings from the floors above them. "Slumlords get discounts and kickbacks, tax breaks go to companies sitting on undeveloped land, hazardous sites are left untreated—and I suppose you think Latino businesses couldn't survive without illegal labor. Well, I've got some news for you, Ms. Nelson: Trenton's strength comes from the diversity and independent spirit of those who call it home, and it's clear they've had enough of business as usual."

"Please get *real!*" Staring at him as though he'd completely lost his mind, she let out a caustic laugh. "Just because you read the newspapers, you think you understand the issues. You're dreaming!"

He smiled inwardly as he replied, "I'm not the only one with a dream."

She would have loved nothing more than to eviscerate him, and had no doubt she could make quick work of it, but she was pressed for time. Leaving him with a phony smile, she turned and walked off, passing Abby at the base of the circular staircase to the second floor portico.

"Maybe you can talk some sense into him," Helen huffed to her protégé as she stormed past.

"What did I miss?" Abby asked Luis with wide eyes.

"You don't miss a trick, do you?" he glared at her before turning to leave.

"Luis, wait!" she implored. "What are you talking about?"

He was incensed. "That bit about my employees, Hector and Felix," he snapped pointing an accusing finger at her. "How could you use something said in private against me like that?"

"What did she say to you?" she asked, following close behind as he paced in circles around the rotunda.

He stopped abruptly. "For one thing, she explained that you were just doing your job," he said angrily, his cold stare burning into her like dry ice.

"Oh, I see," she said folding her arms defensively. "So you think I slept with you on Helen Nelson's orders."

"Well, do you deny it?"

"I thought you knew me better than that," she said and reached for his hand.

"I don't know you at all," he said bitterly, pulling away from her.

The waning afternoon sunlight streamed through the open dome into the gallery below. The combatants paused in their verbal barrage to consider their next moves. While Abby gazed down at the illumi-nated floor mosaics searching for words of reconciliation, Luis waited to hear the truth.

"Let's get one thing straight, Luis," she said finally, struggling to keep her composure. "Helen asked me to talk to you about running for mayor, but sex was never an agenda item." She paused before adding, "That just happened," sharing an insight that she herself had only just realized.

"That doesn't explain the pillow talk, Abby," he said fiercely. "That's unforgivable."

"I never told her anything about your business, Luis."

"I don't believe you," he replied, his tone unyielding.

"I can't say I blame you," she said softly, thinking about how different their worlds were, how she must appear to his eyes. Holding back tears, she said as casually as she could, "May I ask what you've decided about the mayoral race?"

He was looking at the portrait of John Hart, drawing strength from the character of the self-made man.

"Oh, I've decided to run, all right," he said. "But not for *your* party."

With a forced smile he turned and left her standing in stunned silence.

35

Cobwebs and Codices

D arius knew it was wrong, but he couldn't help himself. It made him feel like a secret agent. If he got caught, he'd have to face the consequences, but for now he was too excited to think about anything except completing his "mission."

An hour earlier, he had passed through security on the first floor practically unnoticed. Confidently flashing his winning smile, his school ID, and the visitor's badge he had kept from the previous visit, he was able to slip through the checkpoint without having to sign the guest registry. That meant no one knew Darius Hudson was in the building, or so he assumed.

His plan was simple: Take the last scheduled tour of the day and at some point drop behind the rest of the group for a return to the place of his primary interest. Once he had what he came for, he would blend in with the staff and leave during the five o'clock rush.

By Darius's reckoning, his destination lay somewhere on the top floor, near the engraved relief of the Great Seal of New Jersey overlooking the entrance to the State House on West State Street. Based on what he had been able to piece together from his conversations with Professor Collins, his recent surprise "discovery" in the Trentoniana Room at the library, and his own instincts, the links in the chain led from the cryptic Masonic renderings on the Triumphant Arch directly to the Capitol. The treasure, he presumed, must be somewhere near the Great Seal—though just what the Masons had hidden there, of course, remained to be discovered.

Darius's additional research into Masonic lore provided few new pieces to the puzzle. He knew from his reading that many of the colonial leaders during the Revolutionary War *were* Masons, including

Benjamin Franklin, George Washington, and Paul Revere. He was also aware that recent conspiracy theorists had gone so far as to suggest that the very foundation of the United States was a grand Masonic plot, engineered by the founding fathers who were all pledged to the sacred rites of the order. What secret had the Masons concealed in Trenton?

It was an indisputable fact that there *were* Masons in Trenton during the Revolution. The first Masonic lodge—built a year after the State House was completed—and the current Masonic temple stood within plain sight of each other, and each offered a view of the more famous domed building as well. Surely, Darius surmised, the magnificent stonework of the original Capitol building and the later renovations were examples of Masonic handiwork.

He wracked his brain trying to figure out what connection and, hence, what secret Washington's victory at Trenton and Masonic skullduggery had in common. How did the Arch tie into the State House? He was so completely drawn into this new quest, that for the time being he was willing to set aside his pursuit of the unsolved provenance of the first edition of *Common Sense* he had found hidden in the stairwell at Eagle Tavern. Lately, Tina was of the opinion that he should turn the document over to Professor Collins for a scholarly evaluation. He was grudgingly coming around to that same point of view, but he hated to admit defeat.

The Capitol tour was quite impressive. Seeing the upper and lower chambers of the two houses where state legislators met, argued, debated, and voted in grand democratic tradition was inspiring. The tour guide was a self-confident young female whom Darius presumed was one of Professor Collins's students from Mercer County Community College. Collins had boasted in class several times how proud he was of his students who had been selected for internships with the city and state. In time, Darius hoped to be counted among them.

As the tour was wending its way down the back staircase toward the south entrance, Darius seized his opportunity. He retraced the tour route back up to the third floor, circled around the rotunda portico, and re-entered the north end of the building. He smiled broadly and gave an amiable "hello" or a polite nod to the few state employees he passed along the way.

He stopped in front of a white wooden door leading up the narrow steps that the tour group had descended earlier. He tried the door handle and to his surprise the knob turned easily. He entered the old stairwell cautiously and closed the door quickly and quietly behind him.

The enclosed stairwell was dark, and Darius had to feel his way along the curved wall, climbing up one step at a time. At the top of the stairs, the landing opened into a narrow hallway, dimly lit by fading sunlight coming through a skylight that also gave insiders a view of the dome.

Darius felt his excitement mounting as he located the door to the room that the young tour guide had pointedly not allowed the group to enter. The door led into a small meeting room once used by the governor's staff. It was vacant now except for a few storage boxes. He entered the room, checking behind him to make sure he hadn't been observed. He found the wall switch and flicked on the dull overhead light. Straight ahead of him, against the far north wall, he could clearly see the grooved outline of the Great Seal's opposing side. It was charred and blackened from a long-ago fire.

He crept across the creaking wooden floorboards to examine the grooves more closely. Running his hand over them, he felt along the indented lines hoping the impressions would speak to him of something more. He inspected the lines and the surrounding area for symbols or signs, anything that might lead him to his next clue. All he saw was the imprint of his and someone else's hand against the otherwise blackened exterior wall.

"You're wasting your time," a voice called eerily from across the room. Darius's heart stopped beating. He spun around on his heels to see Professor Collins, arms folded, standing in the doorway.

"Professor Collins ... I—I can explain," Darius sputtered, relieved and surprised at the same time.

"There's no need to, Darius." The professor stepped into the room. "I know why you're here."

"You do?"

"Yes," he said with a wry smile. "I sometimes stop by to see how my student interns are doing, and I saw you come in for Mary Alice's tour. When you didn't return with her group, I checked the visitor's registry and noticed you hadn't signed in or out. You came here to follow the clues you found on the Arch, didn't you?"

Darius shoved his hands into his pockets. "Yes, and it looks like a dead end," he said dejectedly. "There's nothing here."

"I know," said Collins. "That's why I said you were wasting your time. Right church, wrong pew."

Darius gave his history professor a quizzical look. "I don't understand, Professor. The Great Seal has to mean something."

"Oh, it does." Professor Collins moved slowly and dramatically into the middle of the small room. "There's no doubt the clue pointed to the State House, just not this room." He pirouetted around the room and looked up at the ceiling joists. "It's too new. This addition came after the fire of 1885. The Arch scribes would not have known about this room or the Seal's facade."

"Then I don't get it," Darius said, clearly confused by the message.

"Whatever the Masons had to hide, they hid in the State House sometime between 1789 and 1792. I'm sure of that. Come with me, Darius, there is something I want you to see."

Darius followed Collins out into the short hallway, then back down the narrow stairs to the third floor proper. Walking around the rotunda cutaway, the professor stopped in front of a stooped, low-cut wooden door. He jangled a ring of keys from his belt. "Compliments of Mary Alice," he said, smiling as he opened the door and beckoned his student to step up through the threshold.

As fading rays of light filtered into the room through the cupola windows, Darius realized from the cobwebs that he was in an attic, obviously less used but similar to the room behind the Great Seal on the building's north end. This south loft was slightly larger but appeared smaller because of massive, dark hand-hewn oak beams that crisscrossed the ceiling, forming arches and cutting out several feet of headroom.

"These beams," said Collins wistfully, "are actually all that's left of the original 1792 building. The rest was pretty much lost in the fire of 1885. Here, have a look."

"There's something etched here!" Darius said excitedly as he inspected the corner of a crossbeam. "Just like on the wooden arch. But I can't make out what it says."

"*Omnia relinquit sevare republican,*" Collins recited from memory. "He relinquished everything to serve the Republic."

"What does it mean, Professor?"

"It's the motto of the Society of Cincinnatus," Collins explained. "Do you remember the story of Lucius Quinctius Cincinnatus from my class, Darius?"

"Of course, he was the farmer who led the Roman army."

"Correct. And after the war was fought and won, he gave his command back to the Roman Senate and returned to his plow. George Washington modeled himself after Cincinnatus when he turned over his command of the Continental Army to Congress after defeating the British. A weaker man might have held onto the reins of power and proclaimed himself king. In Washington's case, very few would have opposed him at that time. Many actually begged him to consider it."

"So what actually *is* the Society of Cincinnatus?" Darius asked with keen interest.

"The society was formed after the war, by officers who had served under General Washington. It is believed that General Henry Knox and Captain Alexander Hamilton, both ardent Washington admirers, organized the first meeting in New York in 1783. Eventually many veteran officers joined, including Washington himself. They adopted the eagle as their insignia and the aforementioned Latin motto. The Society of Cincinnatus is generally considered the premiere American hereditary society, passed down through the eldest sons of the original members. Present day members must descend from officers who fought in the Revolution. Their professed goal is to care for the widows and orphans of deceased comrades."

Darius looked up at the massive beams and shook his head. "Professor Collins," he began slowly, choosing his words carefully, "I just don't get it. All this stuff—the Masons, the Triumphant Arch, the

Capitol roof rafters, the Cincinnatus motto … are you saying that George Washington is trying to send us a message from beyond the grave?" He laughed nervously, unsure of his own words.

Daniel Collins did not laugh. He stared at Darius intently, as if sizing up the person who had asked the question rather than analyzing the question itself.

"That's an interesting conclusion, Darius," he said without the slightest undercurrent of bemusement. "One I would expect from my star pupil. I could tell from the moment you stepped foot into my classroom that you shared my enthusiasm for a good treasure hunt. You can't help yourself—it's in your nature."

"Then it's true?" Darius asked with unrestrained emotion. "You believe that George Washington is directing us to find something he hid here in Trenton?"

"Right church, wrong pew again." Collins leaned against a musty old filing cabinet and casually folded his arms, relishing what he was about to say.

"Not Washington, Darius," he began, "but *someone* from that time period—and later, perhaps—has gone to a lot of trouble to use these old relics as signposts, encoding them with information in order to lead someone adept at deciphering their significance to something of great importance."

Collins smiled at his star student before continuing. "George Washington was a good guess, based on the clues—the Arch commemorating the General's return to Trenton, the reference to Cincinnatus, the fact that he was a Mason, etc.—but I don't believe this puzzle is about a person so much as it is about a prize. A prize of tremendous historical value."

Darius eyed his teacher from across the room with a mixture of curiosity and concern. "You knew," he began with some misgiving as the light of revelation switched on in his brain, "that day … in the bank … and at the library, too, you already knew about all of this."

"Yes," Collins acknowledged without reservation.

Darius's mind was firing on all cylinders. "Then why include me in the game?"

"Validation, my dear boy," Collins said with a mischievous smile. "You at the bank, Miss Alma and Shelly Reed at the library. What good is a great historical discovery if the discoverer has no one to validate that it was *his* find?"

Darius thought for a long moment. "But you haven't found it. Otherwise it would have made front page news."

Collins's relaxed posture stiffened slightly. "I was right about you, Darius. You are a bright young man and someone I can trust. You truly do share my passion and appreciation for history. Just as we can't let them take Eagle Tavern away from us, we cannot allow the same misguided bureaucrats to come along and spoil our big discovery when it happens, can we?"

"And that's where I come in … but how?"

"The secret may yet be linked to Eagle Tavern."

"The eagle is the insignia for the Society of Cincinnatus!" Darius exclaimed.

"A fact that cannot be overlooked," Collins agreed. "And I believe you and your … ahem, *associates* have ways of getting inside the building while it remains closed to us poor public servants."

Following Collins's train of thought, Darius suddenly found himself wondering: Did the professor know about the copy of *Common Sense*? Was that the "prize" he was alluding to?

"However," Collins continued as if musing to himself, "there is another possibility that remains to be explored—one I hadn't considered before. It may only be a coincidence, but later members of the Society of Cincinnatus in Trenton were among the founding members of the Trenton Battle Monument Association."

"What do you think it means?" asked Darius, dazzled and somewhat overwhelmed by all that he had learned on this unscheduled part of the tour.

"Perhaps nothing at all," Professor Collins said, dismissing the whole notion. He rubbed his chin and added enigmatically, "Except that if memory serves, one of the members of the Trenton Battle Monument Association was both a Mason and a direct descendant of John Hart, Signer of the Declaration of Independence."

36

Game Time

*T*he sun was just beginning to set in the western sky as game time approached. A cool April breeze blew off the river and through the stadium. The night promised to be a hitter's delight as the center field flags rippled with the wind.

"Welcome to Waterfront Park, sir," the youthful ticket taker said to the man next in line at the main gate. "Home of the Trenton Thunder—proud Double-A affiliate of the twenty-seven-time World Champion New York Yankees!"

"Nice sales pitch, Darius," Luis Alma grinned as he handed him the game tickets Dominic Rosetti had given to Roberto. "So that's how you charmed my daughter."

Darius gave him a bashful smile as he tore off the ticket stubs. Luis, Raul, and Roberto moved through the turnstile, but Tina lingered.

"You guys go on ahead," she shouted as they headed up the steps into the ballpark. "I'll see you out there." Roberto and his grandfather just kept going, but Luis looked back briefly, a bit sadly, as if he needed her more than she did him. She watched as he faded into the crowd.

"I brought along some 'common sense,' just like you asked," she said to Darius, patting her handbag. "I'm *so* glad you decided to give it to Professor Collins."

"If anyone can get to the bottom of it, he will," Darius said as she smiled up at him, thinking how handsome he was in his forest green Trenton Thunder polo shirt and khaki pants. "Besides, if this thing is as valuable as I think it is, he might be able to sell it to a collector or a museum and use the money for repairs on Eagle Tavern. That may be the only way to keep the city from having to sell it to those developers."

"It's a noble cause," she said approvingly. "What does Professor Collins think of the idea?"

"Well … I haven't exactly told him about the plan or the pamphlet yet," he admitted sheepishly. "But I know he's committed to saving the tavern."

"I'll just be glad when I don't have to worry about hiding this thing anymore," she said. "So I'll see you later?"

"Meet me right here after the game," he said with a playful wink.

She responded with a seductive smile followed by a kiss on the cheek. He let his eyes follow her tight, pear-shaped derriere as she sashayed up the pavilion steps, taking each step with him in mind.

"Nice ass, you tap that yet?" The raspy voice startled Darius, who wheeled around abruptly.

"What are you doing here?" His tone couldn't have been clearer. He wasn't happy to see Bobby Jackson anywhere, least of all at his place of employment.

"I'm looking for your kid brother," Jackson snickered.

Darius signaled for a coworker to relieve him and stepped away from the line of queuing baseball fans. Jackson moved to the side of the line with him.

"He's not here, and you should be in jail," Darius said with all the venom he could muster.

Jackson grinned. "Got me a smart white lawyer," he said, taunting Darius. "The cop can't positively ID me, and I found that gun in the street."

"Then why did you run?" Darius shot back.

"Shit, you'd run too if you were being chased by a hopped-up spic holding a fucking rake," Jackson snarled.

"That's your story?" Darius inquired with disdain.

"Oh, right, I forgot," Jackson replied with a cruel smirk. "That spic might be your daddy-in-law someday. My condolences."

Darius looked around to see if the park guards were watching them. He leaned in to Jackson and whispered through clenched teeth. "Enjoy your freedom while you can, Bobby, 'cause you ain't got a prayer."

"Don't need no fucking prayer," Jackson said with an arrogant laugh. "Got me some friends in high places."

"Then what do you need my brother for?" Darius asked, softening his tone. "Why can't you just leave him alone?"

"No can do, bro," Jackson replied as cold as ice. "Curtis took a blood oath."

Darius was well aware of Bobby Jackson's "habit" and knew it cost him a lot to maintain. "What will it cost to undo that oath?"

"You ain't hearin' me, Darius. You can't put no price on a brother's obedience. It's a death pledge, man."

Darius knew precisely what the stakes were—he was bargaining for his brother's life and he might not get another chance. "How much would it take to get your boyz to back off, if I could convince Curtis to keep his mouth shut?"

Now it was Jackson's turn to weigh the odds. "Shit, you can do that, man?"

"Sure," Darius bluffed, staring into Bobby Jackson's ruthless coal black eyes. "I guarantee it." Curtis had always been unpredictable and uncontrollable, a loose cannon like their old man. Still, he had to try *something*; he'd figure out how to keep Curtis out of sight later.

"Nah," said Jackson dismissively with a wave of his hand, "you ain't got that kind of scratch."

Bobby Jackson was a heartless, petty thug; Darius was certain of that, but no one had ever accused him of being stupid. He had anticipated Jackson's move and now it was time to play the wild card he was holding—or rather, the one Tina was holding onto for him. She wouldn't be happy about this development, he knew, but once she realized it was a matter of life and death she'd have to understand.

"That's where you're wrong, Bobby," Darius said resolutely. "What if I told you I could give you something so valuable it could set you up for life?"

Jackson gave him a skeptical look. "I don't know, Darius," he said hesitantly, "I got me an eight-hundred-pound gorilla to feed. How much value we talkin'?"

"Enough to buy that white bread lawyer of yours outright and then some."

"Yeah, that's money," Jackson seemed impressed. "You better not be yankin' my chain, bro."

"It's all yours, Bobby. But I want your word that everybody backs off. You leave Curtis to me."

"Done!" exclaimed Jackson sealing it with a ritual handshake that made Darius feel even more nervous and conspicuous than before.

***

"So, how do you like the seats?" asked Dominic Rosetti, plunking himself down at the end of the row as cheers followed the National Anthem. "Welcome to Section 8, home of Trenton's own 'Rivertown Rowdies'!"

"They're awesome," gushed Roberto, returning from the field with his father, wearing his Derek Jeter #2 jersey. "Thanks, Mr. Rosetti!"

"And thank you for arranging to have my boy throw out the first ball," Luis said. "That was really special. I hope you didn't have to go to a lot of trouble."

"No trouble at all," replied Dominic, running a hand through wavy short-cropped gray hair and adjusting the brim of his authentic Trenton Thunder cap. "I just told them they better treat the next mayor's kid right," he said with a sly grin before adding, "It's a damn shame you're not a Republican."

"After Bush, it seemed like that circus left town," Luis said frankly.

Rosetti chortled. "Hey, the fact of the matter is that the Republicans have never had a snowball's chance in hell here—not with a 2-to-1 Democrat margin in registered voters. The Dems have had a stranglehold on Trenton for years, and the only thing that well-oiled machine of theirs is good at is making sure nothing changes."

Luis grew thoughtful for a moment before he spoke.

"The way I see it, both major parties have a vested interest in keeping politics divisive, and there's no reason to believe they'll ever come together to solve the problems facing ordinary people. At the end of the day, it's either big business or big government, and it all falls on the shoulders of the little guy. That's why I decided to run as an independent."

"Mr. Rosetti," Raul interrupted and changed the subject. "What was it you told my grandson about some doctor fish that lives in the Delaware and grows to be as big as a house?"

Dominic let out a loud belly laugh. "That's a sturgeon, not a surgeon, Roberto," he said, mussing Roberto's hair. "And me and Charlie caught him fishing off a house during the flood of '55," he added with a wink and a smile to the others. "I was hoping you would meet Charlie today, but he's a little under the weather. He's got the stories. Here's a guy who actually saw Willie Mays play for the Trenton Giants at Dunn Field back in the fifties."

"*Now* you're talking baseball," Raul acknowledged with pleasure. "Roberto Clemente, Juan Marichal, Orlando Cepeda—those were real ballplayers!"

"A National League fan, I see," Dominic remarked with mild amusement. "So, how goes the campaigning?" he said turning back to Luis.

"Honestly, I'm not sure what to make of it," Luis said. "We're getting my name out there. P. J. Moore and the whole *Trentonian* staff have made good on their promise to support me, and I'm sure Dodd loves reading all these heartwarming stories about me in the same paper that constantly trashes him."

"Well, enjoy it while you can," Dominic said. "Once you get into office, things change."

"How so?" Luis wanted to know.

"Well, for one thing you get to watch the game from the Triumph Club Box," Dominic said with a hint of sarcasm, hooking his thumb toward the covered booths ringing the upper deck behind them. "Speak of the devil, here comes Randal Whittaker now."

"Greetings, all," the nattily dressed developer said expansively as he looked down their row. "Enjoying the game I trust?"

"Absolutely," Dominic replied for all of them. Three generations of Almas appeared to have momentarily lost the ability to speak as they looked up at the exotic beauty on Whittaker's arm.

"Luis Alma and family, may I introduce my wife, Naomi?" Whittaker said with a nod to the willowy, caramel-skinned goddess by his side.

"Nice to meet you all," Naomi said with a warm smile. "Mr. Alma, I've heard so much about you."

"And I heard you might be here tonight," Whittaker said, "so I thought I'd take the opportunity to present this in person." He handed Luis an embroidered salmon-color envelope. "It's an invitation to next month's groundbreaking ceremony for the Alma Arms. Naturally, the invitation extends to your entire family."

"Thank you, Mr. Whittaker," Luis said, "but I wish you would consider another name for the building project. It's a little embarrassing, especially now that—"

"Now that you're running for mayor?" Whittaker finished for him. "At Triumph, we call that vision," he said. "Seeing into the future."

"Mom liked the name," Tina blurted out.

"See?" Whittaker jumped on the comment. "What better endorsement than the approval of your family?"

"If I might say so, Mr. Alma," Naomi ventured tactfully, "your name suggests strength and hope for Trenton's future. I think it's a great fit."

"Thank you, Mrs. Whittaker," Luis said trying not to appear ungrateful; the truth was that he was uncomfortable being lionized for what he considered a trained response rather than a heroic act. "I'll try to remember that if they ever invite me to give a speech in the North Ward," he joked.

"Oh, they will," concluded Whittaker, shaking Luis's hand. "And I'll look forward to seeing you there. Enjoy the game!" With that, he headed back up to his private box, gorgeous wife in tow, schmoozing all the way.

"She's so beautiful," Tina remarked as soon as the couple was out of earshot. "She must be a model."

"At one time, yes," Dominic said. "She got her looks from her mother. Her father was Hollis Markham."

Luis's face registered complete surprise.

"Don't tell me you didn't know that, Luis," Dominic said. "Naomi Whittaker runs the Youth Center and, yes, she's the only daughter of the late Reverend Markham. I'd bone up on the movers and shakers in this town, if I were you." Looking over his shoulder to watch the

Whittakers ascending to their box, he added, "Naomi is a class act, just like her old man."

Luis flashed back to what Abby had said about Hollis Markham over lunch at De Lorenzo's. "Well, I'm glad she won't be running against me," he said.

***

"He worries me," Senator Stevens said as he paced the floor of Triumph's luxury box.

"That makes two of us," Helen Nelson added, raising her third glass of Dom Perignon.

"Let me remind you both," counseled Whittaker as he calmly poured his wife a glass of champagne, "that Luis Alma was *your* idea. Construction on the Alma Arms project is proceeding regardless of who runs for mayor."

"Aren't you moving a little too fast, Randal?" Naomi cautioned her husband. She had been watching the ballgame through the big Plexiglas picture window. "There are still a few families living in those buildings. My father expected everyone to be relocated before any work began."

"It's not my problem," Whittaker said indifferently. "I made a deal with the city to tear down those old rat traps and replace them with modern living quarters at below market prices. The wrecking ball arrives next week."

"But where will those people go?" she protested.

"The state will provide for them," he reasoned. "Isn't that right, Howard?"

"It's Dodd's job to impose eminent domain," Senator Stevens replied. "My hands are tied until all the sanctions are levied."

"Unfortunately, Naomi," said Helen, adding her practiced political view of the situation, "a handful of slumlords are holding out for government money while those poor people suffer in deplorable conditions."

"Not all those homes are held by slumlords, Helen, absentee or otherwise," Naomi countered.

"Where did you hear *that*?" Stevens snapped.

"From my father," she said, looking to her husband for support. "Was he wrong?"

"Not wrong, Naomi, just misinformed," Whittaker said coolly, taking a deep breath. "Your father was a great man, but he was ruled by his heart, not his head. He accepted many things people told him on faith, and they sometimes turned out to be untrue."

"Naomi," Stevens offered as he refilled his glass with scotch, "when we set up Triumph Development and committed resources to the rebirth of Trenton, we did it for the benefit of *all* of its citizens. While public perception has Randal calling the shots as CEO of the corporation, from day one all major decisions have been made by unanimous agreement, and your father—"

"What the senator is trying to say," Whittaker cut him off impatiently, "is that your father was a silent but full partner in Triumph, as is Howard, who as an elected officeholder votes through proxy."

"That would be me," Helen admitted with a knowing nod and a lazy wave of her hand.

"And while we sometimes disagreed on a given course of action," Whittaker continued after taking a sip of his champagne, "ultimately we always came to an understanding."

"So, are you saying my father approved of this project even if it meant putting poor families on the street?" Naomi asked point blank, looking at her husband before turning her gaze on the senator.

The directness of the question caught Stevens off guard. He looked to Whittaker to field the question.

Whittaker cleared his throat. "Given Howard's assurances that no person displaced by eminent domain would end up homeless, your father was in favor of moving forward without delay. Unfortunately, he was taken from us before Howard could tie up all the loose ends."

"I was working on it, believe you me," Stevens pleaded his case.

"Meaning you went ahead without his approval," Naomi said, looking at her husband as if he had just slapped her in the face.

"Like I said, Naomi, it was just a matter of time before—"

"Before *what*, Randal? Before Howard secured the funding to set these people up in new state subsidized housing? Or before you convinced my father that he had been 'misinformed'—that he was letting his concern for the plight of his people overrule his better judgment?"

A sudden rap on the door to the luxury box broke the tension among the occupants inside.

"Am I interrupting something?" Jimmy Dodd let himself in and quickly closed the door behind him. His appearance rendered the group speechless. He looked like Buster Brown, in gray flannel breeches, frilly white shirt, and black silver-buckled shoes. A powdered wig and felt tri-corner hat completed the period look.

"I just auditioned to play the part of George Washington at this year's crossing re-enactment," he volunteered in answer to their stares.

Helen broke the silence with a slightly tipsy laugh. "I don't know what's funnier, Jimmy—you pretending to be Washington or you pretending to be mayor!"

Dodd looked from face to face, clearly wounded by her remark. "I've been a damn good mayor and you know it," he said petulantly.

"And Washington never told a lie," Stevens added, laughing and obviously feeling no pain.

"I've had enough of this farce for one day," Naomi said angrily. She grabbed her Gucci bag and was through the door before her husband knew what was happening.

"Naomi, wait!" he shouted after her, turning around as he reached the doorway. "Jimmy, you better save that outfit—there's going to be another Battle of Trenton."

37

Saving Face

S o, how was the game?" Abby inquired casually, smoothing her shoulder-length blonde hair in front of an ornately framed but otherwise uncomplimentary mirror in the ladies room at Amici Milano.

"The Thunder won in extra innings, but the real sparks flew during the seventh-inning stretch," Helen said in an authentic whiskey voice, applying black eyeliner in the unflattering glare of the restroom's fluorescent lights. "Naomi was really giving it to Randal."

"She deserves better." Abby studied her reflection ruefully.

Helen interrupted her preening to stare at Abby's downcast expression in the mirror. "Since when did *you* become so self-righteous?"

"It was a mistake," Abby offered solemnly.

"Join the club, honey," the older woman slurred. "My life is littered with mistakes like Randal Whittaker." She went back to her makeup. "What did you expect? *Romance?*"

"I'm not like you, Helen," Abby protested unconvincingly. "I thought I was, but I'm not. Naomi is my friend."

Helen applied rouge. "You think Mary Roebling didn't make sacrifices?"

"She didn't sacrifice her principles."

"Grow up, Abby," Helen said with marked disdain. "You don't become a powerful woman in a *man's* world unless you play by their rules. Don't tell me that Mexican gardener of yours has given you a conscience? He'll come around, believe me. *All* men do once you find the right carrot to dangle in front of them." She adjusted her bra to reveal more cleavage.

"He's Cuban, not Mexican," Abby said.

"Like I know the difference." Helen let out a throaty laugh.

Abby didn't respond. She was thinking about her night with Luis, of how his hands and lips had felt on her skin, and of how he'd seemed to care more about her pleasure than satisfying his own lusts. She closed her eyes and sighed, thinking they'd drifted too far apart to ever relive that night.

She looked in the mirror to see Helen smirking at her, as though she was reading her thoughts.

"What exactly did you say to Luis, Helen?" she asked. "What did you tell him about me?"

"You mean, did I say anything about your past? How your daddy never forgave you for your brother's death? How the Tucker line came to an end when you lost the ability to conceive?" She paused in her vitriolic survey to apply eye shadow. "Or is what *really* worries you what I may have told him about Randal? Which is it, Abby?"

Abby's face flushed as she thought of her past indiscretions and loss, but Helen's look was unsympathetic. "Your past is *your* problem, Abby, not mine. Get over it."

"You can't buy a man like Luis Alma, Helen," Abby said adamantly. "He's his own man."

"He may be, but he can't love a woman like you, Abby. You're not his wife, and you never will be." She snapped her compact shut and stuffed it into her purse. "If I were you, I'd hone in on Howard. He's had his eye on you for awhile."

"You've got to be joking!" Abby said recoiling at the thought. "What the hell would I want with that old pervert?"

"That old pervert just guaranteed our funding for another year, and if we play our cards right he'll be good for a plum committee assignment in the fall."

"You're not serious!" Abby responded with disgust.

Helen tried to reel her in. "One night in the sack, and we'll have him right where we want him."

Looking up, Abby saw Helen clearly in the unforgiving mirror.

***

"Were you and my father involved in any other business I should know about?" Naomi demanded of her husband, who was behind the wheel of their luxurious and, in this case, excruciatingly quiet Lexus. They were the first words either had spoken since leaving the ballpark.

"No, Naomi, absolutely not," Whittaker pleaded, hoping to sound convincing.

"What is it with your involvement in the Youth Center?" she asked, subtly turning to observe his reaction. She tried to make her question sound casual although it had been eating at her for some time.

"What about it?" he said, answering her question with a question— a trick he used to play for time when he was painted into a corner.

"Is that business related, too?"

"Of course not," he replied quickly. "Whatever gave you that idea?"

"Oh, I don't know," she said, trying to sort it out in her own mind while dragging what she could out of her shrewd husband. He's dancing, she thought to herself. "I guess it's just the way you pull certain kids aside, for your private little talks."

"When I see young men with potential," he said, "I challenge them to become future business leaders." His tone was defensive. "Is there something wrong with that?"

"Not if that's all you're doing."

"Christ, Naomi, what's that supposed to mean?" he demanded, striking the wheel with his hand. His expression said he was annoyed and struggling to control his temper. He wasn't used to his normally placid wife pushing him like this, and he didn't like it. "What's with all these damned questions, anyway? You're not sore at me because your father kept our business together a secret, are you?" His thoughts suddenly went to Abby. She and Naomi were once pretty tight, and they still spoke occasionally—could she have said something to get Naomi's bowels in an uproar?

"I don't know, Randal, maybe I'm being irrational. Why don't you tell me how I'm supposed to feel, like you always do." She folded her arms and glared at the road ahead.

"You lost me there, Naomi," he said softly, hoping to calm her. "Why don't you tell me what's really on your mind?"

"It just strikes me as odd that the kids you've been spending so much time with at the center are the worst of the lot." She made it more of a question than an accusation.

"Many of these boys have serious behavior problems," he said, his notoriously charming smile back in place. "Sometimes I get through to them, sometimes I don't."

"Is that what happened with Curtis Hudson and Bobby Jackson? Are they two of your failures?" She said it without rancor but with more insight than he expected from her.

He grew quiet, focusing his attention on the road while he considered how to respond.

"Well?" she insisted. "Are they?"

"Your father always tried to lift up those with the greatest need," he said quietly, trying a tack he hoped might win her over. "How can I strive for anything less?"

"My father would have succeeded," she said bluntly, hitting her husband where it should have hurt the most.

"Maybe my mentoring skills are lacking, or I'm just a poor judge of character," he said with mock humility.

"Neither," she said coldly.

"What exactly is it you're implying?"

"I find it odd that so many of the boys you tutor personally end up back on the street, in gangs, or in jail." She pulled no punches.

"And you think that's somehow *my* fault?" he laughed mirthlessly. "What kind of sordid thinking is *that*, Naomi?"

"Well, call me crazy, Randal, but it certainly doesn't hurt your business, does it?"

He swerved onto the shoulder of the road, pulling to an abrupt stop and throwing the car into park. The anger in his eyes sent out sparks as he stared into his wife's beautiful face.

"What the *fuck* is that supposed to mean?" He was enraged.

She didn't flinch. "The greater the gang activity and crime level in the city, the cheaper the asking prices are for the buildings you buy, and the more you make in return on profits from your sales after redevelopment." She fielded her husband's anger calmly, with a peacefulness and serenity that came to her in a moment of pure insight. "I know my father wouldn't have had anything to do with *that* side of your business."

After letting her suspicions come pouring out, she waited. Abby had been right, he had nothing more to say.

***

The ballgame ended in extra innings with the Trenton Thunder edging out the Binghamton Mets four to three in the bottom of the tenth. Despite the late hour, Darius stayed on to help the ushers clean up while Tina watched with amusement and waited for him in the press box.

"If everything goes according to plan, you may have a new bumper sticker for your car: 'I SAVED EAGLE TAVERN,'" she kidded him as the two walked hand in hand to his old brown Bonneville at the deserted far end of the stadium parking lot. She handed him the rare copy of *Common Sense* with a palpable sense of relief.

"Wait a minute, Tina," he grinned as he took the booklet, "when you put it that way, it sounds like I won a drinking contest!"

"And that's how you'll be remembered in history: Darius Hudson, bar savior!"

He opened the passenger door for her and, in the excitement of the moment, she threw her arms around him and pulled him into a passionate kiss. The carefree embrace broke off instantly when Darius saw several shadowy figures emerge from the riverbank. He pushed her into the car protectively, snapped down the lock, and slammed the door shut.

"Going somewhere, bro?" It was Bobby Jackson, dressed in a black hooded sweatshirt. He pulled his hoodie back revealing the Bloods' trademark red bandana covering his head. The five similarly dressed gang members standing behind him followed suit. "I thought we had a deal?"

"We do," replied Darius, quickly assessing the situation.

"Well, then I'm here to collect." Jackson showed more of his teeth than Darius ever wanted to see.

"Now?" Darius said. "Here?" He slipped the booklet behind his back.

Jackson looked past him into the passenger seat of the Bonneville. Tina slid down low in the seat. "Is that your bitch?"

Darius didn't answer right away.

"I'm sure she won't mind waiting for her man to finish up his bidness," Jackson said as his fellow gang members snickered.

"It's not a good time, Bobby," Darius offered, unsure what else to say.

"It's now or never, bro," Jackson said, nodding to his posse. The group spread out revealing a sixth person, a boy, who although tightly bound was twisting and turning to break free from the dog chain wound around his neck. From the swollen eye and bloody lip, it was obvious to Darius that he'd been beaten. A hulking Blood forced the boy to his knees.

"Don't do it, Darius!" gasped Curtis. "Whatever he wants, don't give it to him!"

Pulling out a handgun, the big gang member pistol-whipped the boy. Curtis slumped to the pavement, moaning, then growing still and silent.

"Curtis!" As Darius rushed toward his brother, he was immediately grabbed and held by several of the Bloods. "Here's what you want," he said, holding the pamphlet out to Jackson. "Now let us be!"

"What's this shit?" Jackson spat as he pulled the copy of *Common Sense* out of Darius's trembling hand. He gave his gang the signal to lay off.

"It's what I promised you," Darius said as he knelt down to inspect the gash on his brother's forehead. Curtis whispered weakly, "No use … saw him … kill Markham!"

"A *book*?" Jackson said screwing up his face. "You giving me a fuckin' *book*, Darius?"

"It's a rare first edition of *Common Sense*," Darius tried to explain as he huddled over Curtis, hoping the shockwave his brother's revelation had sent up his spine wasn't showing on his face. "An original copy of Tom Paine's manifesto."

"I don't give a shit if it's the Bible Moses owned," Jackson said. "I need the *cash*."

"You can have it. All of it, after you sell it."

Jackson reached down and grabbed Darius by the collar, pulling him to his feet. As he resisted, the gang members closed ranks. The two former friends from the same hood stood on different paths, face to face with neither one blinking. Rage seethed through Darius's veins. Contempt flashed openly in Jackson's dark eyes.

"Do I look like a fuckin' book dealer, bro?" Jackson said.

"It's worth a *lot* of money," Darius argued.

Jackson snapped his fingers and a Blood brother responded by handing him a cigarette lighter. "Well, then let's see if it's made of gold," he sneered, setting the fragile, dog-eared parchment on fire. He tossed the flaming pages onto Curtis's crumpled body.

Curtis cried out as the flames burned through his clothing and singed his skin and hair. Jackson kicked the boy in the head. "Shut your trap, you little rat."

Darius lunged at Jackson but was once again restrained by his gang. He watched helplessly as the priceless document turned to ashes and his own bright future went up in smoke. In that moment, he knew the only thing that mattered was saving his brother's life. If he had heard Curtis correctly, and he knew he had, then Bobby had already murdered at least once—he couldn't let him kill again.

Inside the car, Tina's eyes were wide open and all of her senses were alert. She was frightened, but not helpless. Looking for her cell phone she discovered Darius's keys in her jacket pocket, where he must have slipped them as he pushed her into the car.

Jackson held out his hand, palm up, and the hefty gangsta who had worked Curtis over passed him a handgun.

"So, Darius, what else have you got to trade for your little brother?" he said lifting Darius's wallet from his pants pocket. He pulled out the cash and spilled the rest of the contents on the ground. "Fifty bucks?" he heckled Darius. "You expect me to spare your brother's life for a measly fifty bucks?" The other gang members laughed.

Jackson aimed the gun at Curtis's head and pulled back the hammer. "Hey … wait—maybe your bitch has something we want." He cocked his head toward the car.

Tina turned the key in the ignition. True to form, the Bonneville backfired and belched out a plume of smoke. The explosion sent the Bloods scattering and running for cover.

Darius knocked the gun out of Jackson's hand and gave him a shove as Tina threw the car in reverse and fishtailed past them. She flung open the passenger door as the car squealed to a stop.

Jackson made a grab for him, and Darius wheeled and landed a blow to his face, dropping him to the blacktop. He swept Curtis up in his arms and slid into the passenger seat as several gang members reached the rear of the vehicle.

The Bonneville burned rubber across the parking lot as shots rang out, shattering the rear windshield. Tina swerved out onto the road and into traffic.

"Police station?" she gasped, her hands at ten and two on the wheel.

"No," Darius said as he felt the warm blood seeping through the fabric of Curtis's shirt. "The hospital!"

As he told his unconscious brother to hold on, that everything would be all right, in his heart he knew it was too late.

38

Coalition of Hope

*T*he execution-style slaying of Curtis Hudson at the hands of Bobby Jackson and his gang hit Luis Alma hard, bringing back all the unsettling images of his wife's violent end and his own brush with death on the steps of the State Museum. As Tina recounted the tale of their night of terror, Luis wondered if he had what it took to be the mayor of this city.

But Luis had already committed to himself that he would run, and there was no turning back now. He knew he would have to bring law and order to a town desperately in need of both and address the root causes in order to succeed. It was a tall order for even the bravest soldier, and he was glad he wasn't in this alone. His family was behind him.

As the campaign got underway, he took inspiration from the notion that *anyone* could run for mayor in Trenton, even without a party affiliation or major party support. In fact, it was a nonpartisan free-for-all, and even candidates from the same party could run against each other. Luis found strength in the idea that he represented the people rather than a party, and he was amazed at how his grassroots campaign caught fire with the support of disenfranchised voters.

It worked exactly the way Abby predicted it would. No one came away with the 51% of the votes needed to win the general election. Dodd garnered the most votes with 27%, while Luis finished second in the polls with 25%. None of the other seven candidates even reached double digits. Now, it would all come down to a mid-June runoff between Dodd and Luis.

Today, however, as he put on his best suit for the Heritage Days Festival where he was scheduled to deliver "the speech of a lifetime," victory was far from his mind. As he tried to twist his red-striped tie into what he hoped was a passable Windsor knot, he wasn't sure if the Luis looking back at him in the mirror was the same man he had always known. His palms were sweaty and the butterflies in his stomach were fluttering in an unfettered free fall.

Life was strange, he thought wistfully. Not long ago everything had seemed so simple. He was happily married to his loving wife of twenty years. They were busy raising two bright kids and caring for his gently aging, widowed father. The modest landscaping business his father had turned over to him was growing, and he was almost at the point where he could realize the dream of moving his family to the country and a peaceful prosperous lifestyle.

Then, less than a year ago, a single tragic event had changed everything. Luis wasn't sure how, but the murder of Reverend Hollis Markham had set into motion a series of unexpected twists and turns that had dramatically altered his life and led him to run as an independent candidate against a four-term incumbent mayor.

As he rehearsed his speech, Luis considered the daunting, if remote, prospect of his becoming mayor of this diverse city of some ninety thousand people. Nearly a quarter of them were Hispanic, but the largest block of constituents by far was African American, representing almost fifty-five percent of the population. Luis needed broad support within the black community to win the election and that would take a lot of work. The remaining twenty percent were likely to go heavily for Dodd, though he would do his best to reach white voters, many of whom were disenchanted with the current administration.

Luis's thoughts drifted to Tina's story about the *Common Sense* pamphlet and how much it had meant to Darius. In addition to having gained an appreciation for the young man's intelligence and bravery, he was struck by his deep respect for American history. Luis recalled the pride he himself had felt the first time he heard the tale linking his own family to one of the nation's founding fathers. If elected, he would work to inspire *all* his fellow citizens to share this same sense of pride in their city's history as the place where freedom made a stand. This was sacred ground, alive with the promise that all men were created equal and shared the same rights, and it was a message he knew he could deliver.

The crucifix above the bed he had shared with Maria caught his eye, making him think about what faith really meant to him. He blessed himself and said a Hail Mary, realizing it was time to bare his soul to the people and to lay out his beliefs in a cohesive platform that he hoped all Trentonians could support.

First on his to-do list was a plan to rid the city of self-serving developers who were queued up like false prophets pretending to strike a blow for the future of Trenton while lining their own pockets. People like Randal Whittaker had a public face and private motives, he now understood. If he were elected, the residents of Tucker Street would be offered low-interest loans to buy or renovate their own properties, and Alma Arms would immediately be renamed Victory Square.

Next on his agenda, Luis would exhort all Trenton's elected officials to be guided by conscience and remind them that they owed it to the people who had elected them to remain free from the influence of special interest groups. "The good-old-boy network isn't good enough anymore. If we want people to have faith in their elected officials, then nepotism and corruption must come to a screeching halt," he recited, then wrote it down.

The educational system was in bad shape. Luis believed that the role of government had to be re-evaluated and in particular that "school board members should not be appointed but rather chosen by their communities for their passion, commitment, and qualifications. Class sizes need to be reduced, students should have access to one-on-one counseling, and corporate citizens must get actively involved!"

Luis believed that city leaders had a duty to ensure that the state acted as "a benevolent big brother," working in tandem to meet Trenton's unique needs. City and state government needed to find common goals and bring an end to the days of deep-pocket politics. For its part, the city had to learn to stand on its own feet and fend for itself fiscally. "Trenton cannot afford to become a welfare city attached to a bloated welfare state!

"I call for the founding of a Coalition of Hope," he continued into the mirror, "in which the many groups whose representatives I've spoken with on the campaign trail—those committed to protecting lives and ensuring the public good, to preserving this city's unique history and natural resources, to revitalizing its abundant housing and building stock, to promoting its cultural diversity and the industry inherent in its people, and to eliminating racial discrimination and discord—are provided the opportunity to join together, to share ideas and resources, to unify and reach critical mass so that important public programs can be effectively funded and managed under one banner.

"We need to rekindle the spirit of idealism that brought this city to greatness in the industrial era. The Roeblings and other civic-minded business leaders proved that it is not only *possible* to build a community where people reach out to help one another, to work together for the greater good, but that this is, in fact, the *common sense* approach to solving the challenges faced by all of us." He paused for dramatic effect.

"I have seen the future of Trenton, and it begins with an appreciation of her glorious past."

"Bravo!" clapped Raul as he stepped through the bedroom doorway. He had on his woven straw fedora, madras shirt, and favorite chinos—the ones Rosa had given him for Christmas that came from a shop called Banana Republic. He always got a chuckle when he thought of that name. Now, he was ready to party. "You sound like a real politician. I especially like your Coalition of Hope."

Luis's face flushed with embarrassment as he realized his father had been eavesdropping on him for some time. "Thanks, Pop," he said, collecting himself. "I just hope I'm the right guy to pull all these people together. Sometimes I wonder if I've bitten off more than I can chew."

"Hey *mijo*, you know how to eat an elephant?" Raul watched as a smile crept across his son's face. "One bite at a time!" They had a good laugh together, then Raul added, "You can start by following your own advice, Luis."

"How's that, Pop?"

"Build that coalition. You've already got the Latinos more proud than they've ever been in this city. You should hear the way they talk about you in the neighborhood. Next thing you got to do is find your-self a sponsor in the black community. Too bad that Reverend Markham is gone—they say he was a good man and he certainly had a lot of influence. Maybe his daughter is someone you can work with. She runs the Youth Center, right? That's good for a few votes."

"Yeah, Pop, but those kids are all too young to vote in *this* elec-tion," Luis joked. "Actually, I have a good feeling about Naomi Whittaker, but I don't want to be indebted to her husband in any way. He's a user, and you can see how he's already trying to use me with this Alma Arms project. He never even asked for permission to use our name."

"Does he need it?" Raul asked rhetorically. "He's got money and connections."

"Lots of connections," intoned Luis, "and I'm not going to be added to the list."

"I don't know why this Alma Arms bothers you so much, son," Raul said with a mischievous twinkle in his eyes. "It seemed to get Miss Tucker's attention. What happened to her anyway?" he probed. "Things get a little too personal?"

"I see the neighborhood rumor mill hasn't missed a beat." Luis gave his father a contorted smile.

"You take a girl to Malaga for lunch and think I'm not gonna hear about it?" he deadpanned.

"Actually she took *me* there, Pop. It wasn't my idea," said Luis recalling the scene uncomfortably.

"You went, though," Raul goaded him.

"She was persistent."

"Yeah, and I'll bet those big beautiful eyes had nothing to do with it. Nice legs and tush, too, as I recall …"

"That's enough, Pop. I get the picture. It's over. So, let's just for-get it."

"Well, no matter what happened between you two personally, I think she'd be good on your team professionally. She seems like one smart lady."

"Abby's with the Democrats, Pop, and by deciding to run inde-pendent I pretty much became the enemy." He sighed. "There are other complicating factors, including the fact that something I told her in confidence about Hector and Felix came back to haunt me."

Raul looked at his son quizzically. "Is that why you sent them to stay with Mrs. Garcia's cousins in New York?"

"I couldn't just let them get deported," he admitted with a note of shame in his voice. "Abby's boss threatened an immigration investigation if I didn't play ball, and as you know, I didn't. She could still make some trouble for me, though she's got to worry it might backfire."

Raul stiffened as he remembered the haughty overbearing Helen Nelson. "She seems like the type who thinks *all* Latinos are illegals. I got a different feeling about Abby, though. She doesn't seem like the type to sell you out. I saw the way she looked at you that night with Roberto on the bridge, after she stood up to that *pendejo* Dodd. I don't know what she said to you, Luis, but there was real feeling there—I think she saw you as out on a ledge yourself. Like father, like son."

Luis stood silently and let the words sink in. He had always respected his father's uncanny ability to read people, not to mention his plain-spoken wisdom. He may have been a gardener with an eighth grade education but in Luis's eyes he was a sage.

Raul put a hand on Luis's shoulder. "Maybe you should stop looking for Maria in Abby and see her for who *she* is."

Before Luis could think of how to respond to this piece of fatherly advice, his cell phone rang. It was Dominic Rosetti with news of a change of venue for Luis's speech; his tone was normal, but when he'd finished rattling off the details and hung up Luis felt there had been something left unsaid.

The original plan was for Luis to appear on the steps of the War Memorial; now, in the eleventh hour, the Heritage Days organizers were moving him to Battle Monument Park. Thinking about it, two things bothered him about the new location: the surrounding neighborhood was rough, and it was some distance from the other major events of the festival. Something smelled fishy, and Luis thought he caught a whiff of perfume in the mix. Whether it was Abby's, Helen's, or a little of both, the bottom line was that the longshot independent candidate would be at a distinct disadvantage right out of the gate.

39

Betrayal

The late model Lexus pulled over and parked across from a section of boarded up row homes on Tucker Street. Like a modern-day version of an impending biblical plague, all the homes slated for demolition had big red X's painted on the front doors, except in this case it wasn't in lamb's blood. A bulldozer and a crane with a wrecking ball sat idle on the adjacent vacant property.

"Why are we stopping here?" Naomi Whittaker inquired in an uneasy tone.

"I've got a disgruntled tenant to attend to," her husband replied. "This won't take long."

"Can't Solomon handle it?" she asked.

"He is," Randal said impatiently. "And I agreed to meet him here. It's a rough neighborhood. Sachs thinks the situation might require some extra persuasion."

So, Naomi thought in disgust, this is what it all comes down to; a *shyster* lawyer relying on an ostensibly *honest* businessman to help muscle some poor slob out of his home in order to make room for progress. Later, the businessman will take his trophy wife to a *charity* jazz brunch at the Marriott and plop down $100 a plate to ease his guilt.

Naomi was dismayed by the distance between them after six years of marriage. They had been growing apart for years, but it had accelerated rapidly since her father's death. Lately, it was almost as if they were strangers, living under the same roof but certainly not together.

Randal was no longer the man she thought she had married but rather the one her father had warned her about. Of course, she knew about his infidelity. He was a rich and powerful black man, and there was no shortage of women drawn to the fantasies they imagined him fulfilling. They would have been surprised if they knew how little physical satisfaction he had given his stunning bride from day one. She once thought things would have been different if they had had children, but the chances of that happening were becoming even more remote as constant bickering and late night "business meetings" did little to inspire greater intimacy between them.

She knew why Randal had brought her along today. He was extremely adept at public relations. The Heritage Days Festival, when more than twenty-five thousand people poured into the capital city for two days of fun, food, and entertainment, was the perfect occasion to showcase his wife, the Sarah Lawrence–educated daughter of the Right Reverend Hollis Markham. She wondered why she had ever accepted the role.

"Wasn't the demolition of these homes scheduled for last month?" she asked him as she collected her unhappy thoughts.

"You can thank Luis Alma for the postponement," Whittaker replied disdainfully, and it was clear to Naomi that he was not happy about the delay. "He convinced the city council to request an injunction, and they found a judge stupid enough to approve a stay of action until after the election."

"Can he do that?" she asked, impressed by the maverick Latino's moxie.

"Legally, no," he sighed. "And we were going to challenge it, but naming rights has its privileges and Sachs convinced me it would be a public relations disaster to oppose the namesake of the future Alma Arms."

"Why don't you just change the name to something else?" she asked curiously.

"Because the public loves it," he said tersely. "I committed to it and right now I can't afford any bad press."

"Sure, now that you don't have my father around to smooth things over for you," she responded with insight.

"There's Sachs now," he said ignoring the affront and nodding to the metallic blue Jaguar XJ pulling up to the curb ahead. Looking totally out of place in these surroundings, a short heavyset white man with an expensive toupee and a three-piece suit struggled out of the driver's seat. He was lugging a chic safari backpack, Naomi noticed.

"Wait here," Whittaker barked at her as he exited the car.

***

Made of white granite turned gray with age and rising some one-hundred forty-eight feet into the air, the Trenton Battle Monument resembles a Roman Doric column crowned with an observatory deck below a thirteen-foot tall statute of George Washington. Strategically located on a small hilltop overlooking the northern approach to the city, the tower stands at the historic junction of five intersecting roads where General George Washington instructed a young Captain Alexander Hamilton to aim his cannon against the Hessians, in the wee morning hours of December 26, 1776.

"The park doesn't open for another hour," said Charlie Stillwater as he opened the heavy bronze door at the base of the Battle Monument. The old man's face was lined with age but his eyes were alert with a hint of kindness. He was dressed in a short khaki jacket, matching pants, a pale green shirt, and a dark green tie. His boots were in need of a shine. When he spoke, he wheezed as if his breath was being squeezed through a set of exhausted bellows. "Come back later."

"Wait!" pleaded Darius Hudson. "Please, I need to ask you a question."

"You too, huh?" Charlie exclaimed opening the door a little farther. "Okay, come in." Darius maneuvered around the door and into the cramped lobby area next to the elevator shaft.

"Hello, Darius," greeted Professor Collins. He was standing in the dim light with Shelly Reed beside him. "I was sorry to hear about your brother."

"A tragedy," Shelly added. "Gang violence is the bane of this city. I hope we'll elect an administration that takes it seriously."

"I hope so, too," Darius said, his eyes downcast.

"Well, young fellah," Charlie said kindly, "what's on your mind?"

"Did the Masons build the Battle Monument?" Darius blurted out. Collins and Reed grinned and nodded as if it was exactly what they'd expected.

"Great minds think alike, eh, Shelly?" Collins said with a broad smile.

"*Masons*?" repeated Charlie, intrigued. "Like I was telling the professor and Miss Reed here, I can't rightly say. Despite how old you all must think I am, I wasn't around when they built this place." He chuckled at his own joke. "I reckon immigrants built it. *Eye*-talians more than likely did the intricate stonework. They were the master masons of the day."

Darius was dismayed. Had he really expected to get earth-shaking information from the old coot on his first shot? No, but he had to try just the same. Obviously, so did Professor Collins.

"Go ahead," Shelly encouraged Darius, watching his mind tick. "Ask him your next question."

"Okay," Darius played along, "what do you know about the Society of Cincinnatus?"

Charlie pondered the question, eyeing his three visitors warily before he spoke. "I don't know nothing 'bout Cincinnati society, son," he said at last, concluding with a long wheeze, "but for what it's worth, the people behind the building of the monument are listed on that wall." He pointed to a bronze plaque dated October 19, 1893, and engraved with the names of the Battle Monument Association members.

"The name you're looking for is John Hart Brewer," Professor Collins said to Darius. "He was the great-great-great grandson of John Hart, the Signer."

"And let's not forget General William Stryker, the chairman of the association," added Shelly Reed. "He was a Scudder like Hart's wife and quite an authority on the Battles of Trenton."

Darius's thoughts went to the precious copy of *Common Sense* he'd foolishly allowed to be destroyed rather than turning it over to the professor when it first came into his possession. It seemed like the right time to come clean. "I have a confession to make, Professor Collins," he began, framing his words carefully.

"Belay that, Darius, we have an announcement of our own to make," Collins interrupted excitedly.

"You two are getting married?" Darius blurted.

"No, no," the professor chuckled with a sheepish glance at Shelly. "We believe we know what it was that our Mason–Cincinnatus–Battle Monument Association friends hid."

"You know—and you're not mad?" Darius asked, thinking of Tom Paine's pamphlet.

"Mad?" Collins seemed taken aback. "Some people may think us mad when they hear what we propose." He winked at Shelly. "Our theory is that one or more of John Hart's sons learned that Tucker had hidden some of the proclamation money … and we're fairly certain they relieved him of it."

"But after the war Continental notes were worthless," Shelly added. "Land was the only thing of value at that point."

"So they stashed the paper away, knowing that some day its historic value would greatly transcend its irrecoverable monetary value." Collins was positively gleeful in delivering his supposition.

"And they left clues behind for nuts like us to follow," Shelly said with equal fervor.

Listening to the two of them now reminded Darius of the night in the library with Tina when they had volleyed ideas back and forth like a tennis ball, sharing their intriguing historical perspectives from both sides of the Atlantic. Darius glanced at Charlie Stillwater, who seemed to be enjoying the rapid-fire conjecturing. For Darius, the old man's weathered appearance completed the sudden surreal sensation that he'd just stepped back in time.

"The question is, where did they hide it?" Darius said, ever the seeker and loving the chase.

The professor's blue eyes brightened. "First in the State House, until the fire forced the secret-keepers to move it elsewhere."

"So where did they move it?" was Darius's easily anticipated response.

Shelly shivered with intensity. "We believe they brought it here, concealing it somewhere inside this very monument. The timing fits.

The Battle Monument was built a few years after the State House fire."

"And what could be more appropriate as a vault than a memorial commemorating the greatest victory of the war that the proclamation money was intended to support?" Collins summarized neatly.

"And what better group to conceal it here than the descendants of the Hart family, whose forbears were charged with the responsibility of the money's safe passage from signer to treasury?" Shelly finished.

"That's one hell of a fancy yarn," Charlie cackled. "How much do you suppose that old money would be worth today?"

"Well," said Collins slowly, "a numismatist friend confirms that New Jersey Continental paper money in mint condition, bearing the signature of an actual signer of the Declaration of Independence could conceivably fetch up to eight hundred dollars per note."

Stillwater let out a low whistle. Darius's eyes widened.

"Now here's the tricky part," volunteered Shelly. "Assume we're looking for about sixty-five-hundred pounds ranging in denominations between six shillings and three pounds. We're probably talking about some four thousand notes. At eight hundred dollars per note, I'd estimate the total value of the cache to be worth more than three million dollars."

Hooting, Charlie did a little jig. "Well, I'll be damned!" he shouted. Darius was speechless.

"This is all hypothetical, of course," cautioned Collins.

"Right," Shelly agreed. "We don't know for sure that it even exists."

"Let alone where within these walls it may be hidden," Collins said. "My best guess would be near the cornerstone. From earliest times, the Masons were known to bury objects of significance when they laid the cornerstones of their buildings."

"That's all well and dandy, but if it's there, that's where it's gonna stay," Charlie concluded. "There are four million tons of block sitting on top of that stone." Glancing at his watch he said, "Now, unless you treasure hunters intend to shuttle up to the observation deck for a look-see, I've got a job to attend to—and I expect the first bus load of festival goers any minute now."

***

"That was really stupid of you, Bobby," Randal Whittaker said to the dark figure huddled in the far corner of the room. So little light entered the room through the plywood covering the windows that it was difficult for him to distinguish between the thug he was addressing and the bundle of old rags and newspapers he had been using for a bed.

"I had no fuckin' choice," Jackson snarled. "The kid was gonna finger me for the Markham hit."

Solomon Sachs cleared his throat. "You mean the night the reverend came home unexpectedly and caught you and Curtis Hudson stealing his silverware, right? Markham attacked you with a knife and was killed in the ensuing melee."

"Yeah, that's right—I stabbed him in the *melee*," Jackson said sarcastically.

"I could have convinced a jury it was self-defense, even if Curtis had gone to the police," Sachs opined in the darkness. "Your only worry was the assault on the cop, and we could have fixed that, too."

"Enough!" Whittaker bellowed. "You had too many witnesses this time, Bobby." Stepping around discarded needles and empty vials he moved further into the room.

"And we are no longer in need of your services," Sachs emphasized the point.

"So give me the rest of what you owe me and I'll disappear," Jackson said defiantly. "Or would you rather I cut my own deal with the DA?"

The lawyer coughed nervously. "That won't be necessary." He looked to Whittaker for support.

"Give it to him," Whittaker said. Sachs dutifully tossed the backpack onto the soiled bedding.

"Remember, Bobby, you've got one more job to do before you go," Whittaker said solemnly. "And you know what that is."

Sachs shot him a bewildered look. He wiped away the beads of sweat that had suddenly formed on his forehead.

Jackson stirred in the corner. "When do I get paid for that?"

"Tonight, here," promised Whittaker. "When it's all over."

"Fine, but I want fifty thousand," Jackson bargained, rising unsteadily to his feet.

"That's preposterous," argued Sachs. "You're not worth—"

"Done," Whittaker silenced his attorney. "You do what you're supposed to, and you'll get everything that's coming to you tonight."

The two men turned and walked out the door without another word.

Out on the street, Sachs pulled his number one client aside. They had worked together for years, rarely disagreeing even when their dealings were on the shady side of the law, but Sachs didn't appreciate the discussion he had just been a party to. Nor did he like being kept in the dark on business dealings his client initiated right in front of him. "What the *hell* just happened, Randal?"

"Don't worry about it," Whittaker brushed him off. "I know what I'm doing."

Sachs was unusually insistent. "Listen, Randal, a little drug money for gang activity to scoop up cheap housing is one thing, but conspiring with a fucking murderer? That's where I draw the line."

Randal stopped cold and grabbed Sachs forcefully by his coat sleeve. "Since when has your conscience ever outweighed your wallet, *counselor?*" he fumed, staring down his longtime sycophant. "If you can't handle the job, I'll find an attorney who can."

Sachs gazed meekly at his meal ticket and swallowed his pride along with his misgivings.

"Have you arranged to have this place torched tonight like I asked?" Whittaker challenged him.

Sachs nodded somberly. "It's been arranged."

"With any luck, our young friend will be inside." Whittaker slapped Sachs on the back.

A chill ran up the lawyer's spine when he realized Whittaker was dead serious. As the two men parted, walking to their respective vehicles, Whittaker was struck by his own tremor of fear.

Naomi was gone.

40

Hart & Soul

*T*he Heritage Days Festival was the brainchild of the Trenton Commons Commission. Back in 1979, the city leaders were looking for a way to celebrate the 300th anniversary of the arrival of Mahlon Stacy and his band of hardy Yorkshire Quakers to an area then known simply as the "Falls on the Delaware."

Capitalizing on the ethnic diversity of Trenton, the Commons Commission designed and organized a multicultural event around the arts and crafts, entertainment, and culinary specialties of the city. Now into its fourth decade, the festival appealed to all nationalities living in the greater Trenton area to come together in celebration of their community.

Although the Trenton Commons Commission no longer existed, Helen Nelson remembered it fondly. It was where she had gotten her start. The experience helped her land a variety of appointments with the State of New Jersey and eventually led to her current position as the capable, some said despotic, director of Historic Preservation and Cultural Affairs. Along the way, associations with powerbrokers like Senator Howard Stevens and real estate mogul Randal Whittaker had advanced her career but also left her in the unenviable position of being both grateful and obligated, no matter how self-confident and independent she pretended to be.

So, reluctantly, at the urging of Solomon Sachs, on instructions from Randal Whittaker, Helen placed a call to her festival contacts claiming that Triumph Development Corporation, a major financial sponsor of the event, was threatening to pull its funding unless mayoral candidate Luis Alma's speech was moved from the War Memorial to Battle Monument Park. The rationale given was that it would be more fitting for Alma's speech to be delivered in the neighborhood where Triumph was building a housing project in his honor. Though Helen was thoroughly skeptical about the motive, she complied with her benefactor's request and the venue was promptly changed.

Sitting in the Archives Restaurant in the well-appointed Trenton Marriott, Helen nervously tapped her perfectly manicured fingernails on the bar while sipping a mimosa. Howard Stevens sat next to her nursing a Bloody Mary and chatting up a pretty young bartender, further aggravating Helen's already foul mood. They were waiting for Randal and Naomi Whittaker to make their appearance before taking their regular table for brunch. The couple was already twenty minutes late.

"This isn't like Randal," Helen griped to Stevens when the bartender briefly escaped his prattle to serve a customer at the other end of the bar. "What the hell could be keeping him?"

"If it's a romp with that Nubian goddess of his, I'd almost forgive him for letting my soufflé get cold," Stevens lampooned.

"Judging from your little tête-à-tête with the barmaid, I'd venture to say your soufflé is still rising," she huffed, grabbing her purse and standing to leave just as she spotted Jimmy Dodd entering the room. "If Othello shows up, you can tell him his instructions have been carried out. I think I'll go mingle with the unwashed masses—they can't be any dirtier than the politics in here." She sniffed and bolted from the room.

"Was it something I said?" the mayor joked to Stevens as he watched her departing backside.

"Pull up a barstool, Jimmy," Stevens said. "It'll be nice to have some rational company for a change. By which I mean *male* company."

"I didn't know I was still wanted," Dodd wondered aloud.

"You know we all love you, Jimmy," Stevens replied disingenuously, peering down the bar to see where that hot little bartender had gotten off to.

***

The Almas attended Heritage Days every year. Roberto was a particular fan of the funnel cakes—deep-fried swirls of light dough covered in white powdery sugar. Tina went for the music, ranging from the cool jazz of Dick Gratton and Barbara Trent to the blues, pop, and rock of colorful local front men like Joe Zook, Ernie White, Paul Plumeri, Billy Hill, and Frank Pinto. The festival offered Raul a chance to join with some of his cronies on the grassy knoll of Mill Hill Park for marathon chess matches. The whole family enjoyed strolling along the main commercial corridor of the city with thousands of other festival goers, admiring the sidewalk art, face painting, magic shows, mimes, jugglers, and stilt-walkers.

Darius became lost in his element, taking walking tours of the Old Barracks as well as cemeteries, churches, and historic homes that were closed to the public most of the year. For this year's event, the Trenton Historical Society had hired a trolley and offered guided tours of the Revolutionary War battlegrounds beginning at the Battle Monument. During Heritage Days, the city came to life, letting down her hair and opening up her "Hart & Soul," as Darius put it, playing with the surnames that, for him, had come to symbolize Trenton's past and present.

While Luis read his speech again and Roberto tracked down Sam the Funnel Man's truck, Tina and Darius sat on one of the park benches beneath the towering Battle Monument waiting for four o'clock when Luis was scheduled to take the podium. The weather was perfect, not a cloud in the sky, and the rose bushes and azaleas were in full bloom. The Trenton Central High School Concert Band was tuning up to get things started.

Darius told Tina about his unexpected rendezvous with Professor Collins and Shelly Reed earlier inside the monument, excitedly recounting their theory about the missing proclamation money.

"Wouldn't it be something if we could find that money!" he said squeezing her hand.

"Did you tell the professor about the copy of *Common Sense*?"

"I tried, but he was preoccupied with their theorizing."

"I really want to know the story behind E. H. and Penny—I'll bet they were the Romeo and Juliet of the American Revolution," she fantasized.

"In that case, we're probably better off not knowing," he reasoned. "Romeo and Juliet didn't end up together, they ended up dead."

"You're such a romantic," she teased him.

He didn't hear the comment, because his attention had become glued to a hooded figure on the Battle Monument steps. It wasn't so much the face, partly concealed by an oversized pair of Oakley sunglasses, but the familiar swaggering gait that caught Darius's eye. He watched as the individual, a large backpack slung across his shoulders, joined with a small tour group entering the monument.

When the group re-emerged ten minutes later, the hooded figure was not among them. Darius excused himself to Tina and headed for the monument door.

"My dad's about to begin his speech, Darius!" she protested as the band struck up a patriotic march.

He didn't want to alarm her, but what he was thinking troubled him deeply. "I'll only be a few minutes," he said hurriedly. "I want to make sure old Charlie gets to hear your dad's speech, too."

Inside the monument, Bobby Jackson was hiding in the small mechanical room that doubled as the operator's "office" when the elevator was not in use. As the last tour group departed, Charlie Stillwater locked the door before discovering the straggler and politely asked him to leave.

"I want a ride to the top," Jackson insisted. "There was no room when you brought that last group up."

Charlie glanced at his watch. "Okay, but we'll have to hurry." He entered the elevator and as Jackson stepped in after him he explained, "I'm supposed to hold all tours during the candidate's speech."

"I'll be quick," Jackson assured him with a metallic grin.

Charlie shuttered the gate to the old-fashioned elevator, pulled the lever that closed the outside door and engaged the drive. Behind his dark glasses, Jackson studied the old man's every move.

Slowly, the cage began to rise. "This is the original elevator," Charlie said above the grinding wheelhouse din. "It was built by the Otis brothers using genuine Roebling cables."

Jackson stared straight ahead.

"What's in the bag?" Charlie pointed to the backpack.

"My lunch," Jackson replied harshly.

"That's a big lunch," Charlie said amiably.

"And that was a big mistake," Jackson said, striking Charlie's head with the butt of a handgun pulled from the small of his back. The old man crumpled.

When the elevator car came to a halt at the top of the monument, Jackson opened the door and shoved Charlie's body out onto the observation deck. Stepping back into the elevator, he mimicked Charlie's operation of the car and headed to the ground floor.

Reentering the mechanical room, Jackson set the backpack on the ground, bent down to open it, and adjusted a mechanism inside. Sliding the backpack out of plain sight beneath the operator's wooden chair, he turned and hurried out the door.

As the door swung open, it knocked Darius backward. He stopped himself from falling and managed to keep the door from closing as the hooded figure hurried past him.

With the band playing in the background, Darius entered the monument and called out for Charlie. When there was no response, he opened the door to the mechanical room then stopped at the little alcove. Drawn to the list of Battle Monument Association members on the bronze plate he had studied earlier with the professor and Shelly Reed, he ran his hand over the name John Hart Brewer before remembering why he was there.

"Charlie!" he called out again but no answer came. It wasn't like the old operator to leave his post, and he hadn't seen Charlie step outside.

There was a sickening feeling in the pit of Darius's stomach as he made his way to the empty elevator. The key ring was dangling from the panel box. "Charlie?" he called up the shaft. And then he spotted what looked like blood on the floor of the cage.

I should go for help, he thought, his fear of heights weighing heavily on his mind. But if Charlie was seriously hurt, every minute counted. Filled with apprehension, he stepped into the car, closing the gate then pulling the lever down. His heart leapt into his throat as the cage jolted upward.

Pressing his body against the wall of the ascending car, he closed his eyes. It seemed to take forever to reach the top. When the elevator finally lurched to a stop, he took a second to compose himself before slowly opening the door. Brilliant sunshine burst into the car, and he blinked as his eyes adjusted to the light. The sky opened up in front of him, his knees buckling as he looked away, melting down onto the safety of the cage floor. At that moment he saw Charlie's body sprawled out on the observation deck, precariously near the edge.

"Help!" he screamed from inside the car, his cries lost against the marching music being performed just below. He pulled out his cell phone and dialed Tina's number. After several rings it went to voice-mail. It was probably in her pocketbook, he thought, her Lady Gaga ringtone drowned out by the music. The old man moaned, and Darius watched in horror as he rolled closer to the edge of the deck.

In his head, Darius repeated the words over and over: "It's time to face my fears," and then realized he was saying it out loud. He had tried and failed to conquer his fear of heights on the Lower Free Bridge for Tina's brother. He had tried to stand up to Bobby Jackson, but not enough to save his own brother. His batting average was zero but now he had another chance; he wasn't going to let his fears keep him down, and he wasn't going to let the thugs of the world win this time.

He pulled himself up off the elevator floor, climbing unsteadily to his feet then inching slowly toward the outside deck. *Try not to look down,* he told himself as a pigeon flew by within kissing distance of his head, reminding him just how high up he was. He swallowed hard and looked straight ahead. Stepping through the threshold, the view was instantly spectacular. In the distance, the city skyline jumped out to meet his gaze. He could see the Capitol Dome gleaming in the sunlight, the downtown commercial district and the rippling Delaware River beyond it.

He chanced a downward glance toward the base of the monument, hoping to spot Tina. It was a mistake. A wave of vertigo swept over him causing him to lose his balance. He reached for the railing but missed. As he stumbled and fell to the floor, he caught a glimpse of a hooded pedestrian turning the corner onto Tucker Street. For Darius, there was no mistaking the evil under that hood. The image burned into his consciousness.

He had fallen beside Charlie's body, and, braving the onset of another panic attack, he got to his knees and began rolling the old man toward the elevator. When he reached the car, he entered it then pulled Charlie the last few feet inside with him. Taking a deep breath to refocus his thoughts, he engaged the lever. The ancient electrical gears and pulleys banged and hissed into action as the car began its descent.

Reaching the first floor, Darius dragged Charlie by his feet into the mechanical room and took his first good look at the bloody gash on the old man's forehead. He flipped opened his phone and dialed 911.

Just outside, as the band finished a rousing rendition of *La Bamba*, Luis was standing on the steps of the Battle Monument between the two lifelike Revolutionary statues guarding the entrance. Introduced by Dominic Rosetti, a reluctant public speaker, he cleared his throat and gazed out into the approving, cheering crowd. To his surprise, there were Abby and Naomi, seated front and center on either side of his father. Raul flashed him a big grin and two thumbs up. Luis returned the smile as he watched Abby move over on the bleachers to make room for Roberto and Tina.

Inside the monument, Charlie was regaining consciousness. Groggy at first, he looked up at Darius with confusion in his eyes. Looking past the young man, his eyes grew wide as they came to rest on the large backpack tucked beneath his chair. As a burst of adrenaline coursed through his system, the old man leapt to his feet, almost knocking Darius over as he grabbed the bag and bolted toward the door.

Throwing the door open, Charlie nearly bowled over his longtime friend Dominic Rosetti. "Out of my way!" he shouted frantically as he raced through the agitated crowd. "Get back!"

"Charlie!" Dominic shouted, taking off after him.

With Dominic close behind him, the old man ran down Broad Street, wheezing as his asthma tightened its grip on his windpipe. Some fifty yards from the monument, he lunged for the curb and hurriedly shoved the backpack into a sewer grate. As he turned to ward off his friend, a tremendous explosion sent a column of smoke and steam along with huge chunks of blacktop into the air.

With images of Desert Storm bombing raids exploding in his head, Luis dove off the speaker's platform looking up in time to see Abby throw her arms around Tina and Roberto, knocking them to the ground as she shielded them from flying debris and the stampeding throng.

Dominic Rosetti lay in the street, bloodied but still breathing not twenty-five feet from where Charlie Stillwater had met an instant death, as sirens wailed the city's grief.

41

Firestorm

*A*fter giving his statement at the Trenton police station and making sure that Officer McKenna escorted Tina and her family safely home, Darius doubled back to Tucker Street. He had defeated one of his demons today. It was time for him to confront another.

The sun had already set as he parked the Bonneville alongside the lit Battle Monument and approached Tucker Street on foot. Although this was an area he was familiar with from having grown up a few blocks away, the sight of so many boarded-up homes on the deserted street made his skin crawl.

He didn't know if he would find Bobby Jackson here, but it was the only place that made sense to him. Studying the dozen or so dwellings from behind the cover of a bulldozer, he tried to imagine what a street thug like Bobby Jackson would be looking for in picking a place to hide. Just then he noticed a shadowy figure moving among some shrubs at the far end of the street, by a corner property next to an abandoned garage or warehouse. It made perfect sense.

As he approached the house cautiously, Darius heard the sound of smashing glass followed by a gunshot coming from inside. A figure darted out of the shadows between the warehouse and the row home, moving quickly away from the buildings to a waiting car down the street.

Watching from his vantage point across the street from the house, Darius could see light shining through the cracks in the plywood covering the windows. As the glow turned brighter it dawned on him: The building was on fire!

He ran across the street to the burning building. He pried away the plywood from an already broken front window and pulled himself up and over the ledge, tearing his shirt and cutting his hand on the jagged glass as he tumbled into the smoky living room. He stood and assessed the scene. There was a light on at the end of a hall, and through the smoke he could make out a dark shape near the floor, possibly a person.

He covered his head with his arms as he moved down the hall. Flames licked up at him, scorching his face and hands. The smell of his own burning hair assailed him as the flames began leaping from floor to ceiling. At the end of the hall, he entered a bathroom that was not yet engulfed, though smoke from the hall was beginning to fill it up. Slumped over the side of the bathtub was the form he'd seen from the living room—a human body, whether alive or dead he could not tell.

Choking and with his eyes burning from the smoke, he pulled the bathroom door shut behind him. Catching his breath, he turned on the coldwater tap at the sink and wet his hands and face with the few drops that remained in the pipes.

Turning his attention to the body, he saw it was a young black man in a dark hooded sweatshirt. He pulled back the hood and peered into the face. It was Bobby Jackson, and it appeared he'd been shot.

Smoke and flames curled up around the bottom of the bathroom door, and Darius knew he couldn't go out the way he came in. Lifting the lid off the toilet tank, he smashed through the thin sheet of plywood covering the small bathroom window.

Shouldering Bobby across his back, he somehow managed to push the dead weight through the window. As the ceiling began falling in around him, he dove headfirst through the window to safety.

***

The light was on in the study of the Tudor mansion across the street from the deer paddock of Cadwalader Park when Naomi turned the key and walked in. Randal Whittaker was sitting at his desk with his laptop on, and the television muted in the background.

"I thought you'd been abducted," he joked without looking up. "I've been waiting for a ransom note all night."

"I imagine you've heard the news," she said, setting her keys down on an end table. Her hair was disheveled and dark eye makeup streaked down her face as if she had been crying. "Someone tried to blow up the Battle Monument while Luis Alma was giving his speech."

Whittaker closed his laptop and reached for the bottle of bourbon on his desk. "Did they catch the terrorist or was it just another gangland disturbance?" he asked nonchalantly as he poured himself a drink.

"Neither," she said, stepping cautiously into the dark, wood-paneled room. "It was the work of a more insidious evil. Someone who manipulates events like a wizard behind the curtain."

He quickly downed his bourbon and poured himself another.

"There's more," Naomi continued, her eyes fixed on her husband, "A little over an hour ago, the Tucker Street housing projects went up in flames."

"That's a shame," Whittaker said, the hint of a smile playing on the corners of his mouth.

"Don't you mean, that's *convenient*?" countered Naomi. "Now you won't have to wait until after the elections to start tearing down what's left."

"The Lord works in mysterious ways, Naomi," he paraphrased scripture. "Isn't that what your father always said?"

"He was also fond of the expression 'God helps those who help themselves,'" she said slyly. "Have you taken a page from that sermon, too?"

"I don't think I care for your tone." He took a sip of his whiskey. "You still haven't explained why you walked out on me or where you've been all day. I'm your husband—I have a right to know."

"My *husband*? That's convenient, too," she said sarcastically, slowly approaching his elegant desk. "I'm just sorry it took me so long to catch on." She tossed a room key card from the Trenton Marriott on the desk and leaned in toward him. "As for why I walked out on you, at least Abby knew she'd made a mistake and had the courage to tell me about it. If there's anything *you* want to tell me, now's the time."

"I've never claimed to be a saint, Naomi," he spat out, "and in my business there's tremendous pressure to deal with."

"I don't even know what your business *is* anymore," she said, adding, "and I don't think I want to know."

"What are you getting at?" he asked suspiciously.

"Would it upset you to learn I was at the Battle Monument when the bomb went off?" she asked directly.

"Well, thank the good Lord you weren't hurt," he dodged the question.

"Your gratitude is misdirected as usual. The old elevator operator gave his life to save ours—mine and hundreds of others." She tossed a piece of charred fabric onto his desk.

"What's this?" He raised an eyebrow at the debris.

"Do you remember the backpack I bought you in Kenya, on our honeymoon? It was made out of a wildebeest's hide."

"Yes ..." he replied hesitantly.

"Do you know where it is?"

"I'm sorry, Naomi," he said apologetically, "but it made me sneeze—I think it was an allergic reaction. Sachs admired it, and I gave it to him."

"That explains why I saw him with it this morning," she acknowledged.

"I was going to tell you," he said, picking up the fabric for closer inspection.

She folded her arms across her chest. "And what was Solomon carrying in it today?"

He took a healthy swig of his whiskey and swallowed hard, fidgeting in his chair. "Legal documents, I would imagine," he said hoarsely as sweat began to bead on his brow and just above his pencil thin moustache. "I really have no way of knowing."

She rocked back and forth while continuing to hold him in a steely gaze. "Since when does Solomon Sachs lug legal papers around in anything that doesn't have three locks on it?"

His breathing was ragged. Dropping the charred fabric on the desk, he loosened his tie.

"I'm surprised you didn't sneeze, Randal," she challenged him. "That piece of charred hide is all that's left of my honeymoon gift to you. I guess this means the honeymoon's over," she quipped.

"I told you I don't know what Sachs had in the backpack, *Naomi*." His tone had turned belligerent.

"Solomon trusted you, Randal," she said taking the offensive, "and you set him up. You gave him that bag last night, but he never looked in it. He assumed he was delivering hush money to Bobby Jackson."

Whittaker nervously met his wife's gaze.

"After the bombing," she continued, "your lawyer came clean. He's admitted pressuring the festival organizers to move Alma's speech to the Battle Monument, and he claims he was an unwitting accomplice to the bomb plot. In both cases, he says he was acting on instructions from you."

"He's lying," he said defensively, jumping up from his chair. "It's his word against mine."

"That's where you're wrong, Randal," she said with a weary smile. "There's another witness. Darius Hudson pulled Bobby Jackson out of a burning row house on Tucker Street. He's been shot, but he's expected to pull through."

"*No!*" Whittaker screamed as he saw his world suddenly crumbling around him. He picked his laptop off the desk and put it under one arm. Opening a desk drawer, he retrieved a small caliber revolver and waved it at Naomi.

"There's just one thing I don't understand, Randal," she said in a voice choked with emotion. "I can see how you might consider Luis Alma an obstacle in your path … in the same way that you thought of my father. But how could you even think of destroying that amazing monument and killing so many innocent people?"

He was unwilling to accept defeat.

"The monument means nothing to me. George Washington was a slave owner, and while *his* history was being written *ours* was being obliterated." He shook his head. "You live in a fantasy world, Naomi, just like your father. You really believe that someday all races and religions will come together to live in harmony."

He pointed his gun at her menacingly and ranted on.

"Well, I have *no* faith in people, regardless of where they come from or what their skin color is. They all have their own agendas, and I wouldn't have gotten where I am today if I hadn't been looking out for Number One. Luis Alma and that monument were in my way, Naomi—I did what I had to do!"

"Then I truly pity you, Randal," she said placing her open cell phone on the desk as all the doors to the house suddenly swung open and the State Police SWAT Team hurtled into the room with weapons raised.

42

Living History

Not since the Revolution had an event rocked the city or galvanized its people into action like the "Bomb at the Battle Monument." Some might argue that the Riots of 1968 came close, but back then once the arson fires were doused and the shattered plate-glass windows repaired, the hearts and minds of the city remained separated along racial lines.

However unsettling, the blast that was intended to topple the revered Trenton landmark and assassinate one of the city's own—an idealistic first-generation American who dreamed of a better city for all its residents—blew in like a breath of fresh air and blew *up* in the face of its conspirators. What followed was the grand implosion of their proverbial house of cards.

So great was the public outcry for justice that voters turned out in record numbers for the runoff election; not so much to vote for the man who stood alone against business as usual, but to vote the man out of office who could no longer guarantee their safety or provide them with law and order. Luis Alma's margin of victory may have been narrow, but Jimmy Dodd's fall from grace cut a wide path.

In the aftermath of the explosion, after recovering from a gunshot wound and smoke inhalation, Bobby Jackson confessed to both the bombing and the murder of Reverend Hollis Markham on orders personally given to him by millionaire real estate developer Randal Whittaker. Others were implicated as well, including state and municipal government employees from senate offices down through the Dodd administration, but most escaped the dragnet. Solomon Sachs, Whittaker's attorney, took the fifth rather than sully the reputation of any of his other clients. It was satisfaction enough for Sachs to know that the kingpin whose friendship he had once cherished, and to whom he had pledged his unequivocal fidelity, was now behind bars wearing a county issue orange jumpsuit instead of his stylish, designer suits after trying unsuccessfully to set Sachs up to take the fall for the attempt on Luis Alma's life.

Justice has a way of spreading her influence in ways inconceivable to those too jaded or too preoccupied with narcissistic endeavors to notice her arrival. That would explain how Senator Howard Stevens and HPCA Director Helen Nelson, along with two hookers calling themselves Gigi and Yvette, found themselves in a local lock-up after the Langhorne, Pennsylvania, vice squad—acting on an anonymous tip—raided a Red Roof Inn on a Saturday night just three weeks after the bombing in Trenton.

A belief in ghosts was not something Darius Hudson was likely to admit to anyone, but weeks after the explosion, he was in a funk over the violent deaths of his brother Curtis and old Charlie Stillwater, the hero of Heritage Days. Having witnessed both brutal slayings first-hand, he could not shake the images from his mind. Something deep inside him had stirred with emotion and presence when he paused in the alcove of the Battle Monument. Whether he was guided by Charlie's comment about "the people behind the monument" or inspired by his brother's desire for redemption—or perhaps a little of both—when Darius ran his hand over the Trenton Battle Monument Association plaque bearing the names of its prominent deceased members, he felt a sensation of cool air emanating from behind it.

Tapping the plaque confirmed his suspicions of a hollow space behind it. In the days that followed the explosion, after he got up enough nerve to return to the monument—this time armed with a Phillips-head screwdriver and accompanied by Tina for moral support—Darius acted on his "hunch" and proceeded to remove the bronze plate. In the cubbyhole behind the plaque, just as Association members had left it more than a hundred years earlier, he discovered several neatly wrapped stacks of continental notes representing more than three million dollars' worth of proclamation money. The discovery not only made national headlines but was hailed by scholars as one of the most significant Revolutionary War finds of the past 100 years.

The ensuing celebration at Eagle Tavern was organized by Professor Daniel Collins, who basked in the glory of his prize student's discovery as Trentonians turned out in droves for the festivities. The phenomenal success of the event, timed to coincide with Luis Alma's swearing in as mayor, was seen as a good omen—a viewpoint buttressed by the announcement that Triumph Development Corporation had agreed to relinquish its claim as bid winners on the historic tavern. Thanks to the infusion of capital generated by Darius's discovery, the Eagle Tavern was to be painstakingly restored as the new home for the eclectic collection of historic memorabilia currently housed at the Trentoniana Room at the Trenton Free Public Library—in effect, being transformed into a living history museum with Shelly Reed as curator.

For his efforts, Darius received a full scholarship from The College of New Jersey, and since he didn't seek any other reward for his historic find, he suggested that any money left over after the tavern was restored should be used for programs to boost Trenton's fragile educational system.

In perhaps one of the oddest twists of fate in a time marked by twists and turns, Reverend Hollis Markham's daughter divorced her newly incarcerated husband and legally reclaimed her maiden name. Now in control of both her father's and ex-husband's stock in Triumph Development Corporation, Naomi Markham became its chairperson and reinvented Alma Arms as affordable, green condominiums. The development was rechristened "Markham Towers" in honor of her father, who from his eminent perch inside the pearly gates would surely forgive his beneficent daughter this one sentimental indulgence of the family's name.

Naomi also went to work quickly on setting up low-interest financing for Tucker Street residents, allowing them to become property owners rather than just tenants of the new project. As she researched the technology and environmental options available for the site, she became excited and committed herself enthusiastically to developing additional cooperative private–public projects. All of this cut into her time at the Youth Center, but an unlikely ally stepped up to the plate.

Dominic Rosetti had had enough of safety studies, storm plans, and local politics. He wanted to spend the remainder of his days working with young people and teaching them the ropes—figuratively and literally—as Charlie Stillwater had once taught them to him. One of the first things the wily old coyote did was to re-establish city ties with the Boy Scouts and set up riverside education programs. He also reached out to Roberto Alma, naming him as his student assistant.

Luis Alma won the mayoral race by a slim margin, becoming one of just a handful of independent mayors nationwide. He knew he would have to work hard to build a coalition capable of reviving public trust in Trenton government, in particular, and restoring pride in the city's heritage more generally. Following his inaugural celebration, he invited a small gathering of family and friends including Darius Hudson, Pilar Garcia, Daniel Collins, Shelly Reed, Naomi Markham, and Abby Treadwell-Tucker to join him and the city's new recreation director, Dominic Rosetti, for their first official act—the christening of the new Capital Plaza Park along the riverfront behind the Capitol Building.

In a surprise Kodak moment worth a thousand-and-one words, Luis's favorite former employees, Hector and Felix, arrived in Abby's Mercedes. Raul had sent them an invitation along with some money to pay for the trip from upstate New York, where they had been staying with cousins of Mrs. Garcia.

Luis may have been even more surprised when Abby sidled up to him and said confidentially, "I didn't think the new mayor could afford to have any skeletons in his closet, so I've started asylum and hardship applications for your two friends."

She held Luis in her wide-set, expressive blue eyes. "I don't know if you believe me, but I never even mentioned them to Helen. Hell," she added, "I'd marry one of them if it would get you to trust me again."

Luis's face relaxed into a heartfelt smile. "Hector might like that idea, Abby, but it won't be necessary. The city's not the only thing undergoing a change around here." He pulled her into his arms, much to the approval of his observant father and daughter. "I saw your true colors when it mattered most."

Nearby, standing on the riverbank, Dominic began a soft mournful Native American chant he had learned from his mentor, as he and Roberto put Charlie Stillwater's ashes into the Delaware. All those gathered by the river watched silently as the current carried him home.

About the Authors

L-R, David A. Hart and John P. Calu. Photo by Shelley Szajner.

Born and raised in Trenton, New Jersey, **John P. Calu** left as a young man to pursue his muse in Santa Barbara, California, where he established SongFactory —a workshop funded by Jane Fonda that led to a critically acclaimed children's album. In addition to performing as a jazz singer and traveling throughout the Americas, he has been a California Artist in Residence, a Dramatic Arts Director for La Casa de la Raza, and a New Jersey Playwright through the Arts Council of Princeton. He currently resides in Lawrenceville, New Jersey.

A lifelong Trenton area resident, **David A. Hart** received his Bachelor of Arts in history and political science from Rider College (now Rider University) where he also earned a master's degree in the school's graduate program for administrators. A published author and poet, he has won several national songwriting awards and other honors. In 1985, he organized the highly successful JAM For Hunger benefit concert held at Trenton's City Gardens with all proceeds going to famine relief. He lives in West Trenton, where he is an executive for a major New Jersey insurance company.

Calu and Hart have enjoyed a productive collaboration as novelists since 2003. Their published work includes a contemporary adventure series featuring enigmatic Garden State sites, obscure local legends, and everyday mysteries along the Jersey Shore and in the Pine Barrens. They are currently at work on a novel set in historic Princeton, New Jersey.

Also From Plexus

THE PHILADELPHIAN
50TH ANNIVERSARY EDITION

A novel by Richard Powell
With a new Foreword by Academy Award nominee Robert Vaughn

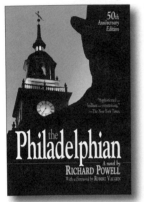

This 1957 national bestseller by the late Richard Powell, a seventh-generation Philadelphian, was touted by its publisher as a "shocking exposé" of Philadelphia and Main Line society. The novel was released to rave reviews and became the 1959 Oscar-nominated film, *The Young Philadelphians*, starring Paul Newman and Robert Vaughn.

Spanning four generations beginning with the emigration of a poor Irish girl in 1857, *The Philadelphian* is a raw and powerful tale of a family of humble origins clawing its way to the top. The story climaxes in an unforgettable courtroom scene, with society on trial and an entire city held spellbound.

344 pp/hardbound/ISBN 978-0-937548-62-2/$22.95
344 pp/softbound/ISBN 978-0-937548-64-6/$15.95

A BOARDWALK STORY

A novel by J. Louis Yampolsky

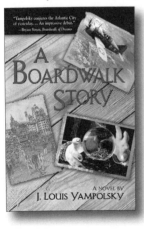

It's 1939, the tenth year of the Great Depression in America, with Europe teetering on the brink of war. In Atlantic City, New Jersey, 15-year-old Jack Laurel is about to see his life turned upside down.

As the annual influx of summer tourists floods the boardwalk, Jack stumbles into commodities trading with two men—one a reclusive mystic, the other a charismatic pitchman and mathematical savant. Inspired by the musings of a boardwalk fortuneteller, the three partners are poised to reap unimagined profits. But a house of cards is about to come down around them and, with it, the wrath of Atlantic City's iron-fisted mob boss.

J. Louis Yampolsky evokes the days when Atlantic City was the "Playground of the World"— the home of gilded Arabesque hotels, parades, pageants, and the famous Steel Pier. *A Boardwalk Story* is a startling debut novel.

488 pp/hardbound/ISBN 978-0-937548-72-1/$24.95

THE NORTHSIDE
African Americans and the Creation of Atlantic City
Nonfiction by Nelson Johnson

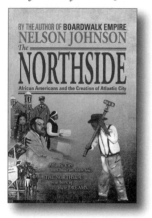

In *The Northside*, Nelson Johnson brings the untold story of Atlantic City's black community vividly to life, from the arrival of the first African Americans to Absecon Island in the early 19th century through the glory days of "The World's Playground." Exploited for their labor and banished to the most undesirable part of town, resilient Northsiders created a vibrant city-within-a-city, a place where black culture could thrive and young people could aspire to become artists, athletes, educators, and leaders of business, politics, and society. As Nelson Johnson shows in this unflinching portrait, Atlantic City was built on their toil—and the Northside was born of their dreams.

November 2010/344 pp/hardbound/ISBN 978-0-937548-73-8/$24.95

BOARDWALK EMPIRE
The Birth, High Times, and Corruption of Atlantic City
HBO Series Tie-in Edition
Nonfiction by Nelson Johnson; Foreword by Terence Winter

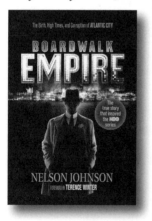

Through most of the 20th century, Atlantic City was controlled by a powerful partnership of local politicians and racketeers. This corrupt alliance reached full bloom during the reign of Enoch "Nucky" Johnson.

In *Boardwalk Empire*, Nucky Johnson, Louis "the Commodore" Kuehnle, Frank "Hap" Farley, and Atlantic City itself spring to life in all their garish splendor. Author Nelson Johnson traces "AC" from its birth as a quiet seaside health resort, through the notorious backroom politics and power struggles, to the city's rebirth as an international entertainment and gambling mecca where anything goes.

Boardwalk Empire is the true story that inspired the epic HBO series starring Steve Buscemi, Michael Pitt, and Kelly Macdonald, with a pilot episode written by Terence Winter (*The Sopranos*) and directed by Martin Scorsese (*Shutter Island*).

304 pp/softbound/ISBN 978-0-9666748-6-6/$16.95

To order or for a catalog: 609-654-6500, Fax Order Service: 609-654-4309
www.plexuspublishing.com